Disclaimer:

This is exclusively my writing.
It lies somewhere in between a humorous erotic romance
and an imaginary tale founded in dreamy fact.

Some names may be actual, yet no situations factual…
It's just a fable of some of the perilous traps that we all
could experience in life that are represented.

Should there be any person, setting or scenario
resembling something which seems real,
perhaps…it's only in your imagination.

This simply is a book of whimsical desire
and plenty of fictional truths.

Revised Version

Book cover: Courtesy of Farfalla Boutique
Proofreader: Cathy Gainer
Tech Master: Kristin Watson

ISBN 9798218448769

Acknowledgements

***

This is usually the page that's
not of interest unless you happen to be
on it…so…without further ado, let me get to it.
I'd like to thank:

The love of my life…

my husband, *Gérald*…who has definitely

demonstrated he has the patience of *Job*.
Living with a story teller can be a challenge unto itself.
Un Grand, Grand Merci mon amour.

And to…

Helga-Liz Haberfellner
You…You stellar literary guru, were the first person
to give me the confidence "not to write like a girl."
Thank you for your input, time, encouragement
and your fabulous sense of Humor.

Shayne, Dena, Amanda,
Chantal, Barbara R, Laura K, Justino,
Eliane, Cathi C, Katy H and The Warburtons
…not forgetting all my many other supportive friends
and customers from the shop ~
Thanks for reading and being there along the way.
It's definitely been a ride…

xx

For Dottie & Domino

Chapter Un

On the rare occasions when Bruce Douglas was in town everyone couldn't help but notice. The yelling that came from his childhood home was so loud it echoed throughout the village. And when he invited Sophie, his live-in girlfriend from San Francisco to join...things got especially interesting.

They were a unique fit...Sophie was thirty-two, ambitious and beyond self confident. She was so beautiful she'd make anyone stop and do a double take...and man did she know it. It also didn't hurt that she was a super successful clothing manufacturer and financially independent. I guess she was a bitch on wheels riding high...if you could call it that.

She always walked tall, shoulders back and chin up. I mean...the girl *really* owned it. She produced her hip collection of women's trends in an overcrowded factory in her hometown of SF and given her fast paced lifestyle, her tightly wound behavior really made her stand out in such a slow-moving French village. It wasn't just the language barrier, the locals found her a bit snobby, rather aloof and remarkably unapproachable. The girl clearly was a foreigner and definitely not from around there. She intentionally gave the impression that their tight knit little community was totally beneath her. She felt the place was so trite and boring...no wonder she was ready to leave as soon as she'd arrived.

The truth of the matter was every time she did come for a visit...she never *really* unpacked. She always kept herself ready for that convenient escape or 'clean *get away*'...always keeping one foot half way out the door so to speak. At least she was consistent...never making concessions in her blatant negativity towards her boyfriend's family in particular. She always looked down on them like they were hillbillies having zero refinement or taste. Let's face it…the girl thought she knew it all when it came to *'those' in the village.*

In true French Fashion, Bruce's parents' house was what would be considered quaint and quite elegant in its simplicity. At least everyone in town thought so, all but Sophie that is. The place had a charming homespun feel to it, that's for sure. It was constructed of large beautiful ancient field stones that were visible both inside and out… They spoke a story like weathered trail maps with centuries of juicy history splashed all over them. When most people think of France they only think of Paris, but believe you me when you find yourself in rural France it's an entirely different ballgame.

It's such a bucolic landscape…mainly focusing on growing crops, whether it be vegetables, flowers, or fields of happy cows eating fresh grass. (let's not forget French Cheese here people) In fact when the surrounding fields needed to be cleared for planting the local farmers would use the field-stones to construct their barns, homes and villages from the earth's given materials. Amazing how most Americans are so charmed by all the stone structures in France…never realizing they were just built from practical necessity. The Douglas' home was no exception. Just like all the other houses in the village, the stone structures meld into an exquisite tapestry created from Medieval times. It was a far cry from anything you'd see in the States, that's for damn sure. The village was <u>really</u> old…

Audrey…Bruce's Mother, was a real beauty in her own right and quite the opposite of Sophie. She was a demure stunner…A quiet, secure, and gentle soul. One of her most glorious talents was her incredible green thumb. She always kept the wrought iron arch surrounding her front door beautiful year round. It was usually dripping heavily with sensuous pink climbing roses or something of the sort. Whatever it was, she made sure the abundance of lacy foliage provided a concentration of color and a deliciously scented fragrance that danced about in most months of the year.

Okay...well the house did have most of the ingredients to be considered 'old world charm,' but Sophie couldn't get over the fact that it didn't have satellite service, cell phone connection, and God Forbid...NO internet. The only saving grace in her opinion were the large exposed timber beams that felt similar to those made of steel in her modern loft-type office space back home.

You see, Bruce's family had long been a contributing factor in the community having planted their roots in deep. Both in their mid sixties now, they'd moved to the village from the States when their eldest, Bruce, was only three. His two younger sisters had been born in the village giving them bragging rights, not to mention French passports...but not 'Ol Bruce. Even though he was fluent in the local language, behind his back everyone always referred to him as 'The American'.

All three kids were raised in the sweet little house yet each couldn't wait to get out and away to begin building their lives elsewhere. Sadly, they seldom came back to visit ...which left Bruce's father Gene, extremely lonely. To fill the void, he became the busy body of the neighbor hood and eventually the entire village. He really was a miserable old coot and his favorite pastime was spreading gossip. He wouldn't dream of passing along any tidbit until he'd had time to stack on his own embellishment to the already juicy tale. However, when it came to anything concerning his wife, he was a well behaved Prince Charming that always brought out his best 'tux' when she was on his arm. Thank God she loved him blindly and could overlook his bizarre eccentricities...

Gene was a brawny type of guy, the kind of man that had obviously been quite a *looker* in his day. Certainly that's where Bruce got his burly good looks from. The rugged and handsome type, you know the one...the kind of hottie that resembled a young Indiana Jones kind of guy. Unfortunately through years of his acting out imagining he was actually the real dude from the action films, he'd developed a substantial limp from all of his rough and tumble. It made getting around a bit more annoying and difficult. In his older years he'd eventually need a walker to help navigate his daily routine…That would only add to his ever so gnarly and grumpy attitude. He'd become a million miles away from the slick polite stud he used to be.

He'd begun wearing the same dark green wool sweater like it was tattooed to his chest…and sadly it'd become his only go-to uniform year round. The boots he wore daily were so heavy, the thick leather soles made echoey clacking noises every time he walked down the lane in front of his house. But the real icing on the cake was his unique hat collection. His favorite cap with the feather was so clownish, it absolutely drove Bruce stark raving mad. You see…Bruce hated his Father, but dearly loved his Mother. It had always been a problem.

Most of the neighbors just shrugged off Gene's oddities until one day it'd become impossible not to take notice. He'd started having boisterous arguments with the Mayor regarding the 'rite of passage' for those using the small lane in front of his house. He couldn't stand all those strangers and merchants walking by and gazing straight into his windows…Especially the medical staff that worked in the nearby retirement home. Seeing their crisp uniforms continue parading by his place…*really* pissed him off…so much so, he'd become adamant the lane become a private dead end.

During those loud and mostly public confrontations he'd always pull out a monstrous sized skeleton key that worked the dividing gate between his place and the street that circled the village named *Tour d'Ville*. He'd obnoxiously dangle the damn thing in the Mayor's face every time they met. He'd become so insolent, he actually began considering himself the exclusive gate keeper controlling the passage. His deplorable conduct continued until at last… he'd prove himself the victor in gaining his way. With having the closure in place, it would finally give his sweet wife

Audrey the opportunity to turn the large blank canvas at the end of the lane into her exclusive private dream garden. Soon it would be filled with fragrant creeping roses, colorful wisteria and aromatic lilac bushes.

Gene's disheveled look must've been intentional is all I can say. He was such a mess that even the villagers couldn't fathom how a guy like that could've landed a woman who always showed up looking like a Ralph Lauren ad. She was so chic, often wearing her long silver hair in a thick braid with her antique turquoise jewelry…She'd always been admired like she was some kind of a local goddess.

Nevertheless, Sophie thought the village was so antiquated and backwards in its approach to accepting anything new that only the world's most ignorant dropouts would've chosen to live there. In addition to her feeling dismayed with the type of lifestyle the village offered, she was increasingly disappointed in Bruce's behavior when there. She felt he always revealed his inner most insecure child when visiting his parents. Even his posture changed when around them. He no longer stood tall showing off his handsome physique nor exposing his confident smile like he'd done in their early days. That's when she'd been so in love and in awe of this Strong, Successful Owner of the most famous poster shop on San Francisco's Fisherman's Wharf.

Sadly…it'd already been a couple of years since wanting to shower him with luxurious gifts like in the beginning. She once even surprised him with a Cartier lighter…and to this day she couldn't get over what a careless klutz he'd been when nonchalantly admitting, he'd lost the super expensive gift. I guess they both took everything for granted then. Those times had been their most exciting days of splendor. It'd been such a joyful period, one full of youthful spontaneity, great sex and constant laughter. While it was a good thing he finally quit smoking, he'd gone from one extreme to the other having become a boring health nut. Forget late nights out with fine dining and martinis, now it was all about 8 hrs of sleep and 'green' drinks. He no longer resembled the fun, sexy adventurous guy she'd once fallen in love with. They'd grown apart and she knew it was the beginning of the end.

Long story short, she felt he'd lost his luster and was no longer exciting. Evidently for her that was the signal… it was time to make a change and move on. Having these new found revelations certainly made it easier to keep her time to a minimum when 'visiting' the small French village. Without some fashion related exhibition or superfluous trendy event happening in Paris that she could piggy-back her visit on, she'd never consider visiting Bruce and his boring family to begin with. 'Visiting' had become more of a convenient stop over than anything else.

Gene absolutely couldn't get over the fact that Sophie was so adored and received such blind faith and dedication from her employees. They were more than happy to take up the slack in her absence when she traveled. That type of unwavering commitment and loyalty was a world away from what he'd known. He certainly didn't think she warranted or deserved it.

He was primarily referring to Gayle, Sophie's design assistant. She'd jump at any directive given her way and never, but never, would attempt to steal the limelight or showboat her boss. After all, Sophie was a true powerhouse. She had sales agents with showrooms in all major US cities and certainly wasn't bashful when it came to calling the shots. But with all that success she still had a few of her own issues lingering about. She gave off a persona of being such a strong high flying eagle, yet it hadn't always been that way. Even with the image of having the world by the tail she still felt a void. She was looking for something or someone to scratch her itch. Bruce's parents had already surmised the end was coming to their son's relationship and astonishingly so…were able to determine that even having no internet…Go figure.

With all that Sophie had, there remained such a wonder why she would still have jealous flare-ups with other women in certain situations. She'd always been a real beauty but with all those years of being bullied as a youth for being 'the tall pretty girl' in class had taken its toll.

Unfortunately…that emotional damage had left her with a chip on her shoulder the size of Omaha. Those jealous insults had primarily been slung her way from other females. That alone left her giving off a fake facade and a competitive nature towards all women. She acted like she was superior when in fact underneath it all she remained self doubting and insecure.

It's sad how that shit happens…some of those nasty things experienced when we're in our adolescence can linger on inside for ages. Having carried around those scars for years, there could be no close relationships between Bruce and his sisters when Sophie was around. She always made it clear that she needed to be the center of his attention no matter what. She wasn't interested in letting 'them' in. Bruce, the poor schmuck sincerely loved Sophie and knowing of her struggles, always adhered and catered to her needs realizing full well it must've disgusted his family to no end.

The ultimate meeting place in town was *Bar Central.* It definitely was the hot spot for cooling off. The place always seemed to be the nucleus for gathering and funny enough it was conveniently located just across from the massive Catholic Church. Literally it was the logical location being that food and wine in France are religions unto themselves. So when Sophie did grace the family with her quick visits, she chose to spend most of her afternoons loitering at the bar with *her type of congregation*. Finally, a place in town where she could 'plug in' and have the freedom to continue with her coveted social media and cell phone use. She set up a 'virtual' office in the booth next to the front window so she could spread out and hold court as they say.

One of the semi regulars that happened to be there on one of those particularly fine days was named Josef. Everyone at the bar either knew him or had heard rumblings about him. Most just respectfully left him to his own. He was kind of a *local elite* who didn't much care for tourists or loud mouthed foreigners. He'd been a patron of the bar on and off for quite a few years, but he was more polished than the others who frequented the main watering hole.

There he stood at the far end of the bar looking like a strong, sexy, six foot refined statue of svelte masculinity. He definitely had presence, especially given his acute attention to detail displayed by his clothing choices…That turned Sophie on in itself. The fact that his defined pecs and strong shoulders were visible under his expensive featherweight cashmere didn't hurt either. In physically summing up this delicious creature, his gorgeous physique was long and lean and resembled a beautifully toned professional swimmer. He had a close beard that was nothing more than a dark sexy stubble that matched his head of long dark loose thick curls he wore swept back from his face. His tanned skin made the brightness of his brilliant white teeth jump out from across the room. And by the way, he just so happened to wear his faded tight Levi's like a runway model…and just the way Sophie liked 'em. My God, where did this hunk of a specimen come from? How was it that she hadn't noticed him before!

Their attraction was instant and it would only take a couple more sightings before they'd take the next step and begin actually speaking to one another…*verbally* I mean.

Due to his fine education, his vocabulary in English was perfect, but his heavy French accent made him so dreamy when he spoke. So let's face it…for a thirsty American girl there didn't seem to be much of a communication problem. Oh contraire, it was as if they'd already been having hot sex just by the gobsmacked glances they'd been shooting one another from across the room. Once their direct eye contact was locked in…they had a bit of an embarrassing difficulty releasing their gaze to look away from one another. Let's just say they were definitely *in to it* and each other, already.

Crazy and fun to think their intense flirtatious vapor infused the bar with something so explosive it was like high octane…waiting to ignite. Their smitten type of laughter was so giddy and playful, it soared…even resonating high above the music. They had some kind of wild coyote kinetic energy brewing about them, but the real *truth in the matter*…is that it all was in his secret plan. You see?…He'd already premeditated luring his target into his love trap and had sought her out intentionally. Everyone in the bar had probably already surmised that fact, all but Sophie that is. The bar just so happened to be the perfect place to set up his Venus fly trap and lure the American in. Voila…Here it comes, wait for it…He finally did it and made his move with a slow sexy strut over to the beautiful blonde. The time to engage had arrived…

"So…ma chérie, what *really* brings you to this little village?" he questioned in his *oh so charming* and sexy accent.…

I'm not kidding, I thought she was going to faint. He was standing so tall and steady at the end of her 'office' … right when he began slowly folding his arms in front of like he was some kind of Nobel Indian Chief. She was so spell bound, thank God she didn't melt and slide under the booth is all I'm sayin'…

With his calm stance and smooth mannerism, she actually felt a wave of panic come over her. His body language was so deliberate, she immediately felt intimidated and vulnerable. It's like he had some weird kind of penetrating x-ray vision with super powers. (including the ability to see her nervously sitting panic stricken in that tacky booth completely stripped of all clothing) It all felt a bit daunting.

It'd been soooo much easier just exchanging flirty glances and making visual innuendos…but now?…She was being forced to reply. She'd have to come up with something if she wanted to make further progress with this dreamboat. She didn't quite know how to handle it, especially when he opened his mouth and all she could hear was his gorgeous velvety voice slithering directly down to tickle her privates. His voice, not surprisingly was every bit as sexy as he was physically, so she made every effort to remain looking cool and collected while feeling the insatiable flutter of butterflies in all the right places. Her immediate secret thought of course when looking at this incredible specimen was to have major throw down sex with him right there. Perhaps he didn't have super powers…but I'm sure he was able to read those obvious thoughts plastered on her face just the same…

Seriously?…What the hell had just happened to our dynamically strong and independent girl? It's as if she'd been struck by lightening and was sitting there still smoldering. Even though she'd fantasized about this moment coming to fruition…now that it had, the entire situation felt overwhelming. The feeling was so heavy she actually had to adjust her position on the booth's bench seat…and I'm sure he noticed that too.

When he'd emphasized the word 'really'…it caused her to breathe faster. Then with flushed cheeks she looked away briefly to compose herself. Good Gawd, who the hell was this creature that was taking her breath away and making her feel like a goofy schoolgirl…Between his looks, his velvety voice and incredibly delicious scent, she felt like she was experiencing a sensory overload. She knew exactly what had hit her. It was the charm that exuded from every pore of this sexy man named Josef Decour the Third. All of this immediate surprising sexual overdrive gave way for her to stumble in her thoughts and immediately find herself reconsidering her previous lack of enthusiasm for the little village.

The shoe had definitely dropped, he'd finally moved the needle and opened the door to conversation. So…as it turns out, this gorgeous hunk came from wine family deeply entrenched in the area. His Grandfather had planted a vineyard and started a winery way back when it wasn't the glamorous life it'd become associated with today.

"Oh, I'm just here visiting with my friend's family," Sophie replied flirtatiously. What a misleading crock of shit that line was, but she said it with such conviction…it *'almost'* sounded believable.

We all know she was really just in the village trying to

survive a few days visiting her so-called 'boyfriend' and his boring family before zipping off to Paris. Of course that was her simple sure fire immediate non-truthful response to this sex God. She couldn't dare explain the real situation, especially after being so conspicuous with her flirty behavior towards this captivating creature.

The thought and anticipation of now seeing him at the bar when she visited had consequently made her visits to the village become more frequent. She was secretly hoping this new intrigue…who wore his jeans 'oh *so right'* could develop into something more. At the very least this flirtatious game temporarily provided a fun bandaid to brighten up her monotonous life with 'boring Bruce' during her visits. But who was she kidding?…What she actually had in mind was finding his replacement, and bingo…there he was, the perfect candidate standing right in front of her wearing a fine gage baby blue cashmere henley that draped his gorgeous sculpted physique like he was a statue in the Louvre.

She'd begun working her very best charms on the Frenchman to lure him in deeper, but this sophisticated shark wasn't such an easy catch. After playing an intense, mutually patient cat and mouse game…they began making every effort to intentionally meet one another at the bar with pre-scheduled dates and times. She absolutely adored… perhaps even relished the challenging chase he was giving. By all means, she certainly wasn't used to that.

At the very beginning, they 'attempted' to make their meetings seemingly look surprisingly accidental. However their 'casual' rendezvous had developed into becoming an expected daily event when she was in town. Sophie was always able to get away from Bruce with one excuse or another. It made spending a couple of hours a day with her new man trophy in attendance so rewarding, and yet sadly…quite easy to do. She loved getting to know all about this Frenchman. His worldliness, his accent, his education, and not forgetting…the reason why and how he filled out his jeans the way he did. Sophie thought he was the ultimate

French fantasy package tidily wrapped up into one.

She and Josef's budding relationship was the catalyst for her to *'innocently'* suggest to Bruce one day…

"Maybe you should consider making more frequent and longer visits to see your parents. After all, they're getting up there and will be needing you around more."

My God, she was Such a sales girl…of course her calculated and deceitful guilt tactic worked. Bruce didn't have a clue her suggestion was only a pretext for her visits to become more frequent as well, especially now that she had other 'special' interests in play.

The freshly minted time that comes with a newly infatuated couple when the sparks begin to fly is truly an amazing thing. It's the space where you feel like you're the only ones in the universe. Remember?…That rare aura and sweet kind of unique period when you think you're in a world all to yourselves and invisible to others.

The only problem with their particular bubble was that they were sitting in the middle of a crowded small town bar with all eyes and ears on high alert. All were waiting and listening with bated breath, anxiously anticipating their next move. It was pretty transparent seeing what was going on, but no one was paying attention right? Ahh Falling in Love or perhaps just in Lust…Isn't it something splendid? The two of them were so over the moon they were unaware of all the other patrons in the bar who happened to be glued to their every word and interaction. It'd really almost become embarrassing…

Sophie was able to keep hiding her growing infatuation with Josef a secret from Bruce, or at least she thought she had. He seemed oblivious to Sophie's new found passion and interest for the village. It could've been that he was either so consumed with his never ending arguments with his Father or perhaps he was just on his way of falling out of love with our girl. Who could say at that point. Apparently, she wasn't the only one that'd become ambivalent about their relationship. Either way, he never questioned her need to be spending her afternoons alone *working* at her 'local office'.

For such a quick minded girl, how could it be that she was so naïve to think no one could see she and Josef's smoldering chemistry had reached its boiling point. If Bruce hadn't noticed any changes in Sophie, at least everyone else in the bar certainly had. This newly found couple…with their mutual playful antics had the other patrons eagerly studying them out of the corners of their eyes every time they 'happened' to get together. Nothing was ever said directly or aloud mind you, that's the way the village worked. They preferred to keep their speculative opinions strictly passed and murmured amongst themselves. This was now the latest underground tremor of juicy gossip and the newest source of amusement for the 'cliquey locals' to feast on.

The fact that they were able to witness the deceptive love story unfolding right in front of their eyes was the most relished tidbit to hit town in ages. This unfiltered kindling romance was being so blatantly displayed for all to see, it'd actually become similar to a local sporting event…(French soap opera style). It had the entire local audience teetering and hanging on to every last detail. Needless to say all bleachers were happily filled secretly watching this love spectacle evolve. The bar owner was always thrilled when the new love birds fluttered about…meaning more clients would 'drop in' when the word got out that they were 'in residence'. When the news broke, it was like a *'paid preview' on HBO* with seats being saved at the bar if you can imagine. It really was a big deal for this sleepy village to experience such a new scandalous event taking place. The 'regulars' had their own secretive underground rumble happen regarding this highly unusual *affair developing*. They passed around their gossip by texting…but when the *show was on…reservations were required*.

It was absolutely all so deliciously deceitful to observe…What fun it must've been for the local bar flies to be provided with such enjoyable free entertainment. It was proving to be the best scandal being played out in a Very long time. That my dears, *is really* saying something given the history of the village. Just lucky Gene hadn't gotten wind of it. That little village was crawling with hidden secrets. And as far as Bruce was concerned?…Why bother letting him know…'The American' had never really been considered *one of them* anyway.

During Sophie and Josef's time apart, they'd begun secretly communicating on a regular basis via text or email whenever possible. The coveted and highly anticipated day…(what Sophie would consider The Big Event) *finally* happened thank GOD. It was during her next visit to the village. Six long weeks had passed since she'd been in town and Josef was more than eager to see her.

She was right on time as she bounced into the bar for their pre-scheduled rendezvous. When their eyes met the energy between them was so strong you would've needed a power saw to cut a measly sliver through it. Consequently, the bar immediately stood still and came to an unprecedented screeching halt. The patrons didn't know what to do…It seemed like the music faded and the entire bar remained in suspended motion, that is until someone *finally* exhaled. Forget about hearing a simple pin drop, they'd moved way beyond that. The place became more than silent just waiting for something to happen between the two. Then…with Josef quietly approaching his prey like a clever sophisticated jaguar, he made it obvious he felt extremely empowered just seeing her.

"Take a drive with me," he boldly said sliding into *her* booth 'accidentally' brushing the nape of her neck softly. He loved it when she wore her hair up.

He began fantasizing about pulling her hairpin out and seeing her beautiful golden locks fall freely. If playful sexy looks could actually speak they'd already be whispering sex talk into one another's ear and shredding their clothes off….

"A drive?…Seriously? OMG" Sophie thought while remaining as outwardly poised as humanly possible. Inside however, she was beside herself. The change of scenery, not to mention a bit of private time could no doubt advance their relationship. Somewhere and just about anywhere other than that crowded little local bar would be a welcomed change. The place was starting to make her feel claustrophobic. She knew going out alone with Josef would definitely be crossing the line, but by that point she was more than ready to go for it. Bruce who?

As I was saying…she'd been using every bit of her charm and wit on the Frenchman, but even so, she wasn't sure if she'd be able to reel him in all the way. Having this initial invite of 'going out' certainly meant she was at least making progress. It was encouraging because Josef was such a sexy big fish…she hadn't been sure if this day would actually ever materialize.

She'd discreetly done some digging into his online history, but unfortunately it was disappointingly obscure. Even though a complete and *total assessment* wasn't fully available, being the tenacious girl that she was…at least she recognized enough impressive info to keep her eye on the prize like never before. It was all so exciting even if it was only for an afternoon 'drive'…but sadly of all the damn times this particular visit was more of a super quick one and wouldn't give them much time alone. It was mid season in the fashion game and she'd already planned a brief trip to Paris the following day before returning to SF. She was going to attend Premier Vision, the only fabric and trend expo that really matters, some say.

By Simply being asked out, she felt a floodgate of emotions simultaneously come rushing in. She was thrilled yet nervous, scared yet weirdly relieved…(And to think, some assume we women can't be multitaskers…)

As her heart began to race around and do back flips…outwardly you would've never known it. After all, appearances in Sophie's world were paramount. On the outside she might've looked like she was managing to keep a calm profile, but on the inside she was jumping off a ten meter high dive with no gravity. Just the idea of being totally alone with this hunk made her flutter like a girl in lustful flight.

After agreeing to their outing, she cleverly began preparing her *'office'* to appear as if she'd just stepped out momentarily. She actually thought no one would be suspicious or notice her absence if it looked like she was still there *'working'.* She thought she was being so discreet, but all the other patrons began quietly smirking in their surveillance. Watching her obvious moves gave them such delight. *'Staging'* her office was quite the seduction production and the peanut gallery were merely happily sitting on the sidelines intrigued and observing more of the amusing love story unfold on center field.

Just as she and Josef were about to make their exit, Sophie conveniently came up with a last minute silly excuse of having forgotten something. She'd reconsidered and thought, "It'd be far too obvious if we left together, much better for me to meet him at his car. Less conspicuous and no one will notice that way"…Seriously? Her fellow patrons by the way were just eating this ridiculous act up. Watching her nervously prepare for her seemingly nonchalant exit was a real show stopper. They even turned their bar stools around for her performance.

After a few minutes of shuffling papers, she finally collected her cell phone and her anxious thoughts…then gracefully walked out of the bar like a princess. She'd left her 'work' laid out on the table in its perfectly chaotic and choreographed positioning, deciding it finally looked as if she'd just stepped out for a few. Within a couple of steps however, her casual walk had accelerated…almost making her break into a sprint. She screeched her fast paced run back down into a slow walk just as she'd arrived at the back of the Church where Josef was waiting. That's when she saw him…he really was the hottest man she'd ever laid eyes on.

He just so happened to be casually leaning against his glistening burgundy DS cabriolet like he was posing for the 'The Sexiest Man Alive' cover. In all confidence, she probably could've used a bit of CPR at that point, the poor girl. She'd begun struggling to conceal her unflattering panting. Seeing her chest emphatically pump up and down…the smooth Frenchman smirked satisfyingly to himself as he tucked her into the bucket seat on the passenger's side. He then casually walked around the front of the car never losing eye contact and slid down into the driver's side. It was such a Hollywood move, I'm surprised he didn't roll over the hood followed by some kind of a cool kitsch dance move.

Between the tight snapping sound of the heavy vintage car door closing (not to mention the one his jeans made sliding down onto the hand stitched leather seat)…it was all becoming a dreamy reality. She'd definitely need to keep her wits about her even if it was becoming increasingly difficult given these sexy circumstances. Sophie felt like she'd been beamed up into an air tight space capsule with her heavenly dream man and no one in the entire world could pierce her euphoric bubble. Her new found universe was all just sitting inside this sexy open cockpit. She couldn't breathe. It was all too perfect and seriously, it was almost enough to give her a heart attack for Christ's sake.

In reality they didn't know one another enough to feel comfortable with the silence…so she'd felt the need to say something…just about anything at that point.

"This car is a masterpiece" she accidentally blurted while exhaling. It came out more like an embarrassing face fart than a compliment. She was horrified. Secretly, all she was really thinking about was jumping across the console and slowly kissing his salacious lips. Thank goodness the moment eloped. So much for playing it cool…

"Merci beaucoup," Josef replied with a smile. "She's a Classic. I've enjoyed this car for years, but she didn't look like this when I got her" he said as he began caressing the leather covered steering wheel.

Sophie looked at his large tan hands moving slowly up and down the wheel and could only imagine what they'd feel like trailing down her spine.

"I had to do a complete renovation on her. She'd been covered up and hidden…just sitting in our family's barn ever since my Father was a boy. She was the pride and joy of my Grandfather's collection, but I never remember him actually driving her. It's funny, even though she's also one of my favorites, I seldom take her out either. I guess she's only meant for these types of special occasions," he responded looking deep into her eyes with a devilish grin.

Good God, even the way he lovingly spoke about his car made her own rhythm beat. She sat calmly, silently expanding her thinking further while pretending to listen to him lovingly speak about his car…(ie: What would his sleek nude torso feel like sliding all over mine kind of thing) And by the way, she became curious what *he'd really* been thinking about when he'd been caressing that steering wheel…Their sizzle had begun to spark.

"I usually drive the Rover" he said turning the key and cutting the tension. The hydraulics kicked in and the car began to rise. Sophie quietly sighed thinking that even his damn car was magic.

Josef's Grandfather had been well loved throughout the region. Amazingly, he was respected by farmers and bankers alike. It'd been he alone who'd rolled up his sleeves …working the land when he first arrived. He'd really shown his chops and done so without owing a cent to anyone. He consistently demonstrated a humble and loving behavior towards the locals and never once acted entitled or above the rest. Josef Sr. had always made a point of helping any distressed neighboring family save their farm during difficult times. After doing so, he was never vindictive even if and when some of those whom he'd helped came back as competitors.

His reputation was flawless and one of an honest man. He always took care of the locals and by doing so was revered by most and accepted by the majority as being 'one of their own'. His Parisian upbringing had not only given him tough street smarts, but a strong backbone as well. After all, he'd arrived in the Dordogne as a single man toting his ten year old boy and not having much of a history that he chose to discuss.

Even though most everyone in the region thought they knew him…very few actually did. One of his big secrets was that his wife, Josef's Grandmother, had a juicy affair and abruptly left him for someone else. The 'other' however, was not a man, but a woman. The haute Parisian Crowd didn't think much of it, but for Josef's Grandfather?…It was the ultimate embarrassing disgrace. He didn't understand it, and sadly…the situation made him feel inadequate. He felt he hadn't been quite man enough. It was a devastating heartbreak, a fissure carved so deep he thought it would never mend. He left his life in Paris feeling completely shattered and took what money he had left, his only son, and escaped to a place where he could get his hands dirty and his mind clear. He bought a dilapidated Château on a large parcel of undeveloped land and got to work. Soon after, he was joined by an orphaned teenager named Michel who'd eventually become his loyal 'right hand man'.

Grandfather tried his very best at raising his young son alone in the country. His ex-wife remained busy living the high life in Paris and her new found lifestyle didn't include sharing the love and sometimes the burden of raising a child. She'd clearly made her choice in the matter.

It was only when Grandfather found a special woman to live in the *Château* that he began to feel whole again. Actually having a new woman in his life who offered a warm understanding with constant stability…(not to mention delicious home cooking) did it help ease his pain and allow him to move on from the past. She also served as housekeeper and nanny to his son. This woman had conveniently become the sole female figure of the Estate. It was with her non-wavering support that Grandfather began to feel happy again…Laetitia was her name.

Now just so you know, Laetitia was a lovely soft spoken type of French woman who was about Sr.'s age. Finding this job allowed her to move back to her homeland and escape an abusive marriage from her British prick of a husband in London. Her ex did his best at damaging her image by demeaning her character with years of stated falsehoods and mis-guided information conveniently given to the courts. Either through the manipulation of his finances and the use of his influential power, she literally was forced to leave her only daughter behind. Even though it was the most difficult decision in her life...she left knowing at least her daughter would be given a good education and need not for anything. In her heart she knew it was worth the sacrifice.

In some bizarre way it was all relatable to her as the boy she was to be looking after would be about her daughters age. Her missing piece or imaginary 'replacement' had subsequently been fulfilled...but then the years passed. It was too late when she'd found out her daughter, being barely in her twenties, had died in childbirth giving life to a baby girl. The sweet little child had been raised by her ex in the UK until his death. Laetitia had only seen her once as an adolescent when she'd come to the *Château* during one of her summer vacations. She'd been introduced as a 'family friend'...with no other questions being asked.

Sadly, Sr. had always been openly disappointed with his son. In fact, they'd never really gotten along. Beginning with the move, and the years to follow, their strained relationship had always been obvious and painful for others to witness. Laetitia especially suffered watching it unfold and knowingly chose to stay on the sidelines. Grandfather's son (Jr.) happened to be a rebellious and antagonistic kid growing up who often craved his Father's undivided attention. The little trouble maker would often act out in the most horrific ways in order to receive it. He showed so much tenacity in his mischief that one time he even snuck out one of the mules from the barn, tethered the poor animal so tightly that with a bit of ingenuity and whip abuse, down went a couple of complete rows of pins holding freshly planted grapevines. The rows of plantings had taken two long weeks of back breaking, painstaking work...yet had been destroyed in one quick instant...just for a bit of *fun* for a devious adolescent. The little shit was always looking for...and getting into trouble.

Jr. found humor in spooking everyone he came in contact with. That is, until one doomed day when the little punk was blindsided and sent off to a strict correctional boarding school in Bordeaux. Unfortunately, that wouldn't be the simple and easy answer either. When the day came for the immature boy to be set free and return home at the mere age of seventeen he most definitely and without question felt the need to continue his self-serving shenanigans. For starters, on the sly he'd secretly begun seeing a waitress from some weird Tiki restaurant in Bergerac. That doesn't take into account the couple of cars he'd already totaled since his return...so it would come as no surprise that he'd 'accidentally' gotten the waitress pregnant.

The girl had no intention of keeping the baby, but Grandfather being the absolute ruler of his kingdom felt the need to intervene. He conveniently worked out the details by paying the girl to become invisible. The lucrative deal came with the stipulation of delivering a healthy child and the promise of never being seen or heard from again. She accepted the terms and generous offer, ultimately fulfilling her end of the bargain. The child was named Josef (III) after the lineage of his Grandfather. The boy was his namesake, his pride...his one and only true joy. The *Golden Boy* had arrived.

Grandfather showered love and affection on his Grandson his entire life. He took him everywhere...Rides on the tractor when working the fields, showing him how to prune the perfect vine, riding lessons, and of course lavish trips to Paris and elsewhere when time allowed. Their trips together also involved a master class in home decor. The Golden Boy was even asked to help with deciding upon fabric choices with anything needing reupholstering in the *Château.* So needless to say, he was granted and exposed to the finest of everything early on. Oh, and that also included a well rounded education of the theater and ballet in Paris and London of course. Grandfather also made it a point to take his precious little Grandson on trips to NYC, beginning with his thirteenth birthday. Good God…there really was no limit. Everything beyond imaginable was within reach for his Golden Boy, the sky included…

Grandfather exposed and taught him what true refinement and luxury was in the manicured upper class. He gave his namesake the world on a silver platter…until the day when it all came tumbling down. Grandfather's cancer diagnosis changed all of that. Luckily, it wasn't a long and drawn out illness, and by design our little Josef would be the only one at the old man's bedside when he passed. You see…it was all in the plan.

When it came to Josef III's Father, (aka: Jr.) he'd sadly become a serious womanizing drunk. It was no wonder his pride made him want to hide his previous male sexual encounters he'd had with a few of the local chaps. Grandfather was always paying off a few men for their discretion and secrets to be kept, but as we know nothing ever stays a real secret for long in a small French village like Issigeac. Stories just get swept under the carpet for a while then re-envisioned for another day with a different audience. Charming isn't it?…Those gossipy little places. What a *sweet* little enchanting village that must've been…

Sr. had always thought his son's only achievement in life had been to produce an heir, even if it'd been getting some random unknown waitress pregnant by accident. The circumstances of the separation between Josef's Grandparents had certainly set the stage for an unbalanced future for 'Junior' that's for sure.

Grandfather always generated such vile ways of acting towards his son, it was unbearable for others to witness. The hatred shown towards the boy probably had nothing to do with the kid himself, but rather the fact of his mere existence. Just seeing the boy was a painful reminder of the betrayal Sr. continued to feel from his own failed marriage, but his cruel behavior was beyond unconscionable. He considered his son a total loser, having no machismo, no ambition, nor any desire to continue running the family business. He made no secret displaying his obvious disappointment and given his blatant disdain…it made things even worse for everyone involved. Bless the poor kid's heart, he'd never *really* been given one iota of loving guidance that would've made him want to follow in the old man's footsteps anyway.

Even as a child, the Golden Boy always sensed there had been some mysterious unexplained invisible wedge between his Father and Grandfather. He knew something serious must've happened to make their relationship so antagonistic towards one another. No way could it have been just his Father's immature personality or his sense of tawny entitlement, there just had to be something else… He'd always been curious about the origin of the unhinged hostility between the two.

Having three generations of men named Josef living in the *Château* was a bit of a complicated issue to say the least. Josef the III always figured that Grandfather must've taken his resentment out on his son, for his own marriage's failure. The Golden Boy's Grandmother had decidedly chosen a new lifestyle and partner years ago, continuing always to show no interest whatsoever in knowing anything that had to do with her past. That abandonment had unfortunately set the stage for her poor little bastard, in fact Jr. had been left out there all alone in the world feeling he couldn't do anything right. The lack of interest for him made for a most disruptive home, and needless to say…for one combative and insecure up-bringing. It really was pathetic. He might've been raised in the 'big' house, but it certainly wasn't a house filled with love. That is…until the Golden Boy, baby Josef came along.

For years Grandfather had conveniently bottled up his feelings deep inside, but that all changed with the arrival of his grand child. He was overjoyed to finally have an outlet to funnel his obsessive feelings into. His son had *finally* done something right even if it were fathering a child unintentionally. Instead of being a 'loser' he'd become a hero. (Temporarily…at least)

That sentiment was only valid until Grandfather was able to get his hooks into his latest namesake. That alone would allow him to dismiss his own 'loser' son for good. He never thought of the baby as a mistake, but rather a child that would secure and protect the family's legacy. He'd more than see to it which was undeniably cruel of the old man to consistently favor his grandson over his own. For the Golden Boy's Father to have felt alienated in his own home, feeling jealous and competitive with his own offspring must've been the most pathetic and depressing scenario imaginable.

Laetitia had witnessed their cruel dynamics for years doing her best to pacify each situation. The toxic manipulation the three male generations continually played out on one another were always kept strictly amongst themselves. Causing grief to one another was the only objective in their exclusive little wicked triangle. Josef III had been so spoiled and brainwashed by his Grandfather having been fed poisonous thoughts and lies about his Father, it made the 'game' that much easier for him. The privileged little boy prevailed at the top of the pyramid and wow...did he ever. He knew where to make it hurt.

It wasn't until the reading of Grandfathers last Will and Testament that it was spelled out so clearly. Simply unbelievable, the old dude had finagled a fail proof way to completely disinherit his own son and leave his entire estate to his beloved grandson by 'skipping a generation'. The way it was written, the *Château*, the winery, and it's one hundred and forty-eight hectares of prime land, his rare car collection...You get the picture...basically the entire enchilada...lock, stock and barrel was to go to his grandson Josef. The Golden Boy, his ultimate joy, his namesake would live on...and he'd made arrangements to ensure that was exactly what would happen. It shocked no one but Grandfather's own son, Jr. The Poor Prick...he never really recovered, but who could seriously blame him.

Learning of his Father's ultimate betrayal, in his deepest depths of depression, Golden Boy's Father committed suicide by locking himself in his room and drinking himself to death. His reckless demise was sadly the result of his complete shock, humiliation and dis-appointment. He died upstairs alone in his room, and not one person even noticed until a few days later. It was the wretched odor coming from the last room down on the right that'd become so intolerable that it made people finally take notice. The poor, lonely rascal…he'd checked out for good.

This tragedy left Josef an orphan. A Single, Selfish, Good Looking, Multi-Millionaire one at that. A successful Vintner at the ripe young age of twenty-three to be exact. His Grandfather had made sure he was to become the sole owner of one of the most beautifully prestigious and sought after properties in the entire region. It'd been seven years since that life altering change had occurred and the business was thriving. Turns out, little Josef was quite the entrepreneur in his own right.

Amazingly, there had only been a few women come and go since he'd become such a major player and presence in the area. He'd always used women as playing cards in a deck needing shuffling on occasion. By design, he'd created a space to intentionally remain secretive and untouchable. With his male dominated upbringing, he'd developed some serious trust issues when it came to women in general…all except for Laetitia that is. He'd always been taught to keep himself on the down low, remaining an independent loner and well above the fray.

When he did go to the bar in town, it was usually just to take a break from his isolated lifestyle. Village life was certainly a change from the world he lived in. Bar Central always offered him an escape with a wide variety of colorful locals to observe. Even though the village was revered as having one of the Best Farmers Markets in France, he preferred to stay away from the village on Market Sundays. He thought they always brought out the distant voyagers and local tourists in full fashion.

He loved being a glorified farmer in an arena where he also needed to be a shrewd businessman. Given his past opportunities, he inherently knew how to play both sides of the field. He'd always stayed to himself when having a drink at the bar…that is until that one fateful day when he laid eyes on the tall raving blonde beauty from San Francisco. He'd only heard about her…but was actually shocked to see how beautiful she was in person.

*

Chapter Deux

Josef put the car in Drive and they were finally off for their long anticipated afternoon together. Autumn was in full swing and there was a little nip in the air. Driving with the top down and heater on, they were surrounded by all shades of sumptuous fall. Such enticing vivid scenery gave way for the most romantic and seductive experience between them. Silently winding in and out through the country roads they were graced by rolling hills filled with endless rows of golden orange and deep burgundy leaves clinging on to meticulously pruned grapevines. Feeling the humming vibration from below, catching captivating whiffs of his musky cologne swirling within the cockpit and promenading leisurely around in this rare French Classic…It undoubtedly offered more than enough satisfaction for a sexy first date. It was their moment at last.

It wasn't until Josef surprisingly turned off the main road and onto a long gravel driveway did Sophie snap out of her euphoric dreamlike state. She sat leaning back and looking up in awe as the car passed through a set of massive towering black wrought iron entry gates.

"Jo…sef? Sophie said, straightening up and turning to him with a seductively sweet voice."Where are you taking me? I just thought we were going for a little tour and would end up back at the bar. I didn't realize our drive had a destination."

To be honest, she loved surprises and the fact he was doing something so unexpected really excited her… Arriving at the end of the long drive, Josef just smiled and turned the engine off. As the car's hydraulics began lowering the immaculate sports car, he slowly leaned over and whispered softly in her ear…"Chez Moi."

Sophie looked up and thought to herself…"Holy Shit!!!…you mean THIS…is…*your* House?"

Josef meanwhile had become distracted noticing

one of the helpers working in the adjacent vineyard as they approached. The field hand was a good looking young buck in his mid twenties named Gilles. He was a new hire and probably needed some 'direction' from the boss is what she figured.

"I'll just be a minute," he said leaving Sophie sitting in the car alone.

I don't think she even noticed she was so overwhelmed. She was utterly taken aback by the gorgeous scene that had just been rolled out in front of her.

The *Château* was so exquisite it could've come from one of the coveted posters she'd had plastered on her bedroom wall as a teenager. Other high schoolers usually had large images of rock stars, but not our girl. Her dream posters were exclusively kept to those of elegant French *Châteaux*. I guess her underlying lifelong desire to live in one was powerful enough for her to use a boring and predictable boyfriend as a vehicle to get her there, after all. The poor dweeb…Bruce actually seemed like he was a pretty nice guy.

Once Sophie opened the heavy car door and got out she stood motionless. Unconsciously she began stroking and gliding her hand across the velvety smooth and highly glossed door panel. It all felt so deliciously rich. She looked around at her surroundings and realized they'd actually arrived in a parking area that was surrounded by large vintage cement urns. All were filled with evergreen shrubs trimmed in perfect topiary style. The uniformity of the tall stacked ball shapes gave an impressive outline to the private open air parking enclosure.

Suddenly a flash whisked by her with lightning speed …immediately bringing her back in to the present. The 'flash' was actually a sleek little black cat with an adorable white patch under her chin. And before she knew it the little feline had jumped up gracefully landing on the leather backseat. Sophie was relieved to see it was only a little kitty…which made her laugh out loud.

"This car is so sexy, even you want in on the action,"

she muffled to the pussy as the feline stretched, rolled and purred with contentment. Just as Sophie was leaning in to give her a belly rub, Josef reappeared startling her.

"She's the boss of the house...I'm glad you've been introduced" he said swooping the cute kitten up in his arms with a loving cuddle.

He stroked her endearingly before letting her jump to the ground where she performed what seemed to be her traditional lacing maneuver of rubbing her scent off onto Josef's pant legs. Her name was Midnight and had been a stray that'd *happened* upon the *Château*. Ever since, she'd become more than just a token mouse trap...she was the beloved mascot of the Estate.

The *Château* was beyond spectacular. As massive as it was its clean lines made all the details really stand out. The front entrance had a simple low cement landing that framed two enormous entry doors. Above the doors and inlaid into the stucco was an engraved cement disk that served as an ancient Family Crest of sorts.

At first sight, Sophie couldn't imagine the full extent or depth of the place, but she instinctively felt it must be like the man who owned it. Larger than life, elegant, mysterious, and full of intrigue. It was only then that she felt she understood why he'd been so reserved and standoffish at first. It must've been that he was just being cautious, wanting to take his time in bringing someone new into his universe. She suddenly realized his world was so much bigger than she'd ever imagined...surely that's why he'd been so aloof at the beginning...She had no clue of his old monied wealth, especially after coming up empty with her online search. He'd obviously been clever enough to bury most of his financial information worthy of the gossipy net that would suggest he was sitting on this kind of fortune. Every detail of the impressive *Château* was built in haute fashion and of the highest quality. The place was beyond Fabulous. It was simply gorgeous, refined and grandiose...

While Sophie stood motionless gazing in awe...in her mind she'd already unpacked, moved in, and was happily living out her dream life there with Josef. She just needed to figure out how to continue with this juicy new relationship and seal the deal. With Josef taking the initiative of inviting her 'home'…at least she knew she was getting somewhere…

The setting was exquisite. The compound…(if you will) combined a few other huge structures creating the footprint of the Estate. One of the adjacent buildings served as the official tasting room, usually only open by appointment only. There was another large stone structure this side of the tasting room that served as the horse barn. Sophie couldn't get over the sheer elegance of the place, especially having horses live in five star conditions. The entire property was pristine and felt like a manicured version of a heavenly Garden Utopia. Even the most monied American snobs would've been impressed…it was all…so *French*. She began losing herself in her ambitious dreams again until Josef gently touched her arm, bringing her back down to planet earth. She had a way of drifting off into her magic dreamland quite often.

"Bonjour, Allo?…Anyone home?" A brief moment passed before he laughed, "Well what do you think?"

Sophie couldn't speak. Her only reply was with a small smile. She had such beautiful lips and the longest eyelashes…Josef could easily read her with a glance. When he saw the corners of her mouth subtly raise, he knew…he already *had her*.

"Let's see what's cooking shall we?" he said as he walked up to the large set of heavy doors and opened one side. He slid his large sexy fingers in between hers and led her by the hand into the foyer. He gave her a quick kiss on the cheek before turning and softly shouting out…"Litty, we're here."

Josef wasn't much on giving an *official* welcome. One that women would appreciate at least. You know…the kind where he would nicely explain a few details about the round foyer entry and/or elaborate on the massive furnishings visible in the adjacent rooms…like the Harry

Potter type library on the right or the over the top huge 'great room' to the left? But Ooh No…Instead, he'd leave our girl standing alone to figure it out on her own. He was already busy making his way through the chiseled stone archway in the back wall of the foyer. The passage would lead him down a long stone hallway that would end up in the kitchen. Laetitia met him at the entrance with a kiss on both cheeks.

"Alors? Well, where is she?" she quietly questioned with a smile and an arched eyebrow.

"She's probably still standing slightly paralyzed in the foyer where I left her. I think she's impressed" his voice echoing as he made his way back to retrieve his *'tourist'*.

Laetitia, or 'Litty' as Josef had always lovingly called her was in her early eighties by then. She didn't get around as easily as she used to, but that didn't stop her from diligently giving Josef her unconditional love and support like she always had. She stood just above five feet tall with a soft calming crackly voice which only added to her elegant charm. A spry and fragile figure of grace, she always looked well put together. Her wardrobe had drastically changed throughout the years and now only consisted of a few cashmere cardigans in various colors and numerous pairs of identical black light weight wool pants. (Most of which had holes that she had lovingly mended several times over) She wouldn't dream of letting Josef buy her anything new because each of her favorite older pieces represented a specific time and a special place in her history. She was adamant in wanting to keep those cherished times alive. It was as if she draped herself in memories, endearingly wearing her past proudly.

Her daily work ritual had ended years ago, so nowadays she mostly stayed quiet in her private suite just off the kitchen. The living room in her suite had a lovely grand stone fireplace that shared a chimney with the one on the other side of the wall in the kitchen. Both were always kept clean and well stocked by one of the workers, usually Gilles the new guy. Seems that young dude did a bit of everything around the place…

Laetitia's living quarters were within ear shot and close enough for her to know when Josef was home rumbling around in the kitchen. She could always sense when he descended down into his coveted wine cave. His cellar was sincerely one hell of a 'sha-wingin' man cave on steroids. No one but Josef ever went down into the abyss of his family's heritage collection without an invitation. It was his secret stash, a coveted place full of his own Estate wines and personal favorites. There were Cabernets from Napa Valley, Malbecs from Argentina, and a few select whites from 'down under'. The entry to this marvelous secret was actually a cleverly hidden faux door panel located in the back right corner of the kitchen next to the end of the fireplace. It blended into the wall seamlessly and resembled something straight out of a Batman movie. No one in their right mind would ever expect to find a hidden passage in the kitchen that led to one of the most exquisite and expensive wine cellars on earth. The vaulted 'cellar' below superseded the concept of 'average' on every level… It was definitely a wet dream come true for any elitist wine aficionado.

Josef was relieved to see Laetitia up moving around easily on the day that'd been 'scheduled' to bring Sophie home for the *big introduction*. Not usually a characteristic in Litty's nature…she'd actually been waiting for their arrival with a bit of nervous apprehension. It wasn't every day that her Josef brought a woman home, especially one who he felt was so special. Litty wanted to greet them graciously and fulfill his days expectations. A couple of times a week when she could muster up the energy, her loving routine would be to prepare Josef one of his beloved home cooked favorites. Today was one of those days and she'd made a monumental effort to do so.

"Hungry? I think there could be a little something waiting for us in back" he said making a sexy move to grab Sophie. She was standing in the exact spot where he'd left her. "But if it's not to your liking, I know where to find something you might like a bit better"…he said with a dry innocent precocious boy look just waiting for her to give him some kind of flirtatious response.

The particular 'spot' where she was standing could've well been a page ripped straight out of Architectural Digest. She'd never experienced seeing such beauty up close and quite frankly she wasn't in much of a rush to move. She looked down to see the flooring was made of massive squares of weathered tumbled travertine. Evidently from the years of wear, they now showed a gorgeous glossy shine with a deep opaque waxy finish. There was a huge sweeping staircase to the right that spiraled way up high to the second floor where at its peak… celadon cotton velvet panels met in the center like a carnival tent and hung to the floor below acting as window coverings…

"I'm sorry Josef, what'd you say?"

He just smiled at her being so lost in his luxury. He then tenderly led his lamb back to the kitchen.

"We can look at everything another time, there's someone I want you to meet." His voice echoing as they made their way back through the arch and down the long hollow stone passage way to the kitchen. It was there that they found a small framed woman with bright blue eyes standing next to the massive wooden farm table. She seemed so petite in comparison…

"You must be Sophie," Laetitia said extending her hand.

Josef did his best to interpret and navigate their meeting. He so wanted their first encounter to go well and didn't want any *'American innuendos'* or *'figures of speech'* to get lost in translation. (The French already think we're crass and undereducated to begin with, so Josef feeling a bit bourgeois in his protectiveness came to the rescue) Even though Litty had been fluent in British English, it'd been years since she'd consistently spoken the language. Truth be told, languages are one of those things: 'unless you use it, you lose it. It's not necessarily like riding a bike. Words go missing and become difficult to find when they get stuck in the multilingual cobwebs. Now where were we…

In the last few weeks, as much as Josef had given hints about his new budding relationship, Litty wasn't so sure. She'd prefer to keep her distance from the American girl to begin with. Why should she give up the familiar and welcoming two cheek kiss so soon? Nope…No way…Not so fast, there would be time for that. Sophie would need to earn that familiarity and closeness.

Anyone who knows anything about French culture certainly understands that keeping a bit of distance and self reserve is ones only real safety net. If one gives their 'familiar' reserve up too easily, (using the Tu grammatical tense for a friend or kids)…that shield of 'educated distance' can never be recuperated. Once you do make the transition from Vous to Tu…you let people in to know your business…Until one passes the test of really getting to know the person, it's so much safer to remain distant and hide who you really are by keeping it at the *Vous* status. (Older peeps also fall into the Vous category when one wants to show respect, Ugh that fucking French Grammar)

"Enchanter" Sophie replied, in her heavy American accent when nervously shaking Laetitia's hand softly.

Such a wrong move to begin with. Nobody likes a wimpy handshake, especially when it's being returned to a strong old French woman who's curious. Funny to think Laetitia then deliberately made an uncomfortable gap of silence to the situation. She'd created that suspended moment of angst in order to *size up* the new girl. She was a seasoned old pro at doing this manipulative maneuver and kept her distance discrete, yet remained poised in order to control the awkward moment. She wasn't interested in any foreigner encroaching…until she had 'cleared' inspection.

You see when Litty had come to the Estate, she'd secretly brought along her own mixed bag of hidden issues. She was so grateful to have finally found some tranquility in life by finding a wealthy and beautiful environment to live in. But whatever her initial motivation might've been, it was like she and Grandfather had rescued one another in some strange kind of way.

"I made one of Josef's favorites this morning. I hope you'll enjoy," Laetitia said turning her back to the couple while directing her attention to the table. She sliced the quiche and placed a healthy sized wedge on each of the two small Limoges plates she'd arranged in anticipation of their arrival.

"Litty...c'est trés, trés jolie comme d'habitude" Josef said, inspecting the French 'egg pie' with delight like it was the first time ever to do so. He continued with an endearing whisper spoken in Sophie's direction, but loud enough for everyone to hear, "Laetitia makes the best quiche in France."

The Grande Dame beamed with pride hearing the familiar compliment and certainly would never disagree. She merely gave Josef her customary affectionate wink. The three sat at the table for quite a while before Laetitia began giving Sophie a rather complete and thorough 'interview'. It was more of a polite interrogation than anything else. Sipping on her cup of tea, Laetitia sat relishing in her satisfaction watching them eat her creation, all while keeping a watchful eye on Sophie's table manners. Her inquisition began with detailed questions pertaining to her origin, likes in art, travel, and last but not least...her opinions on France.

When completely satisfied, Litty stood up, (and so did the 'new' couple) when Laetitia...may I dare say...kissed Sophie on both cheeks before retiring to her suite.

Josef exhaled so deeply you would have thought his toes rattled. Sashaying over to his favorite corner, he found an open bottle waiting and poured two glasses of his latest vintage. As he passed one to Sophie he chimed his glass to hers and said with relief, "Thank God, I think you passed... now please...tell me you liked her quiche." When their eyes met they giggled together in silence...

He sat down smiling wide like a Cheshire Cat feeling proud and grateful that Litty had obviously approved. They remained seated at the table and drank a few glasses of delicious Pécharmant before continuing to devour the balance of Litty's…so called masterpiece.

The kitchen felt rustic yet practical and unlike anything Sophie had ever seen. The entire first floor of the *Château* had the same gorgeous weathered travertine throughout, all except for the massive sized kitchen. That room offered super wide dark polished wooden plank flooring which gave the room an anchor of warmth and grounded everything in the space. The back wall happened to house the show stoppers…two massive identical burgundy *La Cornue* deluxe stoves. For any of you that are a bit less than official culinary specialists…those bad boys remain God's gift to the gourmet cooking world.

When Sophie nonchalantly observed their expensive trimmings she smirked and thought, "wow…just at least one of those monsters must've cost more than my first car."

To say they were just some stunning Eye Candy would be a gross understatement in anyones world. With having culinary Ferrari's parked in your kitchen…no wonder achieving the perfect quiche could be considered child's play, even for the old gal. (Dream on girl, your first car wouldn't have even paid for the brass hardware)

Cleverly disguised were a set of side by side Sub Zero refrigerators filling the once vacant wall cavity between the two doors at each corner of the left wall. With all the hidden cupboards, doors and wall cabinets, you never would've imagined there were two appliances the size of Honda station-wagons secretly hidden behind. Everything just seemed 'too' perfect.

Somewhere in the back of her mind she felt a slight uneasy tinge about everything.The environment was so orderly and manicured, it almost seemed fake. It actually gave her cause to think they were hiding something. The space was so designer sterile even our queen of reinvention, our beloved MS Stewart would've questioned the place. It's a pity Sophie had become so consumed by her own ambitious thoughts of grandeur that she'd let her initial impressions slip and go by the wayside. By only wanting to capture her dream life of luxury…her judgement had become foggy making it impossible to hold on to her gut instincts. Her greed had overcome her logic and sadly, by-passed any of her initial apprehensions.

The mood had definitely lightened up after the little inquisitive 'inspector' finally had taken her exit for the afternoon. It gave Sophie a feeling of giddy enthusiasm. She jumped up and made the size test of standing underneath the imposing mantle and it barely touched her head to give you an idea. Full of playful delight, Josef just watched with amusement as Sophie bounced around the room seeming to have as much fun as a curious child on Christmas morning. It actually gave him a boner…so he stood up and put his arms around her waist and leaned in. He gave her a kiss that was so long and deep, she almost fell over from dizziness. Once she was gently released…she could only imagine what going all the way would feel like. Here was her dreamboat who'd sailed in… (or was it a big ass yacht…)

Even though he was totally in awe witnessing her charming adolescent behavior, he felt giving her a tiny taste of his honey was enough for the time being. He'd never been one to show an over abundance of emotion. He'd always been taught to remain coy…hide his game kind of thing, especially when it came to the locals or anyone he *really* didn't know. Using discretion had always been his religion and to think…not one soul in the Village had a clue, not even an inkling that on occasion some of the worlds biggest and finest wine producers discreetly gathered together at the *Château*. He never let that little fact become well known…

When this impressive and elite guest list did descend upon the place, it was more like bats screeching back into their hidden dark cave at dawn. Seems as though this wealthy group had formed some kind of a club of sorts in years past. They always kept their meetings secretive and a very exclusive thing, only to be shared amongst themselves. Most of the members usually arrived in the region by private jet, leaving their swanky silver wings parked at the small puddle jumper airport just south of Bergerac.

Josef didn't mix his personal life with the Villagers unless he *really* needed something. He'd only been interested in observing them from afar and just like Laetitia, he'd always managed to keep a good ear to the ground. When Litty would be enjoying a fire in her room, she'd listen like a hawk for any movement of the cave's door panel opening. And to think, Josef thought he was the only one to know about his secret hiding den. The walls were thick and even though her hearing wasn't as keen as it'd been in day's past, her other senses remained as sharp as a tack. With intuition being her strong suit she was also blessed with the good fortune of having eyes in the back of her head.

Josef always loved hearing her embellished and over the top stories when she reminisced about the grand events from days past. Like her sweaters, she kept those memories close and very much alive.

Traditionally for the field workers, Grandfather would offer these amazing BBQ pig roasts in front of the tractor barn. All workers were invited and encouraged to bring their entire families along to the event. It was such a festive environment with kids playing precociously while others laughed and danced the night away to the live music. No one else would've dared consider including their farmhands in their Holiday festivities…all but Grandfather that is. He'd always hosted and offered the meal, wine and music as a gesture of his gratitude for those who'd helped in his success. Gratitude parties were all but nonexistent…

The infamous roasts were the most coveted summer extravaganza held on Bastille Day. The Golden Boy always had such fond memories of those BBQ's. After all, it'd been during one of them that he'd received his first kiss from a girl visiting from London…A family 'friend' of Litty's who stayed at the Château for a week or so during her summer break. Those parties were always so lively and fun…they had Quite the reputation. Everybody still reminisces and speaks of them fondly.

"So…tell me…you're seriously considering leaving

for Paris tomorrow?" Josef questioned in a sexy nonchalant manner. She didn't answer immediately...so he continued..."If that's really the case...why don't I meet you there?" he calmly said, laying his glass back down on the farm table. He was such a cool customer in his demeanor... she almost fainted.

That's when the reality of the situation struck Sophie like a lightning bolt. Hearing those words actually come out of Josef's mouth made her realize she'd either have to dive in completely or get out of the pool entirely....After having months pass playing their flirtatious and seductive games... she'd been hopeful Josef would become caught in her snare. But now that he was actually ready to *make the big move* she felt her back was up against the wall. It'd all been a fun challenging chase up until then, but this suggestion made her realize it was now or never. It really was...decision time.

All of a sudden she felt a cold sweat come over her. It's as if the opportunity had flipped and her flirting game of sensual tease was coming at her like a freight train. Slow down right? Ha, let's face it...the idea of having this hottie meet her in The Love Capitol of the Universe was so tantalizing, it certainly wasn't the time to get nervous and back out. Her sexy side had now made the decision.

"What a fabulous place to start our love story together. A hot rendezvous in Paris of all places!" Her temporary panic and trepidation had merely been a fleeting thought...because at that very second she looked at Josef and knew she'd found Bruce's replacement. This entire situation had become something straight out of her fantasy story book. A steamy affair with a Gorgeous Man who could provide a beautiful future...A Man who also happened to be Filthy Rich, Sexy as Hell, and wait for it...*French* to be exact. She never *really* looked back unfortunately. Here was the ultimate Francophile's dream, a real treasure chest in every aspect one might dare to say.

It just simply hadn't occurred to her that the web she'd been so cleverly and meticulously weaving was instead about to circle back around and trap her. Let's face it, there's never a clean and easy way to have an affair. To be a cheat, to be disloyal, it's all a deceitful lie no matter how you spin it. After all, none of this had happened spontaneously…it'd all been something she'd nurtured and calculated every step of the way. But given the opportunity of having an actual physical affair?

Suddenly she felt a pang of guilt. It wasn't about Bruce of course, that would've been too easy. It was more about not having been upfront with Josef concerning her current relationship. Unbeknownst to her, the deeper she got entangled with him, the more he was intrigued. It excited him to no end seeing her fidget and dance around the truth. He was being seduced with her talent of being able to dodge reality and continually conceal the fact that she was indeed Bruce's long term live-in girlfriend. Remember…this player knew it all along.

Given Josef's entitled upbringing, he'd acquired a tremendous sense of self. An arrogance about him so grand it gave him reason to think he was the only talented one in the couple. In fact, the only one shrewd enough to hide something as big as the complicated and deceitful secret he was hiding. He thought it was an incredible asset that Sophie could assume a poker face and not fess up to her current relationship when asked if she were single or had someone special in her life. Watching her try to maneuver and side step a truthful response regarding her status delighted him immensely. He'd egg her on with snippets of subtle questions then let her hang out on the limb for a while. He dangled her out so far, he was playfully amused and curious to see just how she was planning to finagle her way *back in* and figure a *way out* of the situation. He really thought she was so exceptionally clever.

News of just about everything travels fast in a small village the size of Isslgeac. Sophie was an outsider and even though she thought she was so savvy and *in tune,* she sincerely didn't have a clue on how a tiny French village *really* worked. But go ahead…try telling that to a thirty-two year old successful fashionista from California's West Coast. For these *types* of *'know it all'* foreigners like Sophie, they usually needed some kind of powerful rude awakening to suddenly bring clarity to their situation. Teach em' a bit about the in's and out's of how a French Village R*e*ally works kind of thing...

Josef couldn't help but feel a weird sense of guilty pleasure and a slight frisson of sexual charge watching her squirm when asked specifics about her relationships. He knew damn well that suggesting a sexy rendezvous in Paris would create a perplexing dilemma for her. He couldn't wait to see how she'd react. He'd actually been waiting for her to break down and confide in him with her truth. He was so entertained by her thinking she was smart enough to play him. He took great pleasure and actually really liked the challenge of having to wait it out. He was literally savoring the game with this beautiful blonde amateur, but then strangely enough his plan had begun to backfire. Her sheer beauty coupled with her profound sweet naïvety had begun to really get under his skin...he was actually beginning to have feelings for her. I guess her snare had worked.

"Why?" she said feeling dumbfounded at his off the cuff surprising suggestion. She immediately began grappling internally for a more sophisticated response. He thought she was so charming when she was put out of her comfort zone and caught off guard...

"Oh, were you...planning a trip to Paris tomorrow?" she asked hesitantly...with a bit of adorable pleasured panic. Her pupils had become so dilated it was like looking into huge bottomless caverns at someone searching for some inner calm. It was obvious she was trying to keep her heart from jumping out of her chest hearing his latest suggested agenda. The poor girl...she had no idea he was reading her playbook.

"No...but I certainly think it would make our first night together a special one."

There it was. Good GOD, he actually said it aloud. Hearing that shoe finally drop gave her enough confirmation to make what remained of her melted heart...somehow begin lightly pumping again.

"What do you think? Meet me at the Hôtel De Crillon tomorrow late afternoon?" he suggested with a smoldering bit of sexy persistence. "It's on the Place de Concord. Do you know it? We can have a few cocktails there and perhaps dinner if you'd like...before going on to my place" he whispered romantically, lowering his voice into a sweet nothing. It was enough for Sophie's heart to start bouncing around again like she *were* a pinball machine.

Once able to regain her wits about her, she felt so satisfied. Within her alter ego she'd begun thinking the entire situation had played right into her hands. But the thing was...It had definitely become a little bit more complicated than she'd planned. How could she have let herself get in so deep without having the conversation with him explaining her true reason for being in the Village? Their relationship had begun on a pretext, a lie and one big deception. Somehow, she rationalized her actions by justifying her behavior...They were just having 'an emotional affair' up to that point, right? After all, they'd not yet consummated their efforts...it was just a little kiss is all. So my dears, that ridiculous rationale was the only safety net and justification left in her toolbox that would accommodate her absurd denial.

I guess men aren't the only ones that can come up with that stupid bullshit. Somehow, and who knows why... she was still thinking the ball was in her court not realizing she was way out of her league on this one. He really was such a smooth crooner...just like so many of 'em.

"Your place?" she questioned...trying her best to sound blasé and sophisticated. Hearing that little additional detail of him having a flat in Paris confirmed her inner conflicted ping pong game was over. This little 'bonus' of a Paris apartment was more than enough for her to begin revving her engine like never before. She immediately began internalizing again, only this time she could now see her new life unfolding.

Hmmm, now let's see, recapping the inventory 'as one would'...An extremely hot man with a gorgeous *Château,* a super acclaimed multi Award Winning Vineyard located in the picturesque French countryside?...And now? A flat in Paris? For Christ's sake...Forget all about her momentary teetering, she was ready to go for it full throttle. No more flirting and definitely no more looking back even for a second. It was time to get real and see where this thing was *really* going. Snap.

"Sounds fantastic Josef. I'd love to meet you there, but what should I do about my luggage?" she questioned using her best demure girl voice wanting direction. What in the hell had happened to our strong, over the top confidant?...She'd become such a subservient mush under the *Josef Effect. Geez us...*

"Just ask for Antoine when you arrive. He'll be expecting you and will take care of you from there," he said sweetly smiling back at her with an innocent look. It was obvious then, the fucker was gleefully strumming his internal ukulele.

They finished their wine with the last few morsels of Litty's quiche before Josef picked up their dishes and placed them in the sink.

"Laetitia will be happy to have something to do in the morning" the Golden Boy stated inching closer. With his fingers delicately skimming her baby soft cheek, he moved in tenderly sweeping her hair back from her face and intensely stared into her beautifully bright and eager eyes. He took his time, smiled then kissed the tip of her nose ever so lightly. Then came another kiss. This time it was a long, wet intentional kiss. He was so artful and experienced that even his kiss reached down to her tip toes. She felt lightheaded again by the time their tongues had finally finished their slow dance. Their rhythm and chemistry was so frickin' good it felt natural, like they were totally in sync and meant to be. His kiss was as slick as the way he wore his jeans...it actually made her weak in the knees.

Should it have been left up to Sophie, she would've

been more than happy to have their first romp right there on that fabulous kitchen table, which rivaled the one in the dining room by the way. So when it came to it...either would've worked brilliantly for what she had in mind. She immediately went wild with fantasies of them having hot sex all over the place. With his kind of *savior faire* and this type of environment she felt she'd found her true dream match and now? He was giving her what she'd worked so hard on getting. She quickly reigned herself back in...

      "Patience my dear, patience. Keep your cool...he's a big fish and it will take time to pull him in completely, but you're getting close..."

      They made their exit without even a simple goodbye to Laetitia. It was his *Domaine* after all, he came and went as he pleased.

      "I'll take you back in the Rover if you don't mind. I have a few other errands to run in town after I drop you off. I'll have one of my guys move the convertible back in to the garage for the night should they not have already done so. The evenings are coming earlier right about now and are full of humidity this time of year. I always like to keep that little baby warm and dry" he said...gingerly taking Sophie's hand and escorting her to the passenger side of his new beautiful midnight blue Range Rover. Again, once inside she'd need to adjust her seating position like she'd done in the booth. Only this time it was on a luxurious leather seat versus a cheesy replica. Her 're-positioning' had somehow become a necessity worth repeating when he spoke so smoothly...did I say crooner somewhere? *Bullseye*...

      That kiss in the kitchen had her so smitten that even his simple directive of what car to drive was heavenly. She thought his was a voice of subtle command. He wasn't like one of those guys that finished every sentence with a question mark at the end like Bruce did. Sophie loved the fact that she was with a man who could take charge and make decisions. She'd longed for that. Having a strong partner as her equal was what she thought she'd been missing in her relationship with Bruce. He'd always given her the freedom and choice to be the one to make the decisions. Somehow, she'd always viewed that as some kind of weakness on his part. She'd become tired of being the one always to lead the way or at least she'd convinced herself of that for the moment. Silly girl…what the HELL was she thinking?

The following day finally came…but it couldn't have come soon enough for Sophie. She was more than prepared and ready to say her adieu to Bruce and his family. Having had such a fantastic and alluring first outing with Josef, she couldn't wait to make her *exit*. Thank goodness her bags were already prepared (like always) for a quick and easy departure…but this time it was faster.

With plans already secured and in place for a sexy rendezvous in Paris, she was quicker to leave than usual. Bruce and his parents thought nothing of her hasty, flippant rocket speed departure, it'd always been Sophie's style to leave abruptly. They thought her previous departures had always been business related but now, her light-speed getaway had another hidden meaning all together. They weren't even suspect. Sophie was thrilled at the thought of her future with Josef, it had all gone as planned…and her French dream life would soon become a reality. After those smoldering teaser kisses, she was more than ready to be intimate with the Golden Boy. Feeling certain he'd be an incredible lover, he'd also give her the life of luxury that she'd always wanted. She left not feeling the need to look back…only forward.

✳

Chapter Trois

Their anticipated rendezvous set to meet at the Hôtel De Crillon was beyond perfection. No doubt there's a reason why this five star Hôtel remains one of the classiest on the planet. The ambiance was beyond lavish…and dare I say dripping with 'seasoned' sophistication. It wasn't one of those trendy places. Sophie had never stepped one foot inside, but only had heard of its over the top illustrious reputation. It was quite the contrary when it came to the Golden Boy…he'd chosen the Hôtel because he knew it well and felt totally at home there. It'd always been one of his favorite spots and he frequently dropped in for a meal and a glass when in town.

Josef's first introduction to the place was when he'd been young. Grandfather had always adored their resident Michelin Star Chef, so as you can imagine…many elegant dinners had been held in its haute dining room with the kid in attendance. The location of the Hôtel was ideal being that it was only a stones throw away from the family's pied-à-terre conveniently located in the nearby swish 7th arrondissement.

Sophie arrived at the Hôtel at 5:30pm dressed in subtle yet sexy *happy hour* attire. She wanted so badly to make an entrance looking the part of a trés chic, well traveled and worldly woman. Zooming up curbside, her car was received by two bellman who rushed to open the car door as it was rolling up to its final stop.

"By chance are one of you named Antoine?" she questioned, stepping out of the glistening town car. She'd achieved her goal. She *looked like a million bucks.*

Antoine had actually been the one opening the car door. You see?…These people at the Hôtel had their routine down pat. Antoine pleasantly and professionally welcomed her to the Hôtel and reassured her that her bags would be well taken care of. He spoke impeccable Frenglish and had obviously been anticipating her arrival. Within their brief encounter he also gave her directions where to find Monsieur Decour, who happened to be waiting in the lobby's main cocktail lounge.

As she walked up to the main entrance (where both huge doors were being opened for her simultaneously) she had another one of her out of body experiences. The interior was fantasy-like and only something she could've imagined in her candy land dreams.

Now as we know, (or should) Sophie was pretty well versed and traveled…but this *fairy tale landing* of sumptuous wealthy decadence was nowhere to be found in her wheelhouse. She was so overwhelmed in her surroundings, she hadn't bothered to notice her bags hadn't actually been taken out of the car. As I said, they had Josef's program down…anticipating every last detail. It was apparent this wasn't his first *rodeo* at the ultra swank five star digs.

Josef's usual entertaining program (when arriving at the Crillon expecting a guest) automatically triggered his fine tuned protocol to begin like clockwork. The bags left in the car were already being whisked away and delivered to his flat in the nearby 7th. Everyone knew the drill, all except for Sophie of course. Should Josef make the decision to take a room for the evening the manager certainly would've miraculously come up with an available Suite even if the Hôtel was overbooked. The Hôtel was famous for having a certain panache and was very familiar catering to clients as influential as Josef. The concierge had already sized Sophie up in anticipation for any requests or last minute whims of desire. The symphony of discreet back stage moves by the staff was so beautifully orchestrated, it was more than just a well oiled machine in motion…It was simply perfection.

Sophie had barely made it into the lobby when she suddenly stopped…abruptly. She acted like she was Dorothy seeing the yellow brick road for the first time. Nope…not like any dreamworld she'd imagined that's for sure. She'd tried her best to make her arrival look eloquent and refined but once inside the ambiance was so spectacular she froze in her tracks...again. She was making an embarrassing habit of this ridiculous school-girl behavior wherever or whenever she was with Josef. Funny that she'd always taken pride in thinking herself to be so well heeled... especially with any situation that pertained to the upper 'stylish' side of life. This is when in fact, she became a real tourist...thinking she could play along with any level of society. But Josef soon made her realize she didn't know anything when it came to how the _real_ posh and polished _really_ rolled.

She knew very little about the elite, the privileged... those that come from Big Old Money. After all, it takes a while for a self-absorbed barely made newbie to comprehend the difference.

You know the diff...the ones that are well versed in their self-serving elegance...The ones that inherit their future and make their tight knit little cliques very difficult to penetrate. The select few that grow up playing golf at the club, have stables full of polo ponies and are zipping around on private jets for weddings and island parties. We're not talking about the 'regular' upper class of people who are lucky to make enough to go on that nice tropical or ski vacation once or twice a year (maybe)...We're talking about the difference between the 'old school' private side vs the _other side that exists_ for us mere mortals. That old system really can't be taught, you need to be born into it to fully grasp and understand its '_inherited_ breed' of sophistication.

Definitely a prerequisite would be coming from a Prominent (rich generational) family, attend the right schools where your Grandfather happened to dedicate a building and has his name on it, be a member of the right clubs... and beyond all...socialize only where you'd meet big connections. It's a realm that works within itself and is tighter than any whip stitch your Granny ever made I can assure you. The word I'm looking for is...ExClusive, but you must say it only with pursed and protruding lips to be effective.

Josef had been waiting in the bar for over a half hour while keeping a watchful eye out for Sophie's arrival. The minute he saw her in the lobby he stood up and went to recover his awestruck girl. She was so mesmerized by the massive chandeliers and other fabulous details…It just made him laugh finding her 'stuck'…again.

"How was your trip?" He asked kissing her face twice on each side for good measure.

"Stressful," she replied with a smile. "You know how these Parisian drivers can be…my car was a little late picking me up and I didn't want you to think my tardiness was intentional."

"Oh not to worry," he said with a smug laugh. "I would never have thought that. The important thing is that you are here with me now."

What a charmer this handsome guy was. She should have noticed the danger signs then and run for the hills, but instead he swept her arm behind his back and escorted her to the small table where he'd left his half empty flute of Champagne. It was still bubbling from the bottom up just like she was. They were immediately greeted by an attentive server as Josef pointed to his glass and said, "Another one here and one for my lovely lady s'il vous plaît."

They sat with Josef being very focused on giving Sophie his full and undivided attention. "So how long do I have you" he whispered ever so sweetly.

"My return flight to San Francisco leaves tomorrow evening at 6:00."

"Fantastique…then we can spend tonight and all day tomorrow together…How lovely" he said kissing the back of her hand.

She swooned until the server reappeared with their two flutes of Champagne. The bubbles slid down easily. They kept their conversation playful talking their way through one flute after the next. They enjoyed a few canapés that'd been sent over, evidently whipped up especially for them being as they were nowhere to be found on the small bar menu.

After the delicious *hors d'oeuvres* had been pleasantly consumed Josef subtly announced, "Take a walk with me."

It was like phase two of his script had begun playing out. Parisian evenings in the late fall have a certain...'*je ne sais quoi*' about them. It feels like the City of Lights moves in a hyper extended slow motion. The evenings offered an unexpected flurry of an occasional brisk breeze, but over all it felt like a prolonged, lingering Indian Summer. The trees were just allowing their leaves to be blown about and the river boats along the Seine were still providing the very last of their open top tours into the wee hours. Paris is the City for Lovers...and they knew that's exactly where they were headed.

They left the Hôtel and walked along the Champs Élysées then crossed over to Av. Winston Churchill to view what was on the marquis at the Petit Palais. They weren't in any rush. They were laughing and tickling one another while holding hands and walking in unison. Then half way across the Alexandre III bridge, they sat down on one of the benches and spoke about all the locks that'd been attached to the security fencing...

"How many keys do you think are at the bottom of the Seine?" Sophie inquired. Josef just shrugged and continued to sit with his arm securely fastened around her waist. The night was so still and perfectly calm other than the light splashing sound made from the wake of one of the romantic dinner cruises passing below.

"Ready to move on?" Sophie didn't respond, but only stood up and extended her hand to pull Josef up to her level. Then she kissed him, I mean she *really* kissed him. That was the first time Sophie had been the one to physically take the initiative and make the move.

They were no longer playing one another. Both were already in the *love zone* and more than ready to proceed. The night had suddenly become humid and heavy feeling. With a whiff of change in the air, the last little bit of distance to his place felt like miles. Was it really the weather making them pick up their pace? Time for window shopping?... Nope, I don't think so. They both realized their desire and were ready to be on their united way. They only had to walk another couple of blocks to reach Josef's flat on rue Fabert.

"Here we are" Josef said as he punched in his security code on the keypad. The electronic door buzzer clicked allowing their entry into the hidden inner courtyard.

The building had been in Josef's family for decades. Grandfather's parents had purchased the place way back when it had originally been a single family residence. Years later it had been divided and converted into several individual apartments. Grandfather and his siblings each claimed their units...all using them as their part time Parisian get-away. No one lived in the building full time except for the guardian and his wife. They occupied the ground floor unit on the far side of the courtyard. They attended to any of the owner's needs or to any short term renters who visited.

'Ol Gramps kept the little gem as his personal secret playground and used it exclusively for his scandalous adventures. It was mostly used during the time when he was married and living with his family in a more substantial apartment in the elite 16th arrondissement. When life took its twist and his marriage collapsed, he walked away from it all leaving his ex with almost everything. He felt it was a fair exchange just to be rid of her for good. By being so amicable and not causing problems with the monetary aspect in their divorce, it allowed him the freedom to take his son and start fresh by moving to the Périgord region. His ex never knew about the love nest by the way...

That'd been so many years ago that most of the units had already been sold off many times over by then. One apartment after the next, gone for some reason or another leaving Josef as the only original family member remaining. He loved the quaint apartment and it's convenient location. The sexy little abode also had a fantastic unobstructed view of the large green park, 'Esplanade des Invalides' directly across the street which was surrounded by a few of Paris' most monumental treasures. To the right was Napoleon's Tomb and to the left was a marvelous view of the Sacré Coeur on the horizon.

Josef had obviously decided their first night as lovers should be there. The Hôtel De Crillon had delivered Sophie's bags to the Guardians like clockwork who in turn had taken them up to the apartment. They were sitting in the corner of the living room conveniently waiting for the lovers' arrival.

"Oh you sneak!! There they are! I'd forgotten all about them" she giggled. "What kind of spell do you have me under anyway?" She questioned, wrapping her arms lovingly around his neck.

"A spell that I hope lasts for a long time," he said lifting her up, twirling her around and kissing her. As he slowed their spin down...they stopped and stared into one another's eyes. Game on. It was time to begin.

He slipped her jacket off then began slowly unbuttoning her super soft satin shirt. He was either kissing her mouth softly or 'titalizing' her breasts as he began slowly slipping each tiny button out of their embroidered little holes one by one. His hands were so steady as he worked his way down her shirt placket until all that was left was a vertical row of dangling little helpless shiny black buttons. He opened her shirt with dexterity exposing her completely. Her fragrance was so captivating, he found everything about her to be just as he'd hoped and imagined. He'd been patient long enough and now he wanted to touch and caress what he'd been longing for. He thought she was absolutely exquisite and with all of his fantasizing leading up to this exact moment, he'd now become stiff and hard as a rock. He kept his movements fluid and precise. His kisses and sensual touches were all so deliberately slow, it made Sophie's nipples stand erect and point upward. He loved the signs she was giving him.

"I happen to have some nice Champagne chilling. Why don't we meet in the bedroom when you're ready so we can discuss the balance of our evening," he said casually not waiting for a response.

The buttons on her fancy shirt weren't the only

things left dangling. He leaned over and picked up the smaller one of her two bags and placed it in the nearby teeny bathroom, then he made his way to the equally tiny kitchen to retrieve the chilled bubbly.

"Oh My God!"…Sophie mouthed to her reflection in the bathroom mirror. She couldn't help but notice her bottom lip was quivering involuntarily…She couldn't believe this was really happening. She was thrilled to her core but knew she needed to take it easy and stay calm. She couldn't afford to let her emotions get away from her… especially now.

He'd been taking his time and made it quite obvious he was an experienced master in the seductive love game. To be honest…in no way, shape, or form was she accustomed to this kind of man. She'd only been with American men who didn't have a clue what it meant to be truly sensual and romantic. She'd always believed that foreplay should be a beautiful sexy dance of sorts, a sexual stimulation for a prolonged encounter if you will. It was finally happening and it certainly wasn't something her current 'Americano' knew anything about. This type of tantalizing foreplay was something completely new. An utterly delicious and erotic episode had just begun unfolding. She could only imagine what might be coming next. She continued to stare at herself like she was seeing someone else's reflection. She'd changed, she no longer wanted to trap him, she wanted him…to love her.

Okay stop. Stop right there. That's when it gets dangerous for us women. Falling in love with them for their 'potential' is really unrealistic. Our 'fantasy thinking' leads us to believe that he or she will change. That my dears…IS the ultimate denial. In this particular case, this sexy and sophisticated French Man was playing on his allure like a pro. He was so slick leading her on cue into his sticky web that she didn't even realize what was happening. She not only took the honey…but flew into his trap at warp speed. If he was so suave and experienced, how could she be so naïve to think this was something really 'unique' and 'special' to him. Let's face it, when we women let our emotions get too much in the way, even though we swear we aren't…it's usually the recipe for disaster. In fact, when those fantasies begin, you should realize your symptoms and begin to think a bit more like a man. After all, they have the capacity to have two heads but only think with one. We should do the same. A good romp never hurt anyone but oh, oh no…we usually think it's GOT to have more meaning. It's GOT to be love. He's got to feel something deeper Right? Snap out of it, seriously. Okay now where were we…

In Sophie's case, it was far too late. She'd already thrown any last shred of sensible logic out the window. In fact, she hadn't taken one minute of thought in all of this to listen and reflect upon her more rational intuition. Oh yeah… did I forget to mention?…She was already in the midst of stripping down and putting on a fresh lingerie replacement in the bathroom. How's that for a quick reflection? She'd already become completely intoxicated with him.

She pulled from her bag one of her all time favorites. It was a lacy bra with a matching g-string. The combo was in a soft butter yellow, she always felt sexy wearing it. She tossed and fluffed her hair, pursed her lips…then opened the door. She walked into the bedroom where she found Josef standing and gazing through the large picture window towards the park. He'd only a towel wrapped around his waist, so when he turned to face her she didn't even notice the two flutes of Champagne he was holding. It was his huge, supersized flagpole that stole the show. She almost tripped over the corner of the bed getting to the… Champagne was it?

"You're absolutely gorgeous Sophie, what a beautiful sight you are" he said smiling with approval as he extended one of the chilled flutes towards her.

They stood gazing at each other with total approval before turning towards the large picture window to admire the beautiful lights streaming in from across the Esplanade. The ambiance was beyond intimate, so understandably so…as Incredible as it was to have some of Paris' most magical sights lay just outside the window, Sophie was more enthralled with the view on this side of the glass.

(Have to say…couldn't blame the girl a bit)

Josef had lit a single candle which had created the right amount of a dim flickering light for the perfectly romantic ambiance. With the scent of soft lavender dancing through the air, hopefully the candle wouldn't cast a big enough glow to create a backlight for anyone to notice their silhouettes from the street below…But given the immediate circumstances they could've cared less. They were finally together and all alone. Pleasing one another was the only thing they were thinking about. It was scary, It was thrilling, and It was all so deviously reckless. Certainly it wouldn't have fazed them knowing a spectator might've actually caught a glimpse from below. It all felt so naughty, it only added to their excitement. They were two souls colliding in their own sexy fantasy world. Their only intention was to smother one another in their own sexual scents. Their bodies and minds were ready for just about anything. It all seemed so right…it was like nothing was off limits.

After clinking their glasses together and tasting the bubbly, Josef gently took the glass from her hand and placed it along with his on the corner table. He pulled her over to be standing in front of him while both facing the park. She loved the feeling of his muscular and toned physique meld into hers from behind. She'd been fantasizing about touching his gorgeous body since the first day she noticed him wearing that sleek cashmere sweater. That felt like years ago and now with their bodies standing as one, he felt exactly like what she'd imagined him to be. They were the perfect fit.

He released his towel dropping it to the floor. He secured her stance spreading her feet apart, then ever so gently nestled himself between her legs. He slowly outlined her curves with his fingertips like he were etching a lovers map of her body. He began softly kissing her upper back while undoing the clasp of her bra. Once he freed her beautiful small plump breasts, he tossed her bra onto the corner chair and leaned forward touching her upper back with his erect nipples. He began lightly caressing her breasts from behind then pulled her closer by softly threading his fingers through her hair...all the while remaining in position.

Seeing their bodies' reflection in the window made them realize they were the perfect combination made for sensual heaven. It'd all been worth the wait. They were euphoric seeing the other so willing and vulnerable that they drank each other's physical pleasure in one another's touch. She arched and leaned her head back on his shoulder which made him let out a whispery moan. He began rubbing the tips of his fingers over her erect nipples, then cupped her breasts firmly licking and kissing the nape of her neck...

He decisively moved his hands down both sides of her hips when he grabbed her panty strings on either side and lifted her thong up firmly. Then he continued by slightly pulling each side down slowly with subtle authority. He used the strings like a bridle to ride her, just like he would his prized thoroughbred. He began pulling himself forward then backwards ever so slowly letting the taught strings reign him into a slow rhythmic motion. This gave Sophie a sensation like she never could've imagined. Seeing herself standing in the windows' reflection wearing only a g-string and having Josef's sculpted nude torso jockey riding her from behind?

For God's sake people, it was such an erotic scene...she couldn't have dreamt seeing this one play out even in her wildest fantasies. Feeling his incredible manliness slide back and forth in between her upper thighs had her juices flowing. When Josef knew she was ready he rolled her creamy crotched panties down from her hips to her knees, then used his foot to finish pushing them down completely. He instructed her to step out of that poor little string...and she did as she was told. He slowly turned her around to face him, and ever so delicately ran his middle finger high between her legs. Feeling her so wet...he smiled and kissed her mouth sweetly, then led her to the bed.

He quietly instructed her to lay down on her back so he could take his place next to her. His immense size was her dream come true. He was absolutely stunning...He had everything on her desired 'Lovers Checklist' that she'd ever hoped for. Thank Goodness there was no longer any need for just her imagination, it was all on display right in front of her. He was the perfect package all the way down under. Sophie was so thrilled that this major detail had finally been unveiled and her burning question answered. Seeing and feeling his flesh made it real and tangible, his super endowment was as breathtaking as the rest of him...

Her overwhelming satisfaction and delight when seeing his body turned him on. His first reaction was to straddle himself above her and give a full visual by tenderly grazing his stiffness against her stomach for them both to witness. (...and admire? omg...)

"C'est ce que tu aimes ma chérie?"

"Oooh oui...you have exactly what I like my dear... You're beautiful and the perfect size of my dreams" she said, boldly looking into her lovers eyes.

There was no describing how sexy she thought he was. He could read it from his touch...He knew she was ready just by seeing her reaction as he skimmed her belly with such delicacy. It was an evening that would be full of climax. Then as mutual recognition, he seriously kissed her again. Their tongues met and twirled in perfect harmony together while anticipating the inevitable. His lips met hers in just the right way...It's as if they already knew where to find each others inner most sacred spots and pleasing positions. Their bodies meld together naturally, it was as though they'd danced this dance before. It all felt so easy and familiar, like only a perfect pre-destined couple would. The ultimate ballet had finally begun.

He gently opened her legs, got on his knees and slid down between them. He leaned forward and began kissing her breasts...only to move back down on her. He looked up at her thirsty smile and spread her legs wider, then he began kissing her intimate forest slowly. While not yet penetrating her, he made sweet and tender love to her. She'd never felt so uninhibited and appreciated in her life. Seeing Josef's face smothered in her private wilderness was an incredibly sexy sight. It all seemed a bit surreal, a bit crazy, and well...

let's just say…It was un-fucking-believable. The fact that she was actually experiencing *out of this world sex* with her dream man was all a bit delightfully difficult to compute.

His fingers delicately fondled and caressed her delicate velvets so he could slowly separate and admire her soft voluptuous pillows. He wanted to get to know every centimeter of her private sanctuary. Then with perfect timing he plunged his perfectly fitting tongue between them and made his first foray into her velvet cage. Each movement gave a delicious dance of his validation. He gave Sophie time, almost too much time…she wanted him so bad it hurt.

He knew she wanted him, but he'd decided to tease and torment her for as long as she could take it. He wanted her to ask him for it…actually beg for it. Sophie arched her back again and it was her time to let out a groan as she climaxed. It was the first time in her life that she'd honestly ever had a real exploding orgasm from oral sex. She now understood why French Lovers have the reputation they have. She loved the sexual tension and pleasure that he knew how to give. Ooh LaLa…the French.

When Josef finally came back up, he laid back down next to her. Then she rolled over on top of him…gently sweeping his dark curls back from his crystal blue eyes. She spent the longest time studying his face, then gave him a tender and lengthy kiss. She loved the feeling of his body below hers, her breasts perfectly lined up on his.

"It's my turn now," she whispered in a seductive, almost surprisingly aggressive manner. "I'm going to give it to you sooo goood my love…it's going to make your head spin." Her tune had definitely changed. "I want you Josef and I need you…now" she commanded impatiently. He just laid there soaking it up like a Golden Boy. "I can't wait another minute to have you inside me. All the way Josef, I want you and I want all of you."

Using her strong leg muscles, she stood straight up …and straddled over him. She bent her knees and slowly lowered herself down into a crouching position where her sweet spot was just barely hovering above his stiff wand by a tiny whisper. It was now her time to be the manipulative tease.

"Do you like that Josef?...Can you imagine what that's going to feel like when I slide all the way down on your shaft...umm?...Can you?" She watched his face become serious as she lowered herself down on him... taking all of his glory deep inside. It was his time to be overwhelmed...He actually thought it amazing that she could handle taking all of him. He loved it, the sexy bastard. She then found her rhythmic pumping motion and rode his wand up and down...her heals never leaving the sides of his hips. All the while he never stopped melting into her eyes. He couldn't believe what a little sphinx she was...It would actually be Sophie who'd surprisingly turn out to be His dream fuck.

He used his hands to cup her tiny ass and guide her to find their perfect spot in unison. She knew she looked completely vulnerable in this unusual frog-like position, but she also knew he absolutely adored it. He kept repeatedly telling her how unbelievably sexy and beautiful she was..."Tu es belle ma chérie et je t'adore."

She loved hearing and feeling his positive validation of her motions. His constant praise was enough to encourage her to continue using her strong 'slip n' slide' movements on him with no inhibitions. They certainly both must've been experiencing a special type of mutual euphoria...because his eyes were so focused with such immeasurable pleasure, she actually thought she saw them filled with tears at one point. That didn't interrupt her actions though, it only gave her a secret rush.

She knew she was giving him the *ride of a lifetime*. A ride that was really blowing his mind and knowing that made her feel extremely empowered, she felt completely beautiful.

It was as if they were experiencing something so rare, so uniquely intimate...that no one could touch their world of privacy. He made her feel so appreciated, so at that very moment she knew she'd captured him. In and out, up and down, until she'd found her pleasure zone and orgasmed again.

He loved watching her explode all over him. He couldn't get over how exquisite and sexually honest she was. This was the 'first' time in Josef's life when he was the one to feel like a rag doll. He'd met his match and was getting 'properly' fucked like he'd never been in his life. It was a *first* in many ways for the both of them. They were the PERFECT sexual partners and the best sex either one of them had ever experienced. Their Magic had begun spiraling around the room as it radiated from their hot sweaty bodies.

Sophie's legs began to quiver and burn as she slid down for the final time. She loved the feeling of being completely filled with him in every sense. Feeling absolutely exhausted, she laid down on top of his steamy wet body knowing she was the missing piece to their puzzle...She fit right in, and relaxed. It all felt so...*parfait*.

In having had their first real...or should I say...'un-real' physical encounter happen...it was obvious their experience had been far more than simply *a* great one night stand. In fact, it'd been so incredibly fabulous, it'd left them both dazed...(more like spellbound and freaked out perhaps would be more appropriate) Knowing full well they wanted their *'relationship'* to be so much more than just a one nighter...

Having to wait All of that time with all their bottled up energy, ready for take off?...Well, their night had all been far too exceptional to say the Very least...('*Worth It*'...like they say) Quite frankly I think they'd eaten each others sexual souls out of each other if you ask me...but then again, whatta I know...But okay...let's all relax and step back for just a minute to re-cap shall we?...Now wasn't obviously the time to talk about anything beyond the immediate. They'd already checked out and fallen lethargically into a land of hard and satisfying slumber. Until...

"...What time is it?" Sophie questioned feeling a little bewildered and disoriented as she sat up straight. They'd had such a physical marathon that rising from her deep sleep coma was a bit unsettling. She looked around the room only to see his towel and her panties on the floor, her bra on the chair, and their two almost full glasses of flat champagne sitting on the nearby corner table. No, it hadn't been a dream. Her Sex God was still laying right next to her. She actually wanted to pinch herself.

There was a beautiful new day filtering in through the picture window just as Sophie felt Josef's hand barely skim the small of her back.

"Bonjour my sexy fille," he said with a sultry gravel to his voice. He was still laying with a pillow half covering his face. He was so damn sexy she thought she might be dreaming with her eyes open. Lucky girl…

He pulled her back down next to him then rolled on top. He kissed her softly and said, "tu es absolument précieuse Sophie,"…Then out of nowhere he excitedly said,

"I need to show you something."
He hopped off of her with the precision of a military drone taking off…of course and made the perfect bedside landing. He was so smooth…fun must've been his middle name.

"Come on let's make a move," he said with both feet firmly planted. Seriously, it would've been considered a 10 for his landing score alone… "I think we should go down the street for a sandwich. Care to join me?" he said using his boyish and convincing charm. "I'm absolutely starving…" he said enthusiastically. She actually needed a bit of coaxing to rise…He, on the other hand seemed like he had all the Olympiad energy in the world.

"Come on sweetheart, let's get going…I'm sure you already know this being the world traveler that you are…but that weird looking thing that resembles a second toilet in the bathroom might be just what you need right about now. I'm sure it will make you feel better. Turn the faucet on at the back, then slide the lever until you see a cute little fountain sprouting up. Then by all means…take the liberty and sit right down on top of it. The *bidet* was made for times like these in case you didn't know. It will cleanse you and no doubt make you feel more relaxed. If I feel a bit sore this morning, I can only imagine how you must be feeling" he said walking nonchalantly to the kitchen with a little manly macho smirk on his face. He felt he had conquered…but something had changed.

He was finally without an erection and Sophie was able to get a good look and see his entire body in the light of day for the very first time. He was so beautiful but she was shocked to see he'd never been circumcised. That my dears, would take some getting used to.

She took his advice and delicately tiptoed to the bathroom to see about the little fountain he'd been speaking of. When she sat down on the tepid porcelain, she let out a whimper within her delightfully painful inhale. The warm water swishing around on her 'swollen's' gave her immense relief after the initial sting had subsided. She was so sore from their adventurous escapade…but wow, what a time to remember.

She wouldn't have traded that experience for anything. It'd been years since she'd not been able to walk normally after having had a good romp. But then again, she couldn't consider this particular episode to be merely that. It'd been far too good for that. For now, it was the beginning of a relationship with a hidden lover. Josef had turned out to be everything she'd dreamt of, she only hoped he'd feel the same. This was the consummation of a long term chase, but the word *forever* is more like what she had in mind.

After drying herself and taking the time to get her head on semi-straight, she quickly slipped into the living room and discreetly snuck her other bag in to the bathroom. She opened it and pulled out a pair of tan skinny jeans with a matching tonal ribbed turtleneck. She always looked pulled together given her program of packing easy standby travel basics. She kept it classic with items that could work for just about any occasion. Traveling light and keeping it casually elegant had always been her mantra whether it be a fashion exhibition or a small apartment in the 7th.

"Oh My God!! What the hell just happened?" She

said looking at herself again in the mirror. She couldn't believe all what had just transpired. Simply said, it was the most incredible night of her life, that's what…

At the bottom of her bag she blindly searched around until she felt the smooth zip lock baggy containing her perfectly folded vintage Hermes scarf. Her finishing touch was when she tied it loosely around her neck leaving it to drape about her shoulders. A great accessory had always been her crowning jewel. She slipped on her tan leather ankle boots and once she'd given herself a discerning final once-over, she opened the door to the living room and stepped down into the cozy space.

She was shocked to see Josef coming from the bedroom at that very moment wearing no other than a black ribbed turtleneck, black short boots, and a great pair of black designer jeans. (which made his body look so good, she was having second thoughts why in the world she'd agreed to such a simple thing as a sandwich)

Once they caught eyes on one another realizing they were dressed as contrasting yet matching bookends, all they could do was laugh and smile with nodding approval. They appeared with all intents and purposes to be a chic young couple that'd been happily together for years. It was apparent then, they'd mutually found within one another that long lost missing glove that actually fit…(you know… the sock that went missing in the dryer but somehow showed up out of the blue. WTF is that?)

Sophie's bags were already ready of course so she discreetly maneuvered them back to the very spot where they'd been left, only a short *Life*time ago. Everything in her world had changed since then. Love was in the air and in her heart..but as for the little get-away apartment? It suddenly reeked of steamy sex…it was definitely time to move on.

The elevator door opened and they both squeezed in to the typically tiny European *'ascenseur'* standing face to face. It was a quick ride down but *'being that they were still on their own planet'…*when the door opened they were startled to find the Guardian standing there observing them as they were in the midst of passionately making out. I guess the custodian might've been a bit surprised herself… She'd only been anticipating a passive ride up to clean the only other apartment on the third floor next to Josef's.

"Will you be needing me this weekend Monsieur Decour?" she stuttered once her element of surprise had somewhat diminished.

"No, merci. I'd like the place to remain 'as is'. No entry for anyone until further notice, Thank you."

The love birds feeling frisky walked out of the building into a clear, crisp day. They took a left passing the funky Chinese restaurant on the corner, then another left onto the famous rue Dominique. That's one of the most colorful streets in the 7th…it's full of fanciful pastry shops, gourmet groceries and just about every high-end specialty shop to be expected in the super swank arrondissement. During their walk while hand in hand, Josef made an unexpected Fred Astaire move with a side step off the sidewalk landing directly in one of his all time favorite boulangeries. Sophie of course was pulled inside along with him…

"This is one of the best places in the entire world" he said…with an endearing spark of culinary passion. "Their baguettes are exquisite and known throughout Paris. Ham with butter okay with you?" Sophie nodded with immediate approval. Who in the world could say no after seeing his juvenile delight…it was contagious seeing his childish excitement, even if it were…just over a sandwich.

"Deux jambon au beurre, s'il vous plaît," Josef pridefully said to the girl behind the counter.

For some reason Sophie felt when this girl smiled at Josef, she was giving him a look like she was ready to jump over the counter and plant him with a big one. However, he was still flying so high…he never even noticed. Then, when Josef wasn't looking the girl gave Sophie a discerningly spiteful and questioning glance while slightly moving her head from side to side.

Sophie thought, "Hmm this girl must've been eyeing

Josef as a potential just like I once was." Her intentional and disapproving look was like she thought Sophie was stupid for being Josef's latest victim. He never noticed that either. Sophie couldn't help but return the favor with a smirk, a wink and the words…'sorry bitch' folded loudly within their quick layers of silent communication.

Sophie was so blind at that point, she couldn't imagine that possibly the girl wasn't envious, but rather making an attempt to give her a 'girl's hint'. As in…Josef's *usual* was to bring in a different flavor every time he was in town…*that* kind of a hint. But Oh no…sadly, women didn't help other women in Sophie's world…with the exception of Gayle, that is.

"Can't you see?…You stupid blonde American… yeah that's right, you…the one with that appalling accent." That's what the girl behind the counter might've really been thinking as she was busy slowly lathering gobs of sweet butter 'up and down' on their bread ~~loafs~~…woops, I mean baguettes…

Sophie, as we know was never much at seeing the signs and reading between the lines when it came to Josef. Now more than ever her blinders were securely fastened.

"Et voilà, Bon Appetit" the girl said directing her attention back onto Josef as she passed him the two baguette sandwiches with beautiful wrappings around each.

After Josef paid for their lunch, they hit the sidewalk taking an immediate right in the direction of the Eiffel Tower. The simple yet ultimate gourmet picnic of Josef's choice… with the perfect backdrop.

"Just take a bite of that and tell me it's not one of the best things you've ever tasted in your entire life" he said proudly passing Sophie one of the sandwiches.

Even down to its 'presentation'…Each baguette had a double layer of the highest quality of pressed pastry tissue imaginable. They don't even offer that kind of refinement in the States, needless to say wrap a damn sandwich in it. Then to top it off, literally here comes the final layer…a precious little cotton 'serviette'. (aka: small adorable paper thin square napkin) It truly was like a sweater set…they just belonged together. The French just know how to do it is all I can say. They even 'dress' their sandwiches. They took their first nibble while walking. It was all so…very delicious.

His excitement in showing Sophie one of his greatest local favorites was so charming, what could she have possibly said, "Oh *really* darling…don't bore me, it's just a ham sandwich." …I don't think so.

After she took a healthy bite, she knew exactly where Josef's love for the thing came from. When a baguette is a great baguette, there's really something to be said about it. It's that commonality of pride taken similar to a New Yorker when discussing their bagels for example. It's considerably more than 'just the water'…For Christ's sake you'd think it's written somewhere in their anthems DNA.

"Here we are," he said dusting off a small space on the empty park bench with the outer serviette layer of his wrapping. "Another room with a view," he said smiling smugly before bowing like a swash buckler indicating the specific place on the bench was now *ready for his lady*…

Geez-us, was this real?…They were actually picnicking under the Eiffel Tower! Between the creamy pain Sophie felt in her under carriage and the delicious whipped butter she was tasting, this twenty-four hours with Josef would definitely go down as the sexiest and most romantic time ever to be had. His style of doing anything was so unexpected and exciting. Even his spontaneous and charming preparation of her seat on a park bench was something she found to be irresistible and beyond *charming*.

Sitting on the edge of the bench leaning back, (with his long legs extended and ankles crossed) he sat coveting and analyzing every remaining morsel of his sandwich. He was so irresistible, it was enough to make her want to miss her flight. She was so head over heels for this guy…but before the lovey imaginary whoopee cushion could inflate… the bottom fell out.

"Sophie…I don't know about you but I feel safe to

say last night was something we'd both been anticipating. It was beyond 'worth the wait'…agreed? It really was more than perfect…"

Sophie was shocked to hear Josef speak with such tender loving and sensitive words. This was more than a guy admitting his horniness had been achieved then satisfied, it really was a sweet admission…But the timing with his lovers confession was a bit awkward. You see…Sophie had just begun to speak. She'd interrupted his awaited and perfectly timed 'admiration admission' if you could call it that.

"Shhhh, I want to say this before you go on."

She thought he looked so delectable despite whatever was about to leap from his mouth. She was a girl so in love, her head was bobbing in and out of the clouds and her feet had yet to touch ground.

"Okay my darling…go on. Please excuse me"…she said with a nauseating sappy smile. That's when his real sermon began.

He cleared his throat, "I do not…and I mean it my darling…plan to share you with anyone should we decide to continue with a serious relationship. I want to know why you didn't feel you could tell me…admit to me, that you've been living with Bruce in San Francisco."

Whoops. Stop everything…There it was…The record that Skipped and Screeched in her head. That was the very situation she'd never wanted to confront. Those words blasted her back into her hidden guilty present. The elephant…that big 'Ol thing named Bruce she'd conveniently forgotten on the back burner had finally come back and landed on her chest. Hearing those unexpected words pummeled her.

She knew she needed to act fast and respond on all cylinders to recuperate the situation and stabilize her new found position. But unfortunately, all she could utter was "How'd you know? I wanted to tell you…"

He took the liberty of steaming on with his inquiry. While keeping his cool demeanor he said, "Issigeac is a tiny Village as you must know by now. Nothing…but nothing stays a secret there for long. The fact that we've been playing this flirtatious tag game for so long, it must well be past hearsay and old news by now. Even though I grew up just outside the Village I know everyone there, including that asshole Bruce and his hideous family." Hearing this admission…she just about gagged on the last piece of soggy baguette that she hadn't been able to swallow since he began his dissertation. Thank Gawd it finally slid down without needing the Heimlich maneuver.

Sophie was rarely scattered and rattled like that. She'd always been such a control freak, the manipulator in the group as it were…In no way was she accustomed to having someone out maneuver and beat her to the punch. Josef however, had turned the tables. She'd always imagined and dreaded this inevitable moment…but certainly hadn't considered it ever coming up especially under these circumstances.

She felt she'd been 'busted'…her deceptive secret having been exposed…She almost felt defensive like it was too late to come clean. She always thought she'd be the one to decide when the appropriate time would be to discuss her relationship regarding Bruce. Yet the fact that their fabulous fantasy night had been so incredible, discussing that topic was the very last thing on her mind at that particular moment. Their sexy 'night' had changed ever-y-thing. To tell you the truth she'd temporarily forgotten all about the elephant…

Sophie had always imagined Josef to be a fabulous lover but never dreamt a man could ring her chimes like he had. His rare quality of steaminess had thrown a kink into her plan. She felt defenseless like never before and didn't want to jeopardize what they'd just begun. She'd misjudged the situation entirely. She was no longer in it just for the lifestyle, but now…for the man himself. It was all fucked up. With no other choice, she was immediately forced to spill her story and fess up to everything she'd been hiding. She felt a shiver come over her, hating the feeling like she'd been cornered.

He however, just continued to calmly sit looking straight at her like the sex God that he was. He listened patiently waiting for her to fess up or at least give an earnest attempt to weasel out of her predicament.

"Josef" she said, actually finding it difficult to look him directly in the eye…"I don't know what to say other than…initially, I was out for the kill. I was looking for a fling and if it felt good, I was ready to let Bruce go. I don't love him anymore and as for his family? They're definitely not my kind of people. I've held on to him because it was convenient and made me feel safe. I'm guilty of using him and of being selfish.

But what we've just experienced shows me we have the potential to be much more than just a fling. I'm sure of that now. Last night was beyond what you could call 'over the top' love making, and to be completely honest it was the best sex I've ever had in my life. It really touched me like I've never been touched before. You are the someone I want to last. When we began our flirtations at the bar you were a challenge and I wanted you because I thought I couldn't have you. You're not the only one in our duo that's used to getting everything they want. You were such an incredibly gorgeous trophy, but the problem now is that I'm totally, unequivocally hooked on you. All I can think about is you. I want to spend my days making love to you and it was stupid of me to think I could love you…then leave you. That was my ego talking, and simply an unrealistic fantasy. I'd been working my charms on you for months, but what you gave me last night was something I never could've imagined. I want you and I want you forever. Josef, I think I'm in love with you."

Okay people…there you go. So much for playing her cards with finesse. WTF was that? She caved and had totally given in. She'd become so vulnerable, confiding to him her inner most secrets when the fucking bastard, not being able to contain his true self, began to laugh out loud at her expense. He couldn't believe she was admitting her selfishness and game so easily.

He smiled endearingly, like any self serving bastard would, then finally admitted with delight written all over his face, "I've fallen hard for you too Sophie. I absolutely adore you. The fact that you were just so brutally honest tells me I can sincerely trust you. I want you to be mine and mine alone. I've never said that to a woman before, much less felt this way. If we're really going to do this, we need to figure some things out. You need to fully understand and commit to what you're getting in to. I'm not a patient man and when I want and need something, I always succeed in getting it. When I say you're mine, you are Mine. Do you understand? I'm not sharing you. I want to reiterate that so you can fully understand my words. You're going to have to think hard about this and know exactly what I'm saying.

It will be good for you to take the couple of weeks back in SF to decide. I know I'm going to ache, but I understand it's necessary for you to go ahead and leave tonight as planned. That will give me some time to come up with our next move and give you time to kick Bruce to the curb where he belongs. One thing I hope I've made clear… no one can see or touch you intimately. That space is now reserved for me…exclusively. I mean it Sophie. I need to know whole heartedly that I'm the only one in your life who is able to see you, make love to you, and own your sex from here on out. I will NOT share you, Comprends?"

For some insane reason Sophie's normal independent self-serving rationale didn't kick in when Josef began speaking to her like he *owned* her. She'd never had a man 'want' her like that and for some miscalculated reason, his domination and possessiveness made her feel empowered. It gave her the feeling of really being wanted. She felt so flattered, yet seriously…had <u>under</u>valued his words. She heard what he was saying, but hadn't actually listened. She Never considered any consequences that could possibly arise from his demands. Instead, she now had her eye on the prize of having him and the gorgeous lifestyle he could provide. It overshadowed anything he might be dictating.

How could a strong independent woman suddenly accept becoming a possession to a macho man? I think it's called…Sex, SEx, SeX. I guess the thought of a grandiose

Château and a seemingly matching lifestyle didn't hurt the situation either. She was beyond herself happily thinking she'd become 'his'.

"Josef, this is music to my ears. I'm in all the way with you my love, and yes...Okay. I agree to it all," she replied...already calculating her next move.

"You know I'm going to miss you terribly, but my leaving for the West Coast tonight is our best and only real suitable option. This way I'll use the time to untangle a few things and yes my darling, that includes ending it with Bruce...I'll need your help guiding me through to our next phase. I don't want to be left out there to dry as they say."

Sophie might've sounded like a helpless girl but inside she was feeling like she was sitting on top of the world. She felt like she'd won. With her selective hearing she'd just about heard all that she needed. There was nothing much more for her to say...because in her opinion, she'd already clinched the deal.

After their *expectation pact* had been mutually agreed upon, they returned to the Hôtel De Crillon to canoodle and enjoy their last farewell flute before saying their loving goodbyes. Once in the limo, just as it'd been with her arrival, her bags were miraculously already waiting in the trunk. That Josef...he was such a dear...he just thought of everything.

When she arrived at the airport for check in, she was delighted to find her lover had arranged for yet another surprise. Finding he'd paid for a first class upgrade for her long flight was so considerate. So what was a girl to do but spend her entire flight sipping more bubbly and mindfully rewinding their incredibly sexy escapade. When she disembarked, she found a limo waiting for her at SFO. She was in heaven thinking Josef's super caring and attentive behavior was simply him showing her his Love. Not for one minute did she ever think his behavior could be considered a bit manipulative or controlling. Oh contraire, she adored being this spoiled and pampered. It's something she'd always craved and was now happily receiving.

She was quickly whisked away to her shared apartment in Petroleum Hill feeling relieved that Bruce was still in France. It would be so much easier to complete her check list finding the place void of him. Once in, It would only be a few minutes after putting her bags down that her phone began to ring. It was him…'Mr. Thoughtful'.

*

Chapter Quatre

"Hello sweetheart, did you have a good flight?"

"How could I not?" Sophie replied enthusiastically with sexy undertones. "Flying First Class is fabulous. The flight was ultra luxurious thanks to you my love. Merci for all the surprise up-grades…My flight home was the best ever. I drank champagne and thought of you the entire time. I couldn't sleep. I was lost in heaven just thinking about us and our incredible night. It makes me hot just thinking about it.

I only walked in minutes ago and funny enough I'm actually feeling refreshed…but I can tell you…seriously…it's going to be a long two weeks before I can even think of drinking Champagne again. Whew! It's only hot water with lemon in the interim" she sniggered. "It's all so fabulous Josef, I miss you already. It's super early morning there for you isn't it? You're the one that must be exhausted," Sophie said wanting and hoping to hear he was…even for a little bit at least. Josef was an experienced sly dog when it came to performances. He didn't answer her directly but quickly changed the subject to move their conversation along.

"I couldn't sleep either…just thinking about *us*. Those extra perks were the least I could do chèrie. I hope you can relax a bit this evening…Then I want you to sleep like a baby, like…my baby that is" he said in a loving tone. "I'll give you a call sometime late tomorrow night your time. Goodnight sweetheart"…and just like that, they were off to enjoy their own agendas.

When Josef had tucked Sophie in for her return ride to the airport, he secretly had already made plans for his afternoon and evening. Somewhat of an unusual whirlwind shopping excursion was on his particular agenda. While Sophie was waiting to board her plane, Josef had already returned to his flat in the 7th, retrieved a few important items to discuss with his next rendezvous and had just arrived at his destination.

"I don't know anything about sizes but I brought this along for an example" he said to the sales associate as he gently placed his exquisite leather cross body satchel on the glass counter. He reached deep into his soft brown bag and delicately pulled out Sophie's butter yellow bra and adoringly laid it down on the counter. You would've thought he was laying out the Holy Grail for Christ's sake.

He'd decidedly taken the chance of stopping by Loft Couture, the exclusive 'by appointment only' super haute lingerie boutique on rue St-Honoré. He didn't feel he needed to make an appointment like everyone else, he was above that. He had a goal in mind after all. He was on a mission to purchase Sophie a few little surprises for the next time they met. He knew this boutique would have exactly what he was looking for. Her panties were also in his satchel but they never left his bag. They were aromatically concealed in a zip lock for his safe keeping. He didn't want one bit of her sweet scent to escape.

The sales girl was trying to do her best in hiding her enthusiasm having this high rolling delicious specimen of a man just drop in out of the blue yonder. Who needs an appointment when you have an unexpected willing client seriously wanting to *lay it down* and spoil his lady love with a ton of pricey lingerie? She was delighted, appointment or not.

He figured the size for the bottoms by using his personal hand held cupping system figuring all bottoms should definitely be size small. Just seeing those fabulous new little string options resting on the counter suddenly gave him an involuntary kinky little twinge just thinking of their outrageous escapade happening just hours before.

Every additional set decided upon made it more intriguing for the sales girl, especially when Josef whipped out and gently passed her his no limit, thick as a brick black Credit Card. You can imagine, it almost made her five hour work day standing on four inch required heels worth it. Just knowing this one shopper alone would cover her entire month's sales quota was enough to make her swollen feet momentarily feel dance worthy. He'd ended up purchasing several luxe combos of exquisite matching sets and left the shop discreetly. Exhausted, she turned the *open* sign to read *closed* and went directly into the back room to deflate her gravely puffy feet…happily not giving a damn which wall her shoes met.

Josef had always thought Bruce somewhat of an idiot, but now realizing he'd simply never given Sophie the kind of pampering she deserved, it was made quite clear. His major oversight had cleared the way making it easy to swoop in and take his precious prey away from him. Poor schmuck, he'd probably never know what hit him until it was far too late. From way back…these two guys had always had it out for one another. Their *particular game* would continue to play out for just about…forever, I guess.

Our sexy boy left the boutique with a rather large oversized shopping bag absolutely stuffed with incredible lingerie for his new lady love…He had each gorgeous set individually wrapped with simple yet gorgeous packaging. He also made another little detour, catching an early dinner at the well known 'Julien' restaurant before taking an Uber town car to the airport for his chartered flight back home.

The first thing he did when he entered the *Château* was immediately take the huge bag quietly down to the cellar. He'd want to keep the sweet little boxes in hiding for when the perfect opportunities presented themselves.

When Laetitia heard the squeak of the cellar door for the second time much later in the evening, she assumed of course it'd been Josef making another trip down to his man cave for a night cap. After all she'd been expecting him to return that evening so she wasn't concerned. No one in the world would dare go down into his secret cave unaccompanied. Not just 'anyone'…was privileged enough to visit the sacred vault. That simply had always been a given. It was his space.

Meanwhile back in San Fran, Sophie was busy obsessing over her new man. After unpacking, she made her melancholy preparations to relax for the night with a big cup of steaming hot lemon water. She felt it was more than fortuitous that Bruce had planned to stay in Issigeac for a few more days. She'd have time to prepare her exit plan, not to mention have the private space to think how to maneuver her future dream life with Josef. Sophie couldn't wait to turn the page and move on. What an incredible future she saw waiting in the wings. She thought it was her dream knocking on the door and boldly coming in strong.

The phone rang again and feeling a surge of excitement, she answered thinking it must be her Lover calling again.

"Hello?…This is Sue Yolume from the Chinese Garden Spa in the Trocadero. We've received a call from a Mr. Josef Decour and he's reserved a time for you this evening. We are calling to confirm that you will be attending your appointment tonight at 9 pm?"

Sophie was taken aback by the unexpected call, yet delightfully charmed at the same time. It was such a fun and random way to receive such a surprise message from Josef. How romantic…and so much better than receiving a mere flower delivery. Sophie confirmed the appointment and left her apartment in time to park and enter the building she'd driven by at least a thousand times but never once noticed.

It was like a stark white austere laboratory with its extreme cleanliness. It had next to no signage on the windows whatsoever. Once she entered they moved with laser sharp precision when it came to appointment schedules. Thank GOD she wasn't late.

"Now"…said the receptionist. (Not even a hello…) "We have already received payment for a lower body wax, a deep facial cleanse, and a Full Body Massage. Does that agree with your understanding?" she said not waiting for Sophie's response…chop chop.

Sophie was in question about it all, but with Josef having organized and paid for the treatments, it had to be something fabulous and definitely worth investigating. She'd halfway convinced herself that she was excited for the experience. Give me a break…Good God she was actually scared shitless. Josef was such a dear, so considerate wasn't he?

"Yes, I guess that sounds like the schedule" Sophie hesitantly replied, having zero idea of what was to come.

"Okay then…sign here and go to room #1" Madame Yolume quipped on cue arriving at the reception desk and taking the lead. There was certainly no sugar coating going on in this place.

Sophie did as instructed and left her clothes hanging on the rack in room #1 then wrapped herself in the cheesy micro fiber robe that was folded with perfection and left sitting on a nearby small stool. It was all so clinical.

The technician arrived showing her the correct way to mount the table for her treatment. First to come was her waxing. She was instructed to lay on the table backside down with her knees up, bent and spread wide. Once in position, the technician approached Sophie with light speed holding a small pot of HOT bubbling wax. The attendant made a disapproving sound then spread her legs wider. She immediately began smothering her 'pussalaires' with the hot liquid before Sophie even knew what was happening.

No foreplay there that's for sure and once the procedure had begun, turning back was definitely not an option. She didn't have time to say diddly squat before her privates had all been dipped and dabbed and covered with piping HOT paraffin. Then, the audacious bitch had the nerve to immediately place cheap gauze strips on the wax and pull without hesitation. There was no warning given and certainly not a whimper of advance notice. Holy Fucking Mother of Pain…Sophie would never have thought to have this done on her own…but actually, within the pain she found it to have a bit of eroticism. Don't ask me how, but with all of this regimental craziness, she only thought of Josef. Yeah, I would have too, but with an absolutely different sentiment…

Once her initial shock was over, she imagined seeing herself expose her hairless underworld to his liking. Although, unbeknownst to her, the waxing wasn't finished.

What in the hell could possibly be left? The shocking second position required her turning over on the table and balancing on her knees while spreading her legs wide and leaning down on her forearms. She was instructed to lift her ass as high in the air as possible while keeping her knees and tops of her feet stationary on the table. This would have been beyond embarrassing had the technician acted a little less like an army sergeant. Good God…Sophie was scared to death not to get it right.

This ridiculous looking second position amazingly was the only way for the tech to place the wax inside her butt cheeks. Talk about being told to 'spread 'em'…Holy Moly! Sophie didn't realize the amount of hair that even grew in that unknown region until the tech laughed with total enthusiasm and utter delight when showing Sophie the full, disgustingly gross strip of hairy gauze. Gross me out. Who fucking knew? All Sophie thought was 'thank GOD' she hadn't farted. That's called a Brazilian Wax for those of you that don't care to go through life like a bald eagle.

Amazingly…at the end of that excruciating experience, Sophie left the waxing room with a clean slate as one could say. There wasn't a pubic hair left to be seen from the front of her Dallas, all the way back to the crack of her Atlanta. Sophie was gleaming knowing she was smooth all under. It made her feel like she had a special little secret that only she and Josef would know about. (And the no-name technician of course)

She lay reverberating in pain and embarrassment while thinking of the vulnerable positions…when suddenly she was told her regimen wasn't finished. It also included a facial followed by a traditional Swedish massage. Hearing what was next on the agenda was enough for her to take her mind off her pulsating red and swollen areas for a brief second. After all, all the pain was compounded…her personal girl garden hadn't quite recovered from her Parisian romp with Josef to begin with. Now she could focus on another area…but personally…she never would've chosen to have this type of 'maintenance' given the timing.

Didn't someone along the way mention a whoopee

cushion? Fact: Right then would've been the ideal moment to use the thing...

When leaving the spa, she felt a bit devious knowing that she could walk along and the others she saw had no idea what she was hiding below. She loved that, and it made her feel like she had a private sexy secret. It made the physical long distance between she and Josef feel that much closer. This was between them...

Later that evening, just as she was returning from her outing at the spa her cell phone rang again, and low and behold, it was him...the Golden Boy.

"How'd you like your massage?" he questioned with intrigue.

"Oh my God Josef...what a wild experience! I had no idea what to expect...but I can certainly say I've never been this baby ass nude in my adult life, I can promise you that. I'm so pearly soft and clean...I think I need to send you a picture from my phone so you can see for yourself" Sophie said with a hint of seductive hidden pleasure. She was feeling so confident he could hear it in her voice.

"So do me something better...sit on the floor in front of your large mirror, keep your back to the wall and your knees high and bent. Rest your heels on the ground tucked in close to that cute little ass of yours and open your legs wide. Then make a video of yourself touching your clean velvety jewel box so I can have a look. I'd love that so much Sophie. It makes me hard just thinking about seeing you that way. At the very least we could have a ZOOM-a-GASM together. Even though we're going to be virtual lovers for a little while, this would at least allow me to visualize my fantasies until we're able see one another personally. We'll need to figure our situation out pretty damn fast, because I won't be able to take being without you for much longer."

Sophie loved knowing he craved her that much...or at least *hearing* he did. So...she got busy creating the perfect sexy 'stage' for her sexting escapade to begin. As instructed, she sat on the floor with knees high and feet tucked firmly under, but before anything was to be shared from center stage, she took a good look and inspected it all for herself. She'd never really taken the time for an intimate look. Sadly, it would take this to instigate being the first time she actually would. She cherished seeing her own beautiful body in detail…After her 'date' with Sue…she made sure to be her first voyeur. She was so satisfied with her blessings, she felt she looked worthy. The waxing had left her lips so soft and voluptuous she knew why Josef would want to ram his wand in deep. He was going to be so turned on by her baby pink dreamland, the thought of him being so delighted excited her beyond belief. But instead of hitting the record button she stopped, leaned back and thought that no one but Josef could ever love her like she deserved.

Her mind skipped out of sequence for a split second and Bruce popped into her thoughts. She spoke to him aloud as if he were there. "See what you missed…you asshole! All those years together…and you never really *saw* me. I'd always been there, waiting…but you ignored me to the point where I needed to replace you. Now you've missed it…you little Momma's boy. I'm finally serving myself now Mister."

She widened her legs and began touching her nipples before putting her fingers down under. She'd arrived in 'the zone'…and hit the record button. Then she spoke to Josef as she opened herself wider and began flirting with herself. After moments of skimming her inner lips, she raised up off her heels slightly and moved her middle finger back to her Atlanta. "This little area is sacred, but if you are a good boy, it's something to look forward to Josef," she said as she climaxed. She rubbed her roaming hand over her stomach then blew a kiss into the frame for her lover… ending her video.

This would become a recurring event and would definitely provide the lead-in to some phenomenal phone sex on the days without a new complete video. The lovers would continue day and night finding new and exciting ways to play out their fantasies together…that is until Bruce was to arrive back home in San Fran. Now she was really playing with fire.

The following morning Laetitia was relieved to hear Josef rumbling around in the kitchen speaking on the phone. Litty had forgotten most of her English so she couldn't understand the totality of his conversation other than a word here and there. His words: *pleasure* and *massage* certainly stood out. She was intrigued and once she heard him end his conversation she made her way in to the kitchen. She was curious to find out who the mystery person had been on the other end of the receiver.

"Josef, I heard you go downstairs a couple of times last night, everything all right?"

"No Litty, It's me...I'm the one that's not all right. All right!!?" he barked with vigor. He was still caught up in his own thoughts and hadn't fully listened enough to compute what Litty had just said. He continued with what would turn out to be a small solo sermon...

"I don't know what to do. I'm not used to feeling this way. The truth is, I'd heard Bruce...you remember that asshole and his family don't you? Well anyway, rumor had it he lived with an American woman in San Francisco named Sophie. She visits the village on occasion, so I made it my goal to search her out. I spotted her at the bar a few months ago then put my plan into motion. I played her...knowing full well she was in a relationship with that freak. I thought I would fuck with him by taking his girlfriend away from him. I wanted to get into her head and use her before tossing her away. Knowing full well that would hurt him down to the quick and piss him off royally.

The incredibly strange thing about this story is that she happens to be a very special woman. I think she could be my counterpart in a lot of ways. You met her...Isn't she gorgeous? She's my American dream girl and somehow her charms have gotten to me. Now this situation has become absolutely ridiculous! She's driving me insane! She's all I can think about. This girl is making me fucking crazy! I'd organized a nice...I guess I could call it a 'rather typical' night with her in Paris, but it turned out to be anything but that. We had more than an incredible connection, in fact it was something completely out of this world. Sublime…I think would be the word. She's managed to pierce my heart in the most bizarre way. I need to get a hold of myself so I can figure things out. I'm seriously out of my mind over her and hate this feeling of being so out of control. I'm not used to this!" he shouted with an unusual animated look about him before finally taking a breath. His rant continued with force…

"And…as for that wimpy loser of human scum?…I'm absolutely shocked now that I've gotten to know her…find it absolutely unbelievable that it was actually him…that lucky fucking bastard that she's been involved with! To think he could ever catch such a gorgeous creature like her is beyond me. The thought of him touching her makes me sick. That Son of a Bitch better never lay his hands on her ever again. That family has always put their hands on the wrong people," he huffed relentlessly stomping his way around the room without further explanation. He was radiating anger and expelling an uncharacteristic behavior… but then to top it off, rare beads of unbecoming perspiration appeared. Josef had succeeded in acting like a raving lunatic in a one man tirade.

Seeing this unusual behavior (and lack of any poise or composure) erupt, Litty decided to make an aggressive move and interrupt so she could get a word in edgewise. She'd try to put some rationale back into the 'discussion' and give him a bit more than her 'two cents'.

"Josef my dear boy, she actually shouted…this is the first time I've ever seen you like this…and must admit I'm more than a bit concerned! Has this woman put a spell on you?…And of course, I remember that family. Who could forget them? Gene was his name" she said ever so smugly.

Just by the evil quick change of expression on her face suggested she'd just had an epiphany and remembered their hateful history again ever so clearly. But the truth was…she'd never forgotten them. She remembered them extremely well. Gene and his family had always been her nemesis. She'd sworn to Grandfather on his death bed that she'd get them in the end, one way or another.

She continued...reminding the Golden Boy, "In fact it was Gene, that bastard...who tried to have your Grandfather arrested on some frivolous lie just before he passed away. It had something to do with his wife...Some kind of erroneous landscaping issue at the *Château.* Don't you remember that? Personally darling, I don't think I'll ever forget or forgive them. That was such a long time ago my precious boy, why is it You are so concerned about them now?" she said trying to deflect her real feelings. When in fact...she could've chewed on that piece of gum for days...

"It's because they're at the center of my problem, that's why. Sophie's been in a relationship with Bruce for the last few years and they live together in San Francisco! Can you fucking imagine? It makes me insane just thinking about it! I know she wants to leave him, but she's a smart girl and doesn't want to leave without a soft place to land," he said pacing erratically and spewing his thoughts all over the kitchen.

Litty hadn't wanted Josef to know of the venom she'd stored up and reserved for Gene and his family... Unbeknownst to Josef, it seemed the time might've just come to release it.

"I hope you're more than just a soft landing pad," Litty questioned discerningly.

"Of course I am...she's putty in my hands, but we had a strange kind of incredible magic happen between us in Paris that changed everything. That kind of magic doesn't happen but once, or maybe a few times in a lifetime," he said with a boyish dick smirk. He changed his facial expression immediately and became quite focused again once he was able to get off his male high horse.

"We both felt it was something special. I'm just having trouble figuring out the best way to finally get rid of Bruce and his family. They are IN MY WAY and with them being out of the picture, Sophie would be free to move here without any complications. I want her here next to me. I don't want us to have any distractions. I want her to be all mine and only mine."

Laetitia stood awestruck not believing what she was witnessing. She was shocked beyond belief seeing Josef act so frantic obsessing over a woman. However truth be told, she felt it was long overdue. She'd only hoped it could've been with the person of her choosing instead of this American girl. Josef was exposing a new and different side of himself, one that she'd never seen. She hadn't known him to speak so passionately about anyone like this before. Even though his thinking was a bit convoluted in his delivery, his disheveled behavior actually pleased her.

She thought Sophie was nice enough, but she never would've been her first choice. She thought she'd already seen to that given the years of meticulously laying out the groundwork for her Granddaughter to slip in and take over her 'role' one day.

With Josef's unexpected new love interest jumping in...out of nowhere...Litty's secret plan seemed to be darkening by the second. She felt a closeness to Josef like he were her own flesh and blood, so she put on a good front and bit her tongue while presumably going along with his plan...Deep down however, she was conflicted. She was actually relieved and delighted on one hand that her boy had finally met a woman who rattled his cage just like she had Josef Sr.'s all those many years ago. Now it seems there was a fly in the ointment and her name happened to be Sophie.

Given his new found feelings, she was relieved she'd kept Fiona's real identity a secret. Josef would never need to know that she was indeed her Granddaughter. Litty had always encouraged and set the stage so that Fiona had every opportunity to whittle her way into being Josef's 'choice' but if the girl had missed her chance, so be it. Litty was finally too tired to continue her scheming as their matchmaker. She had finally resigned to letting the chips fall where they may.

Honestly speaking, pretending to accept this defeat was a bizarre state of rationale for a tenacious woman like

Laetitia. After some reflection…she'd probably still encourage the impossible match if and when she got her strength back. But it had become apparent that Sophie had penetrated Josef's placid and consistently cool demeanor. She had no doubt hexed the poor boy, making it clear that it was his sexual energy that was driving him. He wanted her. He was consumed by her. All he could think of was her. Her smell, her voice, her laugh, her walk, her sex…and now…to think of her being soft and bare?…He was simply out of his mind.

Sophie meanwhile, being half way around the world was having her own issues. She desperately wanted to be with Josef, yet needed to decide how and when to tell Bruce she was leaving. He'd be home soon and she needed to be prepared with some kind of an exit strategy. She was terrified to think what he might do should he catch a glimpse of her smooth freshly waxed landing strip. Certainly he'd have questions and know she'd not done it for him. She needed to think. She needed to get organized. She needed …to be gone.

Exhausted, Josef retired to his suite. He was stroking himself in bed as he re-watched Sophie's most recent video. They'd only had a few days of long distance sexting before he began speaking to her about her return.

"Sophie ma chèrie, when can I see you again? Waiting two weeks is going to be torturous. This is the last time I ever want to be separated from you for this long. When are you coming back to me?" he said almost whining.

She just lapped his horny misery right up. "Josef, I can't think of anything other than you. My thoughts are a blur and I need to figure out how to tell Bruce it's over. I can probably buy some time and come up with some excuse to be in NYC this week. Do you think you can get away and meet me there? I'm so confused…but I want to get out of this relationship without hurting him. It's been three years now and I want to end it with some decency. I owe him that at least."

Sophie's distress sounded sweet to his ears. He was thrilled knowing she wanted him as much as he wanted her.

The other details relating to Bruce at that particular moment didn't matter. Their conversation confirmed that he still had her where he wanted her…Obviously it wasn't his head attached to his shoulders that was doing all the talking, it definitely was his other…A serious case of pussywhip I'd be safe to say.

"Of course I can meet you in Manhattan, no problem. Don't worry my love, this is all going to work out. I'll get it all organized and be waiting for you at the Gramercy Park Hôtel. How's that sound?"

"Perfect" she replied feeling relieved. This way they could make a plan…

Josef couldn't give a shit about Bruce and certainly wasn't about to expose his true feelings of hatred towards the guy until the time was right, if ever. After the road block of Sophie *officially* ending it with him was complete…the love birds would have the green light to live out their lives freely in France…But in the interim, a stop off in Manhattan to figure things out would just have to do.

Sophie immediately got busy making appointments with a few fabric vendors in New York. That would be a good decoy to validate her falsely 'needed' business trip. She thought it wise to have a paper trail with actual timed meetings should she be questioned by Bruce or any of her co-working employees. Leaving again so soon after Bruce's return would seem suspicious and difficult to explain without some type of planned agenda. What she really needed was more time with Josef to sort it all out and mutually decide how their future together would take shape. It was all happening so fast at that point. The train had begun rolling…

Bruce arrived home late afternoon as expected. By then Sophie had calculated and decided on her next move…It was to pick a fight over some sort of trivia that would create distance between them. That way, he wouldn't have any opportunity, even by accident of seeing her in her sleek birthday suit. That would at least solve problem number one. Then she'd be able to leave town without too many questions.

The following night she left on the red eye and arrived in Manhattan with the cool early morning air. She took what used to be her normal method of transportation (pre-Josef days) into the City. She jumped into the back of a dirty stale cigarette smelling yellow cab and took it straight to her favorite breakfast spot, Best Bagel Co. on 35th. After devouring her customary toasted bagel with lox schemer, she was ready to tackle The Big Apple. She'd made this pilgrimage to BBC religiously when arriving in NYC for the last couple of years to begin her day. It'd become her latest tradition when arriving in the early morning hours. She loved feeling the energy the city exuded when the day was just coming alive. Of course she had other rituals when arriving in the city for afternoon happy hour for example, and others when arriving at night for dinner. Her regular pit stops guaranteed her the privilege of feeling like a long distance local. Once fortified with her morning's first stop, she was ready to move on to the heartbeat of the fashion district.

Her busy morning of appointments were wrapping up when approximately at eleven her phone rang. It was her sexy man calling.

"Lunch is being delivered to our suite in just over an hour. Will you be able to make it?…Just ask to see the manager when you arrive, he'll give you your key," he said making every effort to sound cavalier and not overexcited.

"Oh…in that case, I'll see you in twenty…" Sophie quickly replied with a giggle and hung up.

Josef had checked into the Gramercy Park Hôtel the night before knowing the place all too well. He thought it had just the right amount of panache for them to get lost within themselves for their first US homecoming. Of course he had an ulterior motive for picking this particular hotel. It certainly was for something far more important than simply the fabulous linens and the large bathroom. It had a prime address and was located on Lexington Ave…which just so happened to be in Josef's preferred zip code. He wanted Sophie to get to know and love the neighborhood as much as he did. He had his reasons.

When he heard the door open and saw his lady love enter the room, he swept her up so fast it left her feet dangling. "I don't ever want to be without you again for this long chérie. It's been killing me not being with you," he said smothering her in kisses.

"Oh Josef I know...it's been torture," she replied melting into his arms.

After quickly pushing the door closed with her available foot he carried her over to the overstuffed peach taffeta sofa where they fell onto its many plump matching cushions. With their landing made so soft and easy, they continued making out like it'd been years since seeing one another. Still in perfect harmony, their tongues and physical energy hadn't missed a beat. It already felt deliciously familiar. Once their initial...highly intense fifteen minute make out session had been somewhat satisfied, it was time to give way to their inevitable continuation.

Josef collected himself and said, "While we're waiting for lunch to be delivered, come and let me show you my favorite part of the suite." He stood up, walked over to the bathroom and gently nudged the door open exposing the perfect amount of light that cast an alluring welcome from within. He smiled back and motioned for her to come join him...just like the wolf did when luring little-bo-peep into Grandma's, but this was no place like Grannies digs...

What an absolute showplace this room was. The perfectly placed mirrors, expensive finishes and designer mood lighting...it felt as if everything was made to look and feel sexy. But let's get real...for anyone's understanding when it comes to the common size of a NYC bathroom? This one was seriously impressive in its exceptional size. It felt like it could've been its own apartment if using New York City's standard scale of Real Estate measurements. Having such a rare amenity was only accessible to those in the upper crusted suites. It was an exclusive perk for those who thought it logical to spend outrageous dough to shit, shower and shave with five stars. Personally, I couldn't agree more. It really was the perfect choice.

Once inside the shower room, Josef began the ritual

by tossing his cashmere sweater to the floor and stepping out of his jeans. He wasn't wearing any underwear as usual and Sophie absolutely loved that. She also loved the fact that he was already turned on and was showing it. She pulled off her sweater slowly then undid her belt and slid out of her designer jeans like she was performing a pole dance. (He thought that was fabulous by the way) Finally, there she stood solely in her bra and panty set that she'd purchased online. Yes, it was sexy, but the quality was cheap when it came to Josef's standards. Not knowing the difference, she wore it with confidence and was so proud of her body. She took her time in front of the mirror putting her hair up in a loose top knot, leaving a few wispy pieces to dangle. He loved that too…he had such a thing about her sensual nape. Just watching her make her feminine moves made Josef hurt. He'd become wanting her…thinking she was the most beautiful woman he'd ever seen.

"I need you Josef," she said turning away from the mirror and moving towards him.

"No, not yet my love"…he said stepping into the shower.

It happened to be a huge walk in stone vault with large shower heads hanging above at both ends. Under each were small white marble built in bench seats. Josef entered the shower without as much as touching Sophie on the way in, then he sat down on one of the benches allowing the water to begin trickling down on him from above. He began massaging himself with sudsy strokes which completely turned Sophie on. She stripped off her bra and panty combo and stepped in to join him. She was amused at the size of the shower, it seemed bigger than her entire bathroom back home.

Once she saw Josef demonstrating his sudsy hand dance, she couldn't help but start touching herself with a soapy bubble rebuttal. She was standing with her legs slightly apart when she began stroking herself with both hands so Josef could get a look at her pink baldness. Then she turned her back to him and bent over revealing her entire Atlanta from behind. She was so cleanly stripped of any hair…she stood fully exposed for him to see her in the steamy light. She was his dream image of what sexy should look like. He loved her breasts being fuller in the lower portion and always seeing her pinkish nipples point upward. But it really was her jewel box that he was crazy about. Her sexy smell, its shape, her full lips, and that glorious little ass of hers…he was looking forward to investigating that option completely after their shower like she'd suggested in one of her videos.

"Sophie, you're so beautiful I can't wait," he said standing up and releasing his liquid thunder all over her. They began embracing one another with nipples touching and kissed under the showers rain until he rotated the lever and stopped the flow.

"Let me take care of you now," he said leading her out of the shower.

He lovingly dried her with one of the thick fluffy monogramed hotel towels that sat rolled and ready. He couldn't wait to taste her…so he got her in position by gently leaning her over the sink facing the mirror. As she began resting on her forearms he opened her feet wide and slipped the tip of his index finger inside her Atlanta. That made her velvets twitch and get wet again. Josef knew how to pierce all of her magic spots. Their sex life had taken on a life of its own and nothing was out of bounds. They loved being able to forget their inhibitions. There were no limits nor any embarrassment and that alone was a newly found exciting freedom for them both to explore. They loved it and one another for it.

Josef sucked on Sophie just long enough to get hard again. He stood up straight grabbing her hips…and slid inside her tight vagina from behind. She let out a loud moan of contentment as she was lifted up onto her tiptoes. He leaned forward and cupped her breasts while kissing her shoulders…she loved seeing all of this transpire in the mirror. After watching himself slide in and out, he pulled out of her for the last time and turned her around. He lifted her up so that her little butt was perched on the outer rim of the sink. He held her thighs up high as she leaned back taking in his stiff wand completely. She wanted him in so deep… she wrapped her legs tightly around his waist pulling him in tighter. She wanted every last hard centimeter…

She was looking deep into his eyes when her body began to quiver. "Josef…I'm here" she said as she began having a long intense orgasm. He loved watching her experience his gift.

Once she had settled, he stepped back and began rubbing her down softly with a warm wash cloth. Then he tightly and lovingly bundled her up in a fresh luxurious robe that'd been neatly folded on the shelf next to the sink. He slipped on a matching robe and led them back to the living room where they plopped back down onto the sofa exactly where their day had begun. They finally felt relaxed. Their anxious energy had dissipated, if only temporarily. They were only seated a few minutes before a soft knock was heard on the door…"Room service."

"Oooh yes. I hope you're still hungry…for food, that is" he said standing up with a devious smile. He'd tried his best to tie and secure his robe closure yet it turned out to be a futile attempt to cover his incessant erection. Sincerely, It was no use.

He opened the door to a fresh faced young man waiting to wheel in a little drop-leaf table complete with a crisp pink linen tablecloth. It had a few sweet pink roses in a small clear round vase as a tiny arrangement for the center of the table. The flowers sat amongst the many dishes of gourmet finger sandwiches served up in all kinds of unique and delicious varieties.

"Jo…sef. This is so cute and charming, I just love it!" Sophie gushed with a bit of prep-school enthusiasm while taking a visual inventory of the contents on the table.

Josef however, was busily pre-occupied watching the server nervously fumble around trying to open the bottle of Veuve Cliquot. Josef was beside himself and had become so frustrated that he grabbed the bottle right out of the poor guy's hands. How could anyone blame the young server, he was obviously so jittery and nervous due to Josef's robe not closing that the young buck scrambled out of the room with a much quicker exit than the manner in which he'd arrived.

"Alone at last," Josef said completely unfazed. He pivoted around and smiled at Sophie thinking she was so sexy she could even make a terrycloth hotel robe look incredible.

"Champagne for my baby?" he asked, popping the bottle open. It made a huge celebratory sound as the cork blew off and hit the high ceiling. Not a drop was spilled as the first glasses of the day were filled.

"Oh Josef, what are we doing??...This is driving me insane! More than that...I think it's YOU that's driving me crazy! I was bouncing around my apartment in SF and could't think of anything but you. Thank God I was able to come up with some phony excuse to create distance between Bruce and I. I had to justify this unnecessary trip somehow. If only he'd caught a glimpse of my...I don't know what he would've done."

Hearing this, Josef began to speak calmly yet with a scary tone in his voice, "If that prick ever lays a hand on you, you have to tell me immediately. I want you to leave that pig now without ever going back."

Sophie was a bit stunned with his quick change of demeanor, but nevertheless...when she responded, she did so with a question...avoiding the focus on 'the other' guy.

"Oh yeah?...Now just how do you propose I'd be able to pull that off...just like that," she said snapping her fingers to make her point. "It's much more complicated than you realize. I still have my personal possessions there, not to mention all of my important documents. I don't think I could even get my assistant to go and retrieve them for me they're so well hidden. It'd be way too obvious and risky for anyone else but me to go back there and dig them out. This has been MY life Josef...and I need to end it with Bruce properly.

I'll get everything organized and take care of it on this return trip. Will that suit you? That's when I'll tell him our relationship is over, should he not have already figured that out by now. But what do we do after that Josef?" Sophie asked counting on him to take the lead as he usually did.

She wanted some definite answers and to hear *his* plan as confirmation. Then he started…

"Sophie, I have some rules that we need to discuss before we 'officially' make this commitment between us. I want you to be absolutely certain this is what you want."

Sophie had never been one to adhere to any rules in her life, but since these words were coming from Josef she sat and 'listened' while happily concentrating on her third sip of champagne. He was so full of his own nauseating macho bullshit, whatever he had in mind really didn't matter at that point. She'd already bought in to whatever he was selling. She was literally so captivated by his charm thinking he was so handsome…especially when he looked so serious and passionate trying to explain something. Obviously so submerged in her sense of '*new* world' luxury, she wasn't about to say anything that would upset or jeopardize her new found position.

"What…if any more rules could you possibly have that I've not already agreed to my love?" she questioned, almost in a jovial spirit.

"First and foremost…like I've said, I won't share you. That's My Biggest Rule. We got into this relationship when you were still with another man if you haven't forgotten. It just so happened to be with a guy that I've known and hated my entire life. I will never accept you having a wandering eye like you did when you first laid eyes on me" Josef gloated, making his point effectively intimidating.

"I want you to assure me that you'll never do that again. I'm to be your only one from now on. Then after we begin our life in France I'll need you to promise me that you'll give me numerous children. We can start creating our first baby together soon, and with any luck you'll be giving birth next year to my heir," he said camouflaging his dictatorship with a sexy smile.

Sophie just sat relishing in this 'particular' directive. He'd actually just rattled off exactly what her dream plan had been all along. It'd all worked accordingly. She was going to get everything in life she'd always dreamt of. She'd played her cards right, but it certainly hadn't hurt that she'd been dealt the perfect hand. She was so busy looking at the forest she'd missed seeing the trees. The overall picture was so much more important to her…the lost little soul, she couldn't get out of her own way.

"In addition, I don't want you to have anything to do with that piece of shit or his family ever again. No contact whatsoever. Do you understand?"

"Josef that's going to be a difficult thing to do…so just how would you think I'd be able to do that, huh? I can't stand his crazy family, but they're so present in the Village… I don't know how I can avoid them if I'm ever going to live freely and happily in Issigeac, I can't be looking over my shoulder all the time. They'll just have to get over it."

Hearing this come from Sophie…Josef was actually taken aback by her confident tone and blasé matter-of-fact stance in the matter. She was obviously feeling her oats. A bit more independent and secure than her norm shall we say? So…it's shocking I know but the Golden Boy relented and acquiesced to her for the first time ever. The poor bastard had become so terribly mesmerized by her charm he didn't know which end was up. They traded power places faster than the wind…but all they really wanted was to hop in bed.

"Sophie, I'm not the richest of men nor the most travelled, but I can assure you I'll provide you with what I think will be a beautiful life together. I can actually guarantee that, but there's one thing about me you really must know before we solidify our deal. I really have a dark side to me and one that you haven't seen yet. Our life certainly won't be without complications my dear, but I'll give you a sweet life on a silver platter if you'll go along calmly and not freak out on me with my *sometimes manly behavior.*

My Grandfather, my mentor…may he rest in peace, had a reputation of being a beautiful and loving man. But not everyone knew what a bastard he could be at times. He was capable of doing a lot of…well, let's just say, 'things' that weren't so earnest and good. He exposed and taught me both sides of life, the good and the bad...and now each are a part of me. I always choose the dark side when I need to get something done or use someone to help me get what I want. I'm not saying this to scare you, but for the record I'm telling you...or I guess what I'm actually doing...is warning you...to take heed. I don't want you ever to change, you need to stay like you are...hot, sexy and always devoted to me. If you can look the other way sometimes, we can have a beautiful life together," he continued...

"Then...I want you to sell your clothing company as soon as possible. I know and understand it may take some time so while you're engaged with doing that, I'll buy a little pied-à-terre somewhere here in Gramercy Park or Chelsea. That way we'll have a little crash pad of our own, just until your business is sold. I'll expect you to move into the new place the minute I close on the deal. I've already got a Real Estate agent working on it...but until that happens, I want you to feel comfortable staying here in our Hôtel suite. I don't want to imagine you being around Bruce, not even for one more night. The thought of you staying so far away on the West coast and near him...makes me out of my mind with jealousy. You'll only need a couple of days to pick up your things, but other than that? I want you back here close to me. You'll be safe here and logistically...the East coast makes it so much more manageable for us. You can come and go and meet me in Paris whenever time allows or I'll come here when you can't find the time to join me there. Does this all sound okay my love? It shouldn't take long to achieve our French life together. I love you Sophie and promise to give you all that I can if you'll accept me...and my terms."

Sophie sat half listening. She was so head over heels in love, she was only swooning with admiration when looking at him give his 'pre-nupish' checklist. Seriously...I can't imagine why she didn't leave then. The controlling bastard had just laid it all out on the table, (you're mine unconditionally, no matter what I do) but once he'd finished his ridiculous rhetoric...all she did was casually lean over and pick up one of the perfectly trimmed mini triangles of cream cheese and thinly shaved cucumber. After inspecting it with glee in her eye, she took a tiny nibble out of one corner, then popped the rest of the crust free morsel into her mouth not giving another thought to the reality of his demands.

She'd not seriously heard nor digested the complete list of his rules and regulations…She was still reveling in the word 'babies'. She'd become completely blinded by her *dream image* of him and hadn't really listened to one GD word he'd been preachin'. She only wanted to see the good, the provider and of course, that pearly white picket fence like so many of us dream of. All the bells and whistles that'd come along with the presumed picture perfect lifestyle made her agree to it all. At least with all that she thought she'd heard. It really was mind blowing…Devoted and ready? Why didn't he just come out and demand what he really wanted by using the actual words…subordination as in 'totally submit to me'. I guess when I think about it, he actually had.

"Josef I promise to please you and be true only to you…for the rest of my life sweetheart," she sweetly whispered sitting down on his lap. She then popped one of the minuscule gourmet delights in his mouth and smiled giving a loving touch to the tip of his nose with her index finger.

He was so charmed by her behavior he swept her up and carried her into the bedroom. Fireworks proceeded to run through their afternoon and into the night providing another incredibly long pillow talk experience.

The next morning arrived with a light subtle knock on the door. Josef was already awake and sprang up assuming to meet room service again. The same bellman entered the suite and quickly rolled out yesterday's cart replacing it with a fresh white linen covered table on wheels. This time it was full of gorgeous breakfast platters and a single red rose as its centerpiece. The lingering smell of hot sex had permeated the room to the max, so much so that the fragrance of the perfectly cooked bacon strips didn't stand a chance.

The server made a quick dash for the door and couldn't get out fast enough after Josef signed for the delivery. He was so uncomfortable with their sex den… between the flapping robe situation with yesterdays lunch delivery and today's slight flag pole rising with breakfast, the poor bastard didn't even wait for a tip…either time. Josef smiled to himself thinking he'd never seen a bellhop move so efficiently. He just loved it.

"Sophie, we need to get our energy back" Josef said wheeling the morning table into the bedroom while dropping his slightly closed robe onto the bottom of the bed.

"I could get used to this Josef," Sophie said sitting up and taking a sip of freshly squeezed orange juice that she'd taken from the cart parked beside her.

"Good my love because this is only the beginning," he said sliding a beautifully wrapped package towards her.
He'd been hiding the surprise under the bed since his arrival. It was an elegant shiny black box tied with an abundance of wide red satin ribbon. Inside was one of the gorgeous sets of lingerie that he'd purchased from the swank boutique on rue St. Honore. The copious amount of crisp white tissue within made such an exciting fluttering crinkle sound as Sophie lifted the snug vacuum packed lid.

The set looked expensive and God was it ever. Both pieces inside were beautifully handmade with exquisite blue cotton lace. It was definitely a bra and string bikini set Sophie would never have imagined affording herself. It was her first taste of having the very finest of *French Lingerie*. This set was certainly a major step up from what she could find at her go-to shopping resource 'Mantoria's'. This set was in a different league altogether. It felt so glorious being spoiled and gifted with the best. She excitedly got out of bed, put on the perfectly fitting combo and modeled it with pride for her lover. He was enjoying his personal show while sipping on his first cup of coffee.

"Oh Josef, it's beautiful, I absolutely adore it!" she

gleefully said dancing around the room with seductive stripper moves. "The beginning of many gifts to come," she thought. "Yum, Jackpot…"

She was so wrapped up in showing off, she didn't give a second thought to their prior day's conversation. She hadn't taken one minute to think, consider, or analyze any of the stated rules that were required to become 'his'. Her exciting sex life and greed had obviously overtaken her inner voice.

Later that day, Sophie began spreading the news that her business was for sale. She'd contacted her accountant and requested her well earned healthy looking financial statement be prepared and emailed over asap. It was one that any potential buyer would be impressed with. Then, she called her trusty assistant Gayle to break the news. She didn't quite tell her the whole story…just enough to drop the bombshell that she'd decided on a life change and would be selling the company.

Gayle, needless to say was dumbfounded. Sophie had always been so passionately involved and a hands-on owner since the very day she'd started the company, Gayle simply couldn't believe what she was hearing. Sophie had always been so predictable. Her unfaltering and tenacious work ethic made this impulsive decision shocking. It just didn't add up…this sudden change seemed odd. Gayle figured Sophie must've found something super spectacular to make her want to make such a radical change. The surprising news came from so far out in left field, she thought it must have something to do with some mega rich dude who was obviously from the 'upper crust' and French bred…(no pun intended) Perhaps Sophie's 'dream ship' had really sailed in…big time.

Anyway…the word was out, the existing accounts had begun calling with their concerns about future orders. Gayle as expected, kept a steady hand with a straight face. With her robotic professionalism, she calmly explained to their customers there should be no concerns regarding the company's stability. It was all to be a smooth transition and would remain 'business as usual'. Ha, who was she kidding?...She was lying through her teeth.

Behind Sophie's back however, it'd come time for her brave face to come off. With this new situation being dumped in her lap, Gayle was scared to think what else might be coming down the pipeline. She snapped into more of a rational logic figuring she needed to get hustling double time on making some plans of her own. Loyalty? It was proving to be Dog-eat-Dog after all.

While Sophie was busy networking to those in the industry, Josef met with a few Real Estate agents in Manhattan who specialized in his favored zip codes. He'd already decided exactly where he wanted to look and wasn't interested in any other mid-town or nearby south end areas. He was only dialed in to his two favorites, Chelsea and Gramercy Park. No doubt it's because they'd once again become the latest and trendiest places to live. As we know, (or should) New Yorkers are particularly picky when it comes to 'new' yet old posh zips. (Parisians don't have the exclusive on this one, sorry)

Just let our beloved Gay Boys in to gentrify et voilà...'*bien sûr*'...the area most definitely will become tasteful and fun again. It's a well established cycle. The boyz do their designer make-overs, party down for a while, open a couple of chic shops and bars and before long?...BAM. The spoiled wasps see the upgraded value and move back in only to drive the prices up and voila, the boys will then take flight. On and on the merry-go-round of hip real estate goes...Meat Packing District anyone? Brooklyn by chance?

With every sliver of time and opportunity available, Josef and Sophie would meet back at their fabulous Hôtel suite and make love like it was their first time ever to do so.

"Josef, this has been such a fabulous week, everything seems to be blooming. I have some exciting and fantastic news! In a couple of days, I have an appointment with a Company back in San Francisco that could be interested in buying my label and taking over production! I can't believe it...I'm so excited! Wouldn't that be perfect?

We wouldn't need a place here after all…We could start our life together in France sooner than we thought. I'll need to make a short trip back for the meeting, then I can grab the balance of my things. The timing on all of this couldn't be more perfect! I'd be able to wrap it all up in one fell swoop. Gayle will meet me at my apartment when the coast is clear and we'll take what I can't bring back this time to the warehouse to be shipped later. I'll hurry back to you, I promise," she said prancing around like a debutante at her coming out party. She was almost hyperventilating with enthusiasm given her plan and this latest potential opportunity.

Josef replied in his best upbeat voice, "This is such great news! I know just closing the doors isn't an option, so I hope for your sake this potential buyer works out. You've worked so hard to make the company what it is…I'm really proud of you Sophie."

Blah Blah Blah…Josef couldn't have cared less if she actually sold the company or not. Letting it fall by the wayside would've been just fine with him. He'd said all of those accolades not meaning a damn word. He'd much prefer to begin their life in France immediately also, but with having the lurking complication of Bruce still being in the picture, that too would have to wait. All he could think about was whether Bruce would be home when Sophie arrived in San Francisco. He was obsessing over it and couldn't take the thought of it any longer. He needed Bruce and his family gone and out of their lives for good. Josef didn't want any issues from his past intruding on his new found happiness. Bruce and his family were standing in the way just like they always had. It'd been a long, long story between their two families…a story that obviously had not gone away on its own. It was like Karma was jumping up and hitting back with lightening force.

Josef thought there was no way in hell he and Sophie could live freely in Issigeac while having the Douglas' still loitering about. That family were such gossips, there was no doubt they'd be busy passing judgement on the 'new' couple and spreading nasty vicious rumors to whomever would listen. Josef was secretly forming a plan and now just needed to put it into motion. It'd become weighing heavily on his mind.

"Sophie, It's actually good timing that you go and get things moving along sweetheart. Since you'll be gone for a couple of days, I'll use the time to pop back to the *Château*. It seems we both have some unfinished business to deal with. I've gone ahead, assuming it's okay with you… (like he cared…) and paid for this suite for the next couple of months. It will comfort me knowing you'll have a nice temporary home base to return to. That is just until I find us the real thing, okay chérie?" he said moving closer. (wrapping his arms around her as if they were pliable wet willow branches on their way to becoming dry and hardened)

"Call me when you're ready to head back and I'll try to be here waiting for you. I know they call it "Breakfast at Tiffany's"…but I hope this place will suffice."

"Oh Josef, you're Too cute. I just adore you," she said with a loving giggle. "Agreed, I definitely think it's time to find closure to a few things. I'm ready to move forward and get this plan going first thing tomorrow. Okay?"

My God…she was good. She was quick to feel the tide on its way out and knew it was the time to catch the fast moving undertow. Their plans and timetable had been set. She'd heard all that she needed.

The love birds rode to the airport together bright and early the following morning. They were departing in different directions and from different terminals, so their farewells were said in the car with Sophie being dropped off first. Usually their goodbyes were a long and drawn out event, but not this time. They were both eager to get on with their awaiting battles and complete their missions at hand. Once they'd gone their own ways at the airport, their personalities reverted back to their origins. Sophie no longer acted like the super vulnerable gobsmacked sweet girl. She was back to being a quick stepped aggressive girl boss. She couldn't help but return to her old psycho-bitch business self. She already knew that game well.

Josef meanwhile had taken off his 'lover boy's mask' and regressed back into an aloof, calculating and intense loner. He felt it was time to get his human chess game back in form and get some of his pawns moving. His hidden anger had begun raising its ugly head again and was bubbling just below the surface. But as we know…the guy was so good at hiding things you would've never known.

So at last, they left one another to finish their personal sticky business. Neither knew what exactly was on the other's agenda, but that didn't matter…it was better left that way with no questions asked. It just so happened they'd be cleaning up their *issues* half a world way from each other and this was no time to air out any new dirty laundry. It was time to cleanse their score cards and be finished with their old lives.

Sophie arrived at SFO late afternoon and went directly to her warehouse. Who else but her trusty assistant would be the first person she saw…

"Gayle…I'm so happy to see you. I'm really needing your help. Would you mind coming to my place first thing tomorrow morning?

"Hi Sophie," she said looking dismayed and obviously frustrated not hearing so much as a warm and courteous greeting. After all…this was Gayle we're talking about…Her loyal and trusty right arm.

"Will do…but first talk to me and tell me just what the hell is going on? I can't believe you're selling the company and haven't felt the need to fill me in on any details! You've got to know how shocking this is for me as well, or have you even considered that?…Then just so you know, amongst all this madness happening with the business, something else rather bizarre happened this morning. Out of the blue, Bruce called…and said he was popping down to Los Angeles today, and wouldn't be back until late morning tomorrow. Why would he have done that?…What in the world is really happening around here? Seems like everything is coming unglued at once. I'm confused and more than a bit worried to tell you the truth Sophie."

"I know it's a lot to digest, but don't worry…it's all going to work out, you'll see. Time to make big changes happening in all directions…" Sophie said in a monotone whisper. Gayle couldn't get over seeing Sophie be like that…She actually had the nerve to have a smirk of delight on her face. She'd changed…

"First, Bruce and I are no longer a couple. We haven't spoken making it official yet, but he's got to have figured it out by now. We've had zero communication in the last week. We had a huge fight before I left for Manhattan and we haven't spoken since. But as far as long term, it really hasn't been good between us for a year or perhaps even longer…It's time for us to say our goodbyes. When did he say he'd be back?"

Gayle started fidgeting nervously, "Tomorrow late morning I think he said." Then she had a moment of noticeable panic and fessed up, admitting she might've let the cat out of the bag.

"I let it slip that you had texted letting me know you were coming back in town today. Oh Sophie, I'm so sorry…I had no idea all these issues were happening between the two of you. When I was speaking with him, I was trying so hard to stay my normal neutral self but he pressured me for details…"

"No problem Gayle, none of this is your fault. I had called him earlier wanting to get a feel for the situation and to know his plans. That's when he told me he already knew of my arrival. I was surprised, but so relieved hearing he wouldn't return until tomorrow, or at least that's what he said…He failed to mention anything about LA…or being back Stateside for that matter. This all comes as a bit of a shock after assuming he was still in Europe this whole time. He did nothing to make me think otherwise, oh contraire, he actually led me to believe he was still there. Whatever…" she said flippantly.

"I'm just happy he's not here. That's going to allow me a quiet evening alone to begin preparing and organizing some things for my exit. It'll make it so much easier without him being in the way and giving me any trouble.

Are you sure you're okay to meet me early in the morning? I'd really appreciate it and by the way...please bring along some boxes and packing materials with you. I know it's early, but does 7am work for you? We can finish packing, empty the apartment, and come back to the warehouse with everything before Bruce gets home. I have an appointment with Lesting Wear here at the warehouse at 11:00 after we complete our morning's mission. I must've forgotten to tell you, but they've tossed their hat in the ring and are considering buying the name and taking over production. That would be such a win-win...And I'm sure they'd need you to head up the division. I'll propose that as part of the deal. I wouldn't think of leaving you out on a limb. I'll do the best I can." (yeah...right)

"That'd be great Sophie, but seriously...I'm a bit perplexed and disheartened with all these changes. I thought we were such a good team" Gayle replied with a bit of pensiveness. Then suddenly she had an epiphany...and realized she was being abandoned no matter what Sophie was saying and projecting.

In Gayle's most vulnerable moment...she confided, "I've been so worried with all this sudden news I haven't known what to think...whether I should start looking for another job or what? You are making all of these huge life-changing decisions so fast, it makes me feel in limbo and I hate this feeling of uncertainty! It's been so weird not being able to say anything to anyone in the company about this. Yet at the same time...I really haven't known what to say or think until you shared further thoughts and details...which you have not. All this secrecy...I really hope you're making the right decision Sophie. I wish you would slow down and think..."

"Oh Gayle, I wouldn't be doing any of this unless I found something truly spectacular. I'm really in love with someone special and now, I just need to finish it off with Bruce and move on with my life. I've found my golden ticket and a new life that will fulfill my dreams. Please tell me you can at least be a *little bit* happy for me...(talk about a self centered egoist...My God! Will the real Sophie plz stand up)

"My dream man will be waiting for me in NYC after I finish here, but disconnecting my current life is a lot more complicated than I'd ever imagined. It's difficult having one foot in two continents. I'm so hopeful Lesting Wear jumps in all the way. That would answer so many questions and get me out of here even sooner than I'd imagined. Fingers crossed they'll come through.

I'll see you in the morning. I'll need to be out of the apartment before Bruce gets back so we'll need to be fast. I even thought at one point, I'd have to end it with him over a text should I have found him to be drinking. He can get pretty crazy when that's the case. So much for the converted health nut...right?" Gayle couldn't believe how insensitive and callous Sophie had become. It was like she was speaking to a self serving stranger.

The warehouse was conveniently located in an adjacent neighborhood not far from the apartment. It literally was referred to as the 'Dog Patch'. It was just south-east of Petroleum Hill and it truly resembled its name. Sophie had always loved the funky mix that the colorful hood offered. It was packed full of personality and had quite the unique history. The old 'working man's industrial district' had become a combination of empty warehouses, greasy spoons and run-down garages. It had a few typical row houses sprinkled in, but the most enticing factor when she started the company was the cheap rent. (which of course made it all the more desirable) Since then the 'patch' had boomed like the rest of the city as did her rent...

She'd been lucky enough to snatch a tiny portion of a red brick warehouse when the area was still in one of its down cycles. But that was then, and now?...It was in the midst of becoming a hip and vogue location like it'd been in the 70's. There were new chic eateries and upscale bars popping up monthly. The best news was it was only minutes from Sophie's apartment so after a long day of work, it was either an easy cab or Uber ride home, (or a long walk up the hill) after a few drinks and a late dinner out.

Sophie left Gayle at the warehouse and took a taxi up to her place on Bigsby St. She opened the door and climbed the stairs to the top of the landing exhaling from sheer relief to be home. She dropped her small overnight bag down with a plunk, then went into the dusk filled living room to turn on the lamp next to the sofa. Then she walked back in to the kitchen to grab a bottle of water. Strange thing was that she noticed an open bottle of vodka sitting on the counter and thought, "What a swine...Amazing what he's become recently. Why would he have left a bottle just sitting out like that? Obviously he's back to some of his old tricks before becoming so righteous." She shrugged it off and went into their bedroom where she opened her tightly packed closet and began taking out some choice items and laying them out on the bed. Consumed with organizing her 'exit outfits'...she was lost in her own world of thought...

So you can imagine how shocked she must've been when she turned around to see Bruce standing in the doorway. She didn't like surprises like this. It immediately made her nervous. He'd been drinking and the bottle on the counter then made more sense.

"Well, there you are you little prin...sass...all pretty and standing there picking clothes out like you are going on vacation. What do you think you're doing? Emptying out your closet without discussing any of this with me? You thought you were just going to slip in and out of my life without any discussion?" Bruce said, he was in a highly saddened yet agitated state. It was actually...pathetic.

"Bruce, you're drunk" she responded dismissively.

"So what if I am. We've had three years together and I deserve more than this Sophie. My father gave me a call and said the word in the Village is that you are fucking that evil prick of a man, Josef Decour. Is this true and *really* happening?" he questioned slurring his words.

"We should discuss this at another time Bruce, but I'll tell you one thing for sure, so hear me well...I want to make it crystal clear for you...We Are Over. I'm only here to pick up a few things. I'll be back in the morning for the rest. We can speak over coffee when we both are more level headed and can focus on what we truly have to say."

"I've always known you were somewhat of a snobby gold digger, but since you are so successful…why do you feel the need to be with him of all people!" he yelled grabbing Sophie's arm.

"Let me go! You don't know what you're doing! You're hurting me Bruce. Let go of me!" she screamed wrestling to get away from him. She pushed him back on the bed and quickly grabbed her purse making her way down two steep stairs at a time.

"I'll be here at 7:00" she yelled back up at the top of her lungs before swiftly closing the door behind her. She hadn't been ready for this unexpected and disturbing confrontation…

Obviously shaken, her only thought was to run down to the end of the block and call a Cab. The last thing she'd been expecting was to have a shocking run-in with a drunk and belligerent Bruce. She'd so hoped this type of hurtful exchange wouldn't be a part of their split. (Seriously?…we all know better than that, breakups are never easy. Someone always gets hurt whether we want to admit it or not)

*

Chapter Cinq

Her taxi arrived, and swiftly delivered her down the hill to the Marriott Hôtel on Sutter Street. After checking in she threw her bag on the bed, (which is usually a strict tabu…'cause ya neva know where those dirty things have been) opened the mini bar and called Josef.

"Hi sweetheart, hope I'm not disturbing. I know it's probably the worst time to call…but I couldn't wait to hear your voice" she said craving some comfort especially after that unnerving collision with Bruce. She knew she couldn't mention a word about what had really transpired with her their earlier encounter. By no means did she want to throw fuel on the fire and add to the tension when it came to the Boy's distaste for one another. Bruce would need to sleep it off before they could resume any contact and logically pick up where they'd left off. Hopefully it would be with a clear head and a healthier attitude the following morning.

"Hello ma chérie" Josef replied sounding happy to hear her voice. "I only just arrived a short while ago myself. Everything okay with you?"

"Yes, it's all happening as I'd hoped" she said completely bending the truth. Knowing Gayle was meeting her at the apartment the following morning gave her confidence knowing some back-up support had already been put in place should Bruce pull any more of his bullshit. She was praying she could get everything accomplished without any further issues or bad scenes playing out.

"Since it's late here, I thought it easier to just check in to the Marriott for the night. I'll pop by my old place in the morning after enjoying some room service and wrap it all up then."

"That sounds like a good plan. I'm relieved to hear you sounding so good and that everything is going smoothly. You'll be back in my arms by the time Bruce gets back to San Francisco"…Josef said, not having a clue he'd already returned and had been laying in wait for Sophie's return. He would've gone ballistic had he known.

"Okay sweetheart...then only think of me in your dreams tonight? I'll give you a call tomorrow afternoon, I love you Sophie."

They finished their conversation on that note and hung up. As she put the phone down, she took a long savoring minute to recount what she'd just heard. She couldn't believe he'd finally uttered the words...*Love. I love you. I love you. I love you*...she continued to speak aloud those cherished words as they danced pleasantly and floated around in her head. She went to sleep with the loving sentiment hopscotching through her thoughts and dreams like he'd requested. The fact was, she was spinning out all over the place.

The morning came early and Sophie's cab was a few minutes late delivering her to the apartment. She was greeted by her trusty assistant Gayle, who of course had arrived early and was already waiting on the sidewalk in front.

"OH My God Sophie...When I arrived this morning and knocked on the door, never in a million years was I thinking it'd be Bruce that opened it. He told me aggressively that you were never coming back then flipped me off! I couldn't believe the bizarre encounter. Seriously, it was so unexpected and crazy...Needless to say I was shocked to see him in the first place, especially since he'd told me he wouldn't be back in town until late this morning. Oh My God...was he here when you came home last night?? What happened!! Where did you spend the night? Are you?..." Gayle's questions petered out then took a new direction. "This situation doesn't feel right. What's *really* happening here?"

"Good Morning Gayle. I stayed the night at the cheesy business hotel down the street and yes, he was here when I got home last night and NO, it didn't go well. How's that to answer your questions!" Seems Sophie wasn't the only one to have waken up on the wrong side of the bed…"Our breakup is not going to be as easy as I'd hoped. He was drunk when I arrived, which means I wasn't able to accomplish much. You've seen how he gets. Let me go in now and try to reason with him. Would you mind waiting for me down here for a bit longer while I try to smooth things out? But should you hear me scream…call the police," Sophie joked half heartedly as she put the key in the lock and opened the door. Once inside she looked up to see Bruce sitting on the top stair of the landing looking down at her. He'd been waiting…apparently much longer than Gayle had been.

"I'm sorry for last night Sophie. I hope I didn't hurt you."

"I'll survive," she responded straight faced while climbing the stairs.

She didn't wait for him to move, instead she almost marched right over him making her way to the kitchen. She was back to her power play personality. He, on the other hand, had become the sad and remorseful one out of the two. She walked directly into the kitchen and began making a pot of coffee with Bruce following behind like a remorseful needy child that had just been scolded.

"Do you really know what you're doing Sophie? I know our relationship has been on the rocks for a while but I sincerely don't want you to go. Please take some time and think about it…about us," he pleaded. Taking the longest time…he continued, "But if you think we're really over, I hope you can remember the best of us…all of the good times we've had…at least."

Only moments passed before Dr. Jekyll became Mr. Hyde and changed his tune.

"Are you really leaving me for that bastard? I'm so worried at what you're getting yourself into. The 'Decour trap' is a bigger snare than you realize. Whatever you do, please slow down. I want you to know what you're really facing and dealing with. I've known Josef and his family since we were kids. Did he tell you that?" Bruce questioned with a deliberate conviction as he calmed himself enough to get two clean coffee cups out of the upper cabinet.

Sophie just continued standing quietly with her back to him listening further while she finished preparing the morning brew. She was shocked to know the length of time he and Josef had actually known each other. Knowing each other is one thing, but their heavy animosity towards one another obviously explained there was a painful back story to it as well. What in the hell was this all about? Bruce had never mentioned one word about Josef in the three years together, nor Josef about Bruce. This whole thing between the two had only surfaced and blown up since her explosive rendezvous in Paris with Josef. Everything had been quiet and dormant until then.

Sophie's inner ego started to go wild as she glanced over at Bruce with a pathetic hollow stare and thought, "Wow…Am I that good? Boys bickering over me?" She was devilishly feeling her sexy self and totally delighted in her ego filled self admiration. She'd given Bruce such a particular look…it could've pinned anyone's ears back.

"And I thought Josef was the only protagonist when it came to the relationship between you two." But before Sophie actually had time to verbalize a discerning word out loud, Bruce started to unravel…

"Josef and his family are Really manipulative. They use their wealth to buy false respect and…" he paused… "Tell me, has he ever mentioned his reason why our families have such a history? Did he bother to explain that to you!!?"

"Stop it Bruce!" she yelled. "I don't want to hear your jealousy spew any more hatred against Josef and his family! I'll have to get to know them for myself and make my own decisions and judgements. He's a lot nicer and much more sensitive than you think."

"For Christ's sake Sophie, listen to yourself! You've been blinded my dear…Please…tell me you're kidding?? Has he already got you that fooled? Josef is a clever bastard and I can promise you…he'll run over you, or anyone else for that matter who gets in the way of what he wants. I know him well, he puts on a brilliant show just like his bastard of a Father and Grandfather did. I know all about him and his fucking family. Ask him what the 'real' story is.

Go on, ask him. See if he's able to tell you the truth."

"Enough!" Sophie screamed.

The front door was immediately heard opening from the small vestibule downstairs as Gayle yelled up, "Sophie… everything okay?"

"Oh…now I see…" Bruce said snidely. "You're back to your old usual self. This is all in your master plan isn't it?…You've already made up your mind and are leaving me. Without so much as an honest word…" Selfish bitch…he uttered under his breath as he grabbed his jacket.

"We'll see if this new 'grand' life of yours will bring you all the happiness that you think it will" he yelled back up to her while stomping down the stairs. He stormed out and blew by Gayle who was standing motionless in the entry. He slammed the front door behind him so hard, it's a miracle the door's thin opaque glass panels didn't shatter.

"Oh My GOD Sophie…I've never seen Bruce like that. Are you okay?" Gayle asked entering the kitchen.

"Well, I'm grateful *that's* over…It definitely wasn't as pleasant as I'd hoped, but let's just say, it's now official… we're done, it's history. Here, take this…we need a stiff cup of Joe (pun intended) to get us ready to tackle this project" Sophie said obviously shaken when she handed Gayle one of the empty cups Bruce had intended for himself.

Sophie filled them both up with a hot cup, then led them only a few steps into her pint sized bedroom to begin packing her life up. The apartment was tiny, but had been such an incredible find. It was a small two bedroom yet had million dollar views of the Golden Gate bridge from the dining room and of the Bay Bridge from the living room. The ultimate bonus, besides its views and stellar location, was the fact that it had an old fashioned super sized large garage below. A rare commodity in the hilly city and next to Impossible to find…but for now it felt easier to be done with it and let it all go. Ba-bye…

Sophie began pulling all of her sweaters out from her dresser drawers and throwing them on the bed. She was obviously more upset than she'd let on. She began haphazardly folding and stuffing them in the suitcases she'd brought down from the top shelf of her overstuffed closet. The rest would all go in the boxes that Gayle was busy constructing in the hallway.

"Sophie, I can't believe how many clothes are coming out of that teeny closet. Seems like they are expanding and doubling in size with air" Gayle said attempting to put a smile on Sophie's face.

"Once you finish choosing and organizing what you'll need for this return trip, we can count and estimate how many boxes we'll need to go to the warehouse to be shipped later. I can only fit a few cartons in my car but I'll call the warehouse and have the delivery van sent over to pick up the balance while we're still here. That way it will be done."

Sophie didn't respond, not even with a slight smile of acknowledgement. She could still hear Bruce in her head. They silently continued packing in record speed. Sophie had made it apparent she was ready to close this chapter and get on with her meeting with Lesting Wear. She had a schedule after all. They made it back to the warehouse just in the nick of time.

"Hello Judie. Thank you for coming this morning. Sophie said smiling as she proudly welcomed her potential buyer. I'm assuming you've had time to review our spreadsheet?"

"Yes, I certainly have. I can't believe how profitable you've made this company. Amazing job Sophie…You're to be congratulated my dear. Few in the industry are cashing in like you on simple garment dye production. You chose the perfect time to get into this missing category in the market. The fact that everyone was ready for sexy velvet track suits for the second time around is amazing. What goes around certainly does come around…and obviously that was something people were missing. Judging by your success, it wasn't just because of the timing…your collections have consistently been fantastic. You really created your own design niche" Judie continued…giving Sophie a few well deserved compliments within her response.

"I know right? I was extremely lucky with the timing of it all. Things just seem to have worked out nicely but the stress of handling the growth has really been difficult for me to hold together…In fact almost too much for one person to pull off. That's why I think you've been so blessed to work with your husband as a team. I've never had any support or help from my other half. He's always had his own business to deal with. The only other person that I could've trusted to partner with is my older brother James, but he owns a 'start up' Tech company in the nearby Silicon Valley and already has too much on his plate. Besides, he really doesn't have a clue what we *really* do in the fashion world."

Hearing this Judie cut to the chase abruptly stopping the small talk. She wasn't interested in knowing details…

"Sophie, as much as we love your product and name, unfortunately it's not going to work for us. Our company has been built on printed mesh items and after giving this opportunity much thought and consideration… we've decided to pass. Adding a division with a completely different dye process is too far off our mainstay at this point. We would have to get an entire new team and production facility versus using our current one. Even though your financials are fantastic, it would be too big of an initial investment for us. Our decision is something that hasn't come easy, so I wanted to personally come this morning to let you know our decision" she concluded apologetically.

Sophie felt like she was receiving a back handed compliment. She had invested so much hope and energy in this potential opportunity coming to fruition…that hearing this rejection was not at all what she'd been expecting. Once she was able to really absorb their decision…the word 'no' stopped her in her tracks. Her disappointment was so apparent it was like the word 'loser' was written all over her face with an invisible day glow marker. She was devastated.

She wasn't used to having her life become so chaotic. To merely say she was disappointed would be a gross understatement. The helium that she'd been flying around on immediately vanished from underneath her. Her entire mornings events suddenly hit her like an emotional ton of bricks. She was crushed.

But seriously my dears, let's be realistic. To think she could callously dump her live-in boyfriend in the early morning with no repercussions, then have a slam dunk sale of her business by lunch?...All of these major changes made successfully with no consequences? You have to admit, even for Sophie, her plan was a bit too ambitious. Her desire to get back to Josef made her think she could march right through and stomp over people without any difficulty, having it all play into her hands. No wonder she was slumping. A couple of huge life-changing and emotional events like that could take an adjustment and re-evaluation period for just about anyone wouldn't you think? She needed to slow down and take inventory of herself, not to mention the situation, and perhaps become a bit more... humble and patient, may I dare say...

That would definitely be the difficult part. Both were not necessarily a page covered in her playbook. She'd have to put the idea of retiring to live in the lap of luxury with her hot lover in the SW of France on hold for a while. Easy right? That would be a huge disappointing setback for a girl who was so used to getting immediate gratification with just about everything. Nevertheless, she'd need to maintain her enthusiasm for maintaining her company until the right buyer did come along. The sale could take a while...so she would need to take that time to get re-focused. Let's not forget, Josef was giving her the perfect opportunity to keep her hand on the pulse while living on the East Coast...How sweet he was offering such a beautiful place to *glamp* in total luxury through the transition.

She began to analyze..."Okay, there's no need I should be so worried or feel so hurried. I've worked my booty off for far too long to throw it all away for nada" she began repeating to herself, as if it were her strong new mantra. This would become her internal hymn just until the heart tugging thoughts of Baby, *Château* and Josef returned, running rampant through her mind. (like she were in a 4K race) The disappointment of the sale not happening made it difficult to stay positive, even though she really did have so much to be grateful for. Somehow she felt stuck like her wings had been clipped. Ouch.

Our poor girl…She just hated this new found feeling of reality. After all, when life doesn't go as planed, it does bite sometimes. So after ending her relationship with Bruce, she felt at least she could check off one major item on her mission list.

That one hurdle had given her enough feeling of completion for the moment, so much so that she got on the red eye to surprise Josef with an early return to Manhattan. She'd give him a call from their Hôtel suite to let him know she'd arrived and was eagerly awaiting. It was 6:30 in the morning New York time when she made the call to her lover. She was missing him and curious of his whereabouts. She thought he might be just sitting down for lunch.

"Bonjour darling, I hope I'm not interrupting…I just wanted to let you know I'm sitting here looking out the window at the park. I'm wearing your robe and getting ready to take a long soak."

"Ahh good, does it still have my scent on it?" Josef questioned with a seemingly seductive pleasure in his voice. (knowing full well room service had not been allowed in since they'd left, only the bed had been made and towels refreshed…they liked it that way)

"Yes, it certainly does my love. Your sweet nectar lingers…and I have to say, it's so sexy, it's intoxicating. Perhaps instead of a bath, I'll just take a sudsy shower and think of you…yummmm" she said, using a *certain* intonation. She knew mentioning that would get him aroused and his imagination going in full speed. It worked…

"That makes me hard just thinking about it." Then, there was a moment of silence.

"You're back in NY sooner than I thought… everything okay?" Sophie didn't answer immediately so he continued…

"I'm happy to report, my trip back has also been

productive. I've made a ton of progress on my checklist and Sweetheart, I know…I said I'd meet you there when you arrived, but there are still a few things lingering that I need to take care of. So I'm not sure what exact time tomorrow I'll be able to get out of here. I'll definitely be seeing you in time for a little evening wake up call," knowing full well she knew what that meant.

I was worried not hearing from you last night, but now I know why. Obviously you were en route. Hope your flight was good…How did your business meeting go? I guess yesterday must've been a big day for both of us. Dites-moi…did you see the bastard? Are you two officially finished?"

Josef couldn't help himself…he wanted to get to the point. That was the only pertinent question on his mind whether she'd seen Bruce and *Finished It* with him. The rest really didn't matter, so knowingly she gave him what he wanted to hear.

"Well my love, the good news is I did finish it with him and I'm all moved out. I'll explain more in detail when I see you. I'm just happy to report at least that part is over. As for the business?…Sadly, my meeting was a total bust. The hopeful that I told you about decided it wasn't the right fit for them after all. I'll need to stay diligent and continue to look for the right buyer…Until then, I'll just continue working to keep the business going strong and the sales up. Living on the East Coast will certainly give me the advantage to do so, but I was so hopeful these potential buyers were the ones. As excited as I am about our future stint in Manhattan, I've secretly been praying we could by-pass living here. To be honest, I've been eager possibly thinking the *Château* would be *our first place* together and to have the sale of my business behind me" she said waiting for his reaction…but he kept silent.

The awkward moment before Josef responded was confusing. It made her feel the need to walk back her comment…she didn't want to harp on the subject or sound too anxious so she conveniently took a new tactic.

"But without a buyer in the wings that's going to be impossible. We'll just have to wait and make our experience living here a great one. It'll be fun."

She felt satisfied (for the time being) knowing at least she'd successfully planted the seed about living in the *Château* sooner than later. Just the thought of living with Josef in his Domaine made her feel powerful. Soon to be 'The Woman of the Estate'...her big dream coming to fruition was so close she could taste it. No one would be able to touch her then. Having such privilege, her self entitlement and deservedly lavish lifestyle would soon be at her fingertips. All she needed was Josef to put a ring on it or get her pregnant, whichever came first was inconsequential. It's utterly amazing in fact, absolutely incredible the games some girls play to get what they want...guess it's a two way street when I think about it, but really, so not my style.

"Our day will be here soon enough. All in good time my love" he finally replied.

Thank God she could pleasantly exhale hearing that bit of reassurance. They continued with their sexy play talk when Josef suddenly changed his tone. He sounded strange like he was being distracted.

"Everything okay my love? You sound different. What's happening in that gorgeous kitchen of yours?" she questioned with a bit of humor...(trying to make light of it when in fact she was dying to know what was going on behind the scenes) She didn't want to sound too inquisitive, but when she heard the angst and shift in his voice she became extremely curious. Who was it that was there with him?

Actually, Sophie's suspicions were right. The change in his voice was due to the 'housekeeper' making an unexpected entrance into the kitchen from the dining room. Josef hated his privacy being invaded and having someone overhear his private lovey-dovey conversation with Sophie. Seeing her enter, he immediately stood up and waved her off with an aggressive hand signal, obviously implying for her to get the Hell Out. Once she'd returned to the dining room, Josef and Sophie resumed their intimate conversation followed by their lengthy sweet goodbyes.

When their playful love chat ended, Josef stormed into the dining room half out of his mind to confront the girl who he knew had obviously been eavesdropping in on his conversation. She was standing with her back to him dusting the wall sconces as he entered the dining room.

"I was on the phone, didn't you hear me? I hate being interrupted and feeling like I'm being spied on! Never do that again do you understand?" he yelled venomously. "I fucking detest having anyone sneak around and listen without me knowing. I won't tolerate my privacy being disrespected nor invaded like this ever again...Do you understand? If it does...you'll finally be out of this place for good Fiona. Comprendre?!"

In the midst of his fierce reprimanding, when she turned to respond she saw Josef's cheeks were flushed from his angry outburst. Even though he was upset and showing it, she was happy to see him and thought he was so...absolutely gorgeous...

"Oui, je comprende Josef, I'm so sorry...I assumed you were still out of town. When I heard someone in the kitchen, it was my natural instinct to go see who it was that was making the disturbance. Please excuse me, it won't happen again" she said smiling internally while looking at him in earnest...

"How could he act this way towards me...Had he forgotten how sweet our first kiss was when we were young? At least that should be something worth remembering fondly" she thought while innocently watching him conclude his tirade.

In reality...Their 'collision' if you could call it that... was no accident. She'd actually been waiting for him and grown impatient hearing him canoodle with Sophie on the phone. She wasn't about to let this new girl jeopardize her future. She knew she needed to act fast, especially after the *'talkin' to'* her Grandmother had given her only days before. It went something like this...

"Fiona, if you're ever going to secure your future here, now is the time! It seems that Josef has already set his sights on some ridiculous American girl and it sounds pretty serious. This is going to ruin our plan should he continue to move forward. Think about it...then definitely make your move. If not? I never want to hear another word about any 'missed opportunity' ever again my darling. I'm done.

He actually confided in me the other day. I put on a show so he'd believe I'm going along with his plan to accept his new flame. I have to admit, I actually tried to rationalize it in the beginning seeing how happy he is, but after coming to my senses realized we can not accept defeat. Our family has never been quitters. I don't know how long I can hold him off from going *all the way in* with this foreigner, so you must make your move now! Litty said sounding completely fed up...

And to think...I even brought you here in your youth under the falsehood of being a 'family friend' allowing you your first introduction to the family...Then, all those years of paying for that expensive fancy finishing school in Switzerland to prove you could culturally fit *with his kind*?... Obviously, they didn't teach you much about how to execute a plan and go for the gold when it came to your rightfully given match. Then my dear...to have conveniently slid you in here as my replacement 'housekeeper' and give you the perfect positioning at your current and prime age?...Well!" Litty said with angst, throwing both hands up in disgust.

She continued reprimanding..."Had you been half as clever as I'd thought you to be, you would've already re-kindled and secured a relationship with Josef guaranteeing your future here. You've had plenty of time to make this happen and could've easily done so well before he opened the door to someone else. Especially an American for Christ's sake! I hope it's not too late, but if so? So be it. I'm finished...I've done all that I can do."

So in all fairness...Let's chat about Fiona for just a bit shall we? You see Fiona...as it were, had the attributes of an elegant feminine feline, long, lean and sleek. She moved about any space with the fluidity of a prima ballerina. She seemed to actually float through the place with moves so graceful, it made her presence seem elegant and effortless. She always made it a point to be discreetly hidden in plain sight, all but for that day when she wanted to make herself be seen. Quite honestly…she was more than exquisite to look at once she slowed down enough to get a good look.

She had the longest deep brown, almost Black, super shiny thick voluptuous hair that draped about… usually only visible when not hidden up in a head scarf. She stood 5'8" with stunning clear skin and eyes the color of deep Ming Jade. I mean seriously…this chic had it all. Just her eyes alone were enough one could unequivocally get lost in them once she gave you her unnerving and penetrating direct eye contact. With her breathtaking looks and her perfectly poised and refined physique, she somehow miraculously faded into the tapestry of it all with her soft demeanor. (…Lucky Bitch)

Josef, obviously still perturbed…didn't like having anyone roam freely around the *Château* other than his precious Litty of course. However since Laetitia was no longer able to take care of the place like she once did, she'd conveniently brought in the Natural Beauty as her replacement four to five days a week. It was uncanny, and to think…Josef never saw the 'family' connection.

Since Fiona had always been brought in under the pretext of being a *'family friend'* (including 'visiting' that one time during her youthful school break)…Josef never questioned. But inside, he knew there was something special and *very familiar about her like* he'd already known her. He refused to acknowledge that they'd ever met. (not to mention made out and God knows what else) He hid his feelings…preferring not to openly admit they'd had somewhat of a 'summer fling' in their early teens. Pretending was so much easier. (Did someone say Ostrich?)

Of course she'd changed since then, and as for that first kiss?…Who can ever forget that? Given she'd had a few years to develop, not to mention hone her talents with a bit of savior-faire, he was shocked to see she'd grown into such a full blown swan. I guess it was some kind of a game that ~~they~~ (he) was playing to be honest, not acknowledging her from the past. They both specifically remembered that night way back when…but didn't want to ruin the opaque memory enough to ever bring it back up again and in to the light…much safer to leave that buried.

Josef had lost track of the days, not realizing it was her day to be working. He was acting a bit jumpy and certainly had good reason to be. Evidently it must've been for the fact that he'd only just returned to the *Château* himself. He just so happened to walk in to the kitchen at the very moment his cell phone rang. You see? He'd actually played a bit of 'gentleman's hooky' the night before and felt immediately ambushed once he'd arrived. Instead of returning to the *Château* the night before like he'd led Sophie to believe, he'd actually headed back to his flat in the 7th for another little sexy *overnight stay*. It was coming up close to 1:00 in the afternoon and he definitely looked like what the cat just dragged in.

The perfect storm created the ultimate opportunity for Fiona to spy on him and find out a bit more of what he'd been up to. Amongst other things, hot housekeepers and not so hot nannies can sometimes be known…well let's just say…be *'curious'*, for lack of other words. You know… eavesdrop and always keep a look out for their next opportune moment to take advantage. Perhaps if lucky, become conveniently available to jump into the sack with the boss on occasion. It seemed the sweet little ballerina was up for just about any of the above, on any given occasion. She always kept her eye glued on the prize, just like Sophie had.

The place in the 7th had always been Grandfather's hidden love shack. Even having just experienced the most *incredibly erotic scenario* with Sophie…our Macho couldn't help himself but to follow suit. He was a Chip off the 'Ol Block when it came to having adopted some of the old man's distasteful habits along the way.

Sophie assumed when Josef had texted her a little heart emoji while she was packing up her apartment, he'd done so from the *Château*. She would've never imagined in her wildest dreams he was actually doing so from his flat in the 7th while 'entertaining' another woman. Her naïvety and ego somehow led her to believe the intimacy and amazing hot sex they'd just shared was SO BEYOND extraordinary… it would've been enough to capture him completely. (and satisfy his every need) Mistakenly she thought she'd captivated and reeled in a Big Fish who'd be devoted and faithful. Even though it was mandatory for her to be exclusive, he never once mentioned that he would be. Guess that's just how it was done in the Crillon league.

This would turn out to be merely one of Josef's many secrets. It was only the following morning after entertaining another woman for the night that he'd taken a morning charter back to Bergerac and conveniently picked up his Rover at the airport. He'd just entered the *Château* when the unexpected call came in from Sophie. Of course his first stop had been for a quick coffee at the local bar where he could hear the latest *'local news' before returning home.*

Before leaving Paris he'd given explicit instructions to the guardians to clean the flat. They were to sweep though the place guaranteeing no evidence was left, not even a whisper of his most recent visitor. He'd always paid them well to keep to themselves. His comings and goings had always been considered a private matter…exactly as they'd been with Grandfather. After all there was *'tradition'* to be considered…

Amongst the chaotic confrontation with Fiona and concluding his conversation with Sophie, Josef finally realized he'd missed seeing Litty since arriving. He thought he'd surprise her by taking a tray in to her bedroom, but just as he was getting a few items from the *'station wagon'* her door opened, catching him off guard.

"Bonjour mon petit Josef," she said embracing him with a kiss on both cheeks. "I'm happy to see you. I've got something important to discuss with you. Here my boy, let me finish preparing this" she said taking the tray from him.

"Go on into my living room and relax in front of the fire my dear. I'll meet you there shortly with tea and a piece of my apple tart."

Given her loving tone and direction, he did as he'd always done and made his way into her suite leaving her to finish what he'd barely started. She entered her living room happily carrying her favorite tray that she'd lovingly organized. She'd filled it with a pot of jasmine tea and a plate of Josef's favorite home made pastries. She placed the tray on the low table in front of the fireplace then walked back to the door, closing it quietly. She began poking the logs in the fireplace then calmly sat down on the feather filled chair next to Josef.

"So…how's your affair with Sophie going?" she surprisingly questioned in a blunt matter of fact way of deliberation. While waiting for his answer she poured two cups of tea, then elegantly picked hers up and took a sip with her pinky held high. Laetitia wasn't as naïve and innocent of a woman as she portrayed herself to be. She certainly hadn't come down with last nights rain that's for damn sure.

Her life at the Château began when she was hired as a young housekeeper. She moved up in rank to become Josef's Father's nanny soon after she'd arrived. From there she managed to work her way into becoming Grandfather's trusted consort. The girl just wouldn't stop. She knew a good thing when she saw one.

Her ever present commanding role had conveniently developed through the years. She'd climbed the ladder until at last, she'd stolen Josef Sr.'s heart and was considered to be the Matriarch of the Estate. Given she'd worked tirelessly to obtain that coveted position, she'd been the only consistent female energy that little Josef III had known growing up.

Not only was Laetitia a huge stabilizing factor for Grandfather personally, she also assisted in keeping his property running smoothly and his family intact with a solid reputation. Grandfather truly loved her and did so until the very end. Her presence and love throughout the years had also given the Golden Boy a solid and loving substitution for a Mother…and Grandmother, for that matter. Josef's love for Laetitia had always been a given, as if she were actually blood. He really never knew the difference. Their deep loving feelings were absolutely mutual and their uniquely special and candid relationship was apparent to all.

"Like clockwork" he quipped. "Although one thing is making it very difficult, she's gotten under my skin unlike any other. It certainly wasn't in my original plan when I was luring her away from Bruce. She had no idea of my initial motives…but since then, my feelings for her have changed and it doesn't hurt that she's the best damn sex I've ever had. It's like she's lured me into her trap instead of the other way around. I can't wait to have her live here with me at the *Château*…I mean with us," he said quickly correcting himself…in hopes of not making Litty feel alienated.

"I thought for a moment, I'd buy a little place in New York to carry us over until she sold her business, but when I was there I began to think differently. I don't want to have anything to do with the States where's she concerned. Should something happen, I don't want to give her the option of having a place to conveniently escape to Stateside. The last thing I need is her having a tether line that enables her to keep one foot closer to that asshole ex of hers.

Just the thought of knowing I could steal her away from him was so satisfying in the beginning. Having taken something so precious from him, I considered it to be 'game on' and pay back time. She eagerly walked right into my trap without a struggle…just like child's play in fact. She didn't have one clue, but the funny thing is that as I was working my magic on her…something highly unusual happened. I certainly wasn't expecting it, but actually it was her…(that little sphinx he said endearingly) who gave me a bolt of her magic instead. I definitely didn't see it coming and it's like something I've never felt in my life. I think I could actually be in love. She has me thinking about things I've never thought about. I even think I want her to have my children. How's that? Can you imagine hearing me say that? That's something I've never even considered. I want to keep her here like my cherished love prisoner…just like Grandfather did with you. It wasn't so bad, was it Litty?" he sweetly questioned leaning over to give a tender kiss on her forehead.

Laetitia sat in total amazement…outwardly smiling yet inwardly flabbergasted. It was amazing she didn't spill her tea (literally)…all the while sitting calmly and listening to Josef ramble on about his euphoric feelings for the *American*. It was right then that it was made quite clear Fiona had missed her chance. If she wanted to salvage a glimmer of hope, she'd have to act fast. This was much more serious than Litty had imagined. Josef was demonstrating a rare type of animation and behavior when describing the American, so much so, she couldn't believe what she was hearing. Now he sounded much more distinguished and respectful when speaking of and about her. It wasn't how he'd originally portrayed his new fling like he had in his earlier admission. He was being a bit more thoughtful and sensitive this time and that scared her a bit.

Laetitia was a seasoned old woman by then and had really only been holding on to life for Josef's sake. She'd actually been waiting for him to find true love, (or at least his version of it) even though she'd always secretly hoped and prayed it would've been with her Granddaughter. She'd done everything in her power to get that girl in first position, however knowing Josef had now made his choice in building his life to include having his own family was the sign she'd been waiting for. Now she'd finally be able to let go of her earthly responsibilities and join Grandfather in the here after.

Laetitia had consistently given Josef the tender love and affection that only a Grandmother could provide. She'd always looked over the Golden Boy as if he were her own. She ferociously protected him knowing their bond could never be broken. She refused to allow one drop of outside influence in that tried to damage their special relationship.

Before his final departure, Grandfather had always told Litty how comforted he was knowing she'd keep a keen eye on his beloved Grandson after he was gone. He also told her he'd be waiting for her to join him in eternity once she felt the time was right. Laetitia wasn't about to keep him waiting forever…She felt her day had finally come. She had concluded all of this while pretending to listen to Josef babble on about his love interest and future. The entire time however, she'd only been thinking of Sr.

As usual, not possibly considering anyone else, the spoiled little shit conveniently turned the entire situation and conversation back onto himself and his favorite pet peeve.

"I only have one REAL problem…and that's having Bruce and his low life family hanging around. How can Sophie and I ever go into the Village without that asshole spreading endless rumors and hateful lies about us? The past is definitely something I want to keep buried from her. I can't do that if they're still around. I want that entire family gone once and for all," Josef stated. He stood up and began pacing in front of the fire.

Thank God he finally stopped just long enough to pick up his cup and take a fast sip before exhaling slowly. That gave Litty a brief moment to interject…

"That's exactly what I wanted to speak to you about. I made a pact with your Grandfather just before he passed. We agreed that I'd protect you as best as I possibly could as long as I lived. He made it easy for me and gave me all the resources to do so my dear boy. You know I loved that man deeply. He gave me such a beautiful life here and we had so many years of happiness together…Even though I knew I wasn't his only one. In all of those years he never once made me feel like I was second best or had any competition for that matter.

That's the advice I need to give you. Women that are power players are actually very sensitive deep down. They secretively often want a man to tell them what to do, even though they would never admit they did. Don't be obvious in leading her all the time, just give a directive once in a while mixed with a bit of honest jealously. That would serve you well my dear, should you follow that old rule. It may not be the worst you could do" Litty said, obviously speaking from her personal rule book of manipulative wisdom.

"It might seem true now…thinking you could have a strong enough bond to overcome it all, but never let Sophie know of your other lovers under any circumstances. That would hurt her to her core and she would no doubt strike back at you. 'Ignorance is Bliss' when it comes to that American and whatever you do…Do Not underestimate her for a second. Remember they don't have the same under-standing as we do here in Europe. She would ultimately attempt to ruin you in the end. A powerful woman who is scorned is capable of the unspeakable, and that's not just a wise tale. Do you hear me? Do you actually understand what I'm saying?"

"Yes Laetitia, I understand," he replied in a rather dismissive manner. "Now…did you want to tell me something specific?" he clapped back using a childish snippiness. He was impatient when he felt he was being lectured. He despised being 'schooled' or reprimanded…

"My response to you regarding this will be said one time only, and that's going to be right here and now. Sit back down Josef…I want you to listen well. I think I've taken care of the Douglas family for you. There will be no reason for Bruce to come back to the Village after his parents are gone."

"Lit tee?…What are you thinking?" he questioned in a deceitful and melodious way. "I know that familiar tone of mischief in your voice. What kind of devious scheme are you up to? You know how small the Village is, it's not as easy to cover things up like it was in the old days. Paying those people didn't work the first time and I know it won't work now. Don't you worry or trouble yourself with this my dearest, this isn't your problem…it's mine. This is something I need to take care of" Josef said, feeling in command.

Laetitia sighed apparently dismissing his sermon. "Josef, I won't go into any further detail about this, but I think it's a good idea that you stay in Manhattan with Sophie for a while. You both need to be out of the area for the time being, or at least until the smoke clears and things settle back down. That's all I'm going to say. You need to trust me on this one my boy" she said standing up...She poked the remaining logs again slowly then calmly returned to her place next to Josef in silence.

They continued to sit quietly and listen to the fire crackle and hiss. They often loved spending silent times together while analyzing one another's thoughts. Those two kindred souls could have conversations without saying a word. They really did know one another.

Eventually Josef stood, picking up a small log and gently placed it in the existing low burning fire. He smiled back at Litty ever so sweetly before retiring to his private suite for the balance of the afternoon and evening. The poor boy was trashed. He was so exhausted after his long night and still a bit hungover from his most recent escapade.

Josef's huge bedroom suite occupied the entire upper west side of the *Château*. It encompassed the space above both the great room and dining room below. It had once been Grandfather's private palace, but of course...like everything else, that personal space and all of its rare items had also been passed down within Josef's inheritance.

The entrance to his suite was through a set of tall ebony doors that stood like imposing sentinels. They were a bit intimidating and were absolutely made to feel that way. It's as if they were standing guard only opening to those who'd been invited. It was a grand and impressive entrance leading into his private upper chamber. The round landing at the top of the sweeping staircase that housed the doors was quite the observation deck unto itself. It was somewhere in between a padded luxe vault of silence and a magical world of sensual surprise. It was...beyond.

After entering the actual *sacred kingdom*, one was obliged to be automatically awestruck by the incredibly ornate details of the massive baroque fireplace. You couldn't miss the thing, it was dead center ahead after passing through the stately doors. It provided the first major eye catching focal point into the inner sanctum. It had very little competition other than the two alluring low slung sofas resting perpendicularly in front. They were covered in a shimmering light grey iridescence that lured you in to their sleek sexy tufts. A large rectangular glass top coffee table separated the sleek rayon velvet loungers. The seating combo sat so low to the floor it didn't deflect nor interrupt the full view of the magnificent fireplace.

The entire venue screamed 'luxurious sex'. And believe you me...it really was so seductive you could actually hear it whisper and summon you. But as fabulous as you can imagine this voluptuous vignette to be...well... what stood in the far back of the suite is where the real beacon of decadence lived. The *pièce de resistance* as one could say. It was and remained the ultimate self imposed symbol of the family's manhood. Obviously, we're talking about the bed here...The thing was made from high quality elm and had four massive towering columns on each corner that created its boundaries. They reached to the ceiling and marked the parameter of the heavily carved 'sandbox'. The king sized double thick mattresses for the 'pièce d'Arte' had always been imported from the States. The entire beast was unique...bold if you will, and had been the featured prize of all time for the superior macho men of the Manor. It was their highest pedestal, their showpiece, their altar of success. It reeked of so much fucking masculine ego, you would've thought you could actually smell it. Can you imagine? Why yes...I think I can. The entire Suite was seductive...(but more like a scratch and sniff if you ask me)

As Josef slid onto the masterpiece, he pulled the thick draperies together on all four sides to create total darkness. He began smirking with amusement just thinking Sophie might need a small ladder to help herself up onto his playpen. He was so delighted with the thought of it, he actually found himself laughing out loud. He couldn't wait to see if his image would be a needed reality. Laying alone in his glamorous four poster...he was beginning to miss her.

As he laid his head down on one of the many fluffy feather pillows, he began to organize his thoughts in anticipation for his following morning's rendezvous. Last night had been a pretty rough one, having rocked it so hard in the 7th, it made it easy to fall into a deep sleep with his visuals dancing about.

The morning arrived early and with a bit of anxiety he sprang off the family trophy and onto his feet to begin his day.

"Hello Hervé, I really appreciate you meeting me here this morning on such short notice," Josef said to the small middle-aged man as he entered the car barn.

"No problem Josef, I've always been available to you and your family, you know that. What is it that I can help you with?" he questioned extending his hand for a shake. It was definitely the distant 'Vous' thing playing out.

"Well…to be honest Hervé, it's that never ending problem with the Douglas family that's plaguing me again. I've tried to ignore that bastard Gene for what he did, but now…it's more about his asshole son, Bruce. This time he's the one that's actually causing the problem. It's finally the moment of reckoning and time to be rid of that entire lot for good. I mean…they need to be gone permanently. I actually have a real need now. If they remain living here it means Bruce will inevitably come and visit and be present in the Village on occasion. I can't allow that. I have my reasons. I know in the past you've sometimes tended to the Douglas' electrical needs, correct? Are you still working for them?"

"It's not often that they call, but yes, I still do some work for them from time to time."

"Good…so the next time you have the opportunity, I need you to do something very important for me. I'd appreciate you giving them more than a threat and a scare with some of your 'fancy' electrical. Perhaps…enough to be rid of them for good, no matter how it's done. Do you understand what I'm implying? Am I making myself crystal clear?"

"Oui…loud and clear Josef. I'm terribly sorry it's come to this, but if it's that important to you…when they call again I can do a bit of 'special electric'. My kind of handy work could easily persuade them to move on or perhaps be eliminated. Being as they are such a big problem for you, I can assure you I'll try my very best to make this happen."

"How much do you think this 'handy work' will cost me? I'd like to give you some consideration upfront."

"No need, My family realizes we still owe you. No one has forgotten how your Grandfather saved my older brother's vineyard from bankruptcy when he was just starting out. Even though that was many years ago, we remain grateful and acknowledge our remaining indebtedness. When this deed is carried out, could we then consider our debt to be settled and 'paid in full'? Would that be a safe thing to say and yield a correct assessment?"

"Yes…Thank you Hervé. It most certainly would. This act of loyal service, when successful, will be more than sufficient to erase any debt thought to be owed. I was hopeful you and your family hadn't forgotten."

"Josef no one in the Village ever forgets, you know that. You are one of us, a local, and a man we all need and respect. Your family has a long history here. I can imagine everyone in this valley can say they owe you something. If it weren't for your family, half of this village wouldn't have made it. Don't worry about seeing me around here again anytime soon, it's going to be best for me to stay clear. And for the record…I'll forget all about our meeting and conversation today. Should something happen to make the Douglas' move up or out…so be it. But just to reiterate… once this 'arrangement' has been fulfilled, my family's obligation and debt to you will be considered one hundred percent satisfied, correct?" Hervé said, wanting to hear some repeat reassurance from Josef.

The fact is, Hervé would've done anything to settle his family's debt and get out from underneath the Decour's thumb, including the unthinkable, which he'd just agreed to. The terms of the payoff had now been decided.

They nodded to one another in agreement then shook hands on it before parting ways. Litty meanwhile, had been watching this exchange between the two men through the draperies in her bedroom. Seeing Josef discussing something in secret with Hervé aroused her curiosity. She hadn't seen Hervé on the property in years, but kept her thoughts to herself. She remained silent about viewing Josef's meeting and went about finalizing her own plan.

*

Chapter Six

Josef opened the door to their suite at the Gramercy Park only to find it empty. He dug in his satchel for his cell then hit speed dial…"Sophie, I'm here waiting for you. Where are you chérie?"

"Hello my love!! Can you hear me?" she replied almost screaming. "I'm in Barney's shoe department and it's off the hook crazy here. It's so sad they're closing this location, but at the same time I've never seen such a fabulous sale in my life! It's insanely busy and I've been having a blast! I'm in line to pay for two pairs of the most incredibly gorgeous suede boots you've ever seen!" she shrieked with sheer shopaholic satisfaction. "When did you get in?" She continued without a breath… "I should be out of here and back at the Hôtel in about an hour…that is unless you would prefer meeting me at one of my favorite places on earth named Eataly? That place is so much fun, we could have drinks and a bite…Happy Hour in Manhattan is such a treat no matter where you go, but I just love that place…"

Sophie was so excited to be back in the Big Apple and to be seeing her man, her enthusiasm was contagious. She was so hoping he'd agree to meet her and as funny as it seems…He thought he could actually hear her crossing her fingers through the phone.

"Well, in that case…how could I deny you one of your most favorite things to do in this beautiful city. I think it's a great idea…I'll see you there shortly" he said already making his way down the hall to the elevator.

Sophie sounded so excited, no way did he want to disappoint her. He was happy just to go along with her idea…guilt has long fingers into ones psyche sometimes, even for the likes of Josef. He'd had so much on his mind a nice late afternoon walk would be a soothing way to get his inner calm back and not think so much about his conversation with Hervé.

The days had begun getting shorter. The colder humid early evening air met him abruptly as he made the corner from Lexington Ave. When Josef entered the concept store, he was so surprised to see it was simply a chic Italian themed gigantic warehouse of sorts that had been cleverly divided into small little vignettes of specialized eateries and miniature gourmet boutiques. Everything was gourmet Italian and the place was humming in overdrive. He'd forgotten the beloved American Holiday…Thanksgiving was happening in just a week's time, so needless to say there were millions of tourists all over town enjoying the festive atmosphere. This particular place had wine and cheese displays and small specialty kiosks scattered throughout with every type of seafood, pasta and pizza imaginable. It was a successful smorgasbord of culinary shopping and dining…a place unlike anything he'd ever seen or imagined possible. It gave the American term 'grazing' an entirely new meaning. It was bar hopping and nibbling along the way at its finest.

He was busy reading the history of the company on an engraved metal wall plaque displayed at the entrance, when suddenly…he felt his ass being grabbed from behind. She was early.

"AhHa!…There you are my dear" he said as he quickly spun around and picked Sophie up. It made her large shopping bags flounder wildly about on his upper back. They kissed as usual…making it seem like it was their first.

"This place is fantastic" Josef said finally lowering her to her feet like she were Lois Lane being given a soft Superman landing. "I can see why you love this place and yes there's a ton of things I want to try, but first tell me chèrie…how are you?" Josef questioned, finding himself mesmerized by her beauty. Her nose and cheeks were flushed with a soft rosy pink from her running the couple of blocks to the eatery.

She'd regularly come to Eataly when in town and was so excited to show her French seasoned traveler a new place. One he actually knew nothing about.

"I thought you'd like it, isn't it wonderful?!! It's always on my list of things to do when I'm in town. Let's grab a seat and a glass of that fabulous Italian Vino," she said giving a small laugh and a spring to her step while leading them to a table. "Italian vs French...hmm" she joked with a teasing prance. She was feeling empowered and flirty being in one of *her* familiar stomping grounds...

She headed to the closest venue that sold wine and cheese and sat on one of those high industrial style swivel chairs. She immediately plopped her shopping bags down on the empty chair beside her..."So do tell...give me all the details my love. You look so handsome...what have you been up to at the *Château* to make you look so good? Did you accomplish everything you set out to do?"...she said leaning over with a sweet kiss. The girl sounded so googley goop in love. Seriously, little did she know...

"Oui...I think so. At least I got the ball rolling in the right direction. We'll have to wait and see what becomes of it. How'd it go with Bruce by the way." The smooth crooner questioned while trying his best to stay focused. He couldn't help but show his curiosity when it came to his redundant and relentless obsession with Bruce. Underneath, I guess it really had always been his *real* focus.

The plan he'd discussed with Hervé began resting heavily on his mind. He could barely think of anything else as he stared blanks through Sophie sitting there all smiles. He wanted 'the problem' taken care of now more than ever. He'd definitely take Litty's advice and hide out in NYC for a while. He needed to take cover and not be seen anywhere near Issigeac, at least until the dust had settled. Staying on the East Coast would definitely give he and Sophie a solid alibi if and whenever it be needed.

Like he'd told Litty, he no longer felt any need to have any attachment in the US where Sophie was concerned. That'd only been a carrot he'd tossed her way during his sales speech. His motive having her agree to working from an East Coast base (the way he put it)...was it would make it easier for them to see one another during the transition of selling her company. He failed to mention his main objective was to create physical distance between she and Bruce. Now that the plan for the Douglas' demise had been put into play, it easily justified his decision not to purchase anything in Manhattan. The Douglas' would be gone soon so It actually made more sense...See how nicely this was working out? Once Hervé was able to complete his task, Josef and Sophie would be able to immediately return and live freely in the village. Josef would just have to continue to lead her on regarding his 'thoughtful' gesture... just long enough to buy some time. He definitely didn't want her to know he had zero intention of following through with his original plan of buying something there. He'd need to keep that in his box of secrets, but it was getting a bit crowded in there.

What a douche bag this self-serving bastard was... keeping his devious agenda 100% hidden. As for Sophie, she was just the opposite from the smooth and discreet Frenchman...she couldn't wait to spill the beans. She was ready to tell him every detail of what she'd been doing...but Thank God, she knew enough to keep a few important hidden transgressions to herself. 'Those Stupid Americans' as some say...we just can't help ourselves. We prefer to lay it all out on the table immediately if not sooner...Braggers... or perhaps it's just too much open honesty. Who knows...

The eatery had surprisingly filled up, quickly making it difficult to hear one another above the Loud Buzz. Sophie continued to speak with enthusiastic sign language and lip movements between her nervous gulps of wine. Obviously feeling the stress of hiding what had *really* happened back in San Francisco, she was a bit evasive and didn't expand on any details or specifics of 'The Break Up'. So...she continued with some blasé rhetoric, settling down enough to actually speak and be heard...

"The split with Bruce was easier than I thought. He admitted knowing our relationship had been over for a while so none of it came as a surprise. In the end I think he was a bit nostalgic and sad...but he'll get over it" she said nonchalantly, like a girl that'd already turned the page.

She certainly wasn't about to mention anything that Bruce had spewed about Josef and his family during their unpleasant encounter. Should she have revealed any truthful details that'd been said during their loud and distasteful meeting, it certainly would've ruined their evening. But...she did however, contribute the accurate status regarding her 'business'. After all, the lovebirds were still playing each other and treading lightly. They were only ponying up and admitting what were *their* convenient truths. So...she continued like this...

"The real bummer in all of this was Lesting Wear, sadly passed on the purchase. In the end I guess it was probably too good to be true, but I'd gotten myself so puffed up and incredibly hopeful...it absolutely crushed me when they told me their decision. I'm feeling calmer about everything now, but I really hope to have someone else interested soon."

Josef could barely hear her above the elevated hum of the loud chatter happening in the dining emporium.

"Sophie...We should go ahead and relax, take our time and enjoy Manhattan while we're here. We shouldn't be in such a rush. It could take a while before the right buyer comes along. These important transactions take time" he said almost shouting. He was working his salesmanship on her trying to sound like the selling of her business really shouldn't cause any stress, it would happen in due time. He'd be patient, no pressure, no problem...R. I. G. H. T.

She could feel it...something had definitely happened to make his demeanor seem so different. It's like he was pre-occupied and not totally *in it* like he'd been. Now...he seemed content to 'relax'...hang out...no matter how long her sale took. There had to be something he wasn't telling her. Definitely, there was something else going on.

In keeping with her typical dreamlike status...(and GOD only knows why) when being around this slithering creature…she somehow began rationalizing what her lover was saying.

'He was so considerate, what a sweetheart he was for not pressuring her for a quick sale. Certainly taking the time to find the right buyer was in her best interest, they just needed to be patient'…

Sadly, she had no idea his only intention was merely to 'hang out' until the unconscionable deed was done. He couldn't have cared less about the successful sale of her clothing company. He did remain consistent with one thing in particular and that…like in all other circumstances…was only thinking of himself. After trying to read his thoughts unsuccessfully, she remained puzzled and curious. Then for some inexplicable reason, she couldn't wipe off the fucking smile that was glued to her face. Pool girl.

"I guess it all makes more sense…sticking with our original plan. It's true, it will be much easier for me work from the East Coast. I don't know how I got so far off track trying to rush things. Certainly by having this opportunity of staying here, it will be a more of a convenient way for us to see one another while I'm trying to sell" she said feeling like she was just mumbling to herself while having him present. He was so absent…

"How's the search going by the way," she said in a rather melancholy tone exposing her disappointment. "Are you still looking for places close to my showroom?"

He sensed her happy mood had diminished, so the playboy wizard quickly pivoted back to his rehearsed bullshit of discussing his 'active' search for a place. That always seemed to be a successful tactic in reeling her back in where he wanted.

"Any preference between a brownstone or a loft?" he asked putting on an act like he was sincerely interested in her opinion. He convincingly breezed through a list of questioning motions nevertheless, presuming she wouldn't have a clue he'd actually changed his mind.

The place at the communal table had gotten so crowded it made it nearly impossible to continue a normal conversation. It was time to change the scene.

Josef stood up and came around to her side of the table and picked up her shopping bags…he leaned down and spoke loudly in her ear, "All I do know, is this place is so loud I'm not having fun trying to understand you above all this craziness. Let's get out of here and go back to the Hôtel for some sanity. The Rose Bar will be a nice quiet spot for us to continue our conversation."

With Josef suggesting a move to a more intimate alternative they quickly agreed and made their exit. When they entered the Hôtel he passed their coats and shopping bags to the concierge to be delivered to their suite. The revered *Rose Bar* was located inside and to the back of the Hôtel's lobby. It was a subtle underground NYC hotspot if you will, where only the real movers and shakers made the scene. It was so chic it often had famous musicians stopping by to give impromptu mini jam concerts. That night was no exception. They had a surprise guest…an incredible, super talented famous guitarist was to do a bit of acoustic later. Usually reservations were needed after 9pm, but then again not everyone was a VIP and sold their wine to the Hôtel like Josef did.

"Ahh, this is so much better. We can actually hear one another speak. Let's have a cocktail and a few *hors d'oeuvres* here and if we need a change we can always move on to the 'other' restaurant in the Hôtel….You know I love anything Italian," he said…with a bit of sarcastic undertones and squinted eyes…She knew he preferred her be in love with everything French instead of anything Italian. His words and actions immediately made her giggle.

"Okay my French Man, this talk makes me hungry. Let's finish this drink and go grab a table in the restaurant. I don't care to wait and see who the surprise artist is…I'm starving. Some linguini sounds perfect right about now."

They were quickly seated at a romantic table for two where they dined and laughed the night away. They lingered in their private delight and were the very last table to leave.

"That pasta was delicious" Sophie said arriving at the door to their Suite. "I never realized this was such a hip

Hôtel" she said, sounding like a smitten young groupie…"I can't believe that famous musician Dave Navarro was in the restaurant! I absolutely love that guy! Wonder what he was doing in the Hôtel dining all alone? It was so exciting just seeing him…in person I mean. I've always been such a huge fan. This evening has been so exceptional Josef. All the other times when I've come to the city, my norm had always been to stay at the most ordinary Hôtels after taking my sales people out for our traditional 'market dinner'. It was always so repetitive and predictable having the same boring food at the same boring restaurant, too much to drink…then off to bed, so I could begin the same monotonous routine all over again the following day. It'd become an old record playing the same 'Ol song every trip.

Being with you here has been fantastic, it's changed everything. It makes me feel like I'm getting to know a different side of Manhattan…I've never been able to take the time to be a tourist. Speaking of…care to walk over to the Whitney Museum tomorrow?"

"Shhh…stop being so ambitious chérie, I'm tired" he said smiling to himself in the dark as he pulled the sheets up over them. He couldn't believe…or get over the fact that she could blatantly miss the obvious sometimes. That genuine characteristic of hers continually amused and delighted him. They kissed and were quickly asleep in one another's arms from exhaustion. That is…until the middle of the night when the French Flag was being raised. Sophie knew exactly what to do for the raising ceremony. She hopped on and rode for hours. They romped and moaned so loud it's a miracle hotel management didn't come to see what all the disturbing racket was about. Both had their delicious climax simultaneously and just as they were finally in a euphoric dreamlike state of snooze, the phone rang. A loud and seriously heavy New York accent almost shouting in an upper octave came snaking its way through the receiver. The annoying person on the other end sounded off like a loud obnoxious bullhorn. She spoke so fast it irritated the hell out of Josef, especially at that ridiculous early hour.

"Mr Decour?…I know it's exceptionally early, but you

didn't get back to me like you said you would. Are you available later this morning to look at the listing I sent you? Only a very few…Very select agents know about this place because it hasn't been officially advertised on the open market yet. So…if you have any interest, we should take a look at this *'pocket listing'* as soon as possible" chirped the aggressive and beyond pushy Realtor who was consistently streaming in high pitched nasal.

Josef was about to hang up, but Sophie was within earshot and couldn't help but begin nudging him between the sheets after hearing it was something about seeing a property…

"Yes, yes yes…let's go! This is exciting. Let's go see it"…she said jumping to her feet, clasping her hands together held high as if she were praying.

What could he do? Give in?…Or take the chance of exposing his secret decision of not wanting to make a purchase. He quickly calculated the situation…then surmised the first option to be the only smart decision. (given it was definitely the easier path) Under all circumstances he must continue the charade…

"Okay" he said begrudgingly to the Realtor. "What time shall we meet?" he replied half heartedly.

"I'll meet you in your lobby at 11am sharp and we can go from there," said the loud mouth on the other end. She just couldn't help herself…

"The property that you'll be seeing faces the park and is only a stones throw away from the Hôtel I might add. How's that for a location? You're going to love it" said the Manhattan diva originally from Queens. She didn't wait to hear another word before hanging up. So much for formality.

"Alright my dear we're on for our first viewing, but try not to show any emotion what-so-ever…okay? Est-ce que tu comprends? I don't want to let this pushy agent know our thoughts, especially if we like the place" Josef said throwing back the top sheet and sitting up straight.

As we know, Sophie had a tendency of not listening any further once she'd gotten half an ear full of what she'd 'thought' she wanted to hear. Unfortunately, as sad as it was she'd already lowered every bit of her natural feminine defense mechanisms…so not for one moment did she even consider Josef perhaps wasn't being honest with her. Why would she? She was already *all in*…as enthusiastic as a first year cheerleader when fully committed. Whatever Josef said was her new reality. Blind trust my dears, Blind trust. She'd become so gullible and just like he'd said to Litty…she was putty in his hands. He just fucking ate it up.

Sophie made sure they made record speed getting down to the lobby on time where they were greeted by a short stocky woman.

"Hello Mr. Decour. It's so nice to finally meet you," she said like they'd already been in a long running business relationship. (I think they'd only spoken once prior to that morning) "My name is Alexandra Coz. Here's my card…and you must be?"…

Josef chimed in…"This is Sophie."

The agent was trying her best not to visibly show her disappointment with Josef not having come solo to the appointment. "It'd be so much easier for a sale to happen when there wasn't a pesky little girlfriend involved to complicate things" she thought, grimacing internally. MS Coz, being the true professional that she was, stayed focused like a pit bull in heat mindfully giving them both direct eye contact with an enormous fake smile.

"It's so nice meeting you both. Might we have time for a coffee? I'd love to discuss the comps in the area for this specific property prior to viewing it. I'm sure we won't be the only ones at the showing this morning. I'd rather you have some information about the unit before arriving there if that's okay," she said with a half teetering question mark.

She'd finally came up for air and took her first breath…It was all in her personal sales approach. Kind of like a panting chihuahua dancing in circles so wanting to be cute and noticed. She was determined to do her own digging before wasting any of her time, yet Josef had already passed stage one in demonstrating he had the potential to be a 'real buyer'. Just the fact of having checked in for a stay at one of the chicest and most expensive Hôtels in town was the first box already scratched off her 'client approval' list. It was a great sign of his taste level and buying power. Most definitely there'd be further qualifications needed mind you, because after all... not just *anyone* could buy on the park.

"Well, how much do you know about Gramercy Park?" she asked without waiting for an answer..."It's one of the most sought after enclaves in Manhattan. The park... I'm sure you know is '*Private*'. It's absolutely spectacular," she said in her own rehearsed cinematic style presentation. The wannabe actress ie: Realtor...continued...

"The property we'll be seeing is directly across from the park and with that perfect location, you'll be given direct access...which includes your very own key to the park. It's an exclusive and rightful perk for any owner to a property that surrounds this glorious greenery" she contributed, almost with a gleeful snobby laughter.

The insatiable steamroller was beside herself with delight. She was already calculating her commission while attempting to seem present. She continued giving them back and forth direct eye contact like she was watching the finals at Wimbledon. All the while her inner calculator was fucking running wild. Ding, Ding Ding Ding...

Josef swallowed his steaming hot espresso and stood up. Sophie tried to do the same which left the agent still seated. That caused her to become flustered and consequently fumble around under the table for her briefcase. Silly woman...she'd entered the meeting assuming to take charge of the appointment and had completely mis-calculated her 'potential' client. She had no idea Josef was an excellent architect in negotiations and knew exactly how to maneuver this or just about any meeting. Little did she know he wasn't about to let her *sell* him on anything. He'd heard enough of her sales pitch...and began to lead the conversation.

"Let's visit the property before we discuss any

further details. The minute I see the place I'll know whether I like it or not. There's no need to waste any of our time."

His strong response spoke volumes. He was keeping it totally professional without giving her any personal information or traits that she could expand upon. She quickly reassessed her new client (s) and frantically tried to catch up. They were approaching the bellhop who'd already opened the door for their exit. Once out on the street, Ms Coz quickstepped and made every effort to gain the lead position by herding them towards the nearby apartment they were to view.

"Here we are. Isn't it beautiful? It's the one bedroom on the front left side of the of this fabulous brownstone. Obviously, it comes with this absolutely stunning location having the park just across the street. The original 'maid's quarters' which is the studio apartment located just below street level had never been considered an independent residence until the building went co-op. It's now been Grandfathered-in and is being sold as a combination sale along with the one bedroom apartment above. Strangely enough, there's never been a connecting entrance between the two properties from the inside, but I'm sure that's something you could easily have done Mr. Decour. You look like a man that can achieve just about anything..." Good God the woman didn't even exhale...

"The studio below is a large single room with a nice little bathroom. It's only entrance is from these exterior stairs which services that particular unit exclusively. The little landing at the bottom of the staircase is certainly large enough to support a nice plant or two. I think this combination could be the perfect offering for anyone wanting to get in to the market with '*this*'...address."

Josef was intrigued, but Ms Coz talked so much he'd only listened and absorbed half of her verbal diarrhea. High Pitched Dolphin gibberish he thought it was. She'd become so irritating he'd conveniently blocked her out with his selective hearing. Sophie, on the other hand...beamed with excitement. Her feet were almost off the pavement and ready for take off when Josef visually shut her down with his subtle dismay.

He leaned over and pinched her butt when Alexandra wasn't looking and whispered "Relax my dear… remember what I said? Cool is the Rule."

Josef and Ms Coz walked up the main center staircase while further discussing the building's details. Sophie had consequently been dismissed from the conversation hence his opinion had become the only opinion that mattered. It was Ms Coz's turn to eat it up.

The building's facade was from another world. It actually looked a bit like a meringue shell inspired by the art nouveau era. The place was built during an époque when the general population of builders were true artisans and actually took the time to care about elaborate *finishing* details. Two foot deep by eight foot wide bull nosed orange tinted cement steps for example led up to the three story masterpiece.

The brownstone had been constructed in the early 1900's yet still felt grand even within current high end NYC standards. So many of the old beauties had been torn down and eliminated making way for more and more modern high rises. That practice had always been the cycle of development in The Big Apple. Forget dollar per square foot, now it came down to every square inch having a huge price tag. Building up is the only way to go for the modern developer. Tear down, replace, and repeat the process. Don't forget…if you buy on the top floor…you must buy the air rights above and hope they've not already been sold. No kidding, you've even got to pay for thin air sometimes in NYC. The sky is not the limit, literally…it's a fact.

Gramercy Park was and is one of the few glamorous original neighborhood hold outs to have escaped the wrecking ball. It's always been revered as one of the most savored and best kept secrets for long-term Manhattanites. ('The locals'…*The Real New Yorkers,* as *they* prefer to think of themselves) This particular area, especially surrounding the park had continually been in demand. It'd gone through many phases like **so** many other areas, but somehow had always remained *in Vogue* with the elite. When this particular brownstone had gone co-op, the Home Owners Association felt they were more of a 'distinctive group'… Much more so than just the 'average' upscale New Yorker. After all, they were pridefully sitting on a gold mine and kept the beauty in impeccable condition. The more original details that remained, the higher the price and they made it their business to keep it that way.

With Sophie following close behind, the three quickly landed in the lobby. (if you could call it that) It was nothing more than a tiny vestibule…a minuscule reception area with elegant vintage mailboxes attached to one wall. The door to the apartment they were to see had been left open and there must've been at least eight people frantically scurrying around inside like it was a fire sale. Even though this was a secret *pocket listing* and known only by a few select agents…the word was definitely out. Some 'secret' that was, the place was already crawling with potential buyers.

Once inside, Ms Coz finally slowed down to Josef's methodical rhythm, thinking only of her own goals that is.

"You see what I mean? I'll let you both take your time and wander around the place. I'll be here if you have any questions" she said installing herself next to the small dining room table with a handful of business cards. Always in search of new clients, she'd chosen the perfect vantage point for her expedition to begin. Seriously, there wasn't one subtle redeeming attribute attached to this opportunist. There was only one way out of that tiny place…and it was having to pass by Ms Coz of course.

It didn't take long, their tour of nosing around took all of two minutes to see every square inch of the place. The true asset was the studio apartment below as part of the transaction.

"I've seen all that I need to see. Care if we pop down to the Studio for a quick peek?" Josef said cupping his hands together and whispering loudly towards Ms Coz who was still standing by the dining table. She was beaming like she'd just hit the lotto.

"No problem, I'll meet you down in front in a few. Isn't this place fabulous for a Mill-three?" she mouthed in return.

Josef just pleasantly nodded in agreement knowing at that very second it would be difficult to continue with this ridiculous act any longer. He knew he wasn't interested, even if the place did have a coveted address. Though it could've well been a great investment, in no way shape or form could he ever be interested in having nosey bourgeois neighbors who were indeed…'gate-keepers'. He already knew what that scenario was all about. Only this time, it'd be a small group of 'concerned citizens' that simply had keys to a local dog park. Every one of them undoubtedly would take great pride and interest in delving into the personal business of any and all others possessing a key. Having neighbors gossip about your comings and goings had always repelled Josef…It reminded him of Gene.

As he and Sophie entered the Studio below, Josef quickly closed the door behind them, almost slamming it. He grabbed her…'nailing' her back to the door and began kissing her passionately. He lifted her up and she threw her legs around his waist on cue. He gave her a bit of a dry hump before placing her gently back down to the floor.

"I know this can be overwhelming and somewhat exciting looking for our little dream haven, but I hate this place," delivering his line right on script with perfect timing…"Don't worry sweetheart, our true place is already out there" he stated, knowing it was. (as in his own *Château* for example…) But suddenly seeing the utter frustration in Sophie's eyes, he back peddled. "We need to be on our own sweetheart. I don't want anyone thinking they can easily get to know us. We don't need any busy bodies prying into our business and getting too close. We need to stay independent and keep our privacy sacred. We'll just continue with our search, okay with you?" he said giving her a quick pacifying kiss.

It was already done. We all know he'd previously

made up his mind long before this 'showing'. He opened the door to the apartment and grabbed her hand so they could conveniently exit the place looking unified.

"Okay Josef...but I love this place," she finally said with a protruding bottom lip. It'd become impossible for her to conceal her disappointment. She was so surprised seeing his quick and stedfast final decision, in no way did she think it was fair.

Once they'd climbed the steep metal stairs back up to street level Josef announced, "Listen my love, we have a great little suite at the Hôtel if you haven't forgotten. We have attentive room service with discrete housekeeping. We have a spa with a great masseuse. We have a fabulous bar and restaurant for our taking...and...for Christ's sake we have a key to this little park any time we want it! We should take our time and enjoy this fabulous city. Explore it, spoil ourselves, and take a bite out of the Big Apple right down to its core. We should wine and dine just like we were destined to do. That's all we should be thinking about while we're here. What do you think about that my love?"

Josef said all of this in the most seductively playful and melodious manner...it was impossible for her not to follow along even as he changed the subject. He was definitely bringing his 'A game' in seduction to the discussion. He was displaying his most enticing boy-like maneuvers trying to make light of the situation and get a smile out of Sophie at the very least. He was such a good looking guy and could be so persuasive when he wanted to be. She was so easily swayed by his flirty charm she could never say no...or resist him for that matter.

"Perhaps we can see a warehouse, something a little less traditional in the Flatiron district. Would that suit you Madame Sophie?"...the *bad boy* said attempting to take a step further back. He knew he had to throw her a bone...

This nonsense about looking for a loft or warehouse was just for show. His only real plan was to return to France with Sophie as soon as possible. He wanted her to be with him at the *Château* on a full time basis and he hadn't lost sight of that. But for the time being, until Hervé could complete his 'work'…he'd have to come up with one excuse after another not to leave the States for a while. Once he had the green light knowing the Douglas' had been eliminated from the village, only then would he feel secure enough to return home with Sophie. Until then, he'd just have to pretend to be looking for real estate.

"How about if we have lunch around the Whitney and visit the Museum after. Sound good? I thought your idea about going there was a great suggestion. Let's do it…" he whispered playfully hoping that would change her mood.

"Okay Josef…that sounds fun" she said half-heartedly, clutching his arm tightly.

Josef then immediately dismissed Alexandra Coz like she were an uninvited drunk cousin who'd long overstayed her welcome. Gone they were like the wind, but this time it had a bit of a blister to it. Sophie loved that apartment and was so disappointed she couldn't help but continue to show it.

It took them a good part of the early afternoon casually meandering their way to the nearby west side. They'd been window shopping and doing a bit of purchasing along the way while casually wandering about to their unknown destination for a late lunch. Once they had made their choice and were seated, Sophie relented…

"I love my new necklace Josef. It's absolutely gorgeous. Thank you sweetheart" she said feeling her throat and her new bobble that was brilliantly displayed.

"It's just a little something, I love shopping for you. We should pop by the ABC store tomorrow if you'd like. I need to see if they have my sheets back in stock and I'm sure there'll be a few things there that'll peak your interest."

Sophie was so impressed with his level of polished sophistication, if only Bruce had shown her half the attention that Josef was…Receiving this gorgeous gift made her think and reflect on her ex for a moment…and how he hadn't thought to buy her anything in years.

Sophie's daily routine had definitely changed, she

hadn't been working at all. Instead, spending time with Josef had taken precedent over everything…and he was gleefully making sure of it. She was so enamored and influenced by him, it was like she didn't have a business at all. She'd lost her footing and had been pulled under… again. Fortunately she found solace knowing Gayle was busy *holding down the fort* at home. After all…given her loyalty, she'd never disappoint.

The love birds began strolling through Manhattan in the life of carefree luxury like only those with *real* money do. Those greenbacks when in abundance are always a game changer. Their routine was now shopping, visiting museums, having massages, and of course…enjoying the Macy's Thanksgiving Day Parade.

Soon after, The Christmas Capitol of the US was just beginning to adorn itself. The world class decorations would soon be displayed in full force as Rockefeller Center was having its massive annual Tree delivered. That event alone gave all in the city a rush of magical excitement signaling the holiday season had 'officially' opened. The electrifying energy was felt everywhere. People in the city had become jubilant and the swirling fairy dust had rubbed off on everyone.

Our lovers had become entrenched and completely submersed in the festive season like everyone else. With the money flowing and limitless time on their hands what else could they possibly do but enjoy some fabulous adventures?

They drank bubbles in excess, enjoyed their steamy sex life and frolicked around within their countless five star experiences. Such a bore, right? Gawd…would I love to have that *life*…even if for one guiltless minute, wouldn't you? These two lovers were locked in their own dreamy fantasy…not caring about anything or anyone else in the world.

*

Chapter Sept

But not so long after…the fairy dust unexpectedly blew away with vigor. Their decadent and whimsical visit in Manhattan came to a screeching halt with a surprisingly rare incoming call from the *Château*. Too bad it hadn't been with the news Josef had been anxiously anticipating. They had just entered their suite after a day of frolicking when the phone began to ring.

"Josef?"

"Hello…Michel?…This is a surprise hearing from you. What's going on?…Everything Okay?" Josef nervously questioned. He stood shaken, knowing the unusual call from Michel could only mean something super important had happened. Josef had known Michel his entire life and could tell something tragic had unfolded just by the tone of his voice. Sophie also knew something potentially horrific had taken place just by seeing Josef's body language.

"I'm calling you my friend…about…Laetitia. I'm so, so sorry to have to tell you this Josef, but she's gone. She passed away this afternoon. Fiona found her laying in her bed late this afternoon. She'd gone into her room to make sure her fire was still lit and that's when she found her. It seems as if our precious Laetitia passed away in her sleep. I'm sure it will give you comfort knowing Fiona said she looked at peace."

Josef's knees buckled as he became limp, falling backwards onto the sofa with a puzzling morose look on his face. Sophie was beside herself wanting to know just what the hell had been said on the other end of the line. She nervously crouched down on her knees in front of Josef. She began rubbing his thighs up and down with long relaxing massage strokes in the attempt to comfort him. He was actually so intent on listening to Michel, he didn't even notice. He was so numb he couldn't feel a thing. The entire scenario played out within seconds, but seriously it felt like a lifetime.

There was a long, long pause before any more words were spoken. The silence was staggering. Remember when the pin didn't drop? Well, it finally did big time. And, at that very second...its echo reverberated and seemed to be the only sound on the planet.

Finally Michel began speaking again. "What would you like for me to do?"

Josef couldn't quite wrap his head around it all at that moment. He was unable to utter a sound, he was so shocked. He sat paralyzed with the phone receiver still glued to his ear...as huge teardrops began streaming heavily down his face. It was only after a few minutes that he could collect himself enough to wipe his eyes and begin to speak. He was so devastated hearing the earth shattering news, it's like he'd been beamed up into a different sphere all together. Surprisingly, he forged through the inevitable... All of a sudden, he'd become an alert, mature, decision maker. He was now the master of the kingdom...His Litty was gone and he was finally forced to take control...all by his lonesome.

"I feel so grateful knowing that she went peacefully. Thank you for letting me know Michel. You know how she always loved her naps after lunch" he said speaking with a sad yet light hearted shaky voice. He was lovingly trying to reflect on her daily habits endearingly...ones that they both shared and knew well.

Both must've mutually shared a smile in silence just thinking about her. Michel knew her habits almost as well as Josef. After all, Michel had been part of the estate from way back when. He'd always been considered part of the family, however the thing about Michel was that he'd always observed it from the sidelines. Even though he'd been loved and considered Grandfather's other 'unofficial' son...he was different. He'd always remained outside the jealous fray, keeping humble and not one to gloat like the entitled rest.

His job becoming the winemaker had given him dignity, and enough personal accolades to proudly justify his existence on the property. He'd always stayed under the radar hoping not to create any jealousy from the 'official' men in the house. Blood as we all know, has always proven to be thicker than water… no matter what.

"Call the Funérarium in Castillonnès to begin with. Ask them to gently transport her there and let them know I'm on my way. I'll call the minute I arrive tomorrow."

The gravity of the situation had barely begun to resonate before his mind began racing. It was all so unexpected and shocking. Grandfather was one thing, but this?…THIS, after all…was *HIS* Litty. He actually thought his heavy heart might stop beating. Never in his life had he experienced such feelings of immense loss and emptiness. You could actually see a heavy cloud swirling above him.

"Okay Josef, I'll let everyone know. We'll be waiting for you" Michel said quietly…ending the call.

Josef could only pray that Fiona had been right and she'd gone peacefully. He'd always regret not having been there to have given her his final farewell.

But these things are always tricky. Who knows when one's final days will present themselves.…Now, he'd not a clue of what his world would be without her. She'd always been his rock and map of guidance. His confidant, his balance…and most of all, the most beloved woman in his life…She'd ended up to have been his only family so to speak.

"Sophie, I have some very sad news" said the spoiled brat having not really taken notice of her scrunched down in front of him. He took the longest time to verbalize…"Laetitia…has passed away."

Out of simple convenience, he fell forward and broke down in her arms sobbing uncontrollably before being able to regain his composure. Sophie thought only a 'real man' would expose his raw feelings like that. She knew times would be difficult for a while adjusting to life without Laetitia being around, but secretly…she was grateful thinking the coast was now clear from having another power female at the helm. That would certainly make things easier not having Josef rely on Litty's opinion and approval on everything. At least now…she hoped he'd need hers.

Once he was able to manage his emotions, he sat up…which in turn made Sophie stand. He began running his fingers through his hair like he was clearing the air.

"We should get packing. We need to get out of here and be on the next flight to Paris or Bordeaux. We'll need to arrive in Bergerac no later than tomorrow early afternoon. There's going to be a lot to take care of."

Josef had become an entirely different man in mere seconds. It's as if he'd been catapulted into being the lone survivor on a family quest. Out goes the crying boy…in comes the man to save the Family Estate. It's amazing to see how life can change with a drop of a dime. Sophie couldn't believe the transformation she was witnessing right in front of her and he knew it too…He felt the change happening and really didn't care who else noticed.

Without question Sophie went directly to the bedroom and began packing and within fifteen minutes there was a knock on the door. They were greeted by their familiar bellman who quickly placed their bags on his shiny brass cart. While the guy pleasantly escorted them down to the lobby, he must've sighed a sign of relief at that point knowing the occupants of the '*Sex Suite*' were leaving…

Once downstairs, Josef explained there'd been a death in the family and they'd be checking out prematurely. He requested the bill be forwarded and for the concierge to make flight reservations for their immediate return to France. He'd be waiting for the call with flight details as they were being taken to the airport. That's the kind of service you receive and come to fully expect when you have the money and connections to be considered a VIP. It really is an entirely different world.

The bellman rolled their luggage to the curb where they waited only seconds before being whisked away by a slick limo for their pick up. The driver was placing their bags in the trunk when the general manager rushed out from his office to speak to Josef. He was of course sympathetic and offered his condolences like any proper businessman would who'd want a high rolling client to return.

"We'll be sending you our best thoughts through this difficult time Mr. Decour. We hope to see you again soon under different circumstances"…and as fast as he'd finished his sentence the car door closed and they were off in a dash for JFK.

Josef's cell rang within minutes after departing the Hôtel. It was his favorite concierge who'd already organized two first-class seats. They were to leave on Air France in only two short hours. The timing would be close, but with special white glove check in service available in the elite club lounge, that gold star perk would insure they'd make their flight with no problem.

Josef began making calls to rally *The* troops with the news of Laetitia's passing. It was also time to call in a favor from the Club…getting a ride home from Bordeaux to Bergerac that is. It'd be too late to charter a flight or take a train when they'd arrive, so hopefully Gus could remedy the situation. I think the real issue here was that Josef was needing a little bit of attention and comfort from his cronies.

Once the word was out, he was expecting the entire Club to show up at the *Château* within the next twenty-four hours. It'd be the first time in a long time, (actually ever since Grandfathers departure party) that most Club members would be seeing one another eye to eye. Now… more than ever…it really was the changing of the guard. Not having Laetitia's influence in the mix, there was no question Josef's future was about to change. Litty had always been well known and loved by each and every member of the Boys Club…especially during the early years. Let's just say…they had history.

Litty had always been considered the ultimate catch. Some of Grandfather's good friends had always lovingly teased him that if he didn't take good care of her they'd be more than happy to do so. Litty had touched them all either through her good looks, delicious food, or her flirtatiously witty and clever personality. Ever since Josef was old enough to remember, she'd always been involved in ever*y*thing. She was quite comfortable being at the center of it all…it's as if she'd been a member of *The Club* herself. I guess when I think about it, she actually had been.

Gustav came through as usual and had his Lear waiting in Bordeaux for their pick up only to deliver them to the tiny airport in Bergerac. (where Josef would conveniently find his Rover waiting in his usual parking spot) Gustav was quite the fun and colorful character, a unique and celebrated rarity for those coming from Switzerland…

He would definitely be joining them at the *Château* in the next couple of days like the rest of the Boys. All wanted to gather together for their united final send off for their beloved Laetitia. Gus had been one of the original members of *The Club* and one of Grandfather's closest and most trusted friends. He'd always been a silent rock of support for Josef and Litty…especially after the old man's passing. He'd willingly stepped into the guardian role and had lovingly watched over them ever since.

Fiona opened the front door relieved to see Josef had arrived home safely. When Josef got out of the Rover and saw her, instead of giving a loud and hateful rant like he had the last time he'd seen her, he met her with a soft kiss on both cheeks. He was happy to see her and be able to acknowledge his gratitude for having taking such good care of Littty.

As for Sophie…seeing their warm interaction seemed quite odd. It appeared all too familiar for her taste. The scene made her feel uncomfortable right from the get go. "Who in the frickin' hell was this creature that Josef obviously seemed to know all so well…"

"Merci beaucoup," he gingerly said to Fiona with a pause…before introducing Sophie. Intentionally, Fiona didn't reply directly to Josef but only smiled…turning her focus onto Sophie.

"It's lovely to meet you So…phie."

Her elegant whimsical British accent made Sophie immediately feel on the defensive. Again, let me repeat… Who in the HELL was this woman speaking with such a smooth feline tenor of control? Did she actually have a plum in her mouth or did she just sound like it. (Fucking Brits, they do have a particular enviable swish to them when they *want* to turn it on)

You might as well know…Fiona was originally from England, but was incredibly fluent speaking in her almost song-like French. Litty's ex-husband (Fiona's Grandfather) had definitely made certain that the French language was a part of her curriculum…knowing full well this sophisticated language would be needed one day. (Little had he known, it would be in a French *Château* living with his ex-wife) Given Fiona's exceptional education she spoke with no foreign accent whatsoever. Her French was so perfect, it would've led you to believe the girl was a French Aristocrat raised with a Trés Haute Bourgeois upbringing. Sophie even thought with that kind of superlative talent, this chick could've easily burst into world class operatic song at any given moment. It really was un-nerving.

With all of her God given talents…this young woman immediately made Sophie feel nauseous. She couldn't put her finger on it…but the fact that this girl was so striking… Couple that with her high level of sophistication, it was just enough to make Sophie suddenly feel out of place. She felt an unusually strange sensation come over her, I think you could even be safe to call it what is was…She was intimidated. It was like this girl and Josef *Really* knew one another. I mean really…like they shared some…thing.

Even though Sophie didn't speak French fluently, she knew enough about body language to know that something seemed all too cozy about their chemistry, especially on Fiona's part. Remarkable to think Fiona had been working at the *Château* for more than a year without Josef paying much attention like he'd said…pla leaze…

It was as if Sophie had been given her first slap of reality becoming the odd woman out. On her original visit to the *Château*…Josef had served her up as his most adored and coveted prize. Her feeling of being top dog had become convoluted having been side-whacked by this totally unexpected Brit answering the door. Sophie was taken aback given the *'housekeeper'* and Josef seemed to speak the same language on quite a *few* levels. She automatically felt uncomfortable and sensed there was something not quite right about the situation.

She swallowed her suspicions and tried not to let any obvious jealousy prevail given the sensitive circumstances. She knew instead of giving the 'gorgeous housekeeper' a second thought, her only focus should really remain on her man and his needs at this delicate time. She'd just have to suck it up for a while and discretely cover the standing hair on the back of her neck and delicately brush back the imaginary horns sprouting on her hairline. She'd need to keep it cool...at least until she got settled and knew more. She must be patient. There would obviously be a lot to learn, it was already proving to be an entirely new world...

For the first time, Sophie began to understand the gravity of the situation and just what the *Château* symbolized to the area. Josef had a loyal staff at the Estate and the family had decades' worth of contacts. The flowers began rolling in and the phone didn't stop ringing. Sophie never took in to account how many people the Decour family actually knew in the village, nor their 'position' within the region for that matter. Tourists and newcomers never really do. They don't fully understand how the workings of a small French village really are until a local family either has a death occur or a wedding happen. They don't realize how lengthy the root span of a village can spread until either one of those major events takes place. Given her new found realization, it was certainly obvious...the entire Village would be attending Laetitia's service.

"Lets get settled," Josef said taking Sophie's hand and escorting her up to the second floor.

That strategic move left Fiona standing alone downstairs in the foyer...Sophie meanwhile just gloated on her way up. Josef's decision was enough to falsely give privilege and gratify her confidence again. Being 'selected' and taken to his upper 'kingdom' easily erased any ill feelings she initially might've had.

When arriving at the top of the beautiful winding staircase, (think about the old classic: Gone with the Wind type of staircase) her breath was taken away from the exquisite surroundings. The round upper foyer was spotless and seemed to glisten. You couldn't help but be intrigued by the set of glamorous and imposing double doors that stood commanding the space.

Directly across from the statement entry was a really long and wide cavernous hallway that occupied four large bedrooms, two on either side. The first room on the left had been Josef's childhood room. The two other rooms of non consequence were elegantly prepared as guest rooms…Yet the only room removed from the equation was the one at the far end, down on the right. That'd been Josef's Father's room. It remained with the door locked and in the same state it'd been found at the time of his passing. It was left as a time capsule of sorts, a remembrance if you could call it that. Actually, it was more of a situation that no one wanted to go in.

To Sophie's dismay and astonishing disappointment, instead of being welcomed into his private sanctuary through the set of massive double doors, he surprisingly took a right at the top of the landing and entered the first door to the left. He was so consumed with delight at how lovely his old room had been transformed with its new decor, he didn't even notice the complete and utter look of confusion on Sophie's face. What the hell was this? She immediately felt shunned and humiliated. Could he be serious? Separate rooms for he and his lover? She was so blindsided, she couldn't even see past her immediate… heartbreak.

"You should be comfortable in here sweetheart. I'll just be across the foyer until this is over. I'll make sure the fireplace always keeps you warm when I'm not," he said placing her bags in front of the tall antique armoire. He walked across the room and flung the brocade draperies apart and opened the tall windows to let some nippy fresh air come drifting in to freshen the room.

"I'll let you get unpacked and see you downstairs in a few?" he said leaving the room without so much as a kiss.

"O.m..G…What the hell? Is he being serious or is this some kind of an insensitive joke?" she thought amidst her confused state. She actually didn't know what to think. Somehow, somewhere in her rattled thoughts she realized she couldn't expose her feelings until she actually understood them herself…It was all happening so fast… everything in this new foreign setting was so bitterly unexpected that every bit of it felt disturbing.

In the depths of her devastated and perplexed state, she numbly replied…"Okay, see you downstairs shortly sweetheart." He didn't bother waiting to hear her reply, the Shit was already making his way down the stairs.

He'd actually been so robotic in his behavior, it seemed as if he'd been performing his basic routine of just checking in any 'Ol random acquaintance to a guest room. What the fuck was that about…He was Such a different man, she didn't quite recognize him.

What she did wisely conclude was it was all going to be different. Everything had already changed in one split second. Sadly, she sat down on the comfy bed and watched the sexy plume of her dream cloud evaporate into thin air, funneling its way out of the fabulous wooden window. In one behavioral move, he'd completely deflated her full heart just by dumping her there all alone…And by the way, who in the hell was that woman named Fiona slithering around downstairs leaving her scent everywhere. The housekeeper…? You've got to be kidding…

Sophie immediately felt isolated in this beautiful place. She felt daggers pelting her love bubble for the first time since she'd fallen in love with the man. She suddenly realized what a small part she'd be playing in his world going forward. This was not at all what she'd been expecting. It'd just been her own ego and imagination thinking she could be his only interest.

"So much for 'playing' a man who actually turned out be the ultimate player himself"…she whispered under her breath as she closed the window. She was *seeing the light* by admitting to herself...he loved his human chess-board and preferred keeping his pawns in their *'proper'* place. She began unpacking (completely) while wiping the tears from her eyes. It was her first day of not realizing what she'd actually become was...his love prisoner.

"Sophie, it's almost Ten o'clock and I haven't seen you at all this evening. Why have you stayed up here all night?" Josef quipped as he walked in to the bedroom after one knock.

Sophie had laid down and fallen off into a snoozy trance...when she'd suddenly been awaken by the door opening and seeing Josef enter. She'd finally settled down and taken the time to enjoy her privacy thinking perhaps she could've been over reacting. There was so much to see and learn about with this place. Perhaps he was right giving her a separate space and some time to absorb her new surroundings. Having a private moment of reflection and taking the time to get organized was more of a sophisticated approach. (Personally, I think that's European bullshit if I've ever heard it, but then again...what do I know)

She opened her eyes and said softly, "Hi my love...I thought I'd give you some time to yourself. I know you've had a lot to do and probably have a ton of unexpected emotions to deal with. I'm so sorry for your loss sweetheart" she said, while lovingly reaching out to touch him...He looked right at her and began verbalizing his self-centered thoughts with a less than sensitive attitude...

"That's thoughtful of you my dear, but I really needed your support this evening, but what did you do?...Instead you decided to leave me all alone...Don't you understand this is such a sad and bizarre time for me? I can't believe she's really gone. Thank God...I was able to settle myself down enough to get the service and burial organized for the day after tomorrow. Our priest will arrive the early morning of to make sure we have everything covered for the service. The entire valley will most probably be here on the grounds for the service, which begins at noon. It's definitely going be a community event. As you might know…Litty was a well respected figure in the area," he said…finally sitting down on the bed.

He began stroking Sophie's arm as if his touch were mourning Laetitia…it's as if he wasn't even noticing it was actually Sophie he was caressing. He was off in a different world which gave Sophie an immediate sense of guilt for having only been thinking of herself…

"It sincerely wasn't his intention to hurt me, not escorting me to his room to share a bed, Right?" She began having her thoughts bounce back and forth like a pickle ball on steroids. His guilt tactic had worked…the Bastard.

"I understand how it must cut deep right now Josef. It will all become easier with time. I know how strong your special bond was between the two of you, I know she loved you as much as you did her. These meaningful relationships and feelings in life never really leave us, but they'll soften with time. You were lucky to have had each other," Sophie said almost apologetically. She was making every attempt to once again comfort and console him.

Let's face it, the life altering news was so fresh…it'd only been a short twelve hours since he'd been faced with the news of Litty's passing. He was still reeling and hadn't fully grasped the entire situation.

Feeling spent, the Golden Boy fell fast asleep on top of the bed fully dressed. It was only in the darkness of the night that Sophie awoke and found he'd left her alone sometime during the night. The next morning, she walked downstairs and headed for the kitchen (by way of the great room then the dining room)…to drop in with a quiet entry. Consequently by doing so she surprised the hell out of him.

"How are you this morning Josef?" Sophie said fully refreshed and making every effort to leave yesterday's disappointments behind her.

She walked across the room and without any further words kissed him on his gorgeous lips with a long hot one. She wanted to feel some type of response in knowing where she stood. Her 'welcome back' to the *Château* the day before had been anything but inviting. She constantly had to remind herself to keep the tragedy of Laetitia's passing paramount. It should remain the major pending matter of concern…but she was fast in wanting to know where she fit in amongst his new found title and life that obviously…she knew nothing about. She couldn't help but feel confused given the conflicting messages she'd been given. Why was he now acting like a distant lover, and what the hell was this all about with separate bedrooms? Sophie had been feeling uneasy since her arrival, but thank God…she immediately felt her questions were being answered when her kiss was mutually returned so passionately.

"Better and you? Did you sleep well?" he said holding her really close and smiling into her eyes.

Between his loving kiss that'd been reciprocated and his sweet embrace, she felt comforted. She thought she should probably just chalk it up to a 'bad night' is all. She was so relieved feeling he was back to being his affectionate self again. Her sweet man who gave her his undivided attention was back.

That is, until…the side door opened from the Orchid room (the outdoor patio that'd been enclosed) and there… the creature stood. Fiona of all people, yep that Fiona…the one with her charming non accent. It wasn't enough that she could speak three languages seamlessly, the bitch was to the point where in no way did she sound like a British transplant.

It was quite enough to make Sophie feel that rare little twinge of something she hadn't felt in years. That damn feeling of…Insecurity. There, I said it. Sophie certainly wasn't used to having such an 'in your face' challenging opponent. She definitely had something go haywire in her head every time she was around this British glamour-puss. Fiona knew what she was doing and intentionally shed some strange type of voodoo energy towards Sophie that made her automatically feel timid. She suddenly realized perhaps, she'd arrived in a space where the deck was already stacked against her. For the first time in her adult life, she felt out of step as though she was at a disadvantage. She hated this rather unique and rare feeling. There was definitely an unexpected and uncomfortable situation brewing.

As mentioned, Fiona had been conveniently hand picked and groomed by Laetitia to become her successor. They were two peas in a pod those two. During the bitchy little Brit's time there, she'd been carefully trained to know every little like and dislike of Josef's. It was absolutely uncanny.

Sophie felt Fiona was a manipulator and didn't like her presence whatsoever. She was definitely a clever girl and attempted to make Sophie feel she was out of the loop with every possible opportunity. With all her fake smiles and snide little glances (some loaded with *certain* innuendos, ie: subtle digs)…she obviously was trying to take Sophie off her game. Her behavior would take time to understand, but Sophie was certainly clever enough to realize it had to have something to do with their 'mutual interest'.

"Fiona…Sophie and I will be having breakfast in the dining room this morning. Would you mind seeing to it?" Sophie beamed at his directive hearing him deliberately put the 'housekeeper' in her place…but then…when he continued speaking Sophie didn't quite know how to take it.

"Fiona, I hope you understand your responsibilities in the *Château* have now increased since Laetitia's unfortunate passing. We'll be needing you much more now."

That one significant statement wiped the smile right off Sophie's face. She was so stunned she almost swallowed her tongue. Thank God Fiona didn't notice.

Josef put on a false air of 'the authoritarian' when speaking to Fiona. He knew speaking down to her in that manner would give Sophie the feeling of being superior and the lady of the house. He was so good at playing games, his seasoned talent of working both sides was unbelievable. In this instance…his attitude and elitist demeanor was intentional. Putting distance between his 'employee' and them as a united couple was another move on his chessboard…but asking Fiona to spend more time at the

Château? Sophie didn't like that one bit…

"Let's take a walk out back while she's getting our breakfast together," he said strutting out of the kitchen like he was some overpaid Hollywood Celeb. It was utterly disgusting, but his ploy worked. Sophie was back to feeling empowered and thinking she was on top of the heap. He knew giving her a bit of 'advantage' would do the trick.

When they approached the large stone barn in back of the *Château* Josef stepped up and slid the huge wooden door open. Surprisingly the barn was actually used as his private car hanger. In fact it really was some kind of a mouthwatering designer monster garage. The place was *Lit* as some would say. It was filled with exquisite vintage cars that had also been part of his windfall from Gramps. A car collection so fabulous, any major auto junkie would've been impressed. The sight was truly magnificent. No one could ever imagine seeing such an extraordinary collection hidden in such a rural location. His bit of discreet eccentricity made her *love* him all the more.

Sophie had never been within a mile of such a premier and luxury private auto collection such as this. The cars were all rare and kept in pristine condition. They toured a few rows of the choice collectibles…when Sophie opened the door of a 1967 Aston Martin and got in. It must've made his skin crawl…He was pretty protective of his cars amongst everything else.

"Should we take this for a spin?"

"Why not…of course, but that'll have to wait, I think our breakfast must be ready by now. Shall we?"…he said reaching into the leather tufted womb to help assist her make a graceful exit from the beauty worth a quarter of a mill.

They returned to the house and entered through the glass garden sanctuary. It gave Josef an immediate wave of sadness. "Do you like orchids Sophie?"

She answered with a puffy sigh, "Of course doesn't every woman love the unique beauty of an orchid?"

He was silent and just smiled with a bit of

melancholic nostalgia as if Test number Two had been successfully completed. Josef had been so head over heels in love with Sophie, willing and ready to buy-in to his *new* future, but with Litty's passing his feelings had changed and he'd begun to grow distant. He still loved her, but felt the need to concentrate and focus on the business like never before. He only had room to think of the winery, his family's legacy, and their position in the marketplace. Following his own ambition would become far more important than anything or anyone else...Sophie included. Not having Litty's steady eye looking over the place, his solo performance was now paramount. He felt the weight of the world on his shoulders and no one would be allowed to get in the way of his success. Sophie was to remain at the *Château* as planned, yet his obsessive love and attraction for her had somehow fleeted as fast as it'd come.

His particular type of selective entitlement had begun to play out. His dedication to continue with his Grandfather's dream prevailed and had become his only real concern. Now that it had been left all up to him he was determined to succeed at any cost. If he'd been a self-serving bastard before...the on-lookers would need to take notice. The lion was now off his leash.

Sophie actually thought she'd been guaranteed a beautiful dream life with her dream man. A life that would provide all that she'd desired. (At least that's what he'd promised) It was a heavenly thought, one that she sincerely believed would become true. But given his new sense of self she began to see she'd never be his number one priority like he'd led her to believe. Her pedestal had already been kicked out from underneath her and replaced. The signs had not been so apparent until that very moment.

The *Château* and winery were becoming his one and only world. Sadly, she'd have to accept this before anything else were to happen on her dreamy bucket list. Her life now was to be considered like a fancy bracelet remaining only as his pretty arm piece. It was an entirely new reality she'd be facing.

He'd never converse or admit any of this to her of course…she'd just have to figure it out on her own. As we all know…unfortunately, some things are just too good to be true. Sadly, just like Sophie, some of us are gluttons for punishment and sometimes prefer not to see what's right in front of us. It goes back to that denial thing. She'd just have to adjust and accept being 'second best' if she were to remain in his new life.

Now realizing her future wasn't going to be as picture perfect as she'd imagined, a need to navigate where she would fit in with 'her new' Josef was. She'd need to figure out her place in the puzzle if she wanted to at least keep being a part of it. She knew his recently found behavior wasn't going to be a phase, but rather something that was going to be his new norm. Too bad she'd worked so hard to obtain 'getting there' because turning back now wouldn't be so easy. It'd all become way too complicated.

Entering through the greenhouse they made their way to the dining room through its wall of wooden framed glass paneled doors. Their breakfast had already been carefully orchestrated and was waiting on one of the credenzas. Their place settings at the table had been carefully set with shiny silver cutlery and lovely Gien China porcelain plates. It was all so beautifully laid out. Crystal stemmed glasses full of freshly squeezed orange juice and hot coffee smoldered in coordinating bone china cups. Everything else waiting on the buffet had been presented with such panache.

Even so, Josef felt the regimented need to inspect the spread and give it his critical eye before sampling the goods. He was beyond himself finding the buffet full of all his favorites. Fresh croissants with sweet butter, country ham slices with a medley of different jams and marmalades lined up along with fresh creamy yogurts and breakfast cheeses. Of course, there was also a crisply folded local morning paper sitting beside the beautifully presented breakfast meat tray. It was all so perfect…It was absolutely nauseating.

"It seems that Fiona took serious notes" he gleamed,

grateful to see his customary buffet had been placed just the way Laetitia used to leave it. Of course…it happened to be just the way he liked it.

After seeing the familiar display replicated, he felt another wave of sadness, like he'd had a club hit him in the chest. The reality of not having Laetitia in the *Château* would always leave a hole in his heart, a vacancy he knew would be impossible to fill.

Josef sat down and opened the paper to the obituary section to find what he'd submitted about Litty's service. It was a public invitation for anyone from the area who wanted to pay their last respects and attend her burial service the following day. The plan had been organized to have the Priest conduct the ceremony at the family's gravesite on the property where she'd be laid to rest next to Grandfather.

"Sophie my dear, I still have quite a few details needing attention so I've asked Michel to take you on a tour of the Vineyard today. I think you should see what we do around here. Would you enjoy that?…I'll be busy making further arrangements for tomorrow, but I'll expect to see you back here for dinner this evening sweetheart" Josef nicely said leaning over and kissing her hand. He consistently flipped back and forth between a doting future husband and a complete asshole given how the wind was blowing.

"That sounds wonderful Josef" …taking the bait.

He was giving her just enough affection and sweet sentiments to camouflage his change of heart. What he really wanted was to get rid of her and be alone for the day. For a girl that'd been so savvy, sadly she'd become so completely gullible. They finished their breakfast and Sophie eagerly went upstairs to get ready for her outing.

The plan was for her to meet Michel in front of the *Château* after breakfast. Certain he must already be waiting, she hurried back down after changing. She was pleasantly surprised to open the door and not only find Michel but their touring rides that were all brushed and saddled up in their finest…They'd be taking their tour on horseback. Sophie was beyond thrilled for the adventure.

When she'd gone upstairs to prepare for her outing, Josef had disappeared quietly making his way down to the cellar. It was the first time going down since the brief moment when he had quickly dropped off the bag of lingerie. That felt like a lifetime ago. Sophie called out for him but after not hearing a response, she forged ahead with her tour and left. She had no idea about the cellars existence and didn't know enough about the Estate to imagine all of his hiding places. She was so excited and self absorbed with her own day's agenda on horseback, it'd conveniently given her enough to be pre-occupied and not question his whereabouts. She knew he needed more time to himself (and was taking it) without coming right out and telling her so.

She really could've used a bit of honesty from him right about then…Even though it might've become obvious, it was gut wrenching not to see Sophie read between the lines on this one. You certainly would've thought she'd been able to see this one staring right at her. It was sitting right there in BOLD PRINT.

HE'S NO LONGER IN TO YOU…can't you see?

It was a very confusing time now that things had changed in every which way. For now he'd try to be as subtle as possible and not rock the boat, but his only real play was to continue to use her for his convenience without her noticing. The Golden Bastard was up to his usual deep-seated tricks. His hatred for Bruce allowed him to be evil.

Josef casually entered one of his favorite tasting rooms. It was a small special room that held only the rarest of wines from the *Château* itself. He sat down at the table, opened a bottle and poured himself a glass of his delicious vintage red when he noticed an envelope sitting face down on the table. He turned it over only to see it had his name written on it in Laetitia's handwriting. He was perplexed. He couldn't imagine her ever having come down to his cellar. He opened the sealed envelope, and took his time examining each and every word.

My Dearest Josef,

By the time you read this...I will have already gone to be with your Grandfather. I know what you must be thinking...just whatever you do, please don't be sad or scared. I know when life changes unexpectedly it can leave one feeling a bit lost, but truly there's no need for you to have those feelings my boy. You are a brave and smart man Josef...and much stronger than you give yourself credit for. Fear not, you will make the right decisions.

Before your Grandfather passed, I made him a promise that I'd remain at the Château as long as I thought you needed me. With you now opening up to true love and having the notion of starting a family...that in itself gave me the sign I'd been waiting for. It's a gift knowing you won't spend your life alone. Your revelation has allowed me the freedom to accept it was my time to go. You have to realize life had become so tiring for me, even the simple everyday chores had gotten to be a challenge. You'll understand more about that in time...God willing. Getting old is not so glamorous my boy.

I wanted to leave you this letter to reiterate our last conversation. I hope you've reflected upon it and have actually fully absorbed what I was saying. In those final days when deciding to stop taking my heart medication, I told you that you wouldn't have to worry about the Douglas family ever again and I'd take care of it. That my dear was not just talk...but an actual promise. Rest assured, from now on you will be able to live freely with your lady love and not worry about any hearsay or issues caused by that devious family ever again. That bastard Gene and his entire family will no longer be in the Village to cause you any trouble. I am satisfied in leaving this earth knowing that to be fact. I called in on my last outstanding favor owed to insure this would take place. Your Grandfather will be smiling when I tell him about it.

The other thing I want you to know is that those images you

had in your recurring 'nightmares' as a child were real events. I'm sorry to admit, your Grandfather and I had always misled you by telling you those images were just bad dreams. We wanted to protect you from the truth.

Those images you had of Gene and your Father rolling around in bed together were real events that did happen. It wasn't just in your imagination like we led you to believe. Gene Douglas was responsible for your father liking men on occasion. He initially lured your Father in to a sexual relationship and helped facilitate his homosexual appetite. Whether he already had one or not, I couldn't say, but that 'Ol Gene...he saw to it. He made it his business to consummate your Father's curiosity. In addition to encounters with those of his same sex, your Father also loved women. He was always in turmoil and conflicted over that. Your Grandfather could not accept his behavior, especially after having had a similar circumstance with your maternal Grandmother's choice.

The years of paying Gene to keep quiet were never enough. He continued to threaten your Grandfather with the potential of spreading gossip and humiliating stories as a form of blackmail in order to get more money. When Gene would get low on funds, he tried to use your Grandfather as his personal ATM. As you may remember, when your Grandfather had finally had enough of this tormenting treatment, he refused to pay. About that time Gene came up with an outlandish story that had something to do regarding his wife and an unpaid landscaping bill for work she'd done at the Château. He even had the nerve to try and have your Grandfather arrested from that scandalous lie amongst a list of other false accusations. Those people have only caused us trouble from day one and they've needed to be wiped off the face of the earth for as long as I can remember.

This final deed of getting rid of them is my farewell gift to you my darling boy. Your Grandfather will be so pleased to know that I was finally able to eliminate that sorry excuse of a family for *what they did to us. To think of all those years that Gene's wife preferred to look the other way well, it always astounded me.*

Live your life with no regrets Josef. Have dreams, have love, have children...knowing one day you can leave this exquisite estate to your heirs just as the beautiful legacy your family has left for you. I've loved you as if you were my own from the day I met you. In fact you were the real gift that made me want to survive in life. Thank you for having become the beautiful man that you are Josef. I'm grateful I was able to keep my promise in protecting you until the very end.

With all of my love,
Your Litty.

Josef put his empty glass down on the table then filled it up again, this time to the rim. He repeated this until the bottle was empty, then opened another. Once the second bottle had been left without a drop remaining he staggered his way up the stairs to his suite. He laid down on one of the shimmering sofas and closed his swollen eyes. He rested just long enough to sleep off his binge...He was a seasoned drinker after all.

"That was fantastic Michel. Merci Beaucoup! It's been years since I've been on the back of such a beautiful animal. What an incredible way for me to have viewed the Estate. Our day was priceless and I'm giving you my sincere thanks for such a beautiful tour. I had no idea that you'd been the winemaker here for so many years. Seeing the Vineyard through your eyes was really something special. You must've known Josef's Grandfather for many years" Sophie said, dismounting slowly. She loved the glorious twinging sound that aged saddle leather makes when it rubs together. It's one of those subtle yet familiar chimes that only a seasoned rider has ears for. It's quite delicious and strikes a chord if you are in tune.

"Of course I knew Josef's Grandfather...and quite well I might add. He was such a generous man to me. I've been here working on the Estate since the very beginning. I stumbled upon this place when I was a newbie in the business. Fortunately enough for me, Sr. brought me in and took me under his wing. That's why I became his right hand man early on. We had some kind of a history I'll tell you. He was the only Vintner courageous enough to hire and allow me the freedom to introduce a new grape varietal to the region. Not many men would've been so bold and experimental to allow a young buck that kind of chance. I think it had something to do with my unbridled enthusiasm. He often told me he saw something of himself in me. In the end…being so adventurous with the new varietals, we made a bucket load of money in sales and brought numerous awards to our brand. Certainly Sr.'s close friends from the early years will be around in the next couple of days. I'm sure you'll meet them all, and no doubt they'll have stories for you my dear. The old man will always be missed. He gave this particular bunch of guys some of the early starter vines from our experimental varietals. They all made a fortune from his generosity and they've stayed loyal to this day. They call themselves the 'Boys Club'" he said dismounting Zephyr, the magnificent stallion.

He walked around to the head of Sophie's ride and took her reins. They parted ways with Michel giving her a kiss on both cheeks, before slowly walking back to the barn leading the horses. It'd been such a splendid day, Sophie couldn't wait to tell Josef.

She entered the *Château* only to find silence. She didn't want to create any un-needed disturbance so she quietly slipped upstairs for a quick shower. She dried herself, got dressed and went back down to see if she could find her man. She heard laughter filtering through from the back of the house and it was there, in the kitchen, where she found Josef conveniently sitting with whom other than the Brit. It made Sophie jealous seeing them together giggling. Why in the world was that bitch always encouraged to be around?

"Hello Sophie, how was your ride?" Josef said

standing up straight as she entered the room. His reaction was like he'd been caught with his hand in the cookie jar. Sophie was beginning to think it wasn't just her imagination playing out, she was suspect there was actually something *really* going on between them.

"I just got up from a nap and fortunately found Fiona here...We were just going over the buffet items for tomorrow. After we lay our sweet Laetitia to rest we'll have a few people gathering here for lunch and conversation."

"Oh, will that include the Boy's Club?" she asked with a bit of edgy cockiness like she'd been let in on some privy information to a hidden 'inner circle' secret.

"Yes, it most certainly will" Josef replied nonchalantly..."*The Club* is a group of friends that have wine interests in common. The members are scattered all over the world and I guess you could say they're all considered to be like family. I've known most of them my entire life and practically each one of them has come to my rescue more than a few times over. They've all supported me in one way or another throughout the years. All of them knew Litty. She was well loved by the entire group, you'll see."

Then he turns to the Brit. "Thank you so much for everything. I don't know what we would've done without you," he said opening the door to the orchid gallery for her exit. (I know I mentioned VOMIT somewhere along the lines)

"Where's Sheee going?" Sophie asked with a more than mildly demanding and inquisitive note to her voice.

Josef just smiled and said, "I've asked Fiona to move into the apartment above the car hanger for a while. She's been such a help to us all, I thought having her on the property might be a good thing. Do you have a problem with that my little Sophie?" he asked planting a big kiss on her lips. He was back to playing her like a fiddle.

"Not if you'll continue to explain the situation to me over some pillow talk this afternoon," she said looking down with some sappy pursed lips.

He began to laugh, picked her up, threw her over his

shoulder and carried her upstairs to 'his' private suite. He only stopped at the four poster's edge before gently putting her down.

"Whew, you're heavy! It must be these thick jeans you're wearing...or perhaps it could be just a bit of my hangover still lingering, but either way my darling...let me help you out of these ridiculously heavy things..." he said unbuttoning her fly.

She stepped out of her jeans one leg at a time stomping them to the floor before pulling her sweater off and throwing it a good distance onto the floor. She couldn't wait to feel what his bed was like. She'd begun to fantasize about it becoming her future throne on a daily basis. Everything was so French, but why the initial separate bedrooms? She thought it must be a European thing. She'd gone ahead and disappointedly agreed with his decision for the initial time being, but at this very moment she was relishing in her current opportunity, even if it was just for the immediate. To his surprise, she spring boarded up onto his playpen like she was a bronze medalist thinking she deserved a gold. She did it without trepidation and believe it or not...a step stool was the very last thing needed.

That afternoon they loved on each other all the way into the night with the fortress draperies pulled tight. For a brief moment it'd been *their* inner sanctum, *their* privileged sanctuary ~Far, Far Away from the rest of the world, just like it'd been in the very beginning. Everything else in life had temporarily faded away and been put on hold. The world had stopped on its axis and only the fluttering buzz of imaginary hummingbirds and angels could be heard.

When she finally saw that Josef's eyes were closed she delicately ran her hands sensually over the silky smooth sheets and exhaled with sheer delight. God she loved the feeling of the quality of life that was at her fingertips. She felt it was all so deserving.

When his eyes did open the next morning they were at it again. In between their rolling around and moans of pleasure, they didn't hear or notice the door having been opened and closed. When Josef finally pulled back the draperies of the fortress, he was thrilled to see the fresh breakfast tray resting on the table in between the sofas.

"Oh good! How about a cup of coffee to start this long day?" he pleasingly said stepping down onto the plush area rug that lay below his *throne*. He walked over to the coffee pot with his half monty still lingering and poured them each a *stiff* cup. (Literally, pun intended)

"How in the Hell did that get in here?" Sophie questioned sitting straight up in the fortress.

She didn't quite know how she felt about it. Her emotions left her feeling torn and conflicted. Either she could look at the scenario like she was being treated like a Queen with servants who were waiting on she and her King, or…perhaps the more logical scenario was knowing that the snoopy bitch Fiona had snuck into 'their room' hoping to overhear them in their ecstasy while using a breakfast tray as her excuse. She surmised the situation then made her decision.

"Josef, I don't like anyone coming in on us like that" she said, figuring the second option was more in line with reality.

"Oh Sophie…why be so bothered about Fiona? She's just the housekeeper. She obviously picked up a few of my favorites from her training with Laetitia. Please don't begin the day like this. We were off to such a good start" he said delicately twisting the dangling wisps of hair then slipping them behind her ears. His tone became *almost* wimpy…it was even close to sounding pathetic for Christ's sake.

"This is going to be a very emotional day for me…as it will be for so many others. Just simply be there for me today okay? Could you please do that?"

"Of course I will sweetheart" she said reaching over and grabbing a soft velour throw from the back of the sofa and covering herself.

He struck a match and calmly threw it into the fireplace to ignite the perfectly prepared wood stack. The fire began in such a synchronized harmony…it began to roar like a wild wind in just minutes. (wow…the 'housekeeper' had done it again…) They sat snuggled up together feasting on their tray while admiring the fire and each other.

"Listen my love, this morning's agenda is happening like this: I'll be downstairs at Ten o'clock to meet the Priest. We'll be having a private, intimate family gathering prior to sharing her with the others for her actual burial service outside. So when you do come down make sure to wear something sexy, gorgeous and black. Plan on meeting the entire Village today. Guaranteed, they'll all be here and I'm sure they'll all be curious about you…and want to have a good look my dear. Try to be downstairs a bit before noon" he said walking to the bathroom to begin preparing himself for the somber day. Finished with his speech, it now left Sophie sitting alone…

"OH MY GOD! I hope not everybody will be here," she blurted out running over and flinging the doors wide open. She scampered her way across the foyer towards *Josef's old* room and the throw? Consequently it'd fallen off the pretty little streaker…

She was excited, but panicked…wanting to get her beautification process going asap. Knowing now she'd be on full display for all to see, she wanted to show up looking as glam as possible. She hadn't given a second thought about being excluded from the *private* service…All of those questionable thoughts evaporated *once* she saw another shiny box sitting there waiting…on her immaculately made bed.

Seeing that sexy shiny black box with its familiar red satin ribbon was another unexpected and exciting surprise. The thrill of finding it overshadowed her curiosity of just about everything…including the fact of how the box miraculously appeared and had been left there to begin with…Not to mention the fact that her bed had been made when she'd left it in such a tossed wreck. She quickly opened the box to find another gorgeous lingerie set. As she twirled around holding the contents up to her svelte nude torso, she sang melodiously, "Oh my darling sweetheart…He just thinks of everything."

*

Chapter Huit

Sophie glided down the stairs at Eleven forty-five sharp and surprisingly found a quiet 'great' room. She made the quick decision to detour and slip into the day's events by way of the kitchen. She Conveniently made the vacant tunnel type hallway serve as her personal catwalk, and she strut her stuff so hard you would've thought she was a contestant on Top Model.

She was wearing a tight **Little Black** mini **Dress** with long sleeves and a deep V-front that just so happened to hug her in all the right places. She was certain Josef would approve. The black bra that she'd found in her latest gift box was as elegant as the sheer black stockings, but instead of finding any matching panties, she found a beautiful substitute. Good God…did she feel sexy all under wearing that incredible black garter belt. She absolutely knew she radiated the sentiment. Flat out…she looked and felt sexy and was determined to make a splash.

To complement her look, she wore black leather fitted short boots that had a low block heel. They'd allow her to walk the grounds without looking like such a tourist sinking into the moist mossy earth with every step. She had a dark navy cashmere shawl and a black velvet beret that she'd wear outside for the actual service along with her black square Jackie O sunglasses. She knew, or at least hoped that Josef would be proud introducing her to *The Club*. She understood he'd definitely have other things on his mind, but she also knew once he caught a glimpse of her…he'd imagine what she was or wasn't wearing all under. Of course their sexy little secret would remain private, until later that is.

"You look beautiful Sophie," Michel said as he surprisingly entered the kitchen from the Orchid Solarium. "Josef asked me to escort you and fill in as your date until later, if that's okay with you…" Seeing the disappointment on her face he did his best to make light of the situation.

Presumably, this was another one of those European moves that she couldn't quite wrap her head around. Since she'd not been raised with the refinement to think there was a particular time and place for everything…it'd been her way of thinking she deserved to be in the front row at any event. (that goes for primo parking spots as well) It would sadly take a death in Josef's family to teach her a bit of back seat etiquette…French Style.

"I'd be delighted Michel" she said quickly wrapping her shoulders with her soft and expensive shawl. "You can show me the protocol that I'm obviously in need of understanding."

After she put on her gloves, she tucked her beret under one arm and took his elbow with the other "I'm ready when you are. Merci beaucoup for your escort."

As they stepped outside, Sophie saw Josef was already busy greeting guests. He looked so handsome in all black…but the long mourning coat he was wearing was the sexiest thing she could've ever imagined. Seeing his svelte physique standing there looking as he did made her feel like she was walking straight into a scene of a vintage French film. It made her lust after him more…even under the circumstances.

The scene at noon was absolutely stunning in its picturesque setting. There must've been at least two hundred people huddled around in attendance waiting patiently on the beautiful dark pasture in silence. The *Boys Club* had special priority and a select few had already taken their places as the chosen pall bearers. *The Club's* overflow occupied the first row of the limited seating, leaving Sophie and Michel seated just behind in the second.

For some reason when Sophie was just sitting down, she happened to notice a brief scuffle happening behind one of the big trees at the beginning of the service. Whoever it was, they'd been whisked away so fast it hadn't made anything more than a tiny blip in the radar where the service was concerned. It seems everyone but Josef and Sophie had noticed the identity of the man who'd been swept away in record speed.

The service began without issue. It was a beautiful ceremony held on a crisp, clear and sunny December day. The air was feather weight and blew softly. There wasn't a dry eye to be seen...anywhere. It was a somber and harmonious coming together of all sorts imaginable. The high brow mixing with the low brow, just as Litty would've expected. After all, she'd always wanted to be considered the 'local' people's princess. It was obvious by the turn out ...she'd managed to achieve her goal. She'd long been a beloved and respected local figure and one to be honored.

However, little did they know how well she'd hidden her manipulative game behind the scenes for all those years. She'd been pulling her own set of reins without anyone knowing. She was anything but a kind soul, but there they were...all commiserating together, no matter what their true (or hidden) feelings were about her. They'd all come out to show themselves and give their collaborative support 'celebrating' the life of Laetitia. They felt it their duty to acknowledge a golden era was now changing guard. Her death could have been a very good and convenient thing for many of them, but shushh, just like life was in the village, the carpet would need to be lifted again. Remember those old roots? Sometimes a bit of a major pruning is needed to refresh. Either way you cut it...the hypocrisy ran wild and it was a huge turn out.

Once Litty had been secured and settled into her final resting place, the mood immediately changed and became upbeat. The remaining Villagers, who loved any invitation to a free party, began to drink and sing together until the midnight oil burned. They kept the party rockin' outside behind the car barn with a bonfire in great remembrance and celebration of the Matriarch...I guess.

The Boys Club however, had moved inside and had begun rallying around the dining room table and filtering about in the 'great' room just as they'd done at Grandfather's service. With a house that was normally placid in temperament, cigars and loud mouth stories now prevailed. There were laughs and embraces given from those whom had not seen one another in months or in some cases, years.

Josef noticed Sophie enter the living room but in typical sickening Macho style...he waited. He let her be the one to maneuver the crowd. He patiently watched her navigate through the group of strangers to be next to him. Finally...once able to be standing in front of him he leaned forward and grabbed her hips slowly pulling her towards him where all could see. Only then did he begin introducing her to his immediate circle like she was his trophy. The boy was home and demonstrating behavior that was new to Sophie. She reciprocated by playing her flirtatious game, pretending not to love his power demonstration. Of course secretly she adored being 'his' and on display for all to see.

"This everyone...is my dear love Sophie. She's swept me off my feet gentlemen," Josef bragged. He stood standing with his shoulders back, gloating proudly at his prize. I guess she actually was just that...his prize. He'd gone to great lengths to have her right where he wanted.

She leaned close and surprisingly whispered in his ear..."This might be your time to shine, but I'm wet and I'm going to make you scream later."

With having given him that sexy warning, she excused herself like 'the perfect lady'. She left him with that hungry thought and made her way over to the buffet credenza where she met a man who she found to be very interesting. He was from Zurich.

"So you must be Sophie, the beautiful American we've heard so much about" the gentleman said, welcoming her to engage in further conversation. The two found themselves standing side by side with empty plates observing what was of interest on the exquisite buffet that lay in front of them.

Sophie only responded with a smile and replied, "it was a beautiful service today. Did you know Laetitia well?"

"Oh yes, my dear...Everyone here did. She was a force to be reckoned with" he replied with a smile and a look of endearing remembrance on his face. His wrinkled profile was like seeing a seasoned road map that had traveled wisely.

"She was the only one in the world that could've tamed the old man. Sr. was such a dynamo...and she?... She was *his* lady. Laetitia was such an elegant and generous woman, but did she have a wicked sense of humor! I can remember all the times spent together right here in this very room laughing the night away. She'll be sorely missed, yet I'm comforted knowing she's back with Josef Sr. now. They're finally together again and that's why we're all here. We are celebrating her life and sending her a farewell back to him. We've all had beautiful memories in this place."

Sophie was dumbfounded hearing a man speak so eloquently about someone else's love. She was beginning to understand what Litty's passing meant to this group. It wasn't really about her in recent years, but the long and colorful history she'd shared with all of them. Between Josef Sr., Michel and Laetitia...that threesome of a dream team did quite a bit for the wine industry overall. Back then those three were the first pioneers to make a name for themselves in the region.

"My name is Gus by the way. Have you by chance met Pierre?" he said greeting another gentleman who had just come up from behind. Gus gave Pierre a familiar kiss on both cheeks with a laugh seeing he was also holding an empty plate. Pierre began standing next to the two in front of the buffet when Gus finally made his decision and reached over placing a few small slices of toast piled high with foie gras onto his empty plate. He looked back saying "Bon Appetit" before moving on to mingle with the others in the great room.

"So you must be Sophie, the beautiful American we've heard so much about."

Sophie wanted to roll her eyes, but kept smiling at *The Clubs'* almost pre-recorded intro. She'd better make up her mind on some food pronto and move locations or she'd be stuck being the American welcoming committee all afternoon.

Sophie only responded with a nod and replied, "it was a lovely service today. Did you know Laetitia well?"

"Oh yes my dear, everyone in this place did. I thought she was the toughest 'Ol Broad I'd ever met...but the old man loved her like no other. She was the woman behind the man and Sr. was someone very important to us all. That's why we always honored her...it was actually for him. At least they are back together now. Rest in Peace Laetitia, that's my final blessing. We're come here to close this chapter and to give your Josef our continued support," Pierre concluded...while placing a few plump lamb chops on his plate. He turned around placing a kiss on both cheeks of the man standing behind him. It was Josef.

"Well...I see that you've met a few of the Boys," he said smirking as he watched Pierre jovially network his way to the living (great) room. "I'm not extremely hungry are you? Why don't we meet in the hallway powder room... say...in five? Would that satisfy your appetite my little darling?" he said, nonchalantly placing a few slices of duck breast on his empty plate.

He slowly reached in front of Sophie, grazing her breasts ever so lightly to grab a ladle and cover his slices with a creamy green peppercorn sauce. He turned and looked deep into her wanting eyes and without emotion picked up a dripping piece of duck, opened his gorgeous mouth, and seductively plunked it in. To continue the foreplay, he slowly licked his fingers, never leaving her gaze.

Sophie seeing his sexy culinary demonstration retaliated by placing a few chicken slices on her plate. She calmly reached over in front of him flaunting her beautiful plump cleavage, and began smearing a creamy béchamel sauce all over her dark meat. They stood and ate with their fingers in the most erotic way possible. No words were spoken, just a little moan of satisfaction here and there. I believe it must be called: sex on a plate. (and then some) Literally...it was.

Having all fingers licked and tantalizingly sucked

clean, they went their separate ways knowing full well they'd be seeing one another in approximately 2 minutes. It'd become a subtle race of sorts to the powder room. They each made their way seem nonchalant so no one would notice.(really?) Nothing should be hurried and obvious... being it was a funeral and all.

Josef opened the door to the powder room and dipped in quickly. He felt deceitfully cocky anticipating their rendezvous, having been cleverly sneaky in his approach. He didn't make a sound closing and securing the door behind him. He smiled seeing Sophie already in place, waiting. Thank God it was Josef and not someone else opening the door because Sophie had already slipped off her dress and was leaning back on the edge of the closed toilet seat with her knees spread wide.

Seeing her ready to receive him...sitting in only her boots, stockings and that stunning black garter belt ensemble...he loudly whispered, "Mon Dieu Sophie, you look like my hot little dark angel girl...just waiting for me." She loved hearing him comment on her look and position... appreciating every bit of her hot sexy self.

"Is this what you want?" he said moving his hand over his zipper and stroking the large bulge that was about to pop out of the top of his jeans. "I'm glad I saved room for dessert" he whispered quietly falling to his knees with his mouth already moving in to kiss her velvety soft jewel box.

"Oui Josef...you're exactly what I want. Can't you see that I'm lusting after every bit of you right now?" she whimpered softly while licking her lips ever so slowly. She moistened her index finger and with a gentle tease, stroked her erect nipple through the sheer black lace of her fancy tiny bra. Sophie was determined to be the one to command his movements and performance this time around.

She instructed him just how she wanted it. She looked at him square on, deep into his willing eyes (this time) and grabbed the back of his head cupping it from behind.

"I want it slow Josef. I want it sexy my love, and I want it tender. I want it hot and your magic wand hard.

Quietly intense, got it?"

For Christ's sake the little prick was so aroused by her dominate behavior, he didn't know what to do...thank God he was able to keep it up.

In that particular moment, he wasn't the only cocky one in this dynamic duo. By this time, they both knew she'd prevailed in demonstrating her successful and flirtatious aura of confidence with everyone in *The Club.* Therefore, Josef knew he had reason to please her and understood that every other man there would've loved the chance to be exactly where he was at that very moment.

She was the new talk of *The Club* after having discretely worked her way around the room. She'd put on such a brilliant and hot performance during the ceremony meeting and greeting the global network who were present...she thought it was as easy as taking candy from Horny male sophomores. She'd taken advantage of not only looking fabulous in her LBD, but of her control and her command of the audience. And wow had she played it accordingly. She wanted Josef to know he owed her..., knowing she'd made him proud. If only for a little moment of self indulgence...she was going to get paid for it.

Given the commands, he loved being her sexual servant. Tasting her, stroking her, kissing her...all on her time, as directed. The thought of it made him so stiff he could hardly stand it. It made him want to go so deep, fuck her hard just like he wanted, but no...she took her time and made him wait. She prolonged it all not giving him his pleasure, that is...until she was ready. She took advantage knowing full well he was being missed and searched out by others attending the celebration in the next room. That only made it more exciting. She was sure one of the people looking for him...most definitely had to be that bitch housekeeper who probably wanted to fuck him herself.

After being sucked, licked and fingered in every way possible she finally allowed him to take his own pleasure. She opened her legs wider...but his shaft went in so deep... it was enough for her to give way to that unique and over the top orgasm, that only he could give her. He knew exactly where to find her sweet spot and was always able to make a bullseye every damn time. She didn't bother to wait for him so when his time came, she felt justified looking down on him explode in her while still on his knees.

That was a complete mind twist for our little macho…So after he mustered up the strength to stand, he made his way to the sink to rinse his face and privates. Then the selfish prick casually announced, "Have a good rest of the evening Sophie. You looked beautiful today. In fact, you were absolutely captivating and loved by all. I'll see you in the morning. I need to be with *The Boys* tonight" …and there he went. How's that for love 'em and leave 'em…but in all truth, she'd been the one that had screwed him royally and rest assured, he'd never forget it.

Thankful he'd locked the door on his exit, she continued to sit in a vulnerable position and a state of feeling limp…God was she satisfied. What a fabulous little meeting that had been…It would definitely be enough to satisfy her for the night. She was more than happy to escape upstairs, not regretting missing one more introduction to another character in *The Boys Club*. She was purring on the inside ready to retire into her quiet self for the night. She smiled to herself and only left the powder room when she'd become good and ready.

The early morning had come and gone. It was almost eleven by the time Fiona knocked on the door. "Hello Sophie. Allo? Bonjour…Josef wanted me to let you know he'd like you to meet him in the car hanger at noon. Will you be able to do that?"

"Oh okay…tell him I'll see him there," she responded just loud enough for Fiona to hear while standing on the other side of the door in the hallway.

The bedding and her dreams had been so luxurious that she'd fallen in and out of consciousness since leaving Josef in the powder room. Having a bit of time before her rendezvous, she hopped up and opened the draperies then quickly jumped back in bed to feel the daylight bring an awakening to both she and the room. It was cold and she snuggled down deep in her fluffy feather comforter until there was another knock on her door. It was that annoying Fiona again.

"You must've accidentally left your cell phone downstairs last night. I was surprised to hear it ringing and thought you might need it. I'll leave it here on the floor just outside your door" she said returning downstairs.

Once Sophie figured Fiona was out of sight she leapt out of bed, opened the door and quickly grabbed her phone. She closed the door as fast as she'd opened it then slid back into her warm cozy den of comfort. It all felt so delicious next to her skin.

She was given an awakening shock that ziplined her back into her other reality…A surprise I might say, that she'd not been expecting. Seeing Gayle's name pop up on the phone's ID screen made her quickly realize she'd been lost in an oblivious haze of 'all things Josef'. She'd not given a serious thought about her business or life in the States since arriving back in France for Laetitia's service. She'd become so wrapped up in Josef's world, it was her other life in the States that'd become the one seeming *foreign*.

Sophie figured she'd return the call later that evening when it became morning in California. That would give her some prolonged time to think of an excuse, a somewhat valid and believable justification for her to have been totally negligent regarding her business and life in the States. Her temporary MIA status would need some explaining, but she'd think about that later.

She placed her phone on the nightstand and conveniently snapped back into her current and only priority…"Time to get ready for my date" she sang happily throwing back the thick layers of beautiful billowy soft textures. She made a quick run to the bathroom to begin her beauty routine in preparation for her outing.

When Sophie felt she looked like qualified date material, she walked downstairs only to find a surprisingly clean house. There was not one noticeable remnant, not even a whisper of evidence left from the prior days activities. No cigar smell, no dirty plates, not one darn speck of dust visible...only fluffed sofa cushions and an impeccably prepared fireplace. The wood was stacked so finely, we already know that simply one lit match would start a perfectly balanced flame. Sophie saw the spit shine surroundings and smirked to herself, "The Bitch certainly must've been a girl scout in the UK. Is there anything this witch can't do?"

On her stroll back to the squeaky clean kitchen she noticed the door to Litty's suite had been left open. Sophie couldn't help but to feed her curiosity...So given the open door invitation, she took the liberty and walked into what'd been Laetitia's private world. She'd never been in her personal space before, but could only imagine it remained just as she'd always kept it. It was beautiful in it's simple elegance, perfectly tidy and well organized, just as she'd been.

All the windows had been left open, letting the fresh December air enter and swirl around to freshen the room. Laetitia's energy was no longer present, but strangely enough her scent still lingered. There had always been one expensive self indulgence she'd allowed herself...wearing her favorite perfume, 'Caleche' by Hermes. Through the many years of its use it had permeated every inch of her suite. Amazingly enough her scent remained so strong, it seemed as if she were still there. It was a bit eerie...even if it was a lovely fragrance...

Sophie walked a bit further into her actual bedroom and saw that her closet had been emptied. All of her clothes had been neatly folded and placed in a large box. She soon realized that's where the concentration of her flowery scent was coming from. Sitting on top of the open box was what Sophie figured to have been Litty's favorite Holiday sweater. It was a burgundy cashmere cardigan with black sequin floral appliqués stitched on both shoulders.

Sophie found herself in a trance staring intensely at the sweater...when suddenly she felt a wave of panic come over her. For some strange reason she felt a bit spooked...

and seriously, she couldn't get out of that room fast enough. She didn't know why she'd had such a curiosity to have been drawn in to her space to begin with. But just as she was making a dash out of Laetitia's suite for the kitchen, she was met and confronted by who other…than the British twat.

"What were you doing in Laetitia's room!" she demanded abruptly with a snarky condescending twist. (She sounded somewhere in between a prison guard and an over protective daughter)

"I was just looking" Sophie replied, feeling completely taken aback by Fiona's aggressive behavior. She thought it incredibly inappropriate that she'd have the nerve to be so insulant and interrogate her like that. Especially using such a demanding and authoritative tone…who did she think she was anyway. Where did she get off!

Fiona had gleefully taken that moment to reprimand Sophie and make her feel like she'd been caught doing something covert and sneaky. Fiona relished those times when she was able to make Sophie feel alienated and obviously had seen this as a golden opportunity to do so.

But Sophie wasn't about to wait around and listen to any more of Fiona's irritating bullshit…She left the bitch in mid sentence and blew by her on her hasty way out to the car barn to find Josef.

She was hoping to find a bit of sympathy and some comforting words to calm her from that unnerving encounter. She was feeling so perturbed, wanting to vent her frustrations, and Thank God…there he was. He was busy tinkering around with something under the hood of the Range Rover when he looked up and said, "Hi sleepy girl. I hope you had a comfortable night chérie. Seems as if you did, you look so pretty and well rested."

She pleasantly smiled adoringly. His words might've put the fire out but she was still smoldering.

"Josef the strangest thing just happened…I wandered into Laetitia's room to take a peek and when I was coming out, I was rudely confronted and actually interrogated by Fiona. She made me feel like a criminal for having been in Laetitia's room. She even had the nerve to question my motives."

"Well???...Why in the world did you think you were welcome in her private space to begin with?" he snapped. He did so in such a tone, it was surprisingly harsh and completely unexpected.

Sophie thought it bizarre, instead of coming to her defense, he questioned her intentions as Fiona had. Why would he be siding with her? Quite honestly, he had such a convenient way of always giving that girl the home-town advantage. The benefit of the doubt lets just say, You know...the upper edge as it were. It made Sophie feel like Josef and Fiona had a silent code between them, especially when it came to *'their'* sweet little Laetitia. She hated that... it was *really* starting to chip away at her.

Behind Josef's back, Fiona always attempted to do or say something to make Sophie feel awkward, like she was definitely out of place being there. So it seemed equally as strange when Sophie would try to explain those particulars to Josef and how protective he'd become over Fiona. It's like he'd always defend her actions while telling Sophie she was just being jealous and insecure.

"Oh Fiona would never do that Sophie...she's not like that. It's in your active imagination is all..."

He somehow would turn the tables and place the guilt back on Sophie, always doing it in a sly way...

Josef being such a clever dog changed the subject and tempo quickly. "Sophie my darling...Fiona simply has been helping pack up Litty's closet this morning and I'm sure you must've startled her is all."

Then the fucker made his best effort to console her with more of his bull——."If you wouldn't mind, I'd like you to go with me to the shelter to make a drop off. Then make a stop by at the Retirement Home to take a few special items for her friends who still remain there. There's one friend in particular who was too frail to come yesterday. I'd like to visit her for a moment. I know some of Litty's past peer group would enjoy some of her older books. Same generation you know? Sound okay with you?"

He'd changed his tune back to a loving tone, like he was expecting Sophie not only to agree to the task, but to praise the prick for his thoughtfulness. Men.

"Of course Josef" Sophie said feeling silly for allowing Fiona to get the best of her. (like Josef wasn't?)

"I think that's a lovely thing to do. You knew Laetitia better than anyone and I'm sure she'd appreciate you doing this" she said lovingly while getting into the Rover. The macho smiled to himself in the rear view mirror like he'd just chewed a piece of sweet salt water taffy.

They drove to the back of Litty's suite and stopped. Josef walked in through the unlocked back door that led directly into her bedroom and retrieved the box. He returned placing it on the backseat behind the drivers side and got in, casually shifting the car into D. They made their way off the Estate and onto the main road when Josef abruptly pulled the car over and stopped. Then he surprisingly demanded gruffly, "Did you know Bruce was going to be at the service yesterday?" Sophie looked at him like a deer caught in the headlights...

"What? No! Of course not."

"Really?" Josef questioned, inquiring with both eyebrows raised and having rage reflected in his eyes. She couldn't believe he was disputing her honesty like that.

"What? You don't believe me? I promise I didn't...I had no idea he was even in France. Seriously...was he really there? I didn't see him if he was" she said feeling like a witness being persecuted on trial. "Why are you questioning me like this Josef? Of course I didn't know he was going to show up. Like I said, I had no idea he was even in the country!"

"I told you Sophie...if you want to be with me, there can be no contact with Bruce or his pathetic family ever again. You agreed to that. Should you have decided otherwise, I want you to tell me this very minute!"...his temperament ramping up even higher.

"Josef, I love you. My life with Bruce is over...You know that! What in the world would make you think he was there yesterday?" she questioned sounding truly concerned. She was making her best attempt to de-escalate the situation and 'lower the temperature'…but he began yelling …ramping the volume up even higher…

"It's because some of *The Club* saw him sneaking around and hiding behind a tree, that's why. They dragged him off before he could disrupt the service Thank God! Do you swear you didn't see him or notice any of the commotion?"

A light went off and Sophie put two and two together. That must've been what she'd seen at the beginning of the service. She was more than curious now. Was this jealousy or perhaps something else that Josef was sifting through from his past? Bruce said there'd been a 'history' between their families stemming way back…so what was it? She had no idea but with this continued display of deep hatred for Bruce and his family, it made Sophie begin to wonder what the 'history' *really* could've been.

"Oh…I don't think he would've done anything to disrupt the service Josef" Sophie said calmly, using an even keel to her voice in the attempt to sound neutral. Obviously, that didn't sit right with the Golden Boy…For the first time ever, Josef spewed off a tirade like you wouldn't believe.

"How in the hell would you know that! I don't trust that bastard. He's just as bad as his father. That entire family is crazy and can't be trusted under any circumstances. They're full of lies," Josef snarled looking directly at Sophie like she could give him some pacifying answer to settle his angst.

"I don't know what you want me to say Josef. I noticed some type of scurry yesterday, but I had no idea it could've been Bruce of all people. I'm curious…Why in the world would he have wanted to be there in the first place?"

"Oh don't be so stupid my dear. He was there to spit on Litty's grave and to see you. He wanted to make a mockery out of her, me, and my family…why else would he have been there?" Josef hissed, still scoffing and speaking down to her.

"Please don't be upset at me Josef. This is something I really don't know anything about. It just seems uncharacteristic of my ex-boyfriend to turn up like that is all I'm saying. I'm not sticking up for him, if that's what you're insinuating and are so upset about."

She'd finally had enough of his raging behavior towards Bruce. She didn't understand the root of it all…but it was certainly getting old hearing him rag on and on about him at any given opportunity. It'd become time for Sophie to be the one to turn up the volume…

"If you have such a big underlying problem with him…one that you're not telling me about Cough it up! Tell me! When I met you I had no idea you even knew one another for Christ's sake! What the hell is it?" she screamed back at him.

This was enough of a retort to make Josef settle back down into a cooler zone. He knew he needed to compose himself. He couldn't afford to let this topic of conversation accelerate any further and get more out of hand. He'd never be ready to admit the real reason why he hated Bruce and his family so much. Sadly the devastating embarrassment and confusion he'd felt as a kid had lingered its way into his adulthood. By all means he didn't want to show any sign of weakness or vulnerability to anyone, especially not to Sophie.

Now that Litty had put it in writing confirming his suspicions to be true…all of the humiliation he'd felt due to Bruce's Father's behavior made him more determined to satisfy his need to eliminate Bruce and his 'no good' family. He must make that happen before any leak of their 'history' could be revealed. Under all circumstances…he didn't want to give Sophie an inkling for suspicion regarding the devious plan he'd put into motion with Hervé.

Obviously he was prepared to go to extreme measures to protect his family's reputation, but his hostility had now far outreached his reasoning. His rekindled hatred also encompassed that gossipy bastard of a Father of his who had literally ruined his family.

With Litty having validated his 'nightmare' to have been true, the bile that he'd regurgitated from his childhood was again front and center. There was no turning back…that entire family needed to be eliminated from the village. Now it would be Golden Boy that would *see to it.*

"You're right Sophie. I lost my head for a moment. It must've been the immense pressure from the service yesterday. I'm sorry sweetheart. Forgive me" he said apologetically, reigning back his aggressive behavior…and her of course.

Not another word was spoken until arriving at the retirement home. Luckily, there was a spattering of tenants that were still gathered in the communal dining room. They were so happy to see Josef, you would have thought Santa himself had dropped down the chimney. He knew most guests by their surnames and addressed each and every one with such respect.

He'd chosen one book in particular and grabbed it along with the 'special' sweater for a woman sitting alone next to the window. No words were exchanged only a familiar kiss on both cheeks as Josef laid the sweater and book down in her lap. She knew the meaning of the gesture. Litty was gone…She would've been proud to know Josef had followed through remembering her dearest friends as he had. Taking the time to leave a token of farewell showed that Josef actually did have a sentimental side to him. Sophie was charmed by his display of humility.

"How did you know so many people there?" Sophie asked as they were getting back in the Rover.

"Because Litty used to take me with her to visit on special occasions. We came many times when I was young, usually for someone's birthday, or a major Holiday kind of thing. That's the reason I have a relationship with most who remain…A lot of the seniors don't have any family to speak of, so that place is their family…and I guess I'm considered a part of it. They cherish those of us on the outside who still remember them" Josef said…becoming quiet…and reminiscent.

It was another heart felt reminder of Litty. As they were on their way heading back to the *Château*, Josef suddenly made an unexpected detour, taking an unfamiliar road.

"I have a brilliant idea! Why don't we go to Megève for a little impromptu ski holiday? Wouldn't that be fun? Getting away might be good for us. Having a break from it all could give us a little bit of private time to reconnect. What do you think? Time for a bit of make up sex for lost time?" he questioned leaning over and placing his hand on her inner thigh. His devilish grin made her giggle.

"Sounds fantastic. I've never been, but I hear it's the ultimate playground in the French Alps. I love the slopes but what do we do about ski clothes? As for the make-up sex... I'm sure we can figure that out once we get there Mr. Decour" she gushed, displaying an equally devilish grin. He had a way of luring her back into his web at any moment he chose. It was...disgusting.

"I'm sure the local shops will have everything we need. Let's leave the Rover at the airport in Bergerac and go for a little adventure shall we?"

Sophie couldn't help but let out a little yelp of excitement. She was so busy being seduced by the thought of a glitzy unexpected ski trip, she'd forgotten all about needing to call Gayle. She was back to being lost in her *life with Josef...*not thinking about anything or anyone else. She loved being with him and was so enamored...it seemed like he'd put her in some kind of a hypnotic trance.

The little dream team flew from Bergerac to Geneva. Once there, Josef rented an identical Rover to the one he owned and they set off making their way to the ultimate ski village setting. The picturesque and super glam winter escape of choice for the moneyed jet setters was no disappointment. Skaters filled the outdoor ice rink in the center of town and the bells from the horse drawn sleighs being pulled throughout the village spread the sweet sound of a tinker-bell rhythm. The entire place was a dreamy winter wonderland. Wooden Chalets dotted the mountains like quaint little ornate gingerbread bites…In fact the entire environment shimmered…just like it were a gorgeous twinkly Christmas card.

They didn't stop in the town center, but continued on to a quiet location at the far side of the village and half way up the mountain. Josef pulled up to the front entrance of the exquisite Le Chalet Zannier Hôtel and stopped at the front entrance.

"I hear the spa is out of this world here," he said putting the car in P as the valets opened each of their doors simultaneously. A Hôtel of this standard was a fine oiled machine. Nothing happened by accident. The quality of excellent service was again all choreographed perfectly, just as it'd been in Paris and New York. Now she understood, this type of service actually was his 'standard'.

"How on earth do you think we'll get a room without a reservation at this time of year?" Sophie whispered holding on to his arm as they walked up the heated staircase.

"Easy" Josef whispered back…"I'll just tell them Gus invited us. You know…you met him at the service. He's part owner of this beauty and they always keep a few rooms vacant for VIP's."

In case some of you don't know, Le Chalet Zannier is one of the most luxurious Hôtels in the Alps. The views from the Hôtel are absolutely breathtaking…and how could they not be with Mont Blanc sitting smack dab in front of you. The refined yet rustic furnishings in the Hôtel were all top of the line and definitely 'Minimal Mountain Chic'. It was all so classy and understated, it felt similar to a 5 star senior girl scout camp on design enhancers. Sophie couldn't figure out if she was in a fabulous night club or sexy mountain retreat.

Josef dropped Gustav's name and just like he said, 'boom'…they were checked in and immediately escorted to a beautiful suite upstairs. The 'room' was a two story loft type space with one entire wall being made up of clear windows and tall sliding doors that opened up onto a large wooden deck. What a frickin' *room*…it had stunning mountain views especially when it came to the black diamond runs that went directly beneath their room. (I have never had a 'room' like that in my life…saa weet)

The massive fireplace had a beautiful inlaid river rock facade and had just been lit as they entered the room. The cherry on top to the suite was they arrived by way of their own private elevator. When the bellman finally left the room after explaining the long list of amenities…Sophie ran and took a diving leap onto the overstuffed king sized bed. It was sheer luxury piled high with everything she loved most that was furry, comfy, and feathery.

"Come here and try this heavenly nest out with me! I think this will definitely serve our purpose" she said playfully pitching the many small soft billowy pillows at him one by one.

"Don't get too comfy my dear, I've reserved the spa and the masseuses should be ready and waiting" he said, walking back in from the deck releasing each pillow to the floor as he caught them.

"Oh a massage? Dreamy thinking my dear…Do they do waxing by chance?" she said with a small laugh. (All joking aside…she probably could've used a little touch up) "I'll grab a couple of robes from the bathroom to take down."

"No…Don't bother sweetheart, they'll have everything already prepared he said…clearly already knowing the program. He kissed her lips and pushed the S button for their direct ride down. The elevator door opened quickly…delivering them in to a completely different world.

It was a scented spa room which encompassed a beautiful and wider than normal lap pool in the center of the room. It was a bit freaky landing in such an unexpected environment. The pool had a light floating foggy steam layer lingering above the scented water. On one side of the pool stood two imposing massage tables. They weren't the foldable kind that traveling professionals use…These baby's were solid slabs of heavy French Oak. They definitely weren't going anywhere. There they stood lined up like two obedient soldiers just waiting for their guests to mount.

Each horizontal platform had an inviting padded cotton twill cushion top. The entire place felt a little abstract in it's hidden dreamlike perfection. It was warm, sultry and felt a bit erotic. To experience such a place that felt delightfully soothing yet a bit arousing, bottom line…it was *steamy hot.*

When they'd entered the quiet zen type space they were greeted with polite but aggressive hand signals directing them to their independent changing rooms. Being welcomed with synchronized instructions' seemed in complete contrast to the tranquil atmosphere. It was like watching a pissed off flight attendant demonstrate for the 1000th time where the emergency exits were. Anyway, with that type of surprising demonstration, it was enough to make them do as they were told without hesitation. They both quickly changed and returned to the pool area… wearing matching robes. They smiled and let out a tiny giggle as they gave one another a mutual nod of satisfying approval. What they really wanted to do was laugh out loud and face fuck right then and there.

It was seeing one another wearing identical robes that reminded them of Gramercy Park. The masseuses made it quite clear there was no time to dawdle and trade playful intimacies…they were straight down to business.

The love doves were immediately instructed with authority to lay face down, each on their designated massage tables. *And believe it or not, there were small step stools for each client to use to mount the behemoths safely, and guess what?…they both needed one.*

The atmosphere was so dreamy and seductive, our love birds were totally into the program. They loved this game, it felt like a new adventure. The second their bodies hit the finely woven pique pads and the rubbing began, they were a bit more humble. Josef had a female masseur and Sophie a male. Once they began with their massages everything was then understood.

It was Heavenly bliss. Both had their massage movements given in unison. Every relaxing long stroke came slathered with deliciously scented essential oil. When it was time to turn over and lay on their backs, they changed therapists. The oil flowed and so did another hour until the room was silent. The only faint sound was the door latch being closed behind the masseuses as they quietly made their discreet exit. Sophie was so relaxed, she'd nodded off during her rub down.

But…was she ever brought back to her immediate surroundings when she opened her eyes and surprisingly found Josef stretched out hovering above her like a stiff lightening rod. He was suspended in air and looked as if he was about to do a push up. His body was so strong, and as for his magic wand? Well, let's just say…The dude was pumped, ready and very focused on taking a plunge.

"Oh oui Josef…I'll always be ready for you," she said opening her legs wide for his entry. She kept her elbows bent above her head and both hands gripped to the top edge of the table. He was so deliberate, he pushed himself up and down slowly only allowing his chest to barely graze hers. That made her nipples erect. He came down slowly and kissed her like his tongue was telling her some of his mysterious secrets. She couldn't get enough. Then when he nestled himself so deep inside, she could only lay limp receiving him. Their body oils kept an easy glide going.

That's when he found his perfect position and suddenly let go with a premature orgasm…He slid his oily body down to be resting on top of hers when she began rubbing his back and loving their closeness. His skin was so soft, it had just enough humidity and oil to let her fingers glide with every sexy touch. Out of his selfish appreciation, he filled her mouth with little sweet kisses before pushing himself up again…saying, "I'll need to satisfy you a bit later."

Then, unexpectedly he hopped off of her like a fit gymnast dismounting the Vault. It left her wanting more. That's when he ran over and jumped in the pool.

"Get in here! Let's have a swim!" he enthusiastically said, lightly splashing and playing around like a teenager. He began flicking water at her with his fingertips…"Come on!" he demanded flirtatiously before dunking himself into a hand-stand. He was always doing something boyishly charming and unexpected. She loved how much fun he was to be with.

She exhaled deeply then leapt off the table and jumped in with a splash. They continued to frolic for another ten minutes until both had become shriveled and thirsty.

They happily laughed putting on their matching robes again and made their way back up to their Suite in their private lift. Their clothes that had been left in the changing rooms had already been sent up and were conveniently hanging in their closet freshly pressed of course. As they re-entered their suite, they found a bottle of the finest from Gustav's personal stash waiting on the coffee table in front of the fire place. Sophie was so hopelessly in awe of her gorgeous Frenchman from the Périgord…He really did know how to live. She found every oz of him to be delicious. She wanted him for good…and as far as The lifestyle was concerned?…It wasn't so bad either.

Their trip could not have been more romantic, nomadic and seemingly spontaneous. She had no idea his 'impromptu' adventure was merely a decoy of sorts, but if he'd wanted to get out of town to hide for a few days?… What an incredible choice of places to take refuge. A Seven Star mountain resort with gourmet dinners, cocktails galore, open air hot tubs and night skiing under the stars. It'd been a dream excursion…experiencing the French Alps at its absolute finest…In fact much more than Sophie could've ever imagined, but the spa *'treatment'* had been exceptional, it gave her more than a purring smile every time she thought about it.

When they finally came back up for air, their five day escapade had been enough to cement their intimate feelings again. Their little jaunt had been similar to one of those juvenile acts of playing hooky. Ditching ones responsibilities for the perfect escape offered a bit of fresh air. A little guilty pleasure lets just say. The kind that all of us no matter who you are, wish we could experience more ot. You know…that brief period where you're escaping your 'normal' life…and living it up in your fantasy alternative. It just doesn't happen often enough.

Thank goodness during their trip they'd turned off their phones and gone into hiding for just long enough to get themselves centered again. They were back in their groove and thinking only of themselves. Actually, they had returned from being lost in their own world and were making their way back to their future.

*

Chapter Neuf

Big changes would be made with their return to the *Château*. Nightly, they'd now be sleeping together on 'The Altar'. The first morning back felt so relaxing and natural. The trip to Megève was exactly what they'd needed. That is…until they were awaken by a loud intrusive and continuous banging on the front door. Whoever it was…they Would NOT stop.

This invasion of privacy gave Josef a big slap of his new reality. He suddenly realized there was no longer anyone in the *Château* to do the everyday things like simply answering the door. With Litty gone, the things he'd always taken for granted were now blatantly apparent. Having Sophie next to him gave him comfort, but his new found understanding of it all was really just beginning to sink in. He felt the immense responsibility of the Estate building up and the pressure once again begin to bubble inside like a volcano on the verge of erupting. The pounding on the front door continued…making it obvious some irritating and tenacious person was not giving up nor going away. It made Josef…snap.

"Who in the HELL is at my door causing all this racket!" he yelled angrily throwing back the covers. "Where the hell is Fiona?" he huffed pulling on his jeans and a thick cashmere sweater.

He made his way hastily down the stairs with record speed and flung one of the two front doors open. He spewed gruffly "Yes! What is it!! What do you want banging on my door like this?!"

The two men standing on the cement landing in front were seriously not amused by the lack of a courteous welcome given by this seemingly disheveled man who'd opened the door barefoot. Even Josef had bed head on occasion and…it was certainly proving to be one of those days.

"Josef Decour...I presume?"

"Oui, that's right. Suis Josef Decour" he replied with a cocky demeanor. "Who's asking?"

"My name is Nicolas Tanton. I'm an inspector with Allionz Insurance Co. and this is Officer Cabaux. We're investigating a home fire in the Village. Consider yourself served," said the officer handing Josef an envelope.

Without another word they turned their backs and each walked to their perspective cars then left with a scurry. One leaving a large high flying dust trail behind, and the other with pebbles being spun out everywhere. Their exit moves were obviously intentional and made to give a dramatic effect to their departure. Their aggressive interchange and equally disturbing exits had definitely gotten Josef's attention.

He closed the door behind him with high anxiety and made a B-line back to the kitchen. When he reached the table he anxiously sat down and ripped open the large manilla envelope to read its contents. It demanded he go to the Courthouse in Bergerac the following morning at 9am. There were investigations pending: One from the Police Dept., and the second from an aggressive insurance company. It didn't give specifics, only the address... *'Impasse de Bontier'*.

Josef had just dropped the paper as Sophie was walking into the kitchen. She saw the numb and frozen look on his face, then...seeing the paper lying on the table she knew it must contain some shocking news. She picked it up and began making an earnest attempt to read and decipher it as best as she could.

"Josef...What is this?" she asked impatiently. She was worried..."Who was that at the door?"

She began to read as only an American who didn't quite fully grasp the French language would. She stopped cold when she recognized the large script with the word *Summons* written at the top. That scary international word she most certainly understood. Then she was shocked to see the familiar address.

"Impasse de Bontier, Oh my GOD!" she shrieked releasing the paper for it to surf back down to the table like a slow moving kite. She nervously sat down next to her man.

Josef snapped out of his *lost look* and stood up. "I'm going to the village to find out what's happened. I'll be home by noon. Don't worry, I'll make it quick" he said making his way upstairs to finish getting dressed.

As Sophie was just finishing making the morning coffee…she heard the faint sound of the front door closing. He'd already gone.

When Josef arrived in the Village, he immediately went to Bar Central to hear the *local* news. All the patrons saw him coming, but not one person looked up when he entered.

He scanned around the room for any familiar faces and couldn't believe that not one person acknowledged him. That included an old schoolmate named Virginie who was sitting in a booth in the far back. He hadn't seen her in years but he was so blinded by the lack of recognition, that seeing her was so out of context it passed right over his head like he didn't even notice. It was all a blur…Was this behavior from the villagers intentional? He felt a strange sense of rejection radiating from them for the first time in his life. They all just continued looking down and murmuring under their breath, all except for Dominique, the owner. She quickly zipped down to the end of the bar closest to the front door to greet him.

"Josef where have you been? Everyone from the Winery amongst every other type of creature in the world has been in here looking for you! What the hell's going on? You disappeared after Litty's service and no one knew where to find you. It's been crazy around here. There was a big fire in the Village the day after her service. The Douglas' place on Impasse de Bontier burnt to the ground! Only the stone walls remain, can you imagine? The most shocking thing about it was that Gene and his wife were inside and unable to get out. They even found his walker melted at the bottom of the stairs! Oh those poor people, they were trapped upstairs and perished in the fire. The house went up like a tinderbox due to those old beams inside. I don't have any more details but the police have been in here looking for you a couple of times a day ever since the fire. It's really been intense and has everyone feeling nervous and on edge. They've all been questioning."

Josef was suddenly flooded with fear. Hearing the timing of the fire, then having those two strange men show up unannounced at his door with a Summons? Outwardly he continued to give a cool and calm persona, but on the inside he was shaking in his boots. He began playing a game of lightening speed ping pong in his head with his last conversation with Litty and then the one with Hervé. It'd become a twisted fast mind game of who done it. What really happened? Which one of them had completed the task?

He'd become so overwhelmed, he couldn't stop playing both confusing scenarios over and over in his mind. He didn't reveal one iota of the wave of paranoia he was feeling...he just continued staring blanks at Dominique and watching her lips move. The loud ringing in his ears was deafening. His mouth became dry like the Mohave as his mind continued racing laps in warp speed...Daytona style.

Now that the Douglas' demise had become a reality, he conveniently turned the scenario around in his self-serving logic and began justifying himself. He'd never actually given 'specific' directions with any malice intended towards anyone, had he? No one could accidentally misconstrue his conversation with Herve and think of it as an actual death warrant, could they? After all, he'd only insinuated and spoken between the lines...right? Perhaps it was Hervé that had misunderstood...It'd only been suggested that he give the family some *fancy* electrical should they call...r.i.g.h.t?...right.

But no matter how Josef manipulated and twisted his own version of innocence, the bottom line was it'd been understood between the two men should the house burn down due to Hervé's 'handy work'…so be it. No consequences to their plan had ever been discussed. And, as for the letter from Litty? Had she really made arrangements to eliminate the Douglas' before she passed? Given those couple of possible scenarios…Josef was conveniently distancing himself from it all like he couldn't possibly have been involved, nor had any responsibility in the deed whatsoever. He'd always been good at that… escaping any and all responsibility that is.

He'd prefer to think of it as just a tragic accident. End of story. Josef was running his plea through his mind like a record with a skip. Over and Over it played in high speed like a small 45 rpm vinyl that'd gone astray. No way could it have been his doing…

"Josef, hello…did you hear anything I just said?" Dominique asked, trying to bring him back into the here and now. At one point she'd considered clapping her hands to snap him back…She knew he was out somewhere floating in space at that moment, but dared not bring more attention to their discussion. His behavior had become so bizarre it even made her curious what the real story was…

"Yes Dominique, every word. Thanks for the info. I'll be seeing you," he said quickly exiting the bar. He left feeling like he had a neon yellow post it note stuck to his forehead reading 'guilty'.

He was so shocked and worried everyone was thinking he was involved somehow. It'd been so much easier being tucked away in a luxe mountain retreat and not having to face the consequences of what he'd actually put into motion. He walked around the corner, got in his Rover and nervously sped back to the *Château.*

While driving through the backroads of the Vineyard, the recording of his conversation with Hervé began playing again in his head. Then the questioning began…"Why would those two men have come to the house this morning and served me with a summons? Something is wrong. There shouldn't be any reason or suspicion to trace any of this back to me whatsoever. After all, I've never set one foot in that damn house on Bontier ever since I was a kid!"

He began feeling haunted and questioning himself …"What could've happened to make it all go so sideways?" Josef was still in the midst of having his internal mind battle when his phone rang. It was almost enough to make him drive off the road.

"Are you almost home? You left in such a hurry with not so much as a goodbye…I've been worried sick. Are you okay?"…sputtered a nervous Sophie.

"I'm just pulling up now, I'll see you in a minute," he said leaving dust swirling around the Rover as he reached the front door.

When he entered he found Sophie standing in the foyer anxiously awaiting some news. She looked at him for some explanation. He couldn't help but blurt out the few facts that he did know. (Or that he chose to cough up)

"Sophie…Bruce's parents sadly died in a house fire the day we left for Megève."

What an actor the Golden Boy turned out to be. His only concern was not about the family's demise of course, but being implicated somehow…He was definitely putting on a great show. He was so hopeful she couldn't read the *'post it'* still attached to his forehead.

It was all too much shocking information to digest… Sophie dropped to the ground and began crying hysterically. So much for his sensitive explanation…

"Oh my God Josef, it wasn't a hidden fact that I never liked them, but what a tragedy" she whimpered between her gasping tearful sobs. "I can't imagine that kind of terrifying death for anyone. I'm so incredibly sorry to hear this horrific news. How did it happen?" she questioned still being crouched on the floor. At that very minute all she could think of was Bruce, but certainly couldn't dare admit it. She was flooded with a roller coaster of emotions.

Josef saw how distraught she was and pulled her up to a standing position and cradled her. Then he helped her upstairs to the bedroom and laid her down on the Alter, wiping the tears from her eyes.

"I don't know all the details yet, but I'll fill you in once I do. They say the fire must've started sometime in the early afternoon, the day after Litty's burial. My God...it would've been such an enormous blaze to have engulfed the entire house, but I didn't see any smoke or smell anything did you? It's wild thinking it must've started just about the time we were leaving the retirement home and heading to the airport. But I still can't understand why the police and that guy from the insurance company came to the *Château* this morning. The summons requires me to be at the courthouse in Bergerac first thing in the morning.

I'm going downstairs to make a few calls. You should stay up here and try to relax. I'll ask Fiona to make us a tray and leave it in the kitchen for later when we're ready. Okay with you my love?"

"Fine...but quite honestly, I can't think of anything except for that poor family. This news is so incredibly upsetting" ...she said burying her head in her pillow.

Josef didn't reply but only went downstairs where of course...he found Fiona waiting for him in the kitchen. (Did I happen to mention cunning BITCH somewhere?)

"Josef, I'm so happy to see you. I've been dying to tell you...The entire talk of the Village has been about the suspicious death of the Douglas'. It's really been something crazy. Everyone's been casting their own opinions and stories and they're really flying high. Then when I saw those two strange men here this morning, I became seriously worried. What in the world is going on?...Is everything okay?"

"Yes Fiona. It's all going to be fine, but it's not your place to worry about any of this. You have my sincere thanks for keeping an eye out on everything, but this drama was the last thing I was expecting to find especially after a few relaxing days away. It's like all hell has broken loose. You've probably heard as much as I have at this point" he said, fishing for info.

"Josef, maybe not...there's something else I've been

needing to tell you."

"That doesn't sound good...What is it?"...he said with pause...

"The day of Laetitia's service when I was putting the last touches on the buffet platters, I heard something in the library...so when I went in and saw Midnight scampering away, I didn't think much more about it. That is...until I looked out the front window and saw the back of a man walking away very quickly. He seemed as if he could've just been leaving the house. I think it might've been him that I heard in the library, because I found the door had been left slightly ajar."

"OH MY GOD why didn't you tell me this earlier?!!!" Josef snarled ferociously. "Did you recognize the guy? Who in the F...ing HELL was it?" Josef screamed. He began frantically pacing...obviously feeling beside himself.

"I can't be certain he was moving so fast. I wasn't able to see his face, only the back of him as he darted away. But what I can tell you is that he had short dark hair and seemed like he could've been a tad shorter than you and a bit huskier. It all happened so fast Josef, I couldn't be sure. He was gone before I knew it. I'm only sorry not to be able to give you more specifics."

This complete twist of new and unexpected details threw a huge 'unknown' into the already convoluted equation. Who'd have the gall to come into the *Château* and snoop around? Who was it...and what in the hell were they looking for? Josef was so jumpy he'd become paranoid thinking someone had invaded his home. Nothing like this would've ever happened in his shielded past. For the first time in his life, the Golden Boy felt raw and truly vulnerable.

Fiona by this time had finished preparing lunch, but with Josef pacing around ranting and mumbling to himself like he was, he hadn't taken notice. He left the kitchen for the car barn where he could continue his out of control behavior without any 'concerned' witnesses. It was two hours later when Sophie walked in to find him.

"Aren't you hungry by now Josef? There's been a

lovely spread just sitting on the kitchen table waiting for quite some time. I'm sure we can find a little something that's appealing. Come on...let's go in, have a bite and get warm for the afternoon. You don't need to be out here all alone pacing around, it's all going to be okay" she said lovingly. She approached him tenderly, taking his hand in hers and led them back inside. They took a few full plates and moved from the kitchen to their 'sweet spot' just in front of the burning fire in the great room.

They began their afternoon lunch by opening a bottle of wine, then another. Their picnic on the floor was silent other than the sound of wine being poured and the crackle of the flame. They drank the afternoon away until each had passed out cold on the living room sofas.

When Sophie awoke it was to a room that'd gone dark and had a chill. The fire had gone out hours ago leaving the room feeling cold and empty. She stood up, fumbled around in the darkness until she was able to find herself kneeling beside Josef sleeping on the other sofa.

"Josef wake up. Let's go upstairs and get in bed." He barely moved..."Josef wake up!...Let's go!" she repeated with more of a commanding tone as she yelled back to him zig-zagging her way up the stairs.

He finally moved and was groggily lagging behind. The bed was so warm and comforting, they both fell fast asleep in their cozy *lions den* as soon as they hit the sheets.

The morning had unfortunately come much sooner than expected. When Sophie rolled over she was confronted by Josef's face hovering only inches above hers.

"I'm leaving now. I'll call you after my appointment" he said kissing her forehead in a nervous gesture, just as her eyes were fully opening.

Sophie was just cognizant enough to say, "good luck" before rolling back over and hiding herself under the fluffy comforter. It'd been a really long time since she'd had so much wine to drink in one sitting. Her head was throbbing heavily and any small noise seemed amplified. Her kind of hangover was definitely off the Richter scale...

She was absolutely amazed to think Josef had been able to get up and out on schedule. He was running on high energy and the amount of alcohol still floating around in his system could well have been combustible. Thank GOD he didn't smoke...

Josef had made it a point to be punctual for his appointment in Bergerac. Upon his arrival he parked at the Municipal office Building and entered...He went straight to room 206 as instructed and there he found a desk sergeant who immediately led him into an Interrogation room. It felt like something straight out of a film driven by some trivial textbook citing criminal law. It even had a double sided mirrored wall in the room of all things. It felt surreal...like he was floating above the scene and looking down on himself. He was shown a seat and was kept waiting until the detective in charge finally meandered in.

The guy had taken his time, obviously demonstrating an experienced tactic...making the person waiting nervous, and boy did it ever work. Even though he seemed to keep his calm, his skin was crawling from anxiety. This detective wasn't the same guy who'd shown up at the *Château* the day before...This particular detective was more of a Slick Dick and really knew the drill.

"Good morning Mr. Decour, I'm Detective Inspector Troccaz. Thank you for coming in this morning." Josef didn't reply, only nodded and remained outwardly calm while sitting silent.

"I'm sure you've heard about the tragedy that occurred a week ago in the Village." Inspector Troccaz didn't wait for any acknowledgment...but continued, "We could use your help with a few things. Would you mind if we asked you a few questions?"

His tactics seemed like they were from a typical crack case of cinema detective work. It would've been impossible not to realize it was just a ploy trying to butter up an individual in order to get a bit of information out of them...(whether the clues be verbal or physical) Josef just continued to sit looking cool and listen to what Troccaz had to say.

"We're a bit perplexed with something. We've determined there could be a few different scenarios playing out when it comes to the motive of this crime."

"Crime?" Josef asked sounding a bit shocked.

"Oh I'm sorry, I thought you would've been briefed at the reason why you've been asked here this morning. It's regarding the fire at the Douglas' home last week," the detective casually said.

Josef quickly deviating away from his normally calm demeanor asked, "How can you be so sure it was a crime and not just an accident?"

"Well, we've obtained a few pieces of evidence from the scene that gives us cause to think it wasn't merely an act of innocence, but something that may have been intentional. A pre-meditated kind of thing you know?... That's what we're here trying to figure out."

"Really? Like what kind of evidence?" Josef inquired. (Feeling like he'd just fallen off his chair)

"Do you recognize this item?" Detective Troccaz questioned smugly as he laid a piece of heavy melted silver down on the table in front of him.

The piece was unique in its design having a particular identifiable ribbing texture on the exterior. Even though it had melted completely in place, it still showed enough detailing to know it was a collapsed little case made of pure silver.

"No, what is it?"

"In our estimation it's presumably what used to be a Cartier Lighter. At least we think it is. We're really not sure at this point, but they're quite expensive...Are they not? They're certainly not a common item to be had by a typical *local* household, but I'm sure you've had one...correct?" the detective inquired. He was trying his best to begin laying some sort of an inquisitive trap for Josef.

"Why yes, I have...a lot of people have. I've never used the one that was left to me by my Grandfather. He'd used it for the many years he smoked cigars. Personally, I don't smoke so the one I have has been left sitting in the desk drawer in my library for years. Why do you ask?"

"Because as you may or may not know…every piece that Cartier makes has an assigned number that's registered to its purchaser. We believe this 'lighter' could possibly have started the fire. We're sending this particular piece to Cartier's head office in Paris in hopes they can provide some type of number that can lead us to its owner. Of course…that, and any other pertinent information they could provide would be of assistance.

We're not suggesting or concluding anything here, but until we are able to find out this information…lets just say, we'd rather you stay close to home. Given you have so many international friends, I think it would be best to have an officer follow you back to your place and gather your passport for our safe keeping. You wouldn't mind would you?" the big prick asked with a condescending smile. What could Josef say? He was scared shitless.

Josef left understanding one thing and that was he needed to call Gus immediately. He'd be needing a good fucking lawyer and Gustav would no doubt be able to bring one up from his bullpen. Josef was followed home by the original detective that had knocked on his door the day before.

When they arrived back at the *Château*, Josef went in alone to gather his passport from the bookshelf's hiding spot in the library. It left the officer waiting on the landing outside. After surrendering his passport he returned to the library closing the pocket doors behind him. He watched out the window to be certain the officer had gone before frantically searching through the desk for his Cartier lighter. He ripped though the desk one drawer at a time. Nothing… It was nowhere to be found…the thing was gone.

"That must be it!" he screamed…"This would explain what the mystery intruder could've been after!" He knew it had to have been Bruce…he just *knew it*. He began talking to himself out loud in a muffled and low toned monologue.

"That's it! He must've circled around and come into

the house after being run off from the service. That fucking bastard! What would he have wanted with my Cartier lighter had it not been but to start the fire! That fucker…he's trying to frame me, that's what's going on…And what happened to Hervé?…And all that talk from Litty about some favor she'd called in?"

He closed his eyes and leaned back into the supple leather swivel chair trying to put all the pieces to the puzzle together. It'd all become far too complicated…he couldn't make sense of any of it. He simply wanted to stay low key and hidden for a while until the whole thing blew over.

Not all of them, but definitely some…poor little rich boys love to pretend to be ostriches sometimes…so much easier to hide your head in the sand and not confront the issues, let somebody else deal with it type of thing. Josef wished he could just blink this situation away like he'd done so many other times, but on this particular occasion there wasn't anyone to pick up his mess. Until there was some kind of conclusion to one of the many scenarios in play, he knew he needed to be careful…Everything he said and did was being watched and scrutinized. Suddenly realizing this…he felt trapped and uncertain of anything. He'd truly become frightened and felt completely lost. The poor little prick didn't quite know what to do. This was an entirely new feeling for the Golden Boy…

"There you are Josef…" Fiona said sliding the doors open and entering the library. "I thought I heard you in here. Are you alone?" she said looking around the room. "I could've sworn I heard you having a conversation with someone."

"Yes, it's only me…I guess I was just thinking out loud," he mumbled obviously pre-occupied. "Fiona, I've been ripping the desk apart looking for that damn Cartier Lighter that's always been kept here. Its been parked in the middle drawer for years, and now for some strange reason it's disappeared! Do you have any idea where it is?" he ranted while continuing to pillage through the contents of the drawer aggressively.

"If it's not where its always been…then no, I don't.

Let me see…" she replied walking over to the desk where he was seated. She leaned over his shoulder and shuffled some papers around in the middle drawer pretending to earnestly feel for the lighter. She wanted him to absorb her close presence and literally leave her scent on him just like Midnight had. What a cheap trick if I may say so myself…

After sensually flipping her hair over to one side, (yawn) she *leaned in* placing one palm on the desk and said in a sultry baby-girl voice, "I can't say if I ever actually remember seeing it Josef. When was the last time you did? And by the way I don't have a habit of opening your desk, just so you know. Why the sudden need for the thing anyway? What's so crucial about finding it right this minute?" she said straightening up into a standing position and moving behind him.

"We have to find it! It's imperative we do! That's all I can say. We need to keep looking. Should you come across it anywhere, I mean anywhere, please let me know asap. It's very, very important" he said spinning around to face her. He hadn't realized that he'd just given her free rein to snoop around the *Château* anywhere she chose.

"Okay Josef," Fiona replied with a smile, knowing full well she'd just been given the *keys to browse* at will.

"Oh…before I forget, Sophie wanted me to tell you that she went for a ride. She said she simply needed a break and some fresh air."

Hearing this, Josef quickly got up and walked outside to the horse barn hoping to see that she'd returned. When he entered the barn, a figured shadow came to the forefront and into the light.

"Jesus Hervé…you scared the hell out of me!!" Josef gasped. He'd become so jittery that every move felt like he was standing on a raw nerve that'd been electrified.

"What in the hell are you doing back here on the property!?…Are you trying to give me a heart attack sneaking around like this…Answer me!…What are you doing here?!" Josef said catching his breathe. "Believe you me, it doesn't take much for me to jump out of my skin right about now" he said in a gruff whisper and reprimanding tone. "Someone could've seen you damnit!..."

Hervé let Josef's reprimanding rant blow in one ear and out the other before exhaling deeply..."Thank God you finally showed up Josef. I've been out here waiting for you all morning. I was almost seen by your girlfriend when she left and then by that farm hand of yours. He came in and startled me, but he was in such a rush he didn't even notice me. It made me scared thinking who might be popping in next."

Needless to say, Josef was not amused hearing this...Hervé cleared his throat..."I took the chance of coming because I wanted to let you know it wasn't me... The Douglas' never called me to check on any electrical. I thought it wise to tell you in person now that the latest buzz in the village is everyone thinks you had to be involved with the fire somehow. They're keeping the rumble hush-hush but rumors and stories are flying around as you can imagine. Some of those old flames of fire and gossip have resurfaced with the past issues between your two families. I don't know where these stories are conjured from, but given they are...I wanted to personally confirm, I had nothing to do with the fire at the Douglas' house. My families debt to you is still alive and well."

He felt spooked all of a sudden and quickly said, "I really should get out of here before someone actually does see me Josef" he said with panic in his voice. Then he slipped out of the barn door with caution, leaving without a trace.

Josef nervously walked over to the stall of his prize thoroughbred and began brushing his beautiful thick winter coat with long strong strokes. When the towering stallion began to whinny, Josef saw Sophie enter the barn leading Nuage. He gave a huge sigh of relief seeing her...especially after feeling like he'd been ambushed by Hervé's unexpected visit. He stepped out of Zephyr's stall to greet her and take her reins.

Without saying a word, Sophie fell limp onto a large neighboring pile of loose hay as Josef was sliding off

Nuage's saddle. He became irritated with his findings...

"Wow Sophie, she's really hot and has broken a sweat. She's even got a bit of lather happening on her girth...Obviously you enjoyed your ride," he said sounding annoyed and protective over his favorite 'gentle ride'.

"Oh Josef... the reason she's lathered like that is that we were followed, then chased by a strange car at the end of the road. I cut through the vineyard to lose them and we ran for our lives. It scared the living hell out of us both."

That's all she could get out before falling back again. She was completely shaken and exhausted. It was apparent she'd really been traumatized by the event. What she'd been saying took a minute for Josef to absorb. When the description of her scary ordeal finally clicked in, he fell next to her on the hay pile wanting to hear every detail about her frightening encounter. Nothing of that nature had even remotely happened at the *Château* before...Josef was more than concerned and concluded this was the final straw, literally. (...this time pun definitely intended) It was enough for him to begin feeling panicked and consequently his fear began to affect him physically.

"What are you talking about! What's this crazy story?!!" he said immediately feeling the shocking sensation of having needles simultaneously pierce his body every where at warp speed. Every damn thing that was happening made him feel out of control. His world...let's face it, was moving along at a quick clip of calamities of sorts. It was all presenting itself like the perfect storm for disaster.

Sophie began to speak again explaining her nightmare episode. "We'd gone to the edge of the vineyard and I was taking the same ride that Michel had taken me on when out of the blue, a small black car with dark tinted windows came barreling past me on the exterior road. It startled Nuage and it took me the longest time to settle her back down. When we finally began having a nice rhythm again, the car came back, swerved and almost hit us! Nuage reared up and took off on me! I merely hung on for dear life as she jumped over things that I didn't know she was capable of and ran faster than I thought possible. I was scared for my life and never have I been on a horse that was so spooked. She made a direct shot back to the barn at full speed and here we are. It was terrifying" she said still trembling.

"Sophie, we should go back to the *Château* and stay held up in private for a few days…at least until the dust settles. There's a lot of things we need to discuss," he said sitting up straight.

Then he hopped to his feet and said, "I feel like you and Nuage. I've never felt so unraveled in my life." He sweetly reached down and pulled Sophie up to stand next to him. He turned and lovingly slapped the hind quarter of Nuage and led her to the stall next to Zephyr.

"Where in the hell is Gilles when we need him! He certainly chooses the most inopportune times to go missing. His days are definitely numbered around here."

Josef quickly removed Nuage's tack, left fresh water along with a carrot for both horses that he found in the staff's fridge before leaving the barn. He wouldn't be back for a few days…Gilles would need to tend to the horses if and when he decided to show. The guy had really started to irritate Josef…for more reasons than one.

It'd become time for the lovers to disappear in plain sight. As they entered the *Château* Josef quickly went to the library and stopped at the bookshelf. He reviewed the many leather covered books before bringing one down from the third shelf and opened it slowly. It was another hollow book just like the one he'd retrieved his passport from. It was there that he found the ring of master keys to the *Château*. Not even Litty had known about these secret hiding spots… or at least he didn't think she had. Sophie meanwhile had already walked back to the kitchen not having witnessed any of his secretive actions.

He removed the large ring holding the keys and returned the faux book to its place. He made sure nothing looked out of place…He took a moment and lifted the large heavy ring up to analyze the bulky group of different shaped keys. Years ago when he'd been given the set, he wasn't shown which key went to what specific door lock. He'd never needed to know that kind of thing before, because no one in the valley would dare enter the *Château* without an invitation. After all, I guess receiving the keys had only been a symbol of honor like earning a merit badge.

Josef began going around the *Château* figuring out each key and locking every door behind him. After securing the rest of the house he finally was able to reach the kitchen. The last door to be locked prohibiting anyone from the outside to enter was the Orchid Solarium. After the final door had been secured, he took Sophie's hand and led her upstairs without saying another word. They stripped, crawled into bed, and pulled the bed's draperies closed tight. Both exhaled a cloud of stress as they fell back onto their mound of soft feathery pillows. Having all the doors locked from the inside, Josef had now taken the decision to wake up on his own time. They were officially 'in hiding'.

Settled upstairs in their chamber of silence, Josef drifted off into a subconscious dream land. He'd been twirling in and out, round and round, trying to collect his thoughts and make sense of it all.

"It must've been when we were delivering the books to the Retirement home. It clearly would've put us close to the scene of the 'crime'…and where the hell did I leave that letter from Litty? What if the lighter had actually been Grandfathers? Is Bruce trying to frame me?…" Josef had become wet from thrashing and chanting this crazy talk half aloud. He was awaken abruptly from his sweaty turbulent wrath as Sophie began shaking him.

"Josef sweetheart…Josef!" she said loudly nudging him trying to arouse him back to his worldly senses. "Josef I'm here" she said rubbing the perspiration from his face and upper body. He came out of his trance like state with a look of sheer panic.

"I can't breathe" he yelled, then jumped out of the drapery drawn fortress. "These people have haunted me for years and now…they're winning. I can't fucking believe this!" he continued to scream angrily while forcefully pulling on his jeans.

"What are you talking about Josef?…Come back to bed sweetheart. Where are you going? You were just having a bad dream," Sophie said trying to lure him back into the bed fort.

"You're absolutely wrong my dear, this isn't a dream, it's all one big fucking nightmare coming to fruition is what it is!" He then ran over and flung open the double doors and flew down the stairs to the main foyer below. He arrived at the front door, thankfully having the key still in it. He turned the lock and hastily swung one door wide open. He leapt out onto the cement landing and let out the loudest scream you've ever heard. He didn't care who heard him.

Finally letting his frustrations out in such a blood curdling and echoing loud rant…well, to say it was very unlike Josef to have lost his cool like that would be a gross understatement. He was standing there screaming babble and yelling crazy talk at the top of his lungs. He'd literally become out of his mind the poor little bastard. The dusky evening was just setting in. It'd been proven to be a Very, Very…Long Day.

Miraculously it hadn't been Sophie that'd arrived first, but who other than…Fiona. How convenient for her to have heard his bellowing shrieks and to be first on the scene to *comfort* him. Fiona couldn't believe her luck finding Josef standing all alone in the midst of his turmoil. She quickly surmised the situation and took advantage of the ideal opportunity…It was her first real chance. She'd arrived at the perfect moment, seriously…she was more than *ready and willing* to 'console him'. It didn't hurt that she was only wearing a thin satin negligé…Then she made her move.

"Josef," she said tenderly embracing him. "I'm sorry this time in life has become so challenging." Not verbalizing anything more, she moved her body towards him In a sexual and sultry way giving him a tight full frontal hug. Her breasts lining up with his of course.

They stayed in that position for a long while, that is

until Sophie cleared the last stair and realized it was that fucking Fiona she'd heard with Josef. What the hell was this? Whatever that bitch had in mind, Sophie was intent on interrupting their 'conversation' or *whatever* it was that they happened to be doing.

"Josef, are you all right my love?" she loudly questioned. She knew she'd heard Fiona and expected to see her, but was beyond shocked to see them in an actual embrace!

She was immediately flushed with feelings of confusion. A woman's typical unique and utterly impossible inner combination had arisen. That of jealousy sided by a large serving of insecurity, you know the one, it's possibly the worst self deprecating combo ever to be served up. That instant flash of a woman's own self administered detrimental poison had prevailed.

Seeing them standing as one made her feel she looked like an old nagging housewife arriving on scene wearing a dish rag. With Sophie being wrapped in a simple terrycloth robe, it was a lot less sexy than the forest green satin number Fiona happened to show up in. That Cunning Bitch, it even complemented her eyes. Given the fashion defeat amongst her territorial grab…Sophie wasn't about to let Fiona control this wild situation any longer, and with one phrase dismissed her with lightning speed.

"I'll take it from here Fiona," Sophie said sharply, literally prying them apart with intent.

With Sophie's determined authority, it was enough for Fiona to see she'd been caught in the act so she quickly made her exit from the situation and retreated to her room above the car barn. Sophie continued to comfort Josef while coaxing him back inside. Once standing in the foyer, Sophie gently closed the front door behind them and locked it. Then she pivoted around and blasted the Golden Boy like there was no tomorrow.

"Do you want to fuck her? Is that what this is all about?" she spitefully yelled in his face feeling powerless.

For a family who'd always made a point of being so

discreet…the last thing imaginable was now taking place. What a mess! Two different women standing in their robes outside in front with the man of the Manor who'd just been screaming at the top of his lungs! This was definitely not what one would expect and certainly wasn't the appropriate way to conduct a *quiet mourning period* for a loved one.

Sophie was so pissed and hurt just thinking about what she'd 'accidentally' interrupted that she stormed upstairs leaving the unhinged bastard standing all alone. (Guess she was lucky he followed her instead of going out back to the car barn) Sophie knew damn well Fiona had begun casting her line.

"What the hell Sophie! Do you want me to fire Fiona? Would that make you feel better? I will if you want me to. I don't know how that little thing on the front landing just transpired between us, but I'm sorry if it hurt you. It happened so fast I really didn't see it coming. She was only trying to comfort me in the cold winter air…" (Is this a typical text book reaction from all guilty men caught in the act? Answer: Absolutely….)

"Oh really?…Is that what you'd call it? How was it that she was conveniently there in the first place? Does she lay in waiting to see if she can catch you alone?" Sophie yelled sitting down hard on one of the shimmering sofas.

"Now you're beginning to sound paranoid sweet-heart. Please don't add your insecurities to the pile right now. Can't you see the world is off its axis around here with everything else going on? It's almost too much to deal with. There's nothing going on between Fiona and me. Seriously, you need to know that. I guess my yelling wasn't the smartest thing to do in any event. It was stupid of me to let my frustrations out like that. I just really needed to blow off some steam. Fiona has been the set of eyes and ears around here since working under Litty. I imagine my lengthy outbreak in front not only disturbed her, but a few others as well. She just came to my rescue is all. I know I need to get control of myself. I guess it's me that's actually feeling paranoid…I know they must be watching."

"Now what's really at the root of all of this Josef? I want and need you to be honest with me. I know you've never truly confided in me and just why is that? What is this crazy stuff you're talking about!...Who's watching?...What the hell is really going on!!" Sophie screamed, demanding answers. This little episode with Fiona was the 'coup de grâce' as far as she was concerned...

"The Police for starters, that's who...and perhaps... others. It didn't go well today in Bergerac and I'm worried. My head is spinning just thinking about all the different versions that could possibly play out in this crazy unfolding story. They think the fire was perhaps foul play and not an accident. They actually suspect me for some strange reason but haven't figured it out yet. The major detail is that we were close to the scene when we dropped the books off. What an insane coincidence!

I think Bruce must be involved somehow and is trying fo frame me. He's got to be responsible for this in some way, I'm sure of it. I need time to figure it all out and put the pieces together. There's actually a reason why I've never wanted to confide in you Sophie, it's because I'm ashamed of a lot of things from my past". (Good God...How thick could he possibly lay on this Bullshit!...Disgusting)

"This all may seem perfect on the outside, but there's some heavy baggage surrounding us at the *Château*."

"Oh Josef, we all have some things in our history we'd like to erase..."

"No. Not like mine. There's a long destructive history between Bruce's family and mine. The real reason I feel this hatred for him has to do with his Father. I'd always thought I imagined it, but now it's been confirmed to be true. It was Gene that was responsible for the collapse of the relationship between my Father and his Father. He ruined our family. Turns out Gene was a sexual predator...a real monster. It was him that influenced my Father when he was young. My Father obviously must've had tendencies and liked men on occasion, but Gene made sure there was a continuing sexual relationship that happened between those two. Honestly, I was shocked to find out it carried on and off for years.

I think the entire village knew, but not one person ever spoke openly about it. You know how the village works…they all just smirked and passed whispers amongst themselves as usual. That gave my Grandfather the biggest pang of humiliation imaginable. Gene threw it in his face and because of it, bled my Grandfather out of thousands upon thousands. I have no idea how much it actually was, but I do know that bastard used my Grandfather like a piggy bank. That demoralizing story made Grandfather feel weak and useless for years. That is until one fine day, he finally told Gene where to get off." Voilà…there it was. Josef had finally told Sophie his side of the family drama.

"Oh Josef my love, I had no idea. That's a bitter thing for a child to endure. I'm sure knowing cruel and mean floating rumors circulating around the Village only made it worse." (The topic of Fiona had somehow conveniently drifted away for the moment)

"Exactly…Bruce had always been a close childhood friend growing up, almost like a brother to me until the story about both our Fathers began to surface. Our close boyhood friendship ended abruptly with bad feelings on both sides. Each of us have had our own way of dealing with it. We found a deep hatred for one another because of it, and I know he hated his Father for it just like I did. We've tried to punish one another in some way or the other for years and I know…he hates me for taking you away from him. I'm sure that he knows it was my callous objective at the beginning. I just wanted to take someone he cherished away from him like his Father had from us. I knew luring you away from him would seriously hurt him. The problem then was that I found myself having deep feelings for you and here we are. I want you to be part of my life Sophie."

"So I was just a game for you?"

"Not quite…but let's be quite clear my love… initially we were both in it for the challenge and look where that led us. You can't say initially I wasn't only that for you as well."

For a moment, the stinging words of reality were all a bit too much for both of them to admit and certainly not to expand on. They'd need to ponder on their individual thoughts before any more discussion could be had. Laying and looking at each other from adjacent sofas, having this truthful conversation was the most willing attempt at some honesty they'd ever shared with one another.

The next morning came and Sophie was the first to rise leaving Josef still sleeping on the other sofa. She went down the hallway and into the kitchen and who else did she see but her nemesis.

"What in the world are you doing here inside the house Fiona?" Sophie said harshly. "Josef told me that he'd locked all of the doors." (I think it was payback time for Sophie to have some demanding questions but it didn't fall into her lap so easily…)

"Good morning Sophie. He didn't tell you? Perhaps he'd forgotten"…she said with a smirky grin. "Litty had given me a key to her rooms back door shortly after I began working here at the Estate."

"No…he failed to tell me that. How convenient for you my dear, I'll be sure to discuss that with him first thing this morning. Is our coffee ready?"

"Yes. It's already waiting over there on that tray" said the tart pointing toward the steaming coffee pot. Sophie didn't reply but snatched the tray up with some serious snarky attitude.

As she walked up and into the master suite, she found the room void of the Golden Boy. He'd already jumped in the shower to avoid any further questions or confrontation. She placed the tray on the low table between the sofas and lit the fire. She sat patiently waiting for him to exit the bathroom.

"Oh this will fill my engines with what I need" Josef said, appearing from the steamy bathroom and gazing over at the coffee table. He was wearing his 'matching' robe and proceeded to pour himself a strong one. The little shit…he looked like the cover of GQ Magazine.

"I hope my behavior and our conversation didn't

frighten you last night Sophie. The inquiry yesterday gave me a real scare. Their tactic of keeping me there all day until mid afternoon had me exhausted and made me carry on saying some strange things. Then hearing your news of being chased?…It was all a bit too much. It's a new day and I'm feeling much more like myself." Sophie just sat quietly while watching the fire and sipping her coffee.

"Did you know that Fiona has a key to the Château?"

"No, does she really?…I had no idea. But actually that would explain why she was so quick to find me on the landing last night. She must've come through from the back of the house is my guess. I guess it would make sense Laetitia had given her a key."

"So that doesn't bother you? Her having the ability to enter our place and creep around like she does?"

"Oh Sophie…Don't be like that. Why should it bother me if she has a key? Does it you? She's only here to help us."

"Josef Seriously?…That is such a crock! I can't put my finger on it, but the whole thing around here concerning her reeks. Fiona's trying to work her magic on you and I'm watching it take hold right here in front of me. I can't believe you're not seeing this!…Or are you?"

"That's it! I don't want to hear you speak about Fiona constantly. With the police on my ass, I have more important things to think about. I thought you'd want to support me now versus being envious and jealous of something that doesn't exist" he responded…like the really good and well seasoned liar that he was. He took the opportunity of giving her false guilt, then conveniently left the room.

Sophie meanwhile sat calmly and finished her cup of coffee, then picked up her phone and dialed Gayle.

"Hi, I know it's late and hope I'm not waking you… but If so?…I'm sorry. I'm also sorry for being so out of touch for the last few weeks. How are you?" she said hoping that she could put a bandaid on having been so irresponsible with her neglect. She prayed it wasn't too late to find Gayle as supportive as she'd always been…then Gayle began to speak.

"Sophie, you've made it quite clear that you'd prefer to be lost in your new life. But...there are a few of us that need to continue what we've been doing to make a living. Not all of us have the privilege of jumping off onto a new platform with no rear view mirror. It's been a lot more than a few weeks since you've been 'in touch'. And by the way you're not waking me, I'm not even in SF, I'm in NYC. I just arrived at the gym at the W Hôtel where I'm staying. I have super early meetings this morning and wanted to get a workout in before I start my business day. I hope you know it's 4am here, in case you'd even considered that. It's 1am in SF and as hard as you know I work, it's so very thoughtful of you to call at this hour," Gayle said sarcastically.

"Since no one in the company has heard one word, not even one damn peep from you...we were forced to carry on and you should know it's been in a totally new direction. I began designing a collection for another company last season and most of our past clients have been responsive to coming on board. That's all I have to say. I'll text you my lawyers number should you have any further questions"... then she hung up.

Sophie sat paralyzed holding her phone along with her half empty cup of lukewarm coffee...She was so stunned she sat in frozen bewilderment for what seemed to be a good half hour without moving. She couldn't believe what she'd just heard. She was so shocked hearing those words come from Gayle of all people. Why hadn't she followed through for her like she always had? What in the hell had she done? The nerve!

The reality of the calendar immediately hit Sophie like a lead-pipe. She suddenly realized she'd already missed a full season of decision making and new designs. She'd become so lost in her life with Josef, she'd ignored and forgotten all about her responsibilities Stateside.

Once Sophie snapped out of her fog, she changed out of her robe and went down to find Josef in the library. He was on the phone and signaled for her to sit down as he politely finished his conversation. It made Sophie anxious and thump her foot. Voila…he was finally off…

"Gayle has taken over the lead and sold me out. I never thought this would happen in a million years. I think I should go to NY and see what's going on. I need to leave as soon as possible" Sophie spewed with tearful and hateful disappointment.

"Well, that Lit-tle diva…Just how in the hell was she able to pull that off? I'm sorry to hear this my love, but don't worry about it so much right now. We'll definitely get down to the bottom of it. What exactly was your conversation?" Josef asked rather calmly.

In reality he really couldn't give a shit what Gayle had been doing especially now. He was simply going through the motions of trying to stay focused enough to listen to his girl's problems. Sophie explained everything she'd heard and filtered out of her conversation, but as we all know there are always three sides to every story. Each side has theirs…and then there's the truth.

"I know it must hurt…The feelings of betrayal always do, but you *have to admit you have* been out of the loop for a while, right?"

That comment surprised her…and stung. Then he continued, "Don't worry my love, when it's all said and done, it's you that owns the name. That'll be worth something in the end. Instead of going to NY…I'd much prefer you to stay here and help me navigate through these muddy waters. I have enough money to buy out any of the bastards that are disrupting or trying to get in to your business. Stay here with me sweetheart…we'll go back and address this together in due time. Does that sound reasonable to you my love?"

For some familiar weak reason, Sophie fell back under Josef's spell once again and became subservient to his wishes. It felt so much easier not having to face her own truth. So much easier to continue to hide inside his world especially now, given his current drama. She knew she was needed now more than ever. The minute her conversation with 'her assistant' had ended she'd already compartmentalized her feelings. She'd chosen to be that of a successful business woman who'd been forced to become a victim, a damsel in distress...all because of 'traitors' like Gayle. She didn't want to face her lack of taking responsibility for her actions as being the actual problem, but then again...there Are opportunists lurking everywhere... just waiting for their 'shot' to take it all over.

The other convenient truth was that she didn't want to relinquish her local fight with the household competitor. None of it made sense. She'd completely lost herself in the deep end and had been so out of it for so long, she was scared to return to the mess that she'd left. She'd put all of her pending issues on the far back burner while trying to secure her future life with Josef. But now, it seemingly felt as if it had all gone up in smoke. Bruce would be shocked and disgusted to say the very least knowing what had become of his strong, powerful ex.

Sadly, Sophie remained hypnotized and dependent on Josef...He'd always been like a drug to her. She felt she needed his strong-arm to help guide her through whatever business decisions there were left to salvage. He'd be there to help...Mr. Thoughtful.

"Okay Josef. I guess I can wait for us to go together. Actually, it'll give me support knowing you'll be there to help me sort it all out. Gayle was acting so passive aggressive in our conversation, she didn't even sound like the same person. I'll definitely need you with me."

"Good my love. Now that we have that decided, let's put all of this aside and go for a nice ride together. There's something I want to show you. I'll ask Gilles, if I can find him... to get the horses saddled up and for Fiona to prepare a picnic. It will be good to get out for a bit don't you think?"

After casually dictating their day's agenda, he walked over and gently planted a kiss on her like he'd just given a child a piece of candy. It had become more than pathetic in my opinion, but dare I say...It'd only be a matter of time before she'd finally get her long overdue sense of self back.

✳

Chapter Dix

Sophie zipped down the stairs two at a time, landing in the foyer on both feet. She hurried to the front doors and flung open both to find Zephyr and Nuage saddled up and tied to the post in front. What a beautiful sight…She was so happy to see them that she walked out and planted a big smooch on each of their big sweet sensitive noses.

She'd left the doors open and when Josef appeared he excitedly yelled…"Hey, save some of that for me."

He walked up and kissed Sophie with a sweet peck on the lips before stroking both horses between their eyes. He ran his palm down their long smooth foreheads until he felt their warm breath exhale from each of their soft velvety nostrils.

"Let's have a nice calm ride today shall we?" he said to his beloved animals.

Sophie didn't need help mounting Nuage. Now that she'd had more practice, she'd become the polished equine like she'd been in her youth when riding at the 4-H Club. Once she was securely sitting on top, Josef threw a rolled blanket and the saddle bags full of picnic items over Nuage's hind quarters and fastened up the provisions.

"My boy here doesn't like any extra weight. He's a rowdy type and a lot to handle" he said mounting the incredibly tall, strong stallion.

They were off. Josef took the lead on Zephyr with Sophie following closely behind. He was going to surprise his lady love by taking her on his favorite ride through the property…It'd be a different route than the others she'd been on. After all…this was a special tour of the estate with '*the* proprietor'. It happened to be the most deliciously crisp and perfect sunny day for a ride. It graciously enabled them an escape from the current chaos surrounding them. They allowed both horses to run at full speed kicking up the chocolate colored earth. It smelled and felt like heaven on earth while enjoying such a peaceful winters day.

They slowed it all the way down to a standstill once they'd arrived at the top of the ridge. It was a look-out point where they could easily admire the beautiful rolling hills below while catching their breathe.

"Wow! These horses have obviously been here with you many times before Josef. They know their way around given all your familiar signals. That long gallop getting here was fantastic! Where are we by the way?"

"I'm excited to say, we're now looking at the latest acquisition to my property. See that land down there on the horizon…I signed for the purchase of those adjacent twenty hectares a year ago. We've been seasoning the terroir and working on its development for quite a while in hopes of planting within the next couple of years. We till the soil often because it needs a minimum of three years to breathe and eliminate any toxins left from past fertilizers. This latest purchase will make the estate one of the premier organic properties in the entire region," he pridefully boasted.

"That's incredible! This place is absolutely stunning. The fact that you're looking forward and planning new things for the property is so impressive. Your Grandfather no doubt, would be proud. What's your plan? Additional vines?"

"Yes, for the most part, but I'm also planting a few hectares in fresh vegetables. I'm very excited about the new possibilities and opportunities this experimental land could lead to. Follow me…that looks like a good spot" he said pointing to a cleared area with few trees. (for horse parking)

"Let's have our picnic there and rest a bit. We can discuss and dream of our future over some lukewarm chicken and a bottle of red. Now let's see who'll get the wish bone shall we?" he teased flirtatiously, leading them in a slow walk to the perfect lunch spot.

They dismounted, secured the horses and as Josef began unrolling the blanket he passed one end to Sophie to help prepare their 'magic carpet' for the afternoon. Then out came the saddlebags and the 'beautiful picnic' the Brit had prepared. It just so happened to be loaded with Josef's favorites.

"Hmm. This looks delicious. Litty obviously gave Fiona some tips along the way for my most revered picnic" he said enthusiastically, unpacking the contents. He acted like a gleeful infant. And to think Sophie thought the breakfast buffet was something…but now, picnics? Holy Fuck…

Sophie looked over at Josef with a fake smile and thought, "There's that word again. Fiona, Fiona…frickin' Fiona! What is it with that bitch…I need to find out about this so called 'grooming' relationship. Enough of 'circumstance'…he can't be telling me everything. There is definitely something going on here that needs to be discovered. Her mind… was obviously doing summersaults.

"How's your potato salad?" he asked sounding a bit more interested in the picnic than he was continuing his discussion about the new land acquisition.

"A bit too salty for my liking, but it all looks lovely on the outside,…" attempting to subtly communicate her inner thoughts. Her intended back handed compliment regarding the situation didn't even register…and she wasn't talking about the potato salad of course. She bit her tongue like always, trying her utmost to be on her best behavior and enjoy their lovely outing. She went ahead and ate her pride along with some delicious chicken…and sadly, the damn potato salad was perfect…

"I'm going to do a little bit of work with Michel this afternoon. There are some vines that he's been cultivating so we've planned to meet to discuss when and where to plant. Would you care to join me?…Or should we meet back at the *Château* later in the day?"

The setting was so picture perfect, it was similar to one of those pretentious Vogue covers featuring a Hollywood couple frolicking around looking like they were enjoying the 'perfect' life…But as we all know…pictures sometimes can hide the truth as well as expose it. After lunch had been selectively picked through, Josef laid his head down on Sophie's lap looking up at her like she was the only thing that mattered. She was combing his hair back with her fingers and admiring his beautiful facial features.

"Our children are going to be gorgeous Josef. Once this whole business with the Douglas' is cleared up, I'm ready to start working on a baby if you are."

"You're going to make a wonderful Mother Sophie," he said sitting up and leaning forward to kiss her.

The timing of his confirmation was enough for her to feel their original plan was still on track. For some reason that seemed to have given her enough validation for her suspicions of Fiona to temporarily flee…Again. He'd just confirmed that he still wanted Sophie to be the mother of his children didn't he? All of this pointed in the right direction…Hers.

They returned to the *Château* riding in a slow canter. Seeing his silhouette sitting so tall and erect on top of that beautiful beast made her forget about her earlier upsetting call with Gayle. The vines rambled on for as long as she could see which gave her man in front the perfect profile against the horizon. Amongst the rolling hills, the magnificent *Château* sat visible in the distance. It seemed like her entire panoramic dream was being laid out right in front of her. She was smiling with conceited pleasure as they arrived back 'home'.

"What's that big grin for?" Josef asked as he helped her off Nuage. He untied the blanket and saddlebags sliding them off onto his shoulder like he were a studly western cowboy. Once the horses were secured, he took Sophie's hand and escorted her to the front door. He took his keys out of his pocket and dangled them with prideful ownership before unlocking one of the massive front doors. As they entered, once they'd reached the bottom stair he embraced her sweetly and said, "Enjoy a nice long bubble bath my love. I'll see you for dinner, I'll just pop these things back in the kitchen before I head off for my meeting. The horses must be thirsty. I hope Gilles has decided to finally bless us with his presence today."…His voice fading off as he walked further back down the cavernous hallway…

Sophie sprinted happily up the stairs entering *their* bedroom suite and kicked off her boots. "Whew...what an exquisite day on the property." Lost in her thoughts, she began humming and dancing around on her way to the bathroom where she began drawing a large soaking tubs worth of bubbles.

When Josef went back to the kitchen to drop off the remaining contents of the saddlebags, he thought he might as well pop down to the cave and grab a bottle of the latest vintage for Michel to taste during their 'meeting'. He lifted the corner piece of chopping block counter and pushed the familiar panel behind. As it opened the automatic lighting came on overseeing the exposed staircase that led below. He stood on the top stair of the cellars entrance and covered his tracks behind him, concealing his descent as always. He actually had an ulterior motive in going down to the cave...he also wanted to see if he could find Litty's letter, presumably where he left it. After all he'd been in such a drunken stupor that day, he couldn't be quite sure where it was. He crossed through a couple of tasting rooms before he came to his 'private' cellar. As the door opened, he was beyond shocked to see a sexy creature sitting in a sultry position resting on top of the table. As we know by now... this bastard had no moral compass...a big fat zero.

He recognized the red bra and matching panty set not to mention the beauty wearing it, but how in the hell did she know about his man cave? And how did she know about that bag of lingerie? How long had she been down there just laying in wait?...All these thoughts came racing through his mind...but somehow became inconsequential given her seductive position.

He gave her one look and not a lot of further inner dialog was considered. He walked straight up to the table and pulled her forward, sliding her tight little ass to the edge of the round table before him.

"You little bitch Fiona. What am I going to do with you?"

He did nothing more than undo his belt buckle and

drop his jeans to his knees. He stood there like a real self-centered macho with his riding boots on. She was so hot that he tilted forward and cupped her ass underneath using his hands then pulled her up off the table and onto his wand. She was already so wet he slid right in…deep. He began pulsating her with his stiff rod…so much so, it seemed like he wanted to punish her for this wild behavior.

"Is this what you want you little bitch?" he asked with his eyes closed.

"Yes…This is exactly what I want Josef."

"You like these little crotchless panties don't you," he said ramming himself in further. She was literally suspended hanging on his stiff wand. She was in heaven.

He didn't wait for her answer but only added, "I do too…" The scene was so smoldering hot, he couldn't help but shoot his thunder. He tried to pull out but she made sure that wasn't going to happen. She tightened her thighs around his waist and pulled him in closer. He took a deep breath and placed her back down on the table then quickly pulled up his jeans. Not exactly the romantic encounter she'd been hoping for, but she would've taken anything she could get.

"Put this on" he said pulling her blouse from the back of an adjacent chair. "Why did you feel the need to do this today Fiona? You know when you seduced me a few months ago, I told you it couldn't happen again and now look at you. Sophie is already suspicious of you trying to move in on her territory and our life together. This crazy behavior of yours has got to stop!"

"Oh Josef…don't be silly. It was just a fun little romp that we both obviously needed. Let's not play this game shall we?…You see how I look at you, but okay if that's how you want to play it…it won't happen again. I just couldn't help myself. Litty had told me about your secret cave when she invited me back to the Château a year ago…She explained the method how to come down here and the last time I did was just after you brought that big bag down here. When I saw it was from that swanky shop…It made me curious so I came down here to check it out. Then I saw all of those fancy boxes and thought this little red ensemble had my name on it. Hope you don't mind..." she said devilishly touching herself.

"She gave me this letter to leave here for you as well...for when the time came that is." She tantalizingly raised the envelope up fanning her face with it like a tease. "I left it here for you and you carelessly forgot to take it with you when you went back upstairs. You never realized it could've been me that'd left it here for you to find in the first place."

"Oh my God, there it is. I've been racking my brain trying to remember exactly where I left it...but I figured it must've been down here!" he said seemingly only focused on getting the envelope out of her hands.

When she held the letter up...to Josef's amazement she immediately stopped touching herself and motioned like she was going to rip it in half with both hands. She actually looked ready to do so...

"That is unless you'd prefer I left it all in one piece?" she questioned with a disingenuous look about her. She had already won her trophy unbeknownst to the only other egoist in the room. She'd finally caught what she'd been dangling on her line. He looked at what was happening and quickly snatched the envelope from her grasp.

"Oh I see. That's all you *really* wanted down here" she said with a bit of wicked little false disappointment.

With him having the letter back in his possession she knew her time was up, so she quickly got off the table and slipped on her blouse with cleavage protruding of course. However grateful to have the letter back, he couldn't wrap his head around the fact that he'd created a new and bigger problem to his already complicated life. He couldn't believe the trap that he'd just fallen into. His latest and greatest problem was actually staring right at him.

For the first time in his life he actually felt sorry for having engaged in a couple of afternoon quickies. What had he been thinking?! Those couple of pokes with Fiona would definitely give Sophie cause to leave immediately should she ever find out her suspicions had been acted upon. He could never, ever allow that to happen with Fiona again. In his single minded male thinking, his simple caveman justification chimed in. "If it only happened a couple of times and it was only sex that really didn't mean anything...I could forget all about it like it never happened, right?" Evidently that ridiculous Bad Boy logic prevailed...for now that is.

"Fiona I'm late and need to get to a meeting asap. Why don't you quietly go upstairs now and I'll come up as soon as I know the coast is clear. Please do me the favor... and promise me that you'll Never, but Never come down here again."

She smiled and seemingly took his instructions with the words flying in all directions but hers. She buttoned her blouse, slipped on her skirt and shoes then scurried her way up to the floor above like only a true female cat rat would. Josef took a random bottle of whatever wine he saw on the closest rack, waited a few minutes, then made his way upstairs. He would undoubtedly have his locksmith add a keypad entry to the cellar as soon as possible.

He quietly exited the cellar, only after making sure everything was secure and back in its correct position did he tiptoe his way to the front landing. He was surprised to see both horses were still in front waiting. He led them in a slow walk back to the barn where Michel had been patiently waiting.

"Salut Josef... Did you have a good ride?"

Josef, strangely enough looked at Michel with eyes that reflected a rare pang of guilt. He began rattling off his inner schizoid dialog..."Which ride could he be referring to...the romp with Fiona or the one on horseback. Oh My God is it that obvious? How does he know? Do I smell of sex?" Josef jumped in and out of his thoughts, then responded...

"Yes, and sorry I'm a bit late. Please excuse my tardiness. I had a difficult time deciding which bottle to bring is the reason...It's such a beautiful day, great for a ride. I took Sophie over to give her a glimpse at our new project." He said passing Michel the bottle. "I'm so happy to see how it's looking, it's really coming along. The earth there is so dark it looks and smells like a delicious chocolate malt, rich and prime for planting when we're ready. It radiates success my friend. The additional hectares will make us one of the largest organic producers in the Region. I'm grateful that we'll be doing this project together Michel. Grandfather would be so pleased. So now...let's drink to what new and great things we're doing together."

Once completely inside the barn Josef led both horses to their stalls. "They'll be fine just like they are until Gilles finally decides to show and grooms them..." he said walking to the staff fridge to grab a couple of carrots and a set of clean wine glasses. Crystal glasses were always kept in the fridge for these types of occasions. The two men sat down on a couple of hay bales just like they'd always done for one of their many 'meetings'. In true Vintner fashion, Michel pulled his trusty cork screw from his jean pocket and did the honors. Their close relationship had always been more like family, not one like the 'heir and his employee'. *Instead,* they sat like a wise uncle with his beloved nephew...quietly enjoying a bottle together. They didn't need to speak...it was something within their silence that had always spoken volumes. With the police coming around, Michel had called the 'meeting' just to spend time with Josef and lend his support. Josef didn't want to discuss anything in particular other than making small talk and spending time with his only 'other' unofficial family member...That was comfort enough.

"I'll be going now Josef. Should you need anything, anything at all, you know where to find me. I'm just a whistle away..." Michel said wanting Josef to know he had a loyal friend standing in the wings. They both stood, giving one another a kiss on both cheeks before going their separate ways.

When Josef entered the *Château* he was grateful that the emergency call to his locksmith had worked out. It was so worth the exorbitant price for his quick response. He took the newly minted key from the inside of the front door and used it to lock the door behind him. He gloated simply thinking he'd been so clever to instruct the locksmith to change the front and back door locks and add an entry keypad to the cave. Now, not everyone would be privileged to a fresh set of keys…only he and Sophie. He knew he needed to be more cautious and selective with who would have access to his life, especially after his afternoons reckless 'impromptu' escapade.

"Hi my love, how was your bubble bath?" he said entering the bedroom suite on his way to the bathroom. Sophie was laying down on one of the shimmering sofas where she'd been relaxing. "Delicious my love. How was your meeting?" she said sitting up and sliding down to the floor…positioning herself in front of the fire.

"Great, It's always a pleasure to visit with Michel. I'm just going to jump in the shower and get rid of the horsey smell. I'll join you in a few, okay?" (not waiting for her to answer as usual) What he really wanted to do was wash away the smell of his hot shot with Fiona. The horses had nothing to do with it. When he'd finished his 'cleansing,' he came to sit with Sophie and found her to be mesmerized by the colorful dance of the flame. He sat behind her on the floor and began rubbing her back.

"Do you want me to brush your hair?"

"How sweet Josef…that'd be wonderful. I'd love it, but you've never suggested that once since I've known you. Everything okay?" she said with a light laugh. Thoughtful guy, she hadn't a clue.

"Of course. I was just thinking how much I love you being here…Go get your brush and let me spoil you a bit" he said leaning in for a sweet kiss on her back.

She jumped up and ran to the bathroom to grab her brush, but the minute she was up and making her way…he felt a sudden wave of overwhelming panic flood his every thought. Did he put all of his dirty clothes in the hamper? Could she suspect or notice anything strange pertaining to Fiona? Would the smell of sex be on his clothes? He was beside himself. This, however would become his new norm, …always having to look over his shoulder. He'd entered the trap with Fiona without hesitation and dove in, hook, line and sinker.

Why hadn't he been paying better attention to someone so obvious. The fact?: because the fucker loved having this little secret ego lifting attention and flirtation game going on with the housekeeper, that's why. He wasn't blind, he knew exactly what they'd be doing...on occasion. He'd just never imagined it would've happened again so soon. When you play with fire what else would you expect? It was one big hot mess when it came to anything to do with that girl. He'd hope his quiet afternoon with Sophie could just wash away the rest of his troubles, but as we all know it's not that easy. It gets sticky.

"Josef..." Sophie said with a question mark as she exited the bathroom.

"Oui?" He answered suspect and fearful...praying she hadn't noticed some evidence relating to his quick scandalous adventure.

"What should we do for dinner this evening?" she asked. Relieved to hear her simple question, he exhaled. Not being questioned with any further interrogation...the air came rushing back into his lungs..."I think we should go out. Let me brush your hair and we can discuss it."

"Okay, with pleasure" she said plopping down in front of him. Shen held her brush up by its handle and started waving it side to side in front of her shoulder. Her back was so feminine and beautiful, Josef realized he'd never really appreciated his prize like he did at that very moment...Not until he thought he could lose it that is. He was remembering what Laetitia had told him and was concentrating on her words as he slowly brushed through Sophie's long beautiful naturally blond hair. She could *Never know* about Fiona or any of the others that was for damn sure.

They were just about to dress for dinner when an unexpected call came in on Josef's cell. It was Officer Troccaz.

"Oui...Yes officer" Josef said...then came a long

silence. He listened, then answered, "I'll definitely be there." Then he hung up abruptly.

"Well, that was quick. What was that about?" Sophie questioned.

Josef all of a sudden seemed freaked out and began to bead up with dripping perspiration.

"They want me to go back in and surrender myself to them in the morning. Sophie...this isn't good. They must think they really have something on me. I'm sorry, but we have to stay home tonight. I need to call my lawyer."

"Of course Josef. But what on earth could they possibly 'have' on you that would give them cause to suspect you in this tragedy? It doesn't make any sense."

"There's a major key detail I haven't told you about. They found a burnt shell of what was presumed a solid silver Cartier lighter at the scene. They think it could've been used to start the fire....and more importantly, they think it could've been mine! It's identical to the one Grandfather used to have. The thing was always kept in the center desk drawer in the library, and now it's nowhere to be seen. I can't find it anywhere and the last time I even noticed it was probably around a year ago, I can't be sure. They were tracing the serial number and must've gotten their answer. That's what I think Bruce must've been after when he came into the house during Litty's service. In addition to that potential piece of suspected evidence, we just happened to be at the Retirement Home the day of the fire. Incredibly so...it puts us close to the scene at a most suspicious time. What a fluke! They must have interviewed a few patrons from the 'home'...I'm scared this thing is getting out of control."

"Bruce came inside the *Château*?" she questioned sounding shocked he would've done so.

"Yes, I'm sure it was him. Who else would've been so ballsy? Fiona heard something in the library, then saw someone leaving the house during Litty's service. Her description sounded about right and fits his character. It all makes sense... can't you see? The bastard probably circled back after being thrown out from his disturbance and entered the house knowing everyone was still outside in back. That certainly would explain a few things. You think Bruce is such a nice guy, but there's more to him than you know." Just by regurgitating this possible scenario gave cause for Josef to revamp his hatred for the guy. He began stomping around out of frustration, "I'll be in the library for a few should you need me."

Once Josef was down the stairs and out of sight, Sophie picked up her cell phone and hit speed dial for Bruce. She trembled when she heard his voice. She was either scared of being caught by Josef or terrified of what her ex might have to say.

"Bruce, I know I shouldn't be calling you, but I'm worried about you. I haven't even had the chance to tell you how sorry I am about your parents. This entire situation is so complicated and in no way is it turning out to be a good one. I am so sorry for your loss."

"Don't feel guilt about anything Sophie. It's far too late for that. As far as Josef is concerned…I know you were just bait and caught in the middle. It's too bad you chose not to see it. I certainly did…but it doesn't make the hurt any less painful. I don't know how but I still love you, and I'm worried for you…I think we should meet. There are a few things I need to tell you…things that you should know."

"Don't say that Bruce. I don't want to hear it and that kind of talk scares me. I know everything I need to know. I just wanted to tell you how sorry I am, and for you to be okay through all of this. It's gotten so crazy…Josef is being investigated and it's all a big mess."

"Oh he is, is he…That's interesting," Bruce commented having a certain delight highlighted in his voice.

Sophie thought his response was so curiously bizarre. She hadn't called to open a can of worms but only to give him her condolences, plain and simple. But before they could speak any further, she heard Josef climbing the stairs.

"Bruce I've gotta go. Take care of yourself. I'll call you back one of these days" she whispered…quickly hanging up.

"Were you just speaking to someone?" Josef questioned, entering the suite.

"No I guess just to myself. Everything has gotten me so anxious, I guess I've even started mumbling. Was I being too loud?" she replied trying to make light of the situation and deflect the question.

"My lawyer is flying in to Bergerac in the morning. If they don't have any solid evidence, at least he'll be able to get these people off my back. That'll give us time to organize a game plan. He's also hired a private investigator to help with my case if it comes to that."

"Your case? Oh My God…this is much more than I'd realized. They seriously must think you had something to do with this or you wouldn't be speaking with terms like 'case'. Don't they know you couldn't have been a part of the Douglas' demise?…We were together the entire time and I'm your alibi. Who in their right mind would've wanted the Douglas' dead anyway? Can you imagine?…Personally, I can't fathom such a thing. What a terrible tragedy this whole thing is…"

Josef sat in thoughts of his own while Sophie continued to ramble on with blank sentiments…He thought she was giving a very naïve and typical rendition of her usual 'emotional dialogue'. Of course he couldn't entrust her with any real information, after all…she could be looked at as an accomplice for all he knew and blab her truth to just about anyone who would listen. He couldn't afford to trust her with any secrets. Hiding the truth was his only option.

Josef, the handsome selfish prick…always preferred to keep it that way, so why would he consider changing it now? It was so much easier to keep Sophie clueless and out of the loop on all of it.

*

Chapter Onze

It'd obviously been Litty's last gift of love…writing Josef her death confessional. Needless to say, her explanation letter covered Quite a bit of…ground. He began reflecting on the contents of her letter again now that his panic had subsided…finally recovering the damn thing. What an idiot he'd been being so careless with such a valuable tool. He'd most certainly need to keep it safeguarded from here on out. Within Josef's self centered rationale, he continued to justify everything in the world to help or credit himself. He somehow thought by Litty leaving him the letter explaining her plan, it was her admission of guilt in order to help free him from any implications. The letter would leave Laetitia with the legacy of the Douglas' demise, so instead of him having to admit any guilt…the letter would get him off the hook. That hand written letter of evidence had certainly been left intentionally to save his sorry sweet ass…right?…Case solved.

Holy Fuck…The letter! Oh my GOD…His thoughts became wild realizing he'd left the letter in his jeans pocket …which he'd stupidly left in the bathroom clothes hamper. It all happened so fast, his heart began beating like a hamster running on a hot wheel…He looked up and voila…there she was standing in the bathrooms doorway. He held his breathe.

"Josef I didn't mean to pry but I just found this envelope," she said rather aggressively. "I couldn't help but notice it when I went to put my sweater inside the hamper. It'd obviously fallen out of your jeans pocket, and since the envelope was already open, I read the contents. Just exactly…when were you going to tell me about all of this?"

He sat speechless and petrified. Forget mere beads, Josef was now on his way to bringing a full on *'sweating bullets'* type of thing. He was frozen like a Dairy Queen Blizzard who'd played 27 holes…

He was speechless and couldn't find the words. He didn't know what to say. She'd found it. How could he have been so careless to have left it there for her to discover. He thought Sophie was a great piece of ass, but he'd forgotten how clever our girl actually could be on occasion. At times, she was certainly more than just a beautiful arm piece who could give him gorgeous children. He'd temporarily overlooked her being the snide and sharp girl that she'd been when they'd first met.

When he didn't (or couldn't) answer…she walked over to the fireplace and gently dropped the envelope into the flame. It felt like it was all happening in slow motion. He couldn't believe what he was seeing once he finally realized what she was doing. (Did I say S*L*O* W…motion?)

"What the hell Sophie!"…Josef yelled as he ran to the fireplace, trying to retrieve the envelope from the flames. Poor boy, hope he didn't burn his hands…

It was too late, it had already disappeared into the abyss of the blue and orange blaze right in front of his eyes. He turned to Sophie with a look that was sure to be followed by a vizierial rant, but before he could open his mouth and blow his venomous words, she was smart enough to already be hastily moving across the room.

"I'll be sleeping in my room tonight" she said trying to eek out the words with clarity before making a mad dash towards the huge doors. Thank God she was able to open the heavy's…allowing her to make a run for it, to 'her' bedroom. She locked her door behind her with Josef quick to follow. When finding the door locked, he knew any attempt to engage was futile. Quite honestly…he didn't know how to respond, should she have opened the door and confronted him anyway. He'd need the night to rehearse.

No further contact occurred…he simply returned to his manly *private suite but he* was fit to be tied…and stayed pacing for about an hour before going down to the kitchen. Of course the Bitch would be there waiting. For the life of him, he couldn't understand why he hadn't taken better care of that precious letter. Those words written by Litty on their own were enough to exonerate him. Feeling totally spent by all of this…he found himself in the kitchen again, looking through Fiona and into his future…which wasn't looking so bright at that moment.

"Josef, allo?…Can you hear me!"…Fiona demanded completely agitated. She'd had a minute to digest their earlier romp and felt she could be so bold as to take the liberty and snap her fingers in his face. She'd become scorned and pissed off needing to command his attention.

Sadly, he just sat numb, not actually hearing or seeing a thing. However, it was the loud bells ringing in his ears that took precedent. They had a bit of competition with the heavy thumping happening in his chest. He was definitely sitting in a state of shock. He could only think how incredible it was that both Fiona And Sophie had read Litty's admission letter…And now? It had been destroyed and up in smoke as they say. Realizing there was no longer any tangible evidence that could free him from the situation, (as in throwing a loved one under the bus) he began laughing like he was in the midst of a breakdown. So much for wanting to protect the family's reputation. It had become all out survival mode at this point.

"Hel…lo..ugh…Are you seriously having a meltdown right here and now?"

"What!!! What is it Fiona? What the fuck do you want! What could you possibly have to say to me at this point!!" he yelled, springing up out within his hyper manic state. He suddenly snapped and was zoned in again with a bit of reality back to concentrating on no other…than himself of course.

"Nothing. Nothing at all!" she snipped slamming a plate of charcuterie and a bottle of wine down forcefully on the table in front of him. She left him sitting alone to brew. So much for her attempt…nIce try BItch, not hap en nim…

Josef was awaken the next morning by the soft sunlight gracefully filtering in as he lay on one of the living room sofas. Once he was able to shake off his heavy grog… he sat up, gathered his thoughts and made his wobbly way out to his gorgeous new Range Rover...He actually looked like a gruff sexy bona fide cowboy due to his lack of effort in his usual morning primping. No prep for the day required, no handsome pruning needed, just a speedy exit with determination for this refreshed Golden Boy. The macho had conveniently snapped back in full force and had hit the ground running, as they say.

Sophie heard Josef making some noise outside in back as he slid the car barn door open. She felt relieved and instinctively felt a sense of freedom for the moment. She snuggled down again into her luxurious bedding and reached over to turn on the bedside lamp.

Things were different now...she'd always thought the bed to be so luxurious, only it didn't feel so heavenly like before. What had once felt like silky soft satin now felt more like rough scratchy burlap.

Thank GOD...her itch...was back.

She took her sweet time carefully unfolding the letter she'd placed under her pillow the night before. She wanted to re-read it slowly, capturing every juicy detail. Josef would never need to know the letter was still intact and not in the envelope when she torched the thing...That letter was her insurance...she knew she had to keep it hidden and well protected. Amazing the idiot never questioned whether the letter was actually inside the envelope. Our girl was awake at last, but knew it'd only be a matter of time before Josef would figure it all out. Let's not forget, he was a clever bastard after all.

Josef had arrived at the airport in Bergerac and was having a cup of coffee from the vending machine when he saw his attorney, Olivier Duvet's aircraft land on the tarmac. The airport was so pleasantly quiet that early in the morning. It usually only had a skeleton crew and a single janitor working. Josef knew the place and everyone well. Olivier's jet would be the first to arrive for the day.

"Good Morning Josef," Olivier said extending his hand to offer a brisk handshake.

"Hello Olivier. Thank you for coming on such short notice."

"It's my pleasure. I'll spare you any small talk and get to the point. I knew I needed to get here asap after speaking to the Insurance Company late yesterday. They provided some additional details which made me think we should get down to business and head this thing off sooner than later. Their news was quite surprising. As it turns out...'Ol Gene had a whopping life insurance policy in place. It's all in the fine print, but the policy states that by any chance his demise be accidental, the number one beneficiary of the policy would be his son, Bruce.

If they found it to be intentional, in fact a homicide, it would become complicated and Bruce wouldn't see a dime. His estate would be tied up for years. That alone would give cause to consider Bruce as the number one murder suspect. You see?...He could become a very wealthy man if he did this and was able to get away with it. To convolute the issue even further, the reason the Police are so persistent with getting you in today is because someone has come forward indicating you to have been at the scene about the time the fire broke out. They wouldn't give me any further info other than the 'witness' will be at the courthouse this morning to confirm your I.D."

"What?!!! This is insane! I was only at the Retirement Home for a brief moment and I never went to that house! I know it puts me in the immediate vicinity, but I swear I didn't have a fucking thing to do with any of this," he screamed, his voice echoing through the empty airport...

"I understand your frustration Josef, but we have to keep a cool head about us now. Let's see who this joker is and if he's even credible."

All players were present when they arrived at the courthouse. Josef was shocked to see Bruce was also in attendance. What in the hell was he doing there?

They were all ushered into a larger group type interrogation room when Bruce pointed to Josef..."That's the man I saw around the house...that's him, Josef Decour."

"YOU LIAR" Josef screeched.

"Oh you pathetic thing...You're obviously so jealous about me being with Sophie you can't stand it. You'll go to any lengths...This is all bullshit and you know it!" Josef yelled, then caught himself...Miraculously, he was able to change his tone of delivery and bring it down an octave. Bruce just sat smiling watching Josef squirm.

Olivier then interjected, "Settle down gentlemen, this is just a preliminary meeting. No need getting upset and letting tempers flair. It's way too early for that. We don't have all the real validated facts yet."

"That's correct," Officer Troccaz chimed in. "Thank you for your patience Mr. Douglas. Would you mind waiting in the next room. There are some further questions we'd like to ask you."

"No problem," he said leaving the room like he was confidently sitting on top. It made Josef nauseous being in the same room with the guy, not to mention seeing how he was acting...

"That lying bastard...where was he when the fire started?" Josef whispered under his breath loud enough for everyone in the room to hear his *questioning* statement.

"Josef, you will need to wait here with your attorney for a while. I'll be back" said the Officer leaving the room and closing the door behind him. Then he went next door to the smaller interrogation room where Bruce was waiting.

"So Bruce...he said, (slowly pulling up a chair) Have you ever seen this before? Any idea what it is?" ...placing the same exact melted piece of silver down in front of him that he'd shown to Josef.

The Officer's well thought out plan of having Bruce there to be the one to identify Josef at the scene had played into his hands perfectly. He'd yet to mention to Bruce that he was also being considered a 'person of interest'. Given that fact, they couldn't take Bruce's word as validation for anything. It was just the opposite...After all, it was now known that Bruce was a candidate to be the recipient of a huge insurance policy and he'd love nothing more than to land the blame elsewhere.

After learning through town gossip how deep the two men's hatred towards one another was, the detective thought he'd create a moment to pit them against one another to expose their true identities. The tension and confrontation would allow the truth to prevail and surface easily. But…that'd been an under-estimation when it came to these two seasoned sparing partners. Their animosity towards one another was playing out big time…The sparks flew but somehow, they both were still hiding their game. Only those two knew the rules.

"No, I've never seen that before. What is it?" Bruce questioned. "Why am I being shown a piece of scorched silver?"

It might've been a melted down piece of something unidentifiable, but he knew exactly what it was. The officer cleverly didn't answer his question directly.

"We have reason to believe that you could've been at the house when the fire began Mr. Douglas. Is there any reason why you would have wanted your parents dead?" (Bruce turned the color of the crisp white paper the cop was holding)

"Of course not! What a ridiculous question…Why in the world would you ever think that?"

"Because the talk around the village is that you'd always had an extremely contentious relationship with your Father. Is that true? What was the basis for that type of relationship?"

"What the hell is this type of questioning?…I want to call a lawyer."

"Yes, I think that might be a good idea. It turns out we've received new information. The housekeeper at Josef's place has now identified you as the intruder leaving from the front door of the *Château* the day of the funeral service for Josef's 'Grandmother'. Is there anything about that you'd like to comment on?"

"I won't be answering any questions until I have an attorney present."

"Suit yourself," Officer Troccaz said nonchalantly as he gathered his notebook and left the room. He demonstrated such a smooth, arrogant mystique about him…it was apparent he was the king pin at the station.

Nothing in this scenario was turning out like it should. With all the years that these two men had tried their best to avoid one another, damn if they weren't now sitting in interrogation rooms right next to each other. Ironically both as 'persons of interest' in the same horrific crime! It had become notable, no one would get out of this situation unscathed…it'd all become too intertwined. There was no way out for these two. Their years of bad blood had finally come back to haunt them. It was all going to come out.

After having the entire afternoon pass, Josef was conveniently released into his lawyers custody with the stipulation of not leaving the area. Bruce on the other hand was told he'd be staying over night in jail until he could find proper legal representation. Without being able to provide a passport, which presumably had gone up in smoke…he reluctantly agreed, not having much of a choice. Fortunately he was able to obtain an attorney but the soonest time for a meeting was the following morning. He would then and only then make bail and be eligible for release. He wouldn't end up leaving as you can imagine with the same kush terms as the Golden Boy.

When Bruce's legal representation did arrive and negotiate his release, he'd need a place to stay. It was arranged that he check into the only local accommodation that was open that time of year called 'The Burlier Restaurant & Inn'. It'd be a very secure check-in all right… one that would include a police guard stationed at the door ensuring he'd be staying in place until it all got sorted. It really was turning out to be a complicated nightmare… *believe* you me.

Josef however…had the luxury of going back to his beautiful *Château* with his attorney to leisurely discuss their game plan. Sophie anxiously greeted them curious to hear all about what had transpired. Josef was relieved to see her, yet being his normal self didn't show it, he only played it smug. He wanted her to know he was still pissed for the charade with the envelope.

After introductions had been made, the two men left Sophie in the kitchen and made their way to the library to speak *privately*…as Men often do. Seriously?…Macho fucks. It was a 'closed door' meeting of course.

"Tell me really…what's been going on here Josef? I need to know the truth if I'm going to help you get out of this mess. These charges are really quite serious, you have to know that, right? The police are taking their time…and that means they're actively building a strong and thoughtful case. But obviously they're not positively certain of anything at the moment or they would never have granted you bail and permission to leave" Olivier said, sitting down on the heavily tufted sofa. He crossed his legs and swung his arm casually over the back of the expensive buttery soft leather Chesterfield. He felt right at home.

"Like I've already told you, I took Sophie with me to the Retirement Home to drop off some personal items for Litty's old friends, and that's as close as we got to the Douglas' place. Granted, the retirement home *is* on the adjacent street from the Impasse, but you can't see anything other than the roof of the house from there. It's crazy to think the fire must've started right about the time we were leaving. That's when we decided to catch a flight to Geneva. We didn't see or smell anything that could've given suspect or even relate to the fire. I had no idea about any of it until our return which was five days after the tragedy had occurred."

"I'm happy to know that. Do you happen to have any receipts? You know…Toll roads, parking tabs…anything at all that could be useful in verifying a time line?"

"Well…we flew from Bergerac to Geneva and you can find us on the passenger manifest. I paid cash for the tickets and picked them up at the airport just before the flight. You can also look at the time we checked into the Hôtel in Megève and work backwards from there if any of this helps."

"Of course it does, that's all helpful and needed information. I'll get busy mapping your time schedule of travel to prepare for court tomorrow. But then answer me this if you would…What's the real deal between you and this guy Bruce?"

Josef sighed, "I can't wrap it up in one quick version for you. It's been a long brewing story ever since we were kids. Adolescent rivalry I guess. Nothing more than that"… he said, completely evading a truthful response.

Josef wanted to hide as much as he could. No way did he want to imply or give reason for anyone to see his long involvement and intertwined connection with the Douglas family. He certainly didn't want to expose any of his true feelings towards them visibly, GOOD GOD, no way! If that were to happen it'd be detrimental to his case and show 'cause' due to his animosity…So he remained distant and aloof on the subject without any further explanation.

"Okay that's enough for now, but should you think of anything helpful to add, the sooner the better."

Josef nodded in agreement, "We can resume our discussion later" he said sliding the wooden pocket doors open from the library to enter the foyer.

The afternoon had escaped into early evening and as he led Olivier through to the living room he saw the dining table in the far back had already been set. They entered the magnificent space with the lights shimmering in from the orchid solarium and the wall sconces being lit casting a low glow.

"Now I see…This IS quite extraordinary…I've heard stories about this room. From what Gustav has told me there have been quite a few chic dinner parties held on this gorgeous table."

"It's true and Gus should know. He's attended the majority of events held right here in this very room. He's been a close friend of our family for years as you know. Sorry you missed the times around the table when my Grandfather was still alive. If only this thing could talk," Josef smirked as he slapped his hand down on the mahogany slab. He delivered the sentiment with a devious boy laugh as they took their seats, both men amused at the thought …the pricks.

Josef reached for the bottle of wine that'd been left next to his place setting and after inspecting the label, opened it to his satisfaction.

"Hmm...I guess I won't be the one wine pairing the dinner this evening. Seems as though the choice has already been made, and made quite well I think."

Just as he was pouring the first glass, Sophie entered the dining room carrying a huge ceramic covered pot. She placed it on a metal disk in between the two men and opened the lid allowing the fragrant aroma to escape. A delicious smoldering dish of Pot-au-Feu began wafting its exquisite flavored delicacy throughout the room. The scrumptious scent was familiar being that it was in every French kids culinary repertoire growing up. The boys needless to say, were delighted.

"Wow Sophie, what an absolutely perfect dish for this evening. Did Fiona make this?"

"No darling...I did" she replied nicely, only after she'd carefully placed the heavy lid of the Creuset casserole down on a nearby quilted pad...

"How in the world did you know how to make this classic?" Josef questioned cupping his palm over the dish and waving it in a circular motion towards him to direct the flavorful aroma his way.

Sophie just proudly smiled and looked at Olivier... "He thinks I'm just a pretty face," she said laughing. "Let me serve you gentleman."

After she filled their bowls with the beautiful vegetable broth type stew medley, she then served herself a small portion. After perfectly slicing the baguette in diagonal chunks, she quietly took her seat at the third place setting.

"Where's Fiona this evening?" Josef inquired.

"Oh I gave the help the night off. How is everything progressing?" She said immediately redirecting the conversation...while looking directly at Olivier with a little smile. It was her attempt to deflect any further conversation relating to the invisible bitch in the room.

"Did they find out who's responsible for this tragedy?

Those poor, poor people…Have you buttoned it all up yet?"

Making sure she didn't linger on anything specific… She kept moving the dialog along towards the inquiry in general. Fiona had become an afterthought for the table due to Sophie's quick wit delivery and change of subject. All the while, our hostess subtly used her all so *fake southern bell accent* which evidently made both men take more notice. Some things never change ya'll.

"No, not yet…There are a few things that need further clarification, but we're getting there" Olivier said, loudly sipping his second full spoonful of steaming broth. "This is absolutely delicious Sophie. Did you really make this beautiful classic yourself? My Mother didn't even make it taste this good."

"Now…that's Really sayin' something Olivier. Thank you for that remarkable compliment. How sweet of you to think that, and yes…I made it all by myself. I wanted to offer you gentlemen something nice upon your return from what I can only assume was a long and stressful day. Comfort food always finds a special calming place for me. At least it used to when I was in the US."

"Oh it does here too. This traditional dish is perfect for an early evening supper. It was a fantastic choice my dear. Thank you," Olivier said changing his phonetics.

Surprisingly…but right on cue, he actually began speaking with a mild suggestive Horny Attorney tenor. It's as if he was trying to have an intimate conversation and flirt with Sophie right in front of Josef…(perhaps thinking he wouldn't notice?) God…did she love it. So much for her successful home cooking…It seemed to have hit the right spot and landed where she'd expected. Having Josef be put in a competitive place for a change felt better than any compliment she could've received on her cheffing skills that's for sure. Sophie had put on such an act during dinner…So to *really* take advantage of the situation and irritate Josef, she began openly flirting back with Olivier. Why not? He was so crass and predictable, she merely returned the favor. In any event, they managed to pass a lovely evening together while speaking on a plethora of topics…but then Sophie asked Olivier where he'd be sleeping for the night….Josef then bulldozed his way back into the table talk and took the lead.

"He's staying here tonight…Don't worry dear, I have it covered…I'll show him up to his room a bit later, when we're finished here". Josef wasn't about to let her think she could continue to steal the stage for the entire evening. "Sweetheart, I'll meet you upstairs in our bedroom suite shortly"…he said, dismissing her with a bit of autocratic bullshit. He sounded as if he were excusing a naughty child needing instructions for their 'time out'. Talking down to her was intentional of course…it was his way to 'impress' council, I guess. He always used this type of behavior as some kind of controlling method, but this time she wasn't buying it.

"Okay then…I'll bid you gentlemen a good night. Olivier…hopefully I'll see you in the morning" she said excusing herself from the table like a sophisticated royal.

"Leave the dishes here for Fiona. I'm sure she'll be happy to find a little something for her to do in the morning…just like you thought Litty would've, remember darling? It seems Fiona has a lot of free time on her hands lately and possibly needs more to keep her busy. Bonne Soirée gentlemen" she said ever so graciously before leaving the dining room and making her exit through the living room.

"…My GOD Josef, SHE is absolutely Gorgeous! Where in the world did you find such an exquisite woman… especially way out here in the country?…And wow can she cook! Tonight's dinner was superb in every way, including those Incredibly delicious desserts, and her worldly knowledge is amazing! Not bad for an American…" Olivier chuckled.

"Agreed…but I must admit, all of this tonight was a bit of a shock for me. I had no idea she could even find her way around the kitchen. Sophie's full of surprises, that's one thing I'm certain of" he said with a possessive and gloating smile. He was thinking he needed to get upstairs pronto and give her a good lesson. She had succeeded in making him jealous.

Once Josef had shown Olivier to his room upstairs... the one at the end of the hall on the left, he went into (his) their bedroom suite feeling like he was a suave-bola ready to conquer, but Sophie was nowhere to be found. He pivoted around like a barrel racer...and went directly to his old room where he found her sitting in bed reading.

"What are you doing in here? I said I'd meet you in our suite."

"HaHa...If I didn't know better I'd think you are worried that I might tiptoe down the hall and visit Olivier during the night" she said with a taunting giggle. Josef wasn't amused, he just took off his clothes and promptly got into bed. He couldn't believe she'd say such a thing...

"Don't be such a brat. I can't help myself. Seeing you look so beautiful and being such a great hostess tonight made me crazy. I don't know what to do with you my dear."

"Oh really? I thought we'd already decided and worked that out a while ago...Have you changed your mind?" she questioned, feeling as if she had the upper hand for a change.

That maternal record was playing like an old classic again until Josef said, "What's your plan with the letter?"

"What letter?"...she responded after a few seconds... "Oh, that letter" she replied unconvincingly. "You mean the one that went up in flames?" she said with an equally unconvincing look...

"You may think you can out smart me sometimes, but this happens not to be one of them my darling," he said rolling over on top of her. He gave her a good and satisfying moment, but he was more concentrated on taking his own pleasure. Quite honestly...his physical behavior spoke volumes. This would be the first apparent time Sophie could actually feel he was 'over her'...Things had definitely changed.

After he had found his satisfaction, he rolled back over and fell asleep instantly. All that did was give her time to lay there and contemplate while listening to him snore.

"What would ever give him reason to assume the letter was still intact? He's just trying to mess with my head so let me see"…She stretched her hand up underneath her pillow and of course the letter she'd hidden there was gone. It was then crystal clear Fiona and Josef were in it together. Her mind began to silently explode.

"That witch! That sneaky little British Chick…how dare she search my room…again. She's been in here snooping around on more than one occasion, and this just gives me proof! For those stupid fools to think I'd jeopardize and be willing to lose my insurance? …Fat chance, I knew full well one or both of them would come in here and take that forged letter…This guy is really quite amazing to think he could continue to play me forever. Seriously, that bastard's got another thing coming if he thinks so. I loved our sex life and had gotten so wrapped up in 'the dream,' that I'd gotten lost in it…but your not enough for me anymore you little manipulator…I'm finally on to you Josef and know just how you play. I'll take it as long as you'll give it, but you're not the only one in this *game* now…it's over for me too."

Sophie's inner-dialogue had finally found its voice… It was her rationale speaking. She'd begun to touch her inner psyche. Her racing thoughts began to spin through her head as she lay there, listening to him gargle in his sleep. Why hadn't she ever taken notice of that disgusting habit before? She felt grateful her decoy plan had worked, but hated the fact it had actually been necessary. It made everything so disappointingly clear…

The morning finally came and when Josef awoke he rolled over and casually kissed her…"Good Morning Sophie. How'd you sleep chérie?" he said as if it were a pre-recorded message. She was actually surprised he could speak given the fact he'd miraculously not swallowed his tongue during the night given all the repulsive whistling and grunts that'd come out of him.

"Great…and you?"

Okay…seriously, let's face it. Their game of 'pretend'

had played itself out. They were so full of their own bullshit, it was almost too much for either one of them to take. Their once simple Cat and Mouse game now required each to become a tricky professional. That would include dodging all salacious traps being laid by either party. Each player now needed to bring their most *hyper-clever* recourse and calculating game to the show in order to survive.

"Excellent, I feel refreshed and ready to go," he said stretching his jeans up and on. It's as if they were a banana, being peeled in reverse. He was sexy no matter what he did. Damn.

She just nodded in agreement having laid next to him all night listening to him spew. The fucker actually had the nerve to admit he'd slept like a baby. But baby…what had really happened was she'd had the time to make her decision. And that (drum roll please) was to leave his sorry ass…Finally… Game Over.

"Olivier is going to meet us down in the dining room this morning at 8:00. Are you coming?" He questioned as he was leaving the room. Intentionally, he'd not given her any advance notice of the planned breakfast meeting that was happening in a mere 2 minutes. He wanted to begin the day by taking her off kilter a bit. He definitely wasn't going to allow her any edge or advantage in taking the lead like she'd done the night before. By no means was he going to allow her to perform a repeat performance and orchestrate an open 'flirting session' with Olivier like she'd done during the prior evening's dinner.

Once he was out of sight and on his way downstairs, Sophie stretched her body and felt up under all the pillows for the letter again. She took all the pillows off and searched around only to confirm her findings from the night before. Yep, unfortunately she hadn't been dreaming. The letter was gone. She sat straight up and began to nervously giggle when all she really wanted to do was cry.

"That little sneak did exactly what I thought she'd do. Glad she doesn't know Litty's handwriting as well as Josef does or she would've realized it was a copy that I wrote and left for her to find. That letter is worth nothing in my handwriting. Ha! Got 'cha Miss Fiona. Take your non accent and shove it."

Even though Sophie was falsely bragging to herself, she was quietly heartbroken. Her dream world had shattered. All of the lies and pretending were now being exposed. She reached over to the nightstand and opened the book where she'd left off only to find the folded original. She kissed the letter and returned it to its safe hiding and closed the book placing it back on the nightstand. She hopped out of bed and threw on a lovely floral slip dress topped with a bright fuchsia cashmere cardigan. No bra, No panties…She was finished with all that. Going commando would now be her preference.

"This should be sultry enough for breakfast" she said swishing her hips from side to side as she stood reviewing herself in front of the full length mirror. "I just know how much they love cashmere around here and I'm sure Fiona will like this one too."

Her smile immediately turned upside down and she began glaring at herself while thinking of the Brit. After she put her hair up in a sexy top knot and added a touch of glossy pale pink to her lips, she quickly made her way downstairs.

"Good Morning Olivier. How'd you sleep last night?" she asked gleefully in a half twirl. Her ever so demure and charming presence was to ensure a noticeably seductive entrance into the dining room. She definitely had a spring to her step and a refreshed game face on.

"Perfect night Sophie, Merci. Good Morning to you as well" he pleasantly replied.

She leaned over and kissed him once on either cheek. "Bonjour" she said with a big smile, giving him direct eye contact. They'd obviously graduated from 'vous' to 'tu' given their lovely dinner…and *familiar* conversation the night before.

"Oh doesn't this look lovely…" she said wanting to puke as she glanced over at the incredible breakfast spread sitting on the buffet. "Everything...just looks...scrumptious. Absolutely perfect in fact, right Josef?"

Sophie's lifted eyebrows and her over the top faux gratitude was infectious with just her smile. She was putting on the charm so thick, she reeled Olivier in immediately. It made Josef somewhat suspicious seeing her behavior.

"I see you're having your usual omelette this morning Josef...and you Olivier?...Oh my...that Fiona...she really does know just how to please Josef with all his favorites, isn't that right sweetheart...Is there something here in the mix that you have your eye on?" Sophie questioned teasingly, displaying not so much naïvety.

"I think so," Olivier replied with a wink while looking at Sophie and not at the buffet where Josef was standing.

Sophie loved having this little bit of subtle macho rivalry display happening in front...And over her. It was just enough to give her ego a needed boost after witnessing the strange and protective bond that Josef and Fiona shared. She'd been so stupid...She knew they'd always kept some kind of a secret between them. But now that it'd become so blatantly obvious with the letter disappearing, she could no longer deny it. Their latest little 'event' was the Game Changer.

Once Sophie stepped *into the light* she realized Josef had never really given her the honest and true love that one would expect from one's soul mate. His type of love was something she'd mistakenly masqueraded in exchange for great sex. Her projected image and dream of what was 'the good life' had far superseded reality. It'd all been so very dreamy and glamorous at the beginning...

She knew what she'd really been missing was the sincere loyalty and honor that comes along with the real thing. I'm talking about *true love* here people. She could no longer pretend it was something more than it was. She had finally summed up what she'd really been all along...just one of his pawns.

Thank God, even during the times when she had major waves of self doubt, somewhere hidden way down deep she'd managed to keep a little glimmering slice of her old type of independence alive. Although it may have dwindled into a mere shadow of strength...it had finally begun to percolate. I only wish her woman's emotional vault had been bigger, stronger, and had shown up to the party earlier...it would've made her exit so much easier. Now she had a big dilemma.

How could she *get out* successfully and recuperate some of what she'd so willingly given up? What would she be left with? A defunct business, no savings, no place to live, and no obvious future to speak of. Her options weren't looking so good, but whatever they'd end up to be, she finally realized they'd be a hell of a lot better than continuing with her pipe dream. She'd just have to take her chances and get back out there. As she stood heartbroken...looking all pretty in pink, she began wondering how to pick up her pieces and make her move to leave him...

"Try the crêpes Olivier. I'm sure they'll satisfy you," Sophie suggested with a certain amount of provocative flair. At that moment she happened to be smearing Nutella all over hers with a swirling motion. Her hips...of course, mimicking her spoon's movements. Suddenly she stopped, rolled up her crêpe and took a big, sultry slow bite out of one end like she was devouring a soft, overstuffed...burrito was it?

Olivier and Sophie started laughing together at her provocative actions. She glanced over at Josef who remained sitting at the table submerged in his own enjoyment, coveting his boring cheese omelette. She was curious if he was reminiscing about Laetitia OR Fiona with every bite, but whatever his self-serving thoughts were...at that very specific moment, she saw him for what he was.

"Josef if you don't mind, I'd like to take Zephyr out today for a short ride." Josef was shocked that she would consider getting on the back of such a beast and not take Nuage.

"I don't think that's such a good idea Sophie. I know you have experience, but that stallion is *special* and very unpredictable. I don't want you getting hurt."

"Oh that's really sweet and considerate of you, but we'll be fine. I'll ask Gilles to saddle him up nicely and I'll take it slow and easy. He's such a magnificent animal, I want to experience what it is to ride such a gorgeous creature. I'll be careful and take good care of him, don't worry."

After her convincing spiel and gaining his approval, she excused herself from the table and said her goodbyes to Olivier.

"I hope to see you again. Thank you for all the hard work you're doing for us."

Upon that display of faux loyalty, once Sophie was upstairs Josef surprisingly also said his goodbyes to Olivier.

"Please be in touch by tomorrow with any updates. I'll have Michel give you a ride to the airport. I'm sure you can understand, I can't let my girl ride out in the blue yonder without me."

"Smart man, I wouldn't either…especially while all of this is going on. I'll give you a call tomorrow morning. I feel this has been a good and productive trip Josef. Thank you."

*

Chapter Douze

As Josef was just closing the front door after Olivier's exit, Sophie was dancing her way down the stairs. She was surprised to see Josef about to make his way up to find her.

"I've decided to go with you on your ride this morning sweetheart. It'll be good for us to get out."

"What? I thought you'd be tied up with Olivier for the morning" she said with her best lying eyes. She really wanted to get away and be without him for a while. Turns out she actually had a little something specific in mind...

"I'd rather spend the time with you...that is if you wouldn't mind riding Nuage. I know she likes you, besides I still worry about what happened the last time you went out riding alone. We're still looking for whoever it was in that car that spooked you. There isn't much more Olivier can do here that he can't do from his office. There's no need for him to stick around until we have more updated news from the detective. Michel's taking him to the airport as we speak so now I'm free."

Sophie wisely decided to save the situation and calmly replied, "I love Nuage, I can ride Zephyr another time. I don't want you to think that spooky instance was anything more than it was. It was probably just some lost obnoxious tourist. In this case, let's get going shall we? You can wear the boots you keep in the barn."

She felt her magic strength finally kicking in again. She'd have to remember...laughter and keeping *it light* would always make her the winner. She knew she needed to stop letting Fiona get to her and return to being someone that was fun to be with, at least until she could figure out her next move. Now it was Sophie who was buying time. She was so curious where the chips were going to fall regarding Laetitia's admission, and just who might've been responsible for the fire. Could all of what Litty wrote in the letter really be true? And how was Josef involved in all of this? Sophie knew in her heart of hearts he must've played a part in it. There were so many questions needing answers…

They arrived at the barn and waited for their rides to be saddled up. They sat on sweet smelling hay bales while waiting for Gilles to get all the tack ready…

"You seem like you are on a mission to go somewhere specific this morning Sophie. What's that about?" Josef questioned…pulling a few stray pieces of hay from her hair.

"HaHa…Don't get any ideas Monsieur, I *am* on a mission." She leaned back towards him and gave him a peck on the tip of his nose. He was still irresistibly handsome after all, and even though she was on to him she couldn't allow him to know it. "I want to go back to the area where we had that beautiful picnic. Somewhere in the distance…if I'm not mistaken, I think I saw something that resembled a tennis court, or was that just a mirage?" she laughed, standing up.

"No, no mirage, I'm shocked you could've seen it from that far away Miss Eagle Eye. There is one…out there, but it has to be more than a kilometer away from where we were having our lunch. Why? Do you have an interest in Tennis?…I didn't know that."

"I was on the Tennis Team in High School, I'll have you know. I love the game, but I haven't played in a serious way in years. You're such an athlete, I assume you play?" she said, questioning.

Josef didn't want to seem weak and admit he couldn't…"It's just hitting a ball over the net back and forth isn't it?"

"Exactly…nothing to it my dear" she replied straight faced. "Let's get going."

The horses stood so tall and shone so beautifully in the sunlight. Their manes and tails had been brushed and the duo were saddled up in their finest. When Sophie mounted Nuage, the leather rubbing together once again made that familiar and delicious seasoned song. The reins felt especially good…like holding beautiful long velvety lengths of plump whole vanilla beans. It was heavenly. Their smell, their strength, their beauty…so much to take in that Sophie moaned a sigh of satisfaction. She didn't waste any time galloping off not waiting for Josef, but of course he was quick to catch up.

"What's the hurry?" he said riding up next to her.

"I just want the wind in my hair today, that's all. Yaw!" she commanded loudly giving Nuage a squeeze with her heels.

She went flying. They were both soon riding at top speed and in unison. Josef finally noticed what an excellent horse-woman Sophie was. She was so strong and solid in the saddle, nothing shook her along the ride that she wasn't able to overcome. Even with a stranger scaring her and spooking her horse she managed to stay on like she were glued to the saddle. She'd already proven to be full of surprises, but tennis?…Seriously?

"Oh there it is," she shrieked beaming with excitement. You would've thought she'd just spotted the last egg on an Easter Sunday. "Let's take a closer look. Could there actually be someone playing?" she questioned enthusiastically. She was in a world to herself and proceeded to ride full steam ahead like the seasoned equestrian that she was.

When she arrived she quickly dismounted and tied Nuage to a tree, then quietly walked over to view the players more closely. They were in the midst of a tenacious volley and were so competitively focused, they didn't bother to stop the play even with an unexpected intruder gawking at them. They were at break point and continued their major rally until finally, they had a winner. You would've thought it was the French Open the way they'd been going at each other.

Once the match had ended the victor walked over to Sophie and leaned against the fence. "Hello there"…she said melodiously. "My name is Virginie,"…not being out of breath whatsoever.

"What an incredible volley that was. It was fantastic to watch. Thank you," Sophie replied.

"...And you might be?"

"Oh excuse me, I was so excited I got caught up in the moment and forgot my manners...my name is Sophie."

"Well, I'm flattered Sophie. Do you play? I'm always looking for a challenge should you want to come by some time next week." Just as Sophie was about to reply, Josef appeared from behind the tree and surprised them both.

"Hello Virginie."

"Jos...ef...Is that you? Wow, It's been years..." she said with a chill in her voice.

"Let's go Sophie. The horses must be anxious to get back for their feeding."

"Oh...okay" Sophie replied feeling she'd been put in an awkward and embarrassing position. All she could muster up was a timid smile to Virginie before mounting up and waving a farewell. She was stunned at Josef's rudeness. They rode all the way back to the barn without a look or speaking a word to one another.

"Why didn't you tell me you knew who owned that tennis court?"

"I didn't know I did. I thought Virginie sold and moved years ago. The place never had a tennis court before. You took off so fast, you didn't give me a chance to tell you. When I saw you watching them play, I decided to stay in the background, *never thinking* you would actually strike up a conversation with one of the players."

"That seems strange Josef. Why would you do that? How do you know her?"

"Virginie and I went to school together for a short while before she was shipped off to boarding school. We dated briefly, but nothing more than that. Come on, let's go see what's for lunch" Josef said, side stepping the subject.

Sophie didn't press the issue but went along with his story. They went into the house to find lunch on the kitchen table with a note from Fiona. She wasn't feeling well and wouldn't be available until the following day. That would leave Josef and Sophie alone to enjoy the late afternoon and evening all to themselves.

"OMG…to simply have one night without a glimpse of that British Bitch will be such a reprieve," Sophie thought.

Even though her feelings for Josef had changed, Sophie felt trapped and conflicted having become lackadaisical about making plans for her exit. Her confusion was magnified because she remained addicted to their sex, which made it convenient not to feel the rush to leave. Like anyone in a relationship full of denial, she'd become ambivalent…actually numb from her underlying guilt by staying. Sophie really was in a quandary.

For reasons that were not logical, she allowed herself to continually become seduced and fall back into his sexy lair. She thought she'd be strong enough to escape his sticky web when the time became truly convenient to do so. Until then for immediate gratification, she'd take advantage of a sultry bubble bath after dinner.

This type of backslide would continue just until she was presented with more of a reason to leave. (As if she possibly could need one more…) It takes a strong woman to choose to be alone versus remaining a pawn like Sophie had become. But somewhere in her inner soul she knew she'd been given a window of opportunity by meeting this woman named Virginie. Josef's reaction when seeing her only validated her suspicions. She now saw a friendly face that could possibly give her some needed information. She knew she had to do a bit of detective work and could only do it alone.

The following morning came with a few questions and another excuse. "Josef, would you mind if I drove the Rover to have my hair done in the village this morning?"

"Great idea sweetheart, why don't I drive you?"

"Oh Josef, that's really not necessary. If I'm going to live here, I might as well get a little independent knowledge of the place and start driving myself. I'll be home by early afternoon, okay with you?"

She had phrased it in such a casual and nice way he wasn't suspect…and only pleasantly agreed. Pulling out of

the drive she initially went in the direction of the village…
She felt such relief in her freedom being away from him and
the place itself, it actually gave her an adrenaline rush like
she hadn't felt since the day she'd noticed him. She felt a
sense of empowerment and independence with something
as simple as a drive alone. She circled around a bit and tried
several routes, until finally…she had success in ending up at
Virginie's house. At last, she'd made it. Going there on
horseback was certainly easier than figuring out the little
country roads that could lead her back there. By the time
she'd driven up the long private driveway and parked,
Virginie was already coming out of the house, curious to see
who'd arrived…

"Well, this is a surprise. It's Sophie, right?"

"Yes, that's right. It's nice to see you again Virginie. I
hope I'm not inconveniencing you by dropping by so
unexpectedly," Sophie said with a bit of worried trepidation
in her voice.

"No problem at all, it's nice to see you too. Did you
bring your racket for a bit of a volley by chance?" Sophie
then exhaled feeling welcomed by Virginie's casualness.

"No, not today…instead would you have a moment
and a place where we can talk?"

"Why yes… come on in to the Living Room and I'll
make us a hot cup of tea," Virginie responded in a
comforting manner. Once they were seated and the tea had
been served, Sophie began her questioning…subtly to
begin.

"Virginie, my curiosity pulled me back here for some
reason. The static between you and Josef yesterday left me
a bit perplexed. I was hoping you could shed some light on
a few things."

Virginie nervously replied…"I'll try…if I can."

Given that she'd received the green light…Sophie
began rambling off a slew of comments and questions. She
told Virginie about being with Bruce, then falling for Josef.
The mysterious fire…Laetitia, and the young housekeeper
named Fiona for starters. Sophie explained how after seeing
the interaction between Fiona and Josef, it didn't seem

right...their relationship must have some kind of hidden meaning. Did she know who this British woman really was? She also confided that she felt something was 'off' at the *Château*...and there were a few things that just didn't add up.

Virginie sat quietly amused and thought while staring at Sophie laying it all out...Those Americans...They're such an open book! They can't wait to blurt out their entire life story within ten minutes of meeting a complete stranger... It's utterly AMAZING!

"Goodness my dear, that's a ton of information to digest. You have such a sizable laundry list of questions, I really don't know where to begin...You do realize if Josef finds out you've come here, all hell is going to break loose. This is a tiny village and people talk about everyone and everything that surrounds this place. Gossip is the village's main pastime. It can turn nasty and become quite cruel if you're not careful. I wouldn't doubt if someone even saw you come up my driveway...and if so, it's absolutely possible that now the entire village knows you're here. This place is that small if you haven't figured it out by now. You can't really understand the extent of it unless you were born here. It's a small circuit and most don't like to welcome any outsiders. The old school sticks together like a pasty glue. Josef's Grandfather however, was the exception."

"Oh you knew Grandfather?"

Virginie was shocked at how naïve and in the dark Sophie was especially after having lived in the *Château* for a while. The Village had eyes and ears of its own. It didn't matter if Sophie knew it or not...The villagers certainly did. How could she be living in the *Château* and not know who she was living with? It blew Virginie's mind...so she took pity on the girl and gave her a bit of what she'd come for.

"Well my dear, all I can tell you is...Try to get out unscathed if you still can. That 'beautiful' *Château* has a history of misconceptions and of wrong doings. They always make it out to be someone else's fault. They're a manipulative bunch and always get what they want no matter who's in their way. You should listen to me and be very careful."

Sophie sat staring wide eyed at Virginie...listening carefully to her every word. They made her shiver.

"First, I used to be in a relationship with Josef, I'm sure he told you right?" She rolled her eyes and jokingly grimaced knowing that was the farthest thing from the truth..."Our 'relationship' if you could call it that, lasted for two years. It was one of those high school romances that ended up with me getting pregnant. My parents insisted on an abortion, and to cover it up they shipped me off to boarding school. After getting out of that hell hole...I moved to Sydney for five years as a translator before returning here to the Dordogne. During that period when I was out of the country, that's when my parents sold this house.

I was so devastated at the time with both, the house and that asshole. I never heard another word from Josef after he dropped me like a hot potato, but thank God he did. Seriously, that was the last time I had anything to do with him and that was sixteen years ago. Not surprising, I did see him at the bar in town once, but he didn't even notice me. All this to say...I'm sure he was just as shocked to see my face as much as I was to see his...when you two happened to show up yesterday.

Fortunately, through some inheritance from my grandparents, I was able to buy this place back from the people who bought it from my parents. I had the tennis court put in last year and have been giving lessons ever since. I would've thought Josef knew that, Laetitia certainly did. My parents hate the fact that I've returned to live here. They couldn't stand that old woman, nor Josef, his Grandfather, or anyone else associated with the place for that matter. They think that *Château* and this village is evil, full of the type of cancer that spreads like dye dropped in water. Tainted forever...They couldn't get away fast enough.

As for Laetitia...that spooky 'Ol Grande Dame, she was a real frickin' piece of work."

"Wow…I met her, but can't imagine she was the monster that you make her out to be," Sophie said bewildered…

"It's funny you would say that…I don't know how well you knew her…but that bitch was as mean of an old calculating witch as they come. She had just about everyone in town fooled with her 'good saint act' when in fact, she was a real censorious and spitefully mean person. She was the real Domo of the Estate and ran everything at the *Château* including Josef's Grandfather. She was the one that pulled all the strings and was always conniving her way in or out of something. She knew that place like the back of her hand and manipulated her cards accordingly. She brought her Granddaughter Fiona over from England when she was a young girl, under the pretext of 'being an exchange student'…and some 'friend of the family'…"

"OMG are you kidding me?…Granddaughter?" Sophie was completely freaked out and shocked hearing this…and the other side of the story. "What a manipulative lying bitch she is…" Virginie nodded in agreement then continued…

"Josef's Grandfather was so blinded by Laetitia that he never suspected her grand scheme. It'd always been her intention for that kid Fiona to take her place one day at the helm by having her cozy up to your Josef…just like the old crow had done with the old man. She'd weaseled her way to the top and made herself irreplaceable.

…So I hear this time Fiona has returned to the Château in some kind of a domestic capacity? Ha…but then again, who wouldn't with her background and inside 'coaching'. She knows a good meal ticket when she sees one, just like Laetitia did. She's been back a year or so from what I gather. I'm sure you've seen how she plays. She's as calculating as her mentoring Grandmother ever was….But obviously that all changed when you showed up. I bet you've raised more than a few eyebrows… Turns out, when I was still on the scene years ago, Fiona and Josef had a little thing going on behind my back at one of their summer parties. I caught them making out (and god knows what else they were doing) behind the barn at one of the old man's BBQ's. Josef is a monster…he has no soul. He's a self-serving bastard and is only out for himself no matter what the circumstance. Don't fool yourself into ever thinking otherwise."

Suddenly, the sound of an unexpected visitor rolling up the gravel drive was heard. The timing of the 'intruder' scared the living shit out of them both.

"Shhhh…Listen, someone's here…" They sat motionless, listening intently until Virginie finally sighed with relief realizing it was her next student arriving.

"Peu nez"…she said exhaling…"It's only my 11:00 lesson. Sophie you should get going, but promise me you'll keep our conversation Strictly between us. I would worry thinking anyone, especially Josef, knew that we'd confided in one another…"

Virginie put her hand over her heart then quietly ushered Sophie out. Feeling dazed…Sophie wandered back to the Rover. Once inside she hit the auto lock and screamed, "That fucking Fiona!!…OMG it's not only her *but Everyone* at the *Château*…They're all deceitful liars!"

For Sophie to have heard all of this incredibly painful information, she was shaken to her core. Tears began involuntarily streaming down her face…"This alone explains the reason why Josef rushed us off so quickly yesterday not to mention the weird chemistry that sizzled between he and Virginie…That's the apparent reason why he didn't want me to even speak to her! All of his lies, his secrets…the calculated deceptions and cover ups…" She began to bawl as she drove away from Virginie's place.

"What a tool this guy is. He's just been playing me all along. What a mean bastard…just like Bruce had always told me. I only wish I had listened…"

Between all the information divulged in Laetitia's letter and now to be given a realistic second version from Virginie…Sophie was fit to be tied. She needed to pull over to collect herself. When calm enough to drive, she headed towards the village hoping to pop into the chic little hair salon behind the City Hall. She was praying they'd have time to give her a quick wash and blow out which would at least validate and justify her outing. She needed to regroup and take a breather so she could digest a bit of the tsunami of information that'd just hit her. There was obviously so much more to know and find out, but this plethora of info that Virginie had just supplied must be sadly be only the tip of the iceberg.

Sophie felt anxious and fidgeted through her blow dry and returned to the *Château* at the expected time give or take a few. She parked the Rover in the courtyard and entered the house through the front. She quickly *knowingly* walked back to the kitchen to find Josef sitting with Fiona. Shocking I know, couldn't that chick at least make it a little bit less obvious? It'd really reached the level of no return…

"Wow…Your hair looks gorgeous. Nice color," Josef commented, like she'd be flattered. He didn't know shit.

"Trés, trés jolie," Fiona chimed in. Just hearing that little phrase coming from Fiona's mouth made Sophie feel a slight little bit of vomit come up into the back of her throat.

"Oh, thank you so much…both of you. What a lovely day it's been. How's everyone doing around here?" she said opening the cupboard to grab a wine glass.

"Are you hungry Sophie? Fiona's made some lovely things for a late lunch."

Sophie didn't respond to Josef but looked directly at Fiona and smiled, "That is so thoughtful of you, but I'm just going to have a glass of wine and read in the library for a bit. You both enjoy"…taking her glass and the remaining wine in what was close to a full bottle with her. She'd rather have eaten nails…

"What's gotten into her? She seems like a different person," Fiona said as they continued to sit smiling at one another in agreement. They took their time finishing the gourmet spread until the moment when Josef stood up and announced, "Fiona, when Sophie comes back up for air let her know that I'm meeting one of *The Club* members in

Bergerac and I'll be out for the evening. I'll be available on my cell should she need me. Okay?" He gave Fiona a quick little validating touch on her shoulder before making his exit.

"Oui okay," she replied as Josef had already made his way walking out the Solarium door…

Sophie watched Josef's exit from the front window in the library as he drove off the property. He was driving a little black stylish '63 Alfa Romero. She'd begun to hate his car collection, and even rolled her eyes at his choice for the day. She hastily made her way back to the kitchen where Fiona was eagerly waiting, delighted in fact, to give her Josef's updated afternoon and dinner plans. Instead of any disappointment Sophie shrieked inwardly, "How perfect !"

Fiona loved seeing Sophie's sad reaction (albeit fake) knowing that Josef had just left for the rest of the day without even saying goodbye. She had no idea Sophie's true thoughts were just the opposite, she was actually beaming inside. These opportune moments left alone to continue her detective work were few and far between, so she jumped at the golden opportunity.

"Okay Fiona. Thanks for the message," she said somberly. "I'm just going to pop out to that cute little clothing boutique in the Village for a look before they close. Will I be seeing you later?"

"No, I don't think so. I'm still not feeling a hundred percent. I'll retire for the evening unless you need something."

Play me a river dear, go on… play it. Need something? Give me a break. Sophie could only imagine Fiona would've preferred giving her rat poison at that point. The fact that these two women were looking squarely at one another and lying through their teeth was a 'super bowl event' within itself. An utterly amazing demonstration of two masters in the game of manipulation was being played out big time. They despised one another yet kept up their fake facades until they both knew how to proceed with secure footing.

Sophie waited for Fiona to go in *her* room then she

quietly grabbed her purse. Fiona's privileges by the way had been bumped up by then. Josef had conveniently asked her to take over Litty's suite, he thought it better to have someone else in the house in case any other unexpected visitors or police turned up.

Sophie opened the kitchen drawer and took out the same key she'd placed there earlier when coming back from the salon. Thank goodness the Rover was still parked in front. It hadn't been there long enough to warrant being moved back into the car barn for the evening. Thank God the Brit had already slithered into *her* room…any further trite conversation with her would've interfered with the timing of Sophie's afternoon's plan.

She was off, only this time she took the small road in front of the tasting room. She was finally beginning to know her way around. It was one of the more rural roads on the property. It was flanked by tall thin towering rows of cypress trees on each side. She conveniently slipped off the estate at a snails pace…not making a sound. Once she did make it onto the main road, she was well on her way heading back to her new acquaintance's house at record speed. This time she knew her way…

"Allo Virginie? Hi there, I hope I'm not disturbing you…" Sophie called out to the pretty red head coming out from around the back of the house. Virginie's electric blue eyes were piecing…and showed surprise.

"Oh Sophie, two times in one day? How lucky am I?" She couldn't help her facial expression reflect the sentiment that Sophie was definitely imposing, but Virginie's polite words said just the opposite. Sophie knew damn well she was disturbing her afternoon but felt she needed to be relentless. Let's face it…this was the first time anyone had been straight up and honest with her and she wasn't about to let go of this opportunity. Virginie had been sharing a version of the story that Josef had been keeping a guarded secret. Sophie knew her fluke encounter meeting Virginie was an unbelievable blessing…and she was definitely thirsty for more.

"I was hoping we could take it up again where we left off earlier?" she asked sounding like she was timidly pleading. Virginie changed her tune and took pity on the naïve girl standing in front of her...and tossed her a compassionate glance.

She acquiesced and said, "Welcome Sophie...come on in, but let's not make a habit of this okay?" Her comforting smile and tone gave Sophie a sigh of relief. It was obvious to Virginie that Sophie needed some *real* help and must be desperate for some truthful info or she would never have taken the risky chance of returning. Virginie pulled up two chairs and began laying the facts out as she remembered them. She cut mustard as they say...

"Well, from what I've heard...the talk about town is that your old boyfriend Bruce is getting side walled for something he didn't do. That poor guy losing his parents like that...What a terrible way to go for those poor people. I know his father was a freak show, but given his history, no one could blame him. He had a major nervous breakdown of sorts after being molested" she said without exhaling.

"What?! What in the world are you talking about?" Sophie replied, startled and disgustingly shocked at the thought.

"Oh my poor dear...I'm surprised you didn't hear about that. It was a huge scandalous story in itself. So you didn't know Josef's Father was a predator? One of his victims was Gene Douglas amongst others. That man ruined many a life around here, but Bruce's Father was the only one to stand up to him and continue to publicly shame him. It used to drive Josef's Grandfather crazy! 'Ol Sr. was so pissed, no way in hell would he allow anyone to soil his family's reputation, especially not his son's. So, the old man began throwing money at Gene to shut him up.

It didn't work though. Luckily for Gene, he had a fantastic and supportive wife who didn't run from the situation like a lot of others would have. She was always so loving and compassionate towards him. When he needed to explode periodically with some tumultuous residue remaining from his trauma, he did so with her standing by his side.

That's why I know the fire must've been started by someone in the village that was loyal to Josef's family and not theirs. The entire family at the *Château* is like the mafia here. People pretend to love and respect them, but the reality is they fear them. Their money and power has changed a lot of lives here, for the good and equally for the bad. They probably thought you'd hear the truth from the Douglas' one day and wanted to eliminate that possibility. That'd be my guess, but then again who am I to say"...she said with a smirk. Virginie took a long pause before continuing.

"Given that Bruce had been brainwashed into thinking it'd been HIS father who was the predator, and not Josef's, was such a lie. He somehow believed the vicious tales being relentlessly spread by the loyalists of Josef's family, when in fact, it'd been the other way around. Bruce never completely forgave or believed the innocence of his Father due to all the persistent gossip and the peer pressure that came from it. Sadly starting from that point, Bruce and his Father never managed to regain a healthy relationship. There was always a wedge of mistrust and hatred that stemmed from that lie being spread years ago. But in some twisted way it made Bruce extremely envious of Josef. The loyalty that his family had from most in the village...and ALL that money, the *Château*...and all those connections? I actually think Bruce wanted to change places and be Josef.

Can't you see?...This was all the perfect set up. There was motive, justifiable cause, and a back story that's packed full of those juicy details that these piranha prosecutors love...Only it's impossible. It most certainly couldn't have been Bruce that caused this tragedy. He loved his Mother so...he would never have played with fire, literally. So tell me Sophie...how long did you say you have been living in the *Château*?"

Sophie was so overwhelmed, it took her the longest time to respond. "Apparently not long enough to know any of this. You are such a brave woman Virginie to share all of this information and as painful and confusing as it is to hear, I am so grateful to finally know the truth. And don't worry, I understand your position here and would never out you as my source" Sophie said looking at her watch. "I must be going, I'll try to stop by again if that's okay. There's still a bit more of the story that I'd appreciate knowing."

Hearing all of these wicked truths made Sophie feel increasingly nervous about her visits. Why would the gossip be that Bruce had been involved? Just what could the police possibly consider to be a motive for Bruce? Hatred for his Father? In fact it'd been no other than Fiona who'd indicated Bruce as the one leaving the Library during Litty's service…The missing lighter? Did Fiona start the fire to protect Josef by setting Bruce up? Sophie's thoughts were spinning out of control, but she knew she needed to get back to Virginie's place soon for one final discussion after she'd had time to absorb the days bombshells.

Sophie entered a quiet house. Fiona had remained in her room and Josef was still *out* for the evening. Even though Fiona was not in sight, Sophie knew her ears must've been pressed to the wall out of curiosity. Sophie tiptoed to the refrigerator and grabbed a few things to accompany a cheese plate. Once she'd gathered a full bottle of wine and the tray of nibbles she made her way upstairs. She coveted the thought of a solo dinner in front of the fire. When the bottle didn't have a drop left she went and slid into the 'big bed'. She couldn't relax but began tossing around with too many questions on her mind before falling into a deep sleep.

"Good Morning Sophie" Josef said snuggling her from behind. She moaned and rolled over in to his arms.

"By the looks of it, it seems you had a pretty good night up here all by yourself. Sorry I missed it" he said referring to the empty bottle left on the coffee table.

"Good Morning, I didn't hear you come in last night. Everything okay?"

"Et oui…but you talked so much in your sleep, it

woke me up a couple of times."

"Did I say anything interesting?" she said smiling, trying not to show her nervousness. She was praying to GOD she hadn't mentioned any particularly *'juicy' details* from her conversation with Virginie in her night talk.

"Not interesting enough garble worth repeating," he said rolling over. She was SO relieved hearing she hadn't revealed her thoughts while sleep talking…

Josef took that moment of opportunity and rolled on top of her. They managed to have a quickie that was mutually satisfying, no kissing, no foreplay, just the hard truth plain and simple. It surprised her realizing that now she could use him for sex and not continue to get wrapped up in any mind games. She'd begun acting like an insensitive man. She'd divorced her feelings, but still loved the act. She'd always been curious how men seemed to perform like it is so easy separating the two. Now she understood, it was only sex, right? She thought he must've sensed her not having her emotions and *feelings there with him*…He didn't of course. He hadn't even noticed. Her vale of denial had finally been ripped off and stripped…like she was on the outside looking in.

With knowing all that she'd been told…how could he still want to act like things were 'normal' between them. What a liar this spoiled little rich boy was. He'd lied about everything. His Father, Bruce, Bruce's Father, his history with that British bitch and that's just to begin with. His list of manipulations and untruths were far too long to comprehend. Laying there…she surmised there must be a mountain of surprises on the list that were yet to be uncovered. She knew it was time to get working on her immediate exit plan for her return life in the US. She'd figure out the rest of her future once she made it out of this mess and was safe Stateside.

✳

Chapter Treize

"Sophie I need to go to the airport this morning to meet Olivier," Josef announced as he was coming out of the bathroom after having completed his mornings GQ grooming ritual. "He's flying in for a quick meeting to re-cap our case. He'll be gone by lunchtime...so why don't you meet me at Chef Justifino's at 1:00? It's such a beautiful little restaurant, I think you'll love it. It's easy to find...It's right in the middle of old town Bergerac. Sound good?"

"Certainly does my dear, that's a great idea. It will give me the opportunity to get 'dressed' for a change. I've heard so much about that fabulous little restaurant and their reviews are phenomenal. I'm excited to try it. I'll see you there," Sophie answered from bed. She'd never heard diddly squat about the place by the way.

Josef diligently made his way downstairs to have his morning coffee before leaving. Sophie was still casually lounging upstairs in bed when all of a sudden...she heard all Hell break loose downstairs in the kitchen. The screaming match exploding between Fiona and Josef was simply unbelievable. It'd been so quiet...then out of nowhere came this loud shrieking and extremely aggressive interaction erupt between the two. It was such an explosive interchange, Sophie thought she could actually hear the floor rattle! Our girl was so curious how this could've all started, but she didn't move position...she only pleasingly smiled to herself while continuing to listen to the chaos... She'd purposefully prolonged her descent, but God was she dying to know what had ignited their war of words...

"Those past love birds, they probably had a lot to say to each other right about now"...She murmured aloud.

Sophie had been staying at the *Château* for months by now and probably it'd been just long enough for Fiona to have arrived at her absolute wit's end with the inconvenient living situation. Maybe that was it. The 'ultimatum' from the 'housekeeper' had finally arrived…

Sophie showered and puttered around the suite while getting ready for her lunch date. She put on the prettiest pair of trousers with matching blazer that remained in her dwindling wardrobe. It was the best she could muster up in her current assortment…A far cry for a girl who'd been in the fashion business. Quite the opposite twist for a fashionista who was now wearing an ill fitting two piece suit…but that didn't stop her on this particular day. Between her reinstated self esteem and her thinner than usual physique, she managed to look elegant and totally put together. It was the first day in a long time that she felt she looked like she *owned it*. Confidence in fact, was the suit she was wearing. She was back to her sassy lookin' million dollar self, empowered as it were. She'd finally reached back into her toolbox marked 'hot successful chick' and opened it wide. She felt like she'd found some clarity back in life now that she'd been able to get out from underneath Josef's spell.

"I've been lost in this false world for such a long time…I'm so lucky it wasn't too late to finally reclaim my sense of self. That bastard always manipulated me into thinking I'd be part of his dream world's future, and stupid me…I allowed myself to continue living in that farce with him. Damn it…and Damn him!" she muttered.

You see?…Sophie now recognized and admitted she'd entered the scene with the wrong intentions. She felt Karma had jumped up and was biting back. At least she now saw what a real scoundrel Josef was. She was finally ready to take responsibility, understanding there were also a ton of things she'd need to work out and face on her end. She addressed herself in the mirror as only a strong re-focused woman would who was willing to set things right.

"All of those lies…and what was all that talk about him buying off my business!?"

She was frightened and curious what…if any remnants of her old life actually still existed. Dumping Bruce like she had?…It was all a bad dream of retribution coming back to life. Payback for choosing the wrong man for the wrong reasons.

Once ready for her lunch date, she went downstairs to see if she could notice any trail of evidence remaining from the fight the two might've left behind. She was set to go to Justifino's a bit early. It would give her time for a quick flute of champagne while waiting for Josef to arrive. It would only be fitting to discuss ending it then and there, considering that's where it had all started…In a champagne flute full of bubbles and bullshit of course. I'll say…It'd all been such a misguided dream. No longer did it hold any interest for Sophie, she was ready to get back home. The price tag in France had become way too high. She'd been dancing with the devil and now…at last…she knew it. As Sophie entered the kitchen she found Fiona sitting at the farm table balling her eyes out. (Bien sûr…underneath it all, she was thrilled to see Fiona so distraught and suffering)

"Fiona, what in the world are you crying for? I heard you and Josef screaming at each other down here and couldn't imagine what on earth was happening."

She just smirked and looked up through her tears, "Oh, like you don't know? I'm pregnant with Josef's child that's what!" she screamed hysterically…then ran into her room slamming the door behind her.

Sophie was left standing alone in the kitchen in a state of complete shock. Truly…this was the cherry on top, the *pièce de resistance* as they say. The last nail in the coffin and…Oh baby bababa bay bee…It Was definitely….O..VA. She fell dry eyed onto a chair at the table sitting in utter dismay until her waterworks kicked in. Then amongst her endless stream of tears she staggered her way to the refrigerator and angrily pulled out a bottle of champagne and opened it. She was so shaken that when she popped the cork, almost half of the expensive bubbly spewed all over the pristine kitchen.

"What a fucking shame…the *housekeeper* can clean it up" she screamed. The good news was there was still enough Dom Pérignon left in the bottle to fill her glass a couple of times. She left her last full glass along with the half empty bottle sitting on the sticky table.

Once she was able to stable herself, she went to the powder room to freshen up. Then something happened that played in to her hands like four aces. It made her strike a sergeants stance finding the unusual item that happened to be sitting on the sink. Fiona's pregnancy test that is. The one that she'd obviously either purposely left or perhaps forgotten was just sitting there waiting to be picked up for inspection.

Personally, it grosses me out just thinking about it... but when Sophie first looked at the thing, she did so with an inquisitive bewilderment. However, once her mind was able to process what she'd heard and was now inspecting, she was more than ready to set her plan in motion.

"What a stupid fool I've been," she said wrapping the small tester stick up in a tissue. She took it with her upstairs.

With her mind zipping in hyper drive, she immediately began emptying her closet and gathering her things from the bathroom. She was so done...She couldn't believe she'd hung out for so long and not to have seen this playing out right under her nose. She had no other choice but to leave that moment. Within her packed items, she also included the little red gift box that she'd always cherished. It was from the necklace that Josef had given her in NYC. Those loving feelings she'd felt for him then were a million miles away now, but don't worry...she didn't forget to take her book on the nightstand nor her rejuvenated self esteem with her on the way out.

"It's finally time to fuck with this bastard who thinks he knows everything," she mumbled to herself on her way down the stairs and out of the *Château*. She managed to get all of her bags into the Rover then slammed the car door with a vengeance. "That little fucker, let's see how he's going to squirm out of this one."

She threw the car in gear and sped off the property

leaving a large billowing dust trail behind. She tearfully made her way to Bergerac and found her typical 'Doris Day parking' in the primo spot directly in front of the restaurant. It made for her perfect entrance and already being slightly tipsy, Fiona's shocking news had somehow given her an empowering reliance. Who are we kidding...Let's just say her balance was a bit off from the shock of it all, but the champagne had given her the right amount of bravado needed to get through her lunch rendezvous and execute her not so completely organized plan. Nevertheless, there she went entering the restaurant looking beautiful...where she was greeted by the elegant owner, MS Justifino.

"Table for two please. I think we might have reservations under the name Decour."

"Oh yes, we've been expecting you. Thank you for joining us today" said the rather petite and refined woman. She led Sophie to a charming little square table set for two. The owner was dressed so chic, it made Sophie realize there was so much more style in the region than she'd actually known existed. If only she'd not allowed herself to be treated like a love prisoner. If she had demanded more independence and freedom to explore, she definitely would've noticed her surroundings and opportunities a bit earlier. What a shameful waste it'd all been.

"Compliments of the house," said the chic owner placing a lovely flute of bubbly down in front of her. "Enjoy."

Sophie was left sitting by herself until her empty glass was taken away and replaced with a full one. The soft lighting, the light jazz playing, the crisp linen tablecloths, the polished cutlery, the exquisite stemware...blah blah blah blah blah...it did however, warrant the approval stamp of a Relais Château venue. The cozy establishment absolutely felt like the ideal place for their *last supper*.

Sophie saw Josef enter the restaurant and the way he greeted MS Justifino (with that...oh so familiar kiss) it made it clear they *really 'knew'* one another. Sophie just sat watching him make his way back to where she was seated. Why hadn't she noticed his cocky Guido Glide before?

She'd taken off her rose colored glasses and was finally able to see everything about him with clarity. She now saw him as merely a serpent camouflaged as a man in a suit. (worsted wool sport coat and dark jeans to be specific) She was noticing so many new things about him. The things that she used to find so sexy were now making her cringe. Who the hell did he think he was after all…the Dick.

"I see you've been well taken care of" he said giving Sophie a quick kiss before sitting down with a smile. "Isn't this place beautiful? They have such exquisite taste in everything. Wait until you taste the food!"

With the end of his enthusiastic comments about the place coming to a close, another glass of Champagne arrived and was placed in front of him.

He was so conditioned at playing such a *smooth* and *sophisticated* game that remarkably, he acted as if he didn't have a worry in the world. Pretty amazing for a man who, a) was a 'person of interest' in a murder case, b) was living a double life with his housekeeper (who by the way had dropped the bombshell pregnancy news earlier in the day) and c) was now breezing through a lunch date with his live-in girlfriend.

So just to give you an idea. With all of these major events orbiting around in his life, he just continued staring lovingly at the American seated across from him like he didn't have a care in the world. Imagine…That kind of junk pile would be enough to rock anyone's world don't ya think? Make ones' behavior seem…I don't know, a bit abnormal perhaps? But No…Not this Golden Boy…he kept his swag goin' strong and sailed right on through.

Sophie also did her best at remaining poised while keeping all things pleasant. She didn't expose even a whimper regarding her new found feelings or realizations. Her tactic was exquisite. Her timing impeccable…she was refined in waiting for the perfect moment. The fact that he'd been such an incredible lover was the little (or should I say a rather large) detail that had always made it so difficult to leave. Throw in a fabulous *Château*, etc…and there you have it. The perfect package from the outside had made her dive in deep. Perhaps that's All it'd really been. Great Sex. She'd gotten so caught up in her own image of perfection that it was actually she that had sought after his bad boy type in the first place. She'd forgotten about all the rest including the one she'd been living with in San Fran…

When she allowed Josef to creep into her life, perhaps a male reflexion of self had been all she'd been really looking for. A guy who expected the world to move on his terms just like she did hers. Originally she'd found him to be so sexy and her equal in so many ways. Some of his superficial seductive powers seemed to be exciting and enough for her in the beginning. Because…let's not forget, she'd always loved to dig and be around the gold a bit just like Bruce had said. Even though we love our girl, she'd been somewhat of a power junkie using her sweet naïve girl act all along. But that was then, she'd finally come around 180°.

As they continued mowing down numerous flutes of champagne, Sophie played the part as only an Oscar winner could. She laughed at his jokes, happily devoured her lunch displaying delight with each and every bite, then gave the poor schmuck enough compliments to pump his ego and make him feel like he was the King of the Dordogne. As their dessert was being served, Sophie made her move. She took the small little red gift box out of her purse and placed it on the table next to his full glass. He didn't recognize the box of course.

"For you my love," she said with a face that only a mother could love. When she lied, she looked so beautifully innocent.

"Oh Sophie…I don't deserve anything sweetheart, what have you done…?" He had a smile on his face the size of Scottsdale and picked up the little box with utter delight and curiosity. The poor bastard leaned forward over the table and kissed her lips ever so sweetly.

"It's a surprise silly. I wanted you to be the first to know" she said as she watched him open the box exposing the pregnancy tester stick of Fiona's showing positive.

She sat beaming like a search light just waiting for his reaction. It's a miracle she didn't take out a small pistol from her purse instead and shoot the fucking bastard right then and there. Personally, I would've experienced a real mental break down…but not our girl. She powered through and exhaled, miraculously holding her act together like a pro. Sincerely, it was the perfect performance.

"What is this?" he asked removing the tester from the box. He held it up high and began analyzing it right there in the restaurant where a few others could see. "Is this what I think it is?" He said lowering the tester…

"Oh yes my love, it most certainly is. I know we had discussed this happening a bit later, but here it is. Nature can't avoid these things sometimes. I'm thrilled…are you? I hope so my love, because I'm so excited to become the Mother of your child."

It just so happened the waiter conveniently passed their table within earshot as she was completing her sentence. The word would be out and spread about in no time. It was then his turn for center stage. He lied convincingly even though he'd become flushed and had turned as yellow as the tablecloth.

"This is amazing Sophie" he said with eyes the size of his dessert plate. She'd never seen him look so unappealing.

They immediately made a toast with mutual tears and fake smiles. She almost couldn't contain herself. As much as she thought he deserved this prank, it was difficult to witness him disconnecting from reality to this extent. He truly must've been in one of his super sized self-centered fogs because for not one minute did he think it strange for the woman carrying his child to be sitting there slamming back Champagne flutes one after another. His total lack of consideration for others just added to his existing heap of faults.

She let him stew a bit in his new 'Daddy Reality' before announcing "I'm going to see my girlfriend Sylvie in Paris for a day or two. You remember her don't you? I want to tell her our happy news in person. Are you okay if I leave you for a day or so?" she asked, hoping he'd agree.

If by chance he'd said no…it would put a hiccup in her exit plan. He was so out of it…With the abundance of overwhelming news piling up and settling in, his head must have been bouncing inside like a bobble doll. Somehow her drinking champagne and driving alone to Paris to spread the news seemed logical…

"Of course, if you'd like to. Are you sure? Do you want me to meet you there tomorrow night?" he asked looking straight into oblivion. He had no earthly idea of anything she'd been saying, nor anything that happened to be endlessly streaming from his own pie hole either. Seriously, he really was on auto pilot and the verbal flatulence springing from his mouth were astounding. The gong being hit inside his head must've been so intense it was deafening. Ding Dong…Ding Ding Ding!!!

"Wonderful. That's a fabulous idea Josef. We'll have a blast celebrating! I'll do a bit of shopping and organize a few little things in time for your arrival. It'll be so much fun and a great way to break the news to a few people, don't you agree? I'm assuming we'll be staying at the apartment? Perhaps I'll get a small dinner party together at the restaurant in the Crillon. That would be such an elegant way to share our news."

"Great, he bought it. I doubt he absorbed a word I was saying, but at least I'm free to roam solo for the next few…" Correct she was…Josef was so freaked out he couldn't see or think of anything beyond his own nose at that point. Two different women simultaneously pregnant with his baby? Leaving for Paris to party? Sure, why not?… It all made sense right? What a f- - - …ing jerk.

Sophie knew damn well by the time he returned to the *Château*, Fiona would no doubt be anxiously waiting. In fact, she'd probably already worn a hole in the floor due to her pacing. (or was that her doing pirouettes?…) She was beyond eager to tell Josef she'd spilled her pregnancy news to Sophie earlier in the day…and her test was 'missing'… He'd know then that Sophie sat through the entire lunch knowing the truth and not letting on that the 'test' was actually Fiona's. The whole chain of events would need to be sifted through, but forget the fine toothed comb on this one, it was all pretty blatant at that point. The size of a garden rake would be sufficient for any sifting required.

When Sophie and Josef said their 'loving farewells' at the restaurant, Josef automatically assumed she'd be going back to the *Château* to pack for their Paris excursion. Little did he know that when she got into the Rover, she'd take off in the opposite direction. What in the hell was she to do then? Giving Josef the little red box had been the extent of her entire plan. She'd not given a serious thought to anything much beyond that. Free-styling at that point was not the best decision…but somewhere in her inner chaos, she remembered seeing a little Hôtel hidden off the main road when she'd been making her way to the restaurant. No one would ever think to look for her there. She drove straight to the obscure location, checked in under an alias and payed cash. She needed some time private to think about her next move and hopefully…speak with Bruce in the interim.

Once in her room Sophie hit the mini bar hard. Due to her nerves being tied in knots…she drank in excess and conveniently passed out for the night from cheap booze.

She awoke the following morning with a hangover the size of Memphis and left the Hotel not having called Bruce as intended. She knew she was taking a huge risk being seen returning to Virginie's house, but felt she had to go for it one last time. She was determined to get more useful damaging dirt on Josef. She miraculously found her way…and to her surprise, was met by the groundskeeper who was in the process of blowing off the court. He stopped the noisy machine as she approached.

"Hello…Soph,ie?…Am I saying that correctly? My name is Alex," he said with a nice and welcoming tone. His accent was charming. "I was told to keep an eye out for you in the event that you might be stopping by. Virginie wanted me to tell you hello and to give you her apologies for not being here. She also wanted me to let you know that her lessons have taken her elsewhere for a while. She was given an opportunity she couldn't refuse, and left rather abruptly late yesterday afternoon for an undetermined amount of time. I actually don't know where she's gone exactly."

Sophie was so stunned hearing this her knees went weak. In her state of numbness, she stood speechless with a smile that quickly became a blank expression. She was so taken back by Virginie leaving without any pre-warning… she didn't know what to think. Had it been her decision or was she forced to leave? Whichever it might've been, it all seemed odd and suspicious with her unexpected and untimely exit. But let's face it…it's not like the two women *really* knew one another, or Sophie was owed any type of explanation, but nevertheless, she felt deserted with Virginie's sudden departure.

Sophie got back in the Rover feeling completely lost and full of disappointment. She had weird feelings of an awkward abandonment…Virginie had been the only one with nothing to gain and everything to lose by exposing her truths about the *Château* and its past. She'd generously given the other side of the story, and now?…What was Sophie to do with what she felt was her only ally gone?

She felt a wave of panic hit her like she were pinned to a brick wall with no place to go. She suddenly realized she'd been left out there dangling on a limb all alone. She picked up the hotel phone to call the only lifeline she had left. The phone seemed to ring forever. Sophie was feeling desperate and in need of some immediate support. The bottom had just completely fallen out…of everything. He finally picked up.

"Bruce it's me, don't hang up…please," she begged, hearing the other end answer with silence. Sophie continued speaking anyway, "I need to see you. I'm not that far from the Burlier, but we'll need to be careful and keep it super discreet. Can you meet me somewhere outside of the Village? Please Bruce…we need to talk."

"Sophie, I think we've said all we have to say for the

time being" he finally replied. "I can't leave the B & B. They have me under some kind of a house arrest if you can imagine. Whatever you have to say, say it now."

"I have a letter to give you. It's some kind of admission letter written by Laetitia. I think it could help you. The letter contains all kinds of information that you would find Very interesting."

"Oh yeah? Where'd you get this letter?" he questioned with suspect…"Is this a game? Are you still happy living your life with that bastard?"

"As a matter of fact, I've left him. I won't be going back. I'll be leaving for San Francisco as soon as possible, but not until I've found out who in the hell is following me. I can't figure it out…I've been seeing this weird little black car show up in the strangest places lately. It's like they know where I'll be…Maybe I'm just being paranoid, but this entire place is really starting to give me the creeps. I had a scare when I went horseback riding not long ago, and I can't absolutely be certain, but I think it's the same person that keeps haunting me. I have to get lost tonight and have no idea where to go. I wonder if the person following me had anything to do with the fire. It all feels too timely and suspicious. It's like I have this strange stalker who just appears out of thin air. It's really freaking me out."

"Now it's you that's freaking me out Sophie! This is all very upsetting to say the least. I'm worried about you…or is this just you putting on a drama show like the old days? If this letter is anything that could help me but endanger you, it's not worth it…and what's this about…someone's stalking you? Who in the hell would want to do that? I don't like the sound of this. Have you called the police? You definitely should…if you've not done so already…please Sophie, promise me you'll call them, now!"

"Don't worry about me Bruce, you should be worried about yourself. Losing your parents and now house arrest? I'm so sorry how everything has turned out and become so upside down. I wish you would've told me some truths about this place, your life, Josef…" she said fading off.

"Sophie, like I told you before…you were so

headstrong you thought you already knew everything about him and this place. When you came here for visits you didn't have *time to listen*, not to me, or to anyone else for that matter. There was no 'room' to explain anything to you then. I don't know what you've learned, but whatever it is, chances of it being true are more probable than not. I told you to be careful from the very beginning when you started up with that monster. Josef is vicious and always gets what he wants. I hate that fucker." There was another long silence...

"I met a woman...her name is Virginie."

Bruce immediately came out of his analytical *type of discern* and quickly upped the pace. "We should meet. Can you sneak in here? Put on a hat and glasses type of thing?"

"Ha...what do you think this is?...A spy thriller? I don't think I could just slip in there like it's an old classic detective movie. Even though it does sound fun...(saying that made them both think of the 'old' days) it'd be way too risky. I can't come there, it would just complicate things even further for you. Anyway, that's the first place Josef would look. He's definitely *unwrapping* a few things right about now, and I wouldn't be surprised if he's out looking for me as we speak. I made the excuse that I'd be on my way to Paris in his Rover yesterday afternoon. It certainly wouldn't have taken him long to figure out I didn't go. I'm sure he's already been by your B & B to make sure you're still in place. If he knows you are, he'll assume I'm still in the Village and presume I'm with you.

I really don't have a clue what his next move will be. All I do know is that he detests you...and was always paranoid, actually obsessed...that I'd keep in contact with you. You obviously know Josef a lot better than I do, that's for damn sure. I should've listened to you Bruce, not just about him but about so many other things. I was so blind not to see how deceptive and manipulative he could be. I don't trust *anything* he might do at this point. My God, I've been such a foolish imbecile!"

"I can't say any of this comes as much of a surprise

Sophie. I told you to be careful of him and everything that goes on in that prism of power known as 'The *Château*'. What's going on exactly?...Has something specific happened that's making you sound like this all of a sudden? Hearing your tone and your new found change of heart...It's actually you Sophie, that's making me feel panicked. What's he done to you?"

"Too much has happened for us to speak about on the telephone Bruce." Another prolonged silence prevailed before Sophie gave in...

"Oh fuck it...I'm sure I'm just being overreactive. I'll come to you and be on my way now. We need to see one another and talk face to face. There's so much I need to tell you and I really insist you have this letter! When you read it, you'll understand. It explains a ton of things and offers incriminating evidence against the Decour household. I'll try to hurry so expect to see me in twenty minutes or so" she said hanging up, not giving Bruce the time to respond or suggest an alternative plan.

Sophie quickly got on her way trying to figure out the best route to the B & B. She was feeling lost so began chaotically zig zagging her way attempting to get out of the maze the little unmarked French roads had created. She'd not really been paying attention to anything else. She exhaled with relief when she finally found her way to the main road which would lead her back to the village. That's when she finally took the time to adjust her posture and check the rear view mirror...

Her sixth sense had told her someone was secretly there and sadly...her sensibilities proved her to be right. There they were again out in plain sight. Her stalker was back.

The car seemed to appear out of no where, just like it had with her scare in the vineyard. Only this time it began making specifically dangerous and aggressive moves that really terrified her. The little black souped up car that had super dark tented windows, made it impossible to identify the driver. Whoever it was began flashing their lights, gunning the engine, and racing up closely behind before falling back. They continued to repeat the same dangerous scare tactic and harassing action again and again. Who was this person and what in the hell did they want!!! But whoever it was...she felt they meant business this time.

She began screaming at their intimidating moves emphatically checking her rear view mirror...And that's when she became seriously frantic and sped up. The situation escalated into becoming a high speed chase in just seconds. The car from behind then sped up again and made their best and final move. They made contact with the Rover by methodically pushing its right back bumper just like it were a practiced police pit maneuver. This light but precise action made Sophie lose control and cross over the center line cascading down the embankment and onto the opposite side of the road. That's where she met a tree and her fate head on. Hitting a giant old oak was enough to make her engine burst into flames. Only after seeing this calculated and pre-meditated scenario play out did the car drive off, obviously feeling satisfied with the results.

*

Chapter Quatorze

Bruce was anxiously wringing his hands when Sophie didn't show up as expected. Their earlier conversation had been more than alarming. It'd been a little over an hour since they'd last spoken. She was late and that wasn't like her. He'd begun pacing…"She should've been here by now. Where in the hell is she?"

He didn't know where else to turn other than to call his lawyer for help. Bruce knew the police would think it suspicious and never take him seriously should he be the one who called with a missing persons report…but they'd believe Stephane. Leaving *'The Burlier'* to go find her wasn't an option either. He'd need some help locating his beloved ex. He became so worried…thinking all the wildest possibilities imaginable were coming to fruition. He began feeling flushed with those thoughts racing through his mind and became overtaken with worry…

"Oh Stephane Thank God you answered…"

"Bruce, isn't this a coincidence? I was just picking the phone up to call you this very second. I have some very exciting news! I hope you're sitting down…because you're not going to believe this incredible update."

"But Stephane…I need you to…"

Stephane interrupted immediately steam rolling on with his conversation. "You'll be happy to know that the insurance company and the Police have completed their investigations! They've unanimously concluded the fire was deemed accidental and caused by faulty electrical. After all with so much in question, it's amazing to think the case is officially closed! Turns out the fire started with an old plug downstairs in the living room. This is really a remarkable and an unexpected turn of events. Having them conclude this so quickly is unprecedented. Congratulations! You're a free man Bruce. I couldn't be happier for you. I'm on my way over to pick you up right now. We're going out for a late lunch to celebrate!!"

Bruce remained stunned and silent on the other end of the receiver as Stephane continued, "I was going to tell you this over lunch, but what the hell...why wait! The most outrageous twist in all of this is that you'll be collecting nine million euros from your parents' life insurance policy! ...I know how shocking this news must be...but God love em'...They'd actually taken a massive policy out when you were just a kid. They'd been paying to keep it current for all these years! Of course they also left your sisters a nice chunk so you'll all be provided for. This means not only are you a free man...but you're a rich one at that. To think they lived such frugal and simple lives...and then to have been hiding this whopping policy is unreal! You are one lucky guy to have had parents that wanted to take such good care of you & your siblings. You are definitely the one buying today," he concluded with a self pleasing laugh.

This was way too much for Bruce to absorb at the moment. He'd definitely need a bit of time to digest the abundance of earth shattering, life altering info he'd just had thrust upon him. He could barely focus enough to squeak out the words, "Sophie's missing" before hanging up.

He fell back on the bed so completely overcome , he felt wrung out and began to weep. Having so many emotions hit him at once, he couldn't get his thoughts collected. He was floundering in a state of purgatory, half way in, and half way out of his mind. Basically, I guess you could say he didn't know which end was up...

Only when his phone rang again a half hour later, was he able to pull himself together enough to come back in to the moment. He excitedly picked up the receiver and heard the familiar voice. He was deflated not hearing the voice he was hoping for.

"Bruce...I'm here waiting for you downstairs" Stephane said, sounding quite authoritative and sure of himself on speaker phone. He was acting just like any successful lawyer who'd just prevailed in a big case. He was ready to gloat and dance like John Travolta.

Finding Stephane and not Sophie on the phone...

Bruce couldn't hide his disappointment. He was still in half a daze…"Okay, I'll be down…" He began slowly making his way out of the B & B full of apprehension…It'd be the first time in a week to do so.

Stephane was shocked to see Bruce appear looking so haggard and bewildered. After all, he thought he'd see a man with a happy prance to his step when exiting the Burlier, especially after receiving such phenomenal news.

Stephane swung the passenger door open and began speaking ninety miles an hour in Bruce's direction. His bark was so loud, the only thing Bruce could really hear was the thumping rhythm of Stephane's elevated ego as he approached the car. Regardless, he managed to get in and buckle up while continuing to listen to the sound of this successful egomaniac's rhetoric…

"Hello you free man. What's wrong with you dude? You should be looking like you just won the lotto instead of this calm wimpy persona you're displaying. I just explained the latest news to your police guards at the door and they seemed a lot more eager to leave than you are, believe you me. They were in such a rush to get out of here, it was like they had somewhere very important to be…

Let's try to forget about them and wade in the glory of the moment shall we? Congratulations are again in order my friend! I can only imagine how you must feel, but be patient…it's going to take a while for it all to sink in. The amount of stress that this entire ordeal must've caused would be enough to make anyone crazy. I hope you can now begin the grieving process for your family and find some peace within. Though it certainly was a tragedy, you've got to be grateful the fire was found to be accidental and not intentional as the police had initially suspected."

Stephane rambled on and on before realizing Bruce was still in a coma type state and not hearing a word. His head was obviously in a mine field. Boom shaka laka.

"Where should we go Mr. Douglas?…Initially I was thinking somewhere in Bergerac would be nice, but just as I was arriving in town, I happened to pass a terrible accident. I called the emergency number to report it, but since there were already a couple of people on the scene, I didn't feel the need to stop. That's probably where those door guards went rushing off to so fast. It's rare when something this major happens around here. I'm sure the police and firetrucks are there by now. We can be certain the road is blocked off...which would make having our celebratory lunch in Bergerac next to impossible. It would make it a lot easier for us to stay here in the Village...Any suggestions? Can you think of some place here in town that you'd enjoy?"

Bruce started his reply in a low whisper sounding ambivalent. "Yeah why don't we just go around the corner to *L'Ange de la Village*? The food here at The Burlier is good, but as you can imagine...I could really use a change of scenery right about now. I can't wait to get out of here." Bruce said sounding like he was coming back to life...

"Sorry to hear about the accident...Have any details?"

"Only that it was a dark colored Range Rover and it must've happened only minutes before I passed it. The SUV seemed to have swerved to the other side of the road and flown down the embankment before smashing into a massive tree. That's all I could gather driving past, but it definitely didn't look good. There was a ton of smoke from the fire, but as I was saying since there were already a couple of people who had stopped so I didn't feel the need to."

"Did you say a dark Range Rover?? Oh my GOD!!!... We've got to get to that accident now! It could be Sophie!" Bruce frantically screamed.

"You mean your ex that you told me about? That Sophie? Bruce...really, how could that be? What in the world would even make you say that?" Stephane questioned thinking Bruce was having an overactive imagination given the circumstances.

"Don't give me that pity card look please! There's been so much happening today you can't even imagine! Sophie called a while ago and sounded like she was sincerely in trouble. She was on her way coming to see me and never showed up and that's not like her. When you called spilling the latest news, I guess I let her arrival drift from my mind given all the stress I've been under. Get me there now Stephane, I'm serious!"…Bruce yelled forcefully. He had definitely come back in to all of his sharpened senses.

He was almost panting with anxiety. His heart began beating so fast he thought it might pop out of his chest and run along side the car. He'd feel that way until they arrived at the scene and was able to confirm it wasn't her. How could he have been so casual about her not showing up. He felt a wave of guilt and deep concern come over him. For a brief moment in his overwhelmed world, he could only think of Sophie. Their entire past together flashed in front of him on his mental projector.

They sped in the direction of Bergerac, and there it was…just as Stephane had described. On the main road fire trucks, police cars…it was a chaotic scene with lights flashing and emergency crews scampering everywhere. Nothing much like this ever happened in this sleepy little village, which meant the authorities were available to be on-site immediately. The road consequently had already been closed for through traffic in either direction, so only the distant by-standers and relentless gawkers were able to get a glimpse. It had already become a spectacle.

Once nearer in their approach, Stephane was flagged down to pull over, then signaled to turn around. But just as the car was coming to a stop, Bruce opened the car door and unexpectedly jumped out and began running towards the crash site. Indeed, it was a Rover just like the one Sophie had begun driving. He panicked. It had run off the road and smashed directly into a massive tree. Evidently the front end of the car had been completely engulfed in flames by the look of things, but only the smell of burnt metal along with the foam from the high powered extinguishers remained. The driver was not in the car and was no longer visible as Bruce made his way to the Rover.

Bruce made a running slide down the slippery wet embankment and that's when he saw her. There she was…

laying completely still. He didn't want to believe his eyes. Sadly, it was really her. It was Sophie. His greatest nightmare had become a reality. She lay motionless on the cold frosty grass next to the driver's side of the Rover. The first responders had used the jaws of life to pull her from the wreckage. The ambulance had just arrived in silence with only lights flashing. There were two men running hastily down the embankment with a stretcher.

When the police saw Bruce trying to get to her, they intervened and stopped him. He began wildly shrieking her name hoping for some kind of response. She showed no movement…her beautiful blonde hair still intact as she laid motionless.

The paramedics inspected her, then carefully placed her limp body on the stretcher before spreading a white sheet over her completely. Seriously, I couldn't believe it either, but it's true, Our girl was gone…They pronounced her dead at the scene. Bruce witnessing this began screaming her name repeatedly. He was yelling all sorts of crazy babble before falling to the ground and sobbing hysterically. This had all transpired just as Stephane was able to arrive by his side.

"I'm so, so sorry Bruce. I just heard them say that she was pronounced dead at the scene"…Stephane said… putting his arm around Bruce in the attempt to console him. Obviously a serious state of shock had set in because Bruce began to shake and shiver uncontrollably. The paramedics saw this poor guy reacting to the situation like this and passed Stephane a blanket to wrap around his friend. Once Bruce was able to stand, Stephane escorted him to his car and instructed him to get into the back seat and lay down. They set off following in the direction of the ambulance carrying Sophie's body once the road had been cleared for thru traffic. That silent ride felt like an eternity.

When they arrived at the hospital there were aides that helped Bruce out of the car. He was immediately escorted into the emergency room where he'd be covered in more blankets and given a sedative to calm him. He'd need to stay at least a few hours or until he'd become cognizant of his surroundings and able to acknowledge the reality of Sophie's unfortunate passing. This was definitely not how it was supposed to be. In the back of Bruce's mind, he'd always believed Sophie would come back to him and they'd end up together again. Now having this tragedy immediately follow what had happened with his parents he was turned inside out and left feeling absolutely raw.

Stephane's phone began ringing and as he stepped out of the ER to answer, Bruce was left alone in the hallway laying on a gurney. Going out the door, Stephane looked back to see Sophie's body being rolled into the back elevator, evidently for her last ride...Sadly it was down to the morgue. This had indeed been a surreal day in more ways than one.

*

Chapter Quinze

"Fiona..." he whispered tossing a pebble at *her* living room window. The second pebble was definitely enough to get her attention...

She quickly pulled the draperies back and was thrilled seeing it was Gilles standing there. She'd been anxiously awaiting this moment. She welcomed him with a huge smile and an exhale full of pleasant relief, then quietly opened the window to see him smiling right back at her. They were just about at eye level given a couple of feet.

"Hello my trusted friend" she quietly whispered in his ear when leaning over the windowsill to greet him. Seeing him was finally the confirmation she'd been waiting for.

"It's done Fiona. It all worked according to plan. You won't have to worry about that American tourist ever again" he whispered in return. After hearing that... she straightened back up to a standing position. He continued, "Now you and Josef can enjoy your life together and raise your child without any further interference from that foreigner. The 'incident' just happened a short while ago, I'm happy to report. After all these months of following her every move... the opportunity finally presented itself just like you said it would. I wanted to give you the news personally and collect my fee before I hit the road, he said all proud like. He was acting like he'd just accomplished a major triumph in life.

Fiona remained silently gratified and relieved in her heavenly thoughts. She leaned down again with euphoric pride after hearing his comments and hugged him again. (He was on his tiptoes, the little shit...)

"I'll always be eternally grateful to you Gilles for carrying out this imperative task. I'll never forget your incredible tenacity. For you my dear," she said slipping him a large overstuffed manilla envelope. "Inside you'll find the amount we agreed upon and when you get that front end fixed, let me know how much it is. I'll be happy to pay for the repair and will be sure to include a little something 'extra' for a deed well done. We'll just call it a tip…That's the least I can do."

She released her embrace giving him a wink and a wicked little look of satisfying approval. They'd completed their horrific caper with not so much of a soul even suspecting. Disgustingly so…they actually seemed proud of their deviant selves.

"I should get going Fiona…The Village *busy bodies* and the Police will certainly be circling this place soon like vultures swooping in. They'll have a ton of questions when they begin poking around, but don't worry. If I leave now I'll be long gone and out of sight. I'll be back at my families farm up north within a day or so. The fact that Josef fired me two days ago…it would only make it look suspicious should anyone see me still hanging out around here."

Gilles was so puffed up, he actually had the nerve to begin boasting…"To think of all those times Josef was jealous thinking I was attracted to Sophie…For such a keen guy, it's amazing to think he had zero idea of my real intentions. Your man always thought I had a thing for her. He never could fathom my real reason for always wanting to be close to her. What idiots…They never figured it could've been me that was secretly following her. All those times giving her a *hand and helping her out…it made* for such an easy excuse to know her agenda and goings on…So in retrospect Fiona, bravo to you…You knew just how to play it. Your specific directions allowed me to fulfill the plan and execute it like clockwork. I'm just happy it all worked out… Oh…and one last little thing before I shove off…Sophie went over to a house owned by some woman named Virginie a couple of times. There was a guy there blowing off the tennis court who could confirm seeing Sophie…Thought you should know. Where's Josef by the way?"

"Oh, he came home Very upset yesterday after his lunch date and immediately went down to his cave. He's been down there ever since. He's probably still sleeping off another one of his drunken binges. I told him about the baby before he left for his 'lunch date' with that stupid American yesterday and I haven't seen him since. I hope he's settled into our baby news by now, but no doubt Sophie's death is going to dampen his spirits. I guess that'd be an understatement," she said with a glamorous smile and striking a pose like she were *Madonna*.

"He'll definitely be a wreck for a while, but he'll get over it...I'll make sure of it." This time when she verbalized her new reality, her particular smile reflected a bit of nervous apprehension to it. It was definitely time for Gilles to get a move on, so she could have time to rehearse her reaction and be '*Prepared*' when hearing *the news of Sophie's 'passing'*...

"Be extremely careful Gilles and keep super quiet about this. It's going to be very intense around here for a while, so don't plan on hearing from me anytime soon. You can imagine what a big stir this is going to cause in the village, we'll have to play it extremely cool and stay on the down low until this all blows over. I'm glad you're getting on your way before the news 'officially' breaks. I'll contact you when the coast is clear" Fiona said in her quiet voice, finally exposing her true Cockney accent. Absolutely Amazing to think that now she was finally able to get that fucking plum out of her mouth. Silly me...and I thought she'd swallowed it.

Gilles felt the wave of her immediate dismissal and began walking briskly back to his car where he'd left it sitting on the backside of the tasting room. He quietly got in and drove off hoping and praying no one would see him or hear the rumbling of his bumper.

Fiona, now feeling like a liberated woman closed the window, then the draperies and opened her living room door to the kitchen feeling accomplished. She was beyond shocked to find Josef sitting at the farm table. Her pupils became the size dinner plates and Ice water immediately rushed through her veins.

"Bloody Hell!...He must've come up from the Cellar when I was speaking with Gilles standing outside my window!" Fear and Paranoia quickly reached her every thought. She was beyond terrified thinking he might've seen Gilles or overheard some of their conversation…

Josef looked up at Fiona with the most horrified and intense look imaginable and said, "We need to talk Fiona. Sit down." She felt she could've been on the verge of having a heart attack. Catapulted immediately into being flushed with panic, she nervously sat down next to him as instructed. "What'd he know…What'd he hear? OMG…"

"I just received an earth shattering call from the Police. They want me to go to the morgue to identify a body believed to be Sophie."

He put his elbows on the table and leaned forward placing his face in his hands and began sobbing like a blubbering fool. Guess Gilles had been right about one thing. Thank God 'the idiot' hadn't heard a thing.

Fiona led the situation…like an orchestra leader for the Philharmonic and didn't say a word. Instead, she stood up pirouetted her way over to move behind him. She began gently caressing his back giving him 'comfort' like only a lover would give. She was so grateful he couldn't see her face because she was smiling a devilish grin from ear to ear. She would have him, and all of 'it' to herself from now on. She was so happy to have that stupid blonde bitch gone… No more interruptions, no more silly competition around the house, and no more interference to complicate her future plans. Josef would be hers and hers alone. The plan had worked, but she'd need to keep her calm and not blow what had finally become hers.

"Grandmother would be so proud"…she thought with every gentle massaging stroke. In fact, she was boasting to herself and feeling her self worth for such a success in her brilliantly executed plan.

It doesn't really matter what happens in a small village like Issigeac should you be a 'true' local that is. Somehow all is forgiven and forgotten in time. Things pass, rumors flare then sprout wings…They fly everywhere just until the story gets old and boring or perhaps, gets substituted with something new. Time simply marches on.

Remember, the carpet will simply be pulled up, the story swept under and life soon goes on uninterrupted like the event never happened. Of course should there be a problem or *story* arise from an outsider, then that would fall under an entirely different category and set of rules all together. There would certainly be varied stories that would be actively passed around the bar and whispers repeatedly heard in all the hair salons for years. The gossip would be relentless.

In this particular case no one had really cared to know Sophie…She'd only been a fly-girl with a 'table' at the bar. Certainly no one could say they knew her, and God Forbid…knew any actual details of her relationship with either Bruce or Josef for that matter. Nor did they know any real truth about the accident. But that didn't stop the speculation and wild exaggerations from happening. The locals could not have cared less about her. To consider knowing the truth about the real story was inconsequential. They preferred to add on to the last fabled version of the tale that'd been told by embellishing it with their own additional tidbit. Guess that trait hadn't been exclusive to Gene. That'd always been how it was. It was a long standing tradition, and the way of life in the sweet little village.

The general consensus had always been that Sophie wasn't good enough for their beloved local boy anyway. And as we know, Bruce had always been considered an outsider…so what on earth could he Possibly have to say that could make any difference at all…then to top it off… they'd always thought Sophie was merely a foreigner trying to move in on their turf so why should they have cared about her in the first place?…She simply got what she deserved. That girl named Sophie simply had a tragic accident and that was it. Game over. It *really* was as simple as that.

The village eventually went back to 'business as usual'. The Villagers fully accepted the fate of the new power couple being that of Josef and Fiona. In their eyes that's the match that should've been made from the very beginning. Fiona had always been the exception to the rule when it came to 'un-welcomed foreigners'. She'd been seasoned and loved by *Queen Laetitia for Christ's sake,* and that alone was a good enough endorsement for everyone.

Given their long standing bond, the region knew that Litty would've been delighted and proud of her protégé for taking her rightful position. Fiona had not only played the perfect hand but had won the entire game, just as Litty had originally hoped, planned, and cleverly navigated.

A few quick months had passed and Fiona's belly had grown big. The grapevines were budding and offering the beginnings of fruit to be expected for the next vintage. It was like the fire in the Village and Josef's relationship with Sophie had only been a blip on the radar. Life at the *Château* was now calm and carried on without too much unforeseeable drama. Enough time had quietly passed... which gave Fiona the confidence to assume she'd absolutely succeeded in her ruthless caper. No one knew a thing or suspected her involvement in anything. Not one trace could be pinned on the ballerina...

She'd soon be organizing a grandiose party in honor of her baby's autumn arrival. Of course the big event would be held in the dining room...where keeping with tradition, all remaining Club members would be religiously gathered again. Things would continue at the *Château* just as they'd always been. Not a big change in sight...only some of the players had shuffled. Fiona's long awaited sought out position...the soon to be coveted Matriarch of the Estate was now within reach. Fiona was busy preparing for her role as the grande hostess, the woman to be undoubtedly known and 'respected' throughout the region...just as her Grandmother had been.

*

Chapter Seize

The weather in San Francisco was absolutely breathtaking. That's where Bruce found himself…standing in front of a huge picture window staring out at the gorgeous Golden Gate Bridge…It was such an exquisite day he was simply mesmerized by the crystal clear view.

The repetitive clicking sound made from the lighter he held…snapping it open and closed had him in some kind of a transcendental trance while gazing. The silver ribbing was heavy and the unique design was elegant. Needless to say, it fit perfectly in the palm of his hand. It just so happened it was identical to the one Sophie had given him years ago. That particular gift however, was now only a melted piece of silver…presumably lost in some evidence box in a French police station. After telling Sophie he had lost it…he'd kept it his secret after finding it in the pocket of one of his old jackets. Since he was no longer smoking, why bother?…It could hold some other purpose one day, and man…did it ever.

Holding this beautiful heavy lighter gave him a devious and satisfying pleasure knowing he'd successfully stolen it from the desk of his nemesis. He was delighted to have found it so easily during his quick search when last 'visiting' the *Chateau*. This one, simple piece of beautifully crafted silver had made a life-changing scenario entirely possible. It had given him a golden opportunity…one that he'd fantasized about for years.

The particular picture window he was standing in front of was only one amongst the many others surrounding the oval shaped living room. This unique architectural characteristic is found in some of the grand old 'painted ladies' that remain in San Francisco. Those beautiful original Victorians with their elegantly crafted details continue to grace the city to this day. The big difference between simply admiring them then and now…was Bruce was actually going to own one and call it home. A far cry from the small flat in Petroleum Hill that he'd shared with Sophie.

He was so happy and relieved to be back in NorCal. It just felt right…especially after just returning from a week in New York where he'd purchased a fabulous little beachfront property in South Hampton. With his parents gone, a nice chunk of money still left in the bank, he'd acquired a sense of independent freedom. His mind was clear and he could finally think. Even though he'd decided to use his new found fortune for interesting travel adventures and glamorous real estate purchases, he remained restless. Now it was his turn to have an itch… Seems as if he always had thoughts of Sophie and what could've been.

The sight of whitecaps swirling around in front of him gave him a sensation like he were surfing the crest in his familiar stomping grounds. It really felt like the perfect place to re-group. No one in the States would ever know anything about his family's hidden dramatic secret in France. That complicated truth would always need to stay buried, especially now…given the additional *'real'* reason and cause for the fire. The knowledge of how it had all unfolded was no one else's business but his…Vendetta…Soon, like all the others, this 'Ol story could be considered ancient history and be conveniently swept under the carpet…He was now a wealthy man and not one person on earth could touch him…not *even* Josef Decour.

He was certain he'd return to Issigeac one day to dig around and uncover the truth surrounding Sophie's demise. That whole tragedy just smelled of wrongful doing. He knew in his heart Josef was to blame somehow. He just had to be connected to her death in some way, he was sure of it. He was definitely going to expose that bastard once and for all…but all in good time. Bruce had only just begun to work on his next plan. Those two could not let the past be a bygone…

Bruce had always thought once he had the money, Sophie would eventually come to her senses and they'd get back together. You see?...He'd known about the insurance policy all along. His Mother had always confided in him. One of his unexpected sorrows in all of this was having to lose his Mother in order to obtain that insurance money. Now he'd be haunted having to carry the burden of guilt for the rest of his life for that innocent, beloved bystander. Don't worry...he'd soon get over it.

The Bay was so blue, the day so crisp, the entire area in Pacific Heights could not have been more poetic. The colors of the city were so vibrant they seemed to be in spectra vision. It was so clear it felt like he could literally jump in or out of the pictorial scene (like Dick Van Dyke and Julie Andrews did in Mary Poppins) that lay in front of him. Bruce stood tall seeming as if he had a new purpose in life. He'd finally found a feeling of clarity like he'd never sensed before. Sadly, it would take him receiving the insurance money from the death of his own parents to have these temporary feelings of personal success. I guess for some people in the end...it's called MONEY. Bruce exhaled slowly...letting go of the last little bit of air in his lungs before strongly inhaling. Then he turned to the Real Estate agent standing behind him...

"I'll take it. Let's write a full price offer. I'll name it 'Sophie's Place'. She would've loved this view had she lived to see it."

"Excellent decision Mr. Douglas, I'll have the offer written up for your signature this afternoon. What an exquisite home this is. Sophie, whoever she was would've definitely loved it."

Then the agent thought to herself while looking straight at Bruce..."How lucky this girl named Sophie must've been to have landed such a wonderful and kind man like you. You're such a prince, it's obvious you don't have a bad bone in your body."

Bruce really was a great salesman when he wanted to be. He'd put on a really good show for the agent, but as we all know...appearances can be deceiving.

"By chance Mr. Douglas"...she said, now continuing to focus on him instead of her commission..."Is that a vintage Cartier lighter you are holding? It's absolutely beautiful. I don't think they make them like that anymore."

"Why yes, it most certainly is. Let's just say it's a lovely keepsake on loan for the time being, but I have plans to return it to the home of its rightful owner one day."

Bruce had found his own voice again, but his suave and nonchalant behavior wouldn't last long. Indeed, he did close escrow on the place, and actually did move his toothbrush in, but soon after...he found himself unable to function any longer at that pace. It hit him all at once with triple force, The guilt, The envy and...The loss. It took many months of clearing his head to properly get out of his deep depression. When that glorious day did arrive, he finally found the strength to reach out to the unexpected.

The fog horns' billowing sounds echoed like a well rehearsed symphony throughout the frigid mid-summer's days and nights. The familiar bay area's rhythmic lullaby gave notice...things were visibly difficult and the summers chilly fog had now begun lofting throughout the city. This marked the summer season in SF had officially opened. Like Mark Twain always said, "The coldest winter he'd ever spent was a summer in San Francisco." Truer words have never been spoken...(or written)

So as difficult as it was for Bruce to leave his cozy comfort zone, he rolled over throwing off his down comforter and slapped his morning alarm buzzer for the second and final time. He hit the steam shower hard... carefully grooming himself to look his very best. He wanted to present himself as polished and sophisticated as he possibly could for his anticipated lunch meeting.

He'd made reservations for 12:30 on the terrace at the Auberge du Soleil Resort in Rutherford and didn't want to be a minute late. Deluxe patio seating on a beautiful warm day in Napa Valley's wine country was a hot ticket to come by. He cleaned up like a rusty nail needing to be polished and left his home looking sharp, brushed and buffed to perfection. It'd been so long since he'd been ready and able to return to France...and he was counting on this lunch date to change all that. He needed some info.

He rarely had much use for the pristine red 65'Fiat convertible stored down in his garage. He'd always been envious of Josef's car collection, so this little beauty had been his first to start his own…This particular gem was only used for special outings like today when it would come out of hiding spit shined and ready to roll. He hopped in, slid the top back, put the radio and heater on full blast then made his way out of the city.

Once over the Golden Gate Bridge and through the rainbow arch, the heater was no longer needed as Marin County gave way to the beautiful late summer sunshine and a gorgeous drive to the wine country. Bruce continued his way up Highway 101 before winding his way over to the valley. Not an inch of vacant space was visible on the lush rolling hills that didn't have a vine growing on it. It's a world class super pricey area when it comes to celebrity farmers that love to drink. The rows were so full of thick green leaves and sagging plump fruit, the bumper crop was certain to offer up a banner year. After driving the width of the valley through Carneros, he turned up onto the Silverado Trail. Then he made the hill to the right following the signs to the Resort never leaving third gear.

Upon arrival, he casually tossed his keys to the valet not bothering to wait for a claim check. He walked through the lofty breezeway making somewhat of a sauntering Cary Grant type entrance. His arrival was truly somewhat of a slick performance in itself. Now…here was a guy who'd landed in his element. He was right on time and looked the part of a chic high roller that deserved to be there. Bruce was back to feeling himself and he was really showing it. He walked straight back to the hostess' podium with confidence prevailing to announce his arrival. It was he that *owned it* this time.

"Hello Mr. Douglas, we've been expecting you. Right this way" she said quickly ushering him back to the beautiful panoramic dining deck. It was full of charming tables with burnt orange umbrellas, and offered a magnificent view of the valley's floor below. As far as you could see there were rows of meticulous lush growing grape vines. When scanning the beautiful dining terrace, he noticed his guest had already arrived and was enjoying a cocktail. He made his way over not waiting for the hostess.

"Well, I certainly appreciate you taking the time off in meeting me here," Bruce said with a jovial and welcoming smile as he approached the table.

Sophie's older brother James stood up, "Hello Bruce...My God, how long has it been?" Bruce didn't reply, only concurred with a mutual nod and smile before giving James a 'bro' hug.

"It's great to see you James. It's been way too long is all I know." They both took their seats and as Bruce sat down, he unfolded his napkin snapping it out before spreading it slowly back onto his lap for a stylish and classy landing.

He took that moment to hide how captivated he was seeing James sitting next to him. Bruce had forgotten how much James and Sophie resembled one another. They shared so many features and mannerisms it was uncanny. Somehow, it eerily felt as if he were sitting with her instead of her brother.

His memory of Sophie often became opaque and convoluted due to his obsessive hatred for Josef. Sadly that underlying negativity always took precedent. Sitting there observing James however, he was reminded how her funny quirks used to make him laugh. James definitely had an alluring charm about him, just like she'd had. It made Bruce reflect on all the good times he and Sophie shared...it made him begin missing her...again. The two men sat silently observing one another before their conversation 'officially' began. I guess they both were feeling a bit nostalgic...

"You're looking rather well Bruce. This was such a great idea meeting up. I haven't been to this place for lunch in...I can't even remember it's been so long. I'd forgotten how beautiful this place is, I definitely won't let so much time pass before my next visit. I actually stayed here a few years ago and the rooms are gorgeous.

So…tell me…how are you? I mean really…How have you been doing since Sophie's passing? I know for us, our family has had a difficult time of it, but I heard you also suffered another unexpected tragedy…I'm truly sorry for you and your sisters Bruce. I can't imagine that kind of immeasurable loss happening at the same time. My God…"

"That's a very kind and understanding thing for you to say James. It's certainly been a crazy time in life, I can tell you that…experiencing so much trauma at once has been extremely difficult.

Turns out…in the end, I couldn't handle it alone. I needed to 'drop out' for a while and get myself centered again. Thank God I did…because now I'm feeling ready and willing to get back into *living*. After taking some needed time out for some deep reflection, I'm actually feeling stronger and better now than I did as my *old self*. That's part of the reason why I invited you here today, I was hoping we could discuss a few things that have been resting heavy on my mind. Shall we get started by ordering some lunch with a nice bottle from the area…What do you say?"

They proceeded to enjoy catching up with one another while having light conversation over a bottle of superb wine, but once lunch was served Bruce subtly began with his inquiry. The kind of questions that would explain why he'd invited James in the first place.

"First and foremost, I want you to know how sorry I am not to have been able to attend the funeral service for your sister. After all the loss I was so freaked out I flippantly bought a couple of pieces of real estate, not realizing at the time I'd reached a personal dead end and couldn't go on like I was. That made me think I needed to check myself in to a rehab retreat in Mendocino for a couple of months to get myself stable enough to focus again…and to think a year and a half has now passed since all of that tragedy happened is unreal.

I can't believe I'd become so lost, I felt like I couldn't find my way back without some professional help." (just so you know…his stint in the coastal town of Mendocino was nothing more than an extended five star spa treatment if anything, but of course he failed to mention that small detail)…

"I know losing Sophie must've been a huge shock for you as well James. You and your family have my sincere condolences…And to think what a brave soul you were to bring her body back home and go through all that…Well, I can't imagine how difficult that must've been for you. I'm so sorry I couldn't 'show up' as the man I should've been," Bruce admitted. All this BS was made in the attempt to depict himself as a sensitive and caring man that was feeling remorse for his lack of mature and compassionate behavior. Sincerely, he was giving it his all to secure a good performance.

"Bruce, it was such an incredibly difficult thing for me to do, burying my little sister. The poor dear had her whole life in front of her,…but I got through it. She remains in my daily thoughts God love her. Growing up here in the bay area really gave me the support I needed. With so many people wanting to help, it made a really difficult situation much easier to deal with. I don't think I could've gotten through it without my community of friends. Accidents happen in life, I accept that now…but if we're being honest, I'm just grateful Sophie had found happiness after you left her."

"What are you talking about? I didn't leave Sophie, it was the other way around! I'm surprised she didn't tell you. It was actually a man named Josef Decour that was instrumental in our breakup. I'm shocked you didn't know… I'm sure you met the guy when you went back" Bruce said, fishing for details.

"No, actually… I didn't. There was no need for me to go back. Josef's assistant, someone named Fiona helped organize Sophie's body being transported home along with her belongings."

"Oh really?…Did she send you everything?"

"I think so, all except for a box the Police kept with the items that were with her at the time of the accident. That's still sitting with the Police in France until I'm able to pick it up personally. They wouldn't send it given all the regulations the French have. There's such a strict protocol for everything in that Country…and the amount of red tape is unbelievable. It's required I physically be present for them to release those items to me. I was only responsible for everything once Sophie's remains arrived Stateside. All the paperwork was done between both Countries, so all I really had to do was sign the receipt for her physical being and the possessions shipped. But like you, I've also had a difficult time facing all of this until now.

As a matter of fact all of her belongings that Fiona sent are still stored at my parents' first rental property in South San Francisco. You remember that little place on Maple Drive don't you? Sophie was living there when you first met, right? I automatically inherited her managerial rights to the place when she passed. All of her things are just sitting in the attic. My family has such sentimental values attached to that place, we haven't wanted to think or broach the delicate subject of dealing with its future. We don't know quite what to do with the property now that Sophie's gone, so I've continued to rent it out until we can decide whether to sell or not. I'm sure the tenants would never think to go upstairs through the trap door.

Was there anything in particular you're interested in having? I'm sure it's all covered with a thick layer of dust by now, but if there is something, I'll be happy to take you over for a look. It's funny that we're discussing this Bruce, I was actually thinking now might be a good time for me to go check on the place. It's finally time to purge the past" James said excusing himself for a quick visit to the men's room.

That left Bruce sitting alone at the table having a faux look of compassion and understanding on his face. The incredible view gave him the limitless space to have his guilty and reckless thoughts begin selfishly twirling around in his self centered mind. He'd heard all that he needed and all that he'd come for. The box of items that were found in the Rover were still secure and sitting in France. Evidently that must include *the letter*….When James returned to the table Bruce proposed an idea.

"I know this might sound a bit crazy, but I've been thinking…Would you be interested in joining me on a quick trip to France? There's some unfinished business I have in the Village and it might be a good time for you to see where Sophie spent so much time. It might also be the perfect opportunity to retrieve the box from the Police. I don't know if you could take the time off, but it's a beautiful time of year to travel there," Bruce said giving his best convincing sales pitch.

"One thing I need to accomplish while visiting is to complete my 'walk through' of the re-build of my family's cottage. What do you think? Care to see a bit of France?"

Bruce certainly wasn't going to discuss anything pertinent regarding his so called 'unfinished business'. He'd already begun laying his framework, but we can all assume his only true reason for going back most certainly had to do with his nemesis and getting his hands on that letter. His burning flame of hatred towards Josef Decour remained burning hot. The coast was clear, enough time had passed not to be suspected and now was the time…He could slip back into town under the radar so to speak. It was finally time to extinguish that Decour bastard completely. Bruce knew he'd never be able to live happily until he'd seen some closure to it all. Basically, he needed to ruin Josef and his family's name for good was more like it.

"Actually Bruce, I'm due for a vacation. What the hell…I can squeeze in a few days away. I can always work remotely if something major comes up and I'm needed. I'd love to join you.

By the way…while we're there, I'm going to meet this man Josef, and figure out a few things. I've always thought Sophie's death had to have something more to it. She was such a good driver, I've never understood how the crash could've 'accidentally' happened like the Police report indicated. As a matter of fact, I think I'll hire a private investigator while I'm at it. I absolutely insist on finding out more information on everything while we're there, including the horrific fire that took the lives of your parents. I'm going to be double checking every detail until no stone is left unturned. That's the least I can do. I think knowing the truth about everything will bring us both the internal peace and tranquility we need to *really* move on. Getting to the bottom of it all, will for me. Sophie would expect me to do this. What perfect timing for our trip…This is a great idea. I won't leave France until I've uncovered it all for myself."

Bruce sat mortified hearing this determined dialogue come from James. This was absolutely NOT in the plan. Bruce had created his own monster without knowing it. After sitting there calmly thinking he'd gotten away with murder he realized…he might've just opened pandoras box.

xxx

...to be continued.

About the Author

**Claire Saint-Claire
is an American storyteller living in a tiny
Village in the
Southwest of France.**

**When she's not putting her tales down on paper,
she's tending to her boutique 'The West End'
that she shares with her French husband.**

**Preferring the lifestyle of the bucolic
French countryside…
they chose to re-locate
from Los Angeles in 2019**

**…and have
never looked back.**

www.ingramcontent.com/pod-product-compliance
Lightning Source LLC
Chambersburg PA
CBHW050458160726
48003CB00001B/63